The
Templar Lance

R.A. Johnson

The Enclave Series
Book One

CROW Books

Fifth Edition
September 2023

eBook ISBN 978-1-959480-07-5
Paperback ISBN 978-1-959480-08-2
Hardcover ISBN 978-1-959480-09-9

CROW Books and its crow-and-book logo are imprints of CROW-IP, LLC, all rights reserved.

To Ona, Carly, and Wes—the other parts of CROW.
You are the reason I do all that I do.

PREFACE

This edition of *The Templar Lance* has been a long time coming, and the story it tells has followed a long and twisting path. I turned fifty-five years old in 2014 and had a bit of a midlife moment. I knew my career as a software engineer had about another ten years to run. Deciding what to do after that gave me pause.

I've always written. As a kid, it was bad science fiction, which became pretty good non-fiction: design documents, trade magazine and academic journal articles, marketing copy, project proposals, and patent applications. But always, in the back of my mind, stories scratched and clawed to get out.

So, I decided I would spend my retirement years writing what I wanted to write, but I knew I had a lot to learn. I wrote the first version of the book you're holding in about a year and self-published it in 2015 to resounding silence. I still had a lot to learn.

Several revisions and a sequel, *Lady 355: Mother of Freedom*, later, I lost momentum and moved on to other projects. But leaving The Enclave Series incomplete has always gnawed at me. Every time I looked at the previous editions of this book, however, I found the task of updating it to my standards, such as they are, of almost ten years later very daunting. Still, there was the rest of the series arc to explore.

Then a wonderful thing happened. One of my favorite writers, Joanna Penn, announced on her podcast, *The Creative Penn*, that she was rewriting her first novel. I figured if such a successful author, speaker, and writing coach was willing to

i

take the time to bring a first-in-series novel up to snuff, why shouldn't I?

This, the final edition of *The Templar Lance*, is the result of a year's effort of redoing some pretty cringe-worthy prose and restructuring what was essentially a travelogue into what I sincerely hope is a compelling kickoff to an epic series—and a kickass story in its own right.

I present to you, Faithful Reader, this new and improved edition of *The Templar Lance*, the first book in The Enclave Series.

Enjoy!

Faithfully,

R.A. (Rob) Johnson
Pennsylvania, U.S.A.
August 2023

TIMELINE

1119
Hugh de Payens
leads nine knights to
Jerusalem

1129
Knights Templar
order created

1187
Fall of Jerusalem

1307
Templars
arrested

1347-1350
Great Mortality

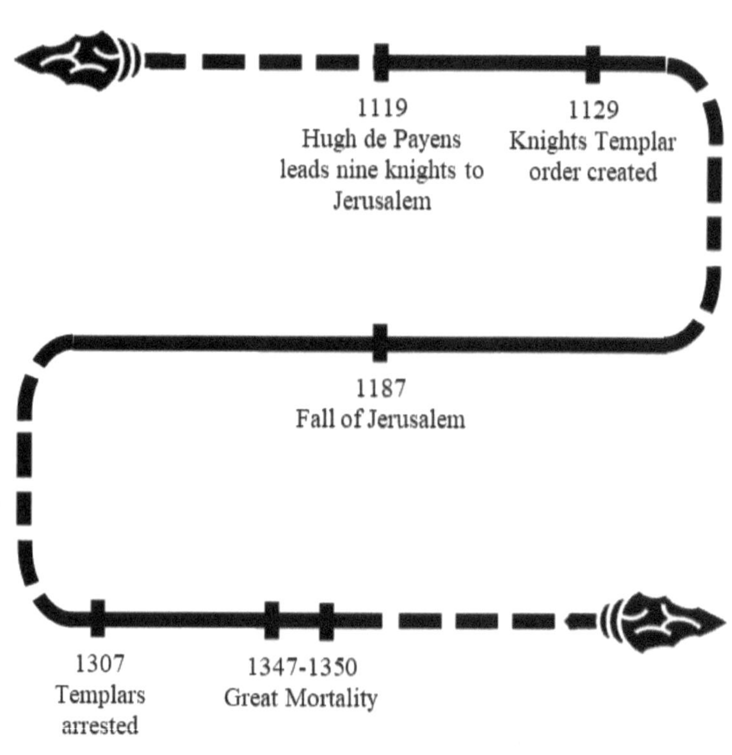

PART I

Codex Incognito
1350 A.D

How do I begin a tale such as the one I wish to tell? There is the beginning, my youth before I came to know, though not necessarily understand, a few of the many mysteries this world holds. But I will get to that part of the tale soon enough. There is the middle, when I was pursued across the face of Europe, charged with protecting a most precious artifact with the power to change the course of human history. Then, there is the end which, until this last year, I thought might never arrive. We will get to the beginning and middle, but let us start here at the end, what may well be the end of all things.

But first, let me set expectations. If you, whomever future you may be, are reading this, I congratulate you. I have written this chronicle in the most devious cypher I could devise, hoping that one day someone with your skills would see through my subterfuge and decode this most unusual manuscript. So, I say, "Well done."

Now that we have finished congratulating ourselves for being so clever, let me teach you lessons that are so strange as to be at first unbelievable, but which will seep into your mind and erode whatever faith in the Almighty you may hold dear. Let me assure you that no harbor is safe from the momentous revelations contained in this missive.

I have decided to document the events of my life thus far, as recent events have shaken my comfortable faith in the continuation of my long life. Indeed, I fear the world, or at least a large portion of it, is dying and the End of Days may be upon us. In the past year, the population of my fair England has diminished by nearly two in three. A pestilence lays over the land that strikes men, women, and children, regardless of the height nor depth of their station nor of their piety. Whole villages stand empty. Fields of wheat, barley, and beans all lay fallow and untended. Cattle wander feral through the land, and the lords of those lands, those few who remain alive, have no bound serfs to collect and husband them.

Even I, who has survived most of two centuries, was taken to Death's door, once again, by this plague, this Great Mortality. Either my blessing, which is also my curse, kept me from knocking or, more likely, Death himself was busy elsewhere. In either case, I awoke in my sickbed, which I had fouled, a stinking, sweating near-corpse. The buboes that are the hallmark of this disease subsided, leaving behind black scars that mark me as a survivor. Reports that have come through my network of spies tell me these scars, which do fade slowly, are treated as either the blessed fingerprints of God Almighty or as the mark of Cain, depending on local superstition. I can tell you, rather, that they are simply the flesh proudly proclaiming victory over this most vile pestilence.

Thus, you know the circumstances in which this codex has been so hastily written. You know the When, Where, and How of it, but you have yet to learn the Why, the reason I have put quill and ink to the finest vellum and written this history in the most obscure way I can imagine.

Bending over the vellum, trying to decide in what language I should commit these words, I was taken again by the Fever and fell senseless into another delirious dream.

In this fever dream, I met again companions of mine with whom I have not conversed for many years. Each spoke in turn in his own tongue, but the words that came from their mouths were gibberish spoken in a halting stutter. As I strained to make out what each was saying, their faces blurred and merged together into a single countenance. Their mouths, still speaking nonsense in their own tongues, now complemented each other, filling the gaps and combining into a single voice, as their faces had. It was the face and voice of a man I had once thought of as my brother, though we were born worlds apart and had, at different times, each called the other Master.

His voice spoke to me clearly in his native Arabic, "Your story is too precious for any but the most enlightened, and too dangerous to far too many. Use my voice to tell it, and I will keep its secrets until the one with the proper talents is ready to hear it."

My purpose is simple, yet contradictory. I write to preserve and protect, yet also to reveal to the worthy, a secret. A secret that could, and perhaps should someday, if revealed, change forever the course of humanity on this Earth. Whether that change is for good or ill will depend entirely on the enlightened one who decodes and reads this missive. Will they use the secret to gain power over the rest of humanity, as this secret could certainly facilitate? Or will they use it to benefit all the people across this wide world? This knowledge and the physical manifestation of it can accomplish either of those goals. Or, as I so fervently hope, will the reader pledge to keep the secret hidden and safe, as I have these many decades?

This illness has shaken my complacent belief in my immortality. I no longer believe in that false and unearned blessed curse. I return to the understanding, as all others of the human race come to realize, that my time on the Earth is finite, and that someday I may well have to answer for my earthbound failings.

Until then, I present my story, written, not as a memoir, but as a history, a travelogue of sorts. It is, fundamentally, a test. A test of erudition, a test of intuition, a test of forgotten knowledge. But most of all, a test of faith. You will be forever changed when you read it. That I promise.

Our story, or at least this part of it, begins in the twenty-eighth year of the reign of King Henry II of England. The year was 1178 Anno Domini.

Chapter 1

England, 1178 A.D.

T he wind blew back my hair as I followed my father on horseback.

"Try to keep up, Little Brother," my brother Stewart said. "As soon as the hounds catch the scent, he'll be off like a crossbow bolt."

We two brothers were as different as our mounts. Stewart, at fourteen years old, was already filling out his tall frame. He got his reddish-blond hair and freckled complexion directly from our father, while I owed my black hair and dusky skin to Mother's roots in southern France. Our contrasts were not limited to our hair color, though. While Stewart could easily pass for a young man several years older, I was small for my ten years, short of stature, with a correspondingly slight build.

Our horses were similarly mismatched. Stewart rode a high-spirited gray stallion who would let no one but Stewart sit astride him. His stallion stood sixteen hands at the shoulder, while my mare was barely more than a pony.

But though we differed greatly physically, no two brothers loved each other more. I idolized Stewart as the model of a noble knight-to-be, and, for his part, Stewart considered it his sacred duty to protect and aid his Little Brother in any way he could. Our temperaments were similarly matched, having learned from observing Father's quiet competence and strong hand.

The first baying of the hounds came from ahead, and Stewart, his voice tinged with excitement, yelled, "Here we go."

Our father, Sir Edwin of Rollingford, the liege lord of Rollingford Castle, spurred his horse into full gallop as the hunting party crossed the field at the edge of the forest.

The hunt had stretched into the afternoon without a good chase, and Father was impatient. When the hounds' baying rose in pitch and intensity, the knight knew they at last had a worthy quarry, hopefully one of the wild boars known to inhabit his lands.

I kicked my mount's flanks, trying to keep up with Father, but to no avail. His charger had born the knight, both in full armor, during many battles. Thunder's feathered hooves pounded the hard ground as he broke into a full gallop. With no steel plates to encumber him, Thunder raced headlong across the field. In fact, no one in the hunting party except Stewart could keep pace with Father.

It was only Stewart, then, who witnessed our father's steed stumble as it gathered itself to leap the stone wall at the edge of the open field. Perhaps it was a hare's hole, or a misplaced field stone that caught Thunder's hoof. Whatever the cause, the result changed our lives forever.

Having lost its footing at a critical point, the charger tried to regain his balance by turning abruptly aside and refusing to clear the wall. Father, having stood in the stirrups to absorb the shock of landing, had no chance to keep contact with the stumbling horse. As Thunder veered to the right, Sir Edwin's right foot pulled free, while his left one twisted more deeply into its stirrup. The result was that he pitched headfirst off the left side of the saddle.

The impact of his head with the stone wall stove in Father's skull, and the sound further startled Thunder into a gallop which dragged the dying knight across the field. As my slower mare was only halfway across the open field, I angled to my right to intercept the runaway, but Stewart reached Thunder first. I reined in and jumped to the ground as Stewart grabbed Thunder's bridle. Only then did the charger stop our father's inadvertent torture. Untangling his broken body from the saddle, together we cradled Father in our arms until we felt him take his last breath.

Sir Edwin was a warrior, one of the King's best. When campaign season came around each year, he was first to be called upon by his brother and liege lord Geoffrey, Baron of Sowich. But Father was also an intelligent, thoughtful man who managed the Rollingford estates well and treated his bound serfs with a firm but fair hand. So it was that as word of his demise spread, the others of Geoffrey's knights and minor lords scrambled for control of the lands our family had held in the King's name for generations.

Being but fourteen years old, Stewart was too young to run the estate, so Uncle Geoffrey chose another of his knights, Sir Robert Enderhite, to manage the estate until Stewart came of age. It was a particularly bad choice.

Upon hearing of Sir Robert's assignment, and knowing his reputation for cruelty, especially to women, my mother immediately sent word to the Baroness, her sister-in-law Margaret, asking her to take us into Geoffrey's household. The reason, she said, was so my brother and I could be trained to serve my uncle as knights. This appealed to Geoffrey's ego, so he readily agreed. The real reason was Robert Enderhite's penchant for treating women as his playthings, and my mother's recent widowhood made her fair game for his unwanted attentions.

"Why are you packing?" he asked upon his arrival at Rollingford. "A young widow, such as yourself, needs a protector."

I knelt outside my parents' bedchamber, ear pressed to the door.

"The Baron has taken my sons and I into his care," she replied. Her tone was firm, but not defiant, which would have ignited his volatile temper.

"Nonsense. This is your home. I insist you stay and run the manor house, as you always have. In fact, you can keep these rooms. I can make do with another—for now." His leering tone left no doubt that he considered that a temporary arrangement, and that soon they would be sharing a bed.

"No. I insist. My boys need training, and Geoffrey's court is the best place for that." She had crossed the line into defiance, and I feared Robert's reaction. To my surprise, though, he laughed.

"I agree, totally. They do need to be sent away…to be trained as knights, as is their birthright. You, on the other hand, are not required at Geoffrey's court, and frankly, being *French,* you will not be much welcomed. On the other hand, I, personally, do not care about your foreign heritage, as I find your exotic looks quite…appealing."

Even at ten years old, I knew the course this conversation was taking. I rose to my feet and felt for the small dagger I carried at my belt. Before I could yank open the door, however, Mother's voice rang out in a tone I had never heard her use before.

"I am *Lady Rollingford,* widow of Sir Edwin Rollingford, Baron Geoffrey's *brother.* I am *not* some serving wench or one of the whores you are accustomed to. You will treat me and my sons with the respect we deserve." Her voice shook with fury.

Robert matched her tone with scorn. "Or what, woman? Geoffrey is miles away, and *I* command Rollingford now. I will do with you and everyone else here as I please."

My hand was on the latch, but I froze when I heard Mother say, "Then you best stay awake, because as soon as you sleep, my *French* poniard will find your heart."

I stepped back from the doorway as her running footsteps approached and she threw open the door. She rushed past me, but stopped and grabbed my arm.

"Where is your brother?" I shrugged in response, keeping my diminutive self between Mother and Sir Robert. "Find him. We are leaving. Now."

I slowly backed away as she hurried down the hallway. Sir Robert, clearly astounded by my mother's resistance, stood red-faced.

As I turned to go find Stewart, I heard him mumble, "Be gone with you, then. You and your French spawn."

Chapter 2

England, 1179 A.D.

I do not remember the day we arrived at Castle Sowich. Or the day after, or several months after that. The days passed in a blurred whirlwind of activity. My mother Sadie, my brother Stewart, and myself—call me Liam, by the way—moved in with my uncle and his family. Uncle Geoffrey and his wife Margaret had two children. My cousin Gerald was the same age as Stewart, and his sister Cecelia matched my years. Aunt Margaret welcomed us with open arms, happy to have another noble lady, in spite of Mother's foreign blood, as a companion. Gerald and Stewart became fast friends, while Cece and I shyly flirted under our mothers' watchful eyes.

Stewart had already begun his training under my father's tutelage, as Gerald had under Uncle Geoffrey's sword master. I, being but ten years old, first needed to learn the duties of a knight's squire. A less glamorous vocation I cannot imagine, as I spent my days shoveling manure, grooming the horses in my uncle's stable, polishing my brother's and cousin's armaments, and generally doing the work of a stable hand bound to my uncle as if I was a serf. Of course, unlike the poor serfs who would toil through their short lives of unrelenting hard labors, I knew that if I learned what I needed to, and did all that was asked of me, I too would someday be a knight, and ride the horses I was grooming.

Gerald and Stewart were of an age, and were equally matched in strength and cleverness, though not so much in personality. Gerald was gregarious, laughing loudly at everyone and everything that struck him as funny. Even at such a young age, he had a silver tongue which the ladies of the court—and the kitchen—drew great enjoyment from. By contrast, Stewart had a more solemn view of the world, having been with the hunting party and witnessing the death of our father. Being displaced from the estate that he expected would someday be his legacy made him even more circumspect. His reticence hid a fierce determination to excel at his training, though, so he might return us to our home as soon as possible.

The sun was hot, even for England, as it beat down on the dusty training grounds. A wiry old man parried Gerald's thrust with ease, then delivered a backhand blow with the flat of his sword to the shoulder of his overextended arm. Gerald, already leaning too far forward, stumbled to one knee.

"Yer dead. Why?"

Gerald climbed to his feet, sword arm hanging at his side. "I lost my balance, Master Grimm."

"Aye, but why?"

Gerald looked confused and his eyes flicked to where Stewart stood, poised in a defensive posture a few feet away. Stewart flexed his legs, the muscles of his calves and thighs standing out in sharp relief.

"Oh, my base. I got outside my base."

Master Grimm nodded his bald head, then flicked his blunted sword upwards and in one motion whacked Gerald on the other shoulder, then whirled about and swung full-speed at Stewart. Steel clanged on steel as Stewart easily parried the attack, using his momentum to spin and launch his own counter. Moving more swiftly than his age and bowlegged frame should have allowed, Master Grimm blocked Stewart's slash, but as the blades clanged again, Grimm felt Stewart's blade slide off his own and barely leaped out of the way of Stewart's upward swipe aimed at his groin.

Regaining his composure, Grimm returned his attention to Gerald. This time, however, Gerald managed to clumsily, but effectively, block the sword master's attack. The three faced each other in a triangle, each in their defensive stance.

"Hold!" Grimm called out and relaxed into an upright stance. "What'd ya learn, eh?"

Gerald, looking abashed, said, "Maintain good balance at all times."

"Aye, and…?"

"Keep your guard up," Gerald mumbled as he rubbed his shoulder where the edges of the blade's fuller had left a double welt.

Grimm turned to Stewart, who, despite the command to relax, still stood at the ready. The old man squinted at the young man until Stewart straightened, though he still gripped his sword warily.

"Good stance 'n parry." The sword master nodded appreciatively. "A feint to contact can be 'fective, but only if ya' stay clear o' his guard." Grimm tapped the cross-guard of his sword with its curved quillons.

Stewart spoke up for the first time. "You like to block with the flat of your blade. Keeps the edge sharp."

Grimm eyed Stewart for a moment, then raised an eyebrow. "Aye, ya' maybe right. Habits are bad in combat. Gives yer 'ponent a way to pr'dict yer movements." He nodded appreciatively, then sobered. "But 'tonly works if'n ya know the bloke yer fightin'.'"

Stewart nodded his understanding, then Grimm continued, his tone chiding but also respectful. "An' ya coulda cut me balls off with tha' slash."

The corner of Stewart's mouth curled into a half-smile. "Those bow'd legs are still limber. I knew you'd jump clear."

Grimm chuckled as Stewart's meaning became clear. *If the slash was a second feint, he would have been caught mid-leap.*

"'At's enough o' this fer today," Grim said, and Gerald, who had looked confused during Stewart and Grimm's banter, brightened. Grimm saw his smile and shook his head. "Yer na done yet."

He walked out to where a banner pole on top of the training grounds wall cast its shadow. He then paced off ten long steps and drew a line in the dirt.

"Work wi' the French Gadget 'til the shadow reaches here. Switch on ten scores." He sheathed his sword, walked to a shaded corner, and dipped a ladle into the bucket of water resting on a bench. Gulped the water, he watched as Gerald and Stewart prepared the *French Gadget*.

The training device we called the French Gadget was built by Uncle Geoffrey's Master of Horse, a Frenchman my father's men captured during a campaign many years before. When the French captives were ransomed back to their king, Francois begged my father not to return him, but rather to keep him on as a servant. Having seen Francois's prowess on horseback, he recommended him to his brother Geoffrey as a groom. Within a few years, having demonstrated his ability to tame and train the wildest of Geoffrey's stable of warhorses, he was elevated to Master of Horse. It was under his tutelage that I began my own training, not with a sword, but with shovel, brush, and comb as a lowly groom.

The French Gadget was constructed of a tree trunk, representing an opponent, about four feet high and two across, hung from a scaffold by five ropes tied to iron rings driven into the wood. One rope at the top raised and lowered the body, while two attached to each side moved the faux opponent to either side and twisted it left and right.

Attached to each side of the body was an articulated arm holding an interchangeable sword, one of wood, blunted steel, or razor sharp. The arms were each rigged with ropes to stab or slash up, down, or sideways.

All the rigging ran through a series of cleverly shaped block and tackle pulleys that moved the various components in coordinated, yet random, ways. The number and asymmetric nature of the pulleys resulted in unpredictable movements of the body and swords, presenting wildly variable attacks that the trainee had to defend against and penetrate to land a scoring blow to the tree trunk body.

The whole gadget was driven by a heavy loop of chain through another block that allowed a second trainee to vary the speed and direction of the gadget's movements. Stewart and Gerald alternated positions, switching when the fighter scored a number of blows against the gadget—ten for this session.

Of course, Gerald made a game of it, counting how many times the gadget landed a strike before they switched positions. It was Gerald's nature to make a game of everything, even though Stewart handily beat him every time. Stewart, for his part, took the training much more seriously, knowing that once he achieved his goal of knighthood, he would be serving in Uncle Geoffrey's vanguard as our father had, while Gerald, being the heir-apparent would almost certainly be in a rear echelon.

Whereas Gerald was rebuked by Master Grimm for not practicing enough to hone his skills, Stewart was often reprimanded for being overzealous and risking serious injury to himself and our cousin, when they sparred each other. Despite these nearly opposite natures, or perhaps because of them, Gerald and Stewart became two halves of a whole. Their friendship became kinship and ultimately attained a brotherhood that I, being so much younger, could not yet share.

Chapter 3

England, 1179 A.D.

My days working in the stables were not all drudgery, however. My teacher there—yes, cleaning stalls, brushing horses, and oiling tack do take some training—was a Frenchman called Francois, with his own tale to tell. He had been a sergeant in the retinue of a French nobleman when he was captured by my uncle's army during one of the many wars fought between England and France for control of the Low Countries. When the French were ransomed, Francois, having been ill-treated by his nobleman and wishing to see a bit of the world, petitioned my father to remain with Uncle Geoffrey's troops and return to England with them. His mastery of the art of cavalry, and his knowledge of French strategy and tactics were seen as valuable, so when those with whom he had been taken captive were sent back to France, my uncle spirited him away to England.

After many years of loyal service, during which he demonstrated his ability to calm and train the great chargers Geoffrey's knights rode in combat, he became Uncle's stable master, which is why I fell under his tutelage. He treated me, not as a distaff noble, but as he would any other stable hand, until one day when we were struggling to repair a saddle and he swore to himself in French. When I responded in kind, he stopped and stared at me. He continued staring at me and spoke something in fast French, which I barely understood. I told him, in the rudimentary French my mother had taught me, that I did not know the language, but wished to learn to speak it like a native. Francois smiled and henceforth added French lessons to my many other duties. After a few lessons, he joked that either I had a strong proficiency for languages, or he was an excellent teacher. To me, though, it just seemed to come naturally.

We soon spoke only French when alone together, as I also began to do when with my mother. She was delighted to hear and respond in the language of her birth, though she had been without it for so long that she at first stammered like a rusty iron gate. In no time, though, her proficiency returned, and we spent many an evening reading the few books she possessed and writing the flowing French script. It was my great fortune that she, having been born into a minor noble family in Provence, learned to read and write as well as the more mundane womanly skills of embroidery, weaving, and managing the household.

I quickly noticed, though, the differences in cadence and pronunciation between the High Provence version of the language spoken by Mother and the more pedestrian Burgundian form Francois used. It amused him and scandalized Mother when I would inadvertently mix the two into a *patois* that instantly branded me as a foreigner to both regions. I quickly learned to treat the two dialects separately. Within months, I could pass for a native of either region.

My talent did not pass unnoticed by Uncle Geoffrey, and he sometimes asked me to translate letters he received from the continent—a task easily accomplished by Mother, but one which my uncle believed was unsuitable for a lady. Thus, I came to understand the importance of informants and spies who could provide intelligence prior to the frequent military campaigns.

These breaks from the routine of caring for Geoffrey's stable of chargers, draft horses, and fine equestrian mounts were few and far between, however. More frequent were the many religious feasts and market days.

～

I stepped from the cold waters of the River Trent, scrubbed clean of weeks of sweat, grime, and a fair share of horse manure. I paid special attention to my fingernails, for I knew Mother would examine them first, and if she found them unsatisfactory, she would take a brush to them until every brown bit was gone.

Next, Francois marched me up to the castle, wrapped in a clean sheet, much to the delight of the many workers—the manor's blacksmith, baker, farrier, cobbler, and many of the other tradesmen needed to run the Baron's estate.

In my meager quarters, Mother had laid out a fancy suit of clothes, which told me we would have honored guests at this festival. I dressed quickly amid the noise of the household servants making their last-minute preparations. But that was not the only reason I hurried to make myself presentable. Despite the fuss, I looked forward to feast days with great anticipation, but not because of the meal, since the kitchen maids kept us well fed thanks to Francois's ready smile and exotic accent. Neither was it because of the break from work, but rather because on feast days, I was allowed to sit at the long head table, along with the honored guests, the Baron and Baroness, Stewart and Gerald, Mother, and—most important of all—my cousin Cecelia. Mother and Aunt Margaret always arranged the seating so Cece and I were together at the table's end.

Cece was a half-year younger than me, and as I was beginning my training, however humbly, for knighthood, she was learning the skills expected of a noble lady. But, when we were seated at the end of the long family table, as the freely flowing wine made the adults louder and louder, Cece and I were able to sneak away to play like the children we still were.

"Oh, no," Cece said when she saw Sally, the serving maid, bringing the mutton course, the greasy meat, still sizzling from the brazier. Cece wrinkled her nose and said, "How disgusting. Besides, I am full to bursting."

For my part, I would have eaten anything put in front of me, and despite the fact that the crispy fat ringing the tough meat was a favorite of mine, I, ever the gentleman, waved it away. Sally smiled knowingly, and her nod told me to stop by the kitchens before the fires were put out for the night.

Serving wenches, hired from the town's two taverns, grinned at the two of us pretending to be lord and lady, and mockingly offered us the wine they carried in earthenware pitchers, only to shake their heads when I held out my cup. Of course, they poured the wine freely for the adults, who grew louder with each round.

Playing my part, I stood and bowed to Cece. "My Lady, shall we escape this mayhem?" I nearly had to shout for her to hear me.

"Oh, yes," she said, fluttering her eyelashes. "Please, Kind Sir, take me away from this debauchery."

We both giggled like the children we still were and ran out the side door of the hall into the castle warrens.

Taking my hand, Cece led me to the library, which I had seen only briefly from the hallway a few times. She took a lit taper from a sconce on the wall and entered the dark room. As she lit several candles, I stood in the doorway, amazed. The room was not overly large, but the walls were lined floor to the high ceiling with shelves filled with books, maps, stuffed birds and small animals, and other objects too numerous and unfamiliar to me to describe. And the smells. The smell of fine, old leather mingled with that of the parchment and vellum it bound into row upon row of codices. In my young, inexperienced life, I never imagined there were that many books in the whole world.

"I never knew that the Baron—"

Cece scoffed. "Not my father. Oh, definitely not him. He never steps foot in this room. I think all of this knowledge scares him." She threw her arms to the side and twirled around, clearly enthralled by the riches surrounding us. "This, My Lord, is Mother's doing. This is her—and my—haven. Our escape from the world of war and famine."

She grabbed my hand, and her smile and bright eyes infected me with her rapture.

"Come, see what we are reading now."

She dragged me to the long table in the center of the room, where a large book lay open in an intricately carved book stand. The Latin script was handwritten in a beautiful, flowing style surrounding an illuminated letter dripping with leaves and fruits and flourishes of all sorts.

"It's…beautiful." Stunned as I was, no adequate words would come.

"Oh, this is nothing compared to some of the bibles Mother has collected."

"What is this book?"

Cece smiled at the wonder in my voice. "It's a Latin translation of a treatise by the Greek historian, Plutarch." She pointed to another leather-bound volume lying open on the table. "This is the same book in the original Greek."

I turned to this, much more plainly written, book. It had no illuminations or illustrations, and the text was composed of strange symbols I had never seen before.

"You can read this?" I asked, incredulous.

Cece laughed, clearly happy that I was so impressed. "The Latin one, yes. I'm learning Greek by reading the two side-by-side."

I looked into her smiling face, practically glowing in her joy of being in her element. Taking her hands in mine, I whispered, "Teach me. Please."

Her smile broadened. "It would be my pleasure, Dear Sir."

When Aunt Margaret and Mother collected us at the end of the evening, they found us reciting the Latin text. Our reluctant parting was obvious to them. I had heard and repeated rote Latin phrases at Mass, of course, but I otherwise had had no exposure to the language. In those few hours that evening, and the many more Cece and I spent together in that magical place, I learned first Latin, then Greek. Cece and Margaret were excellent teachers, and my penchant for language was on full display.

Cece and I knew they had plans for us to be wed one day. My mother wished it to consolidate our family's claims. My aunt wished to protect her daughter from some purely political union, since she was afraid that the Baron would marry her off to the son of one of his many enemies. Cece and I were both perfectly happy with such an arrangement, and we assumed in our naivete that nothing would disturb what seemed to be the natural course of events.

Chapter 4

England, 1180 A.D.

Besides training in arms, my brother and cousin also passed their time learning the management of an estate, how to command men in the field of battle and, among other pursuits, hunting. As my father did, Uncle Geoffrey loved hunting, and Gerald followed in his father's footsteps in that regard. For my part, and Stewart's, a hunt brought back difficult memories. Memories of our father lying broken and dying in our arms. Whenever Geoffrey announced hunting days, we exchanged knowing glances, but kept our reluctance to ourselves.

Besides the deep emotions they evoked, hunting days were long, with much preparation beforehand and cleanup of horses and tack afterwards. As a groom and squire-in-training, I was kept busy from dawn to dusk for several days, first preparing the Baron's and his court's mounts and the thrusting lances, throwing spears, and other weapons the hunters used to bring down the boars and deer populating Geoffrey's hunting grounds.

Then, once the sun set and the hunters returned to the castle for the evening's feasting, Francois, I, and the other grooms worked late into the night feeding, bathing, and brushing the horses.

As we tended each animal, Francois inspected them minutely, pointing out any scratches and scrapes from tree branches, thorn bushes, and overzealously applied spurs. I followed behind with a pouch of salve that I spread generously over the wounds. Next came the liniment, spread over the joints and flanks. The burn of the wood alcohol and strong smell of Francois's secret recipe of comfrey, St. John's wort, and other herbs often made the beasts skittish, but a bag of oats or a sweet honeycomb usually calmed them. Unfortunately, I always smelled of the strong medicine for days afterward.

Between the preparation and aftermath were many hours spent riding over fields and through forests in pursuit of deer or boar. Being the Baron's kin, I was not required to precede the hunters and beat the underbrush to flush out the prey. This was by far the most dangerous job on those days, as you could just as easily flush a wild boar from its den as a stag from its bed. Instead, I rode behind the hunters, always ready to repair damaged tack, retrieve wayward arrows, or tend to the horses during rest periods.

On one such outing, while the hunting party broke for refreshments and waited out the heat of the day, I wandered into the nearby woods. I had seen what I believed to be a game trail, unnoticed and uninvestigated by the others. I quickly found the suspected trail and began to follow it into the woods. It was well-concealed by brambles and undergrowth, but showed clear, recent tracks of what I judged to be a doe and two of her fawns. The moisture that was still clinging to the sides of the impressions in the mud told me they had passed by only minutes before. Dropping to all fours, I carefully picked my way through the brambles as silently as I could manage.

My stealth was rewarded when I emerged from the undergrowth into a small clearing among a stand of hemlocks. Their low-hanging branches nearly swept the ground as they swayed in the breeze, and their rustling helped to disguise my approach. There, nestled beneath the boughs of one, I saw the spotted pelts of two fawns. Although their mother doe, having left them in such a secure place to browse nearby, was probably close-by, my careful sneaking along had avoided her notice.

Without relaxing my stealth, I crept ever closer. As I slowly lifted a hemlock branch—the final barrier to their lair—I realized I was quietly humming between breaths. Completely unconsciously, my tuneless music seemed to have soothed these most skittish of beasts. Emboldened with this knowledge, and continuing the droning hum, I reached my left hand to touch the flank of the nearest fawn. The muscles under its hide rippled at my touch, but it was otherwise undisturbed. I looked into the eyes of the one I touched, and those of her sister. They both stared back, frozen in place, not from fear, but rather as if mesmerized.

The spell lasted but a moment, but seemed to go on forever, as if time itself was suspended. Like a clap of thunder, the sound of twigs brushing a flank, followed by the crush of dried leaves beneath a hoof, broke through the thrall in which all three of us were held.

Knowing that Mother Doe would smell my presence and expecting her to burst into her fawns' lair with razor hooves flying, I scurried backwards, still humming my tuneless drone until I could stand, turn, and run. As I did, I heard the fawns flush from their beds and bound for the safety of their mother.

My hurried escape had not been nearly as silent as my approach, so I was not surprised when I looked back and saw Mother Doe eyeing my retreat threateningly. Once her babies had passed her in full flight, she barked once at me, spun around, and with white tail raised to warn others of my threat, she followed at full speed.

As I gathered my breath, I somehow knew that singular event would come to define the rest of my life.

"Where did you get lost?" Cecelia offered me a plate heaped with food and a mug of cider when I emerged from the wood. Her smile seemed to light the day brighter than even the brilliant sun shining overhead. I wanted nothing more than to tell her about the magical moment I had just shared with Nature.

"Cece, you'll never believe what just happened," I began, but before I could tell my tale, Gerald noticed the twigs and brambles stuck to my blouse and leggings.

"I hope you didn't wipe your arse with any stinging nettles," he shouted.

The Baron, my brother, and the other men—even the beaters—laughed loudly at Gerald's coarse jab. Cecelia did not, however, and for that, I was instantly grateful. Instead, she blushed a little, threw a look of disgust at her brother, set my plate and mug on the feast table, and turned back to return to the other girls and ladies.

"But, but..." I stammered, then fell silent as another wave of laughter washed over me. Abashed, and knowing the tale of my encounter with the deer would never be believed by the men and other boys, I bit my lip and kept silent.

I have never told that tale until this moment when I have put quill to lambskin. I relate it now to lend credence to some of the more unbelievable parts of the tale to follow.

Chapter 5

England, 1181 A.D.

My duties as a squire-in-training changed as I grew older. On my thirteenth birthday, Francois excused me two afternoons every week to attend Master Grimm to begin my training in small arms.

"Yer a bit o' a runt, ain't ya." The old sword master regarded me with his ever-present squint. Nervous, I kept my own council. I could feel the eyes of Stewart and Gerald on me from where they had been sparring. After a few heartbeats, he continued, "Quiet, too. Like ya br'ther, I see."

Without a word of warning, he jabbed at my side with the blunted sword he held. Having watched many of Stewart and Gerald's training sessions, I was prepared.

I twisted to the side and raised my wooden practice sword to block his thrust. With a flick of his wrist, he avoided my block and, while my arm and the sword it bore continued upward, he looped his weapon under it and struck me in the belly with the flat of it. I stumbled backwards, but managed to keep my balance.

"Yer dead," he said, without a hint of emotion. "Why?"

I struggled to catch the wind his blow had knocked from me. "You feinted," I managed to gasp.

"Aye, but 'at's not why."

I replayed the sequence in my mind. "I missed my block."

"'Ndeed ya did. Why?"

I thought of what I did wrong. "My block was out of control."

Grimm squinted even deeper, then nodded. "Three 'whys'," he said. "'At's better'n yer dolt of a cousin did." His face scrunched into a scowl, his sun-borne wrinkles deepening into crevasses in his cheeks. "But worse'n yer br'ther's too. What's the lesson?"

My mind raced, but the answer seemed obvious. "Keep control of one's weapon."

"Always." He nodded. "What else?"

Think I cajoled myself—*Oh!*

"Think," I blurted. "Ah, anticipate the feint."

Grimm was nodding even before I finished. "Aye, but 'spect the poss'bil'ty o' a feint."

He repeated his attack, but slowly this time. I managed to stop my raised sword in a position that would have blocked both his feinted thrust and the real attack.

"'At's good," Grim said. "Better'n yer br'ther, ev—"

The flash of pride I felt at his praise evaporated when he attacked again at full speed. I managed to block his swing, but the force of his blow knocked my sword from my hand and drove me stumbling backwards. He spun his body to follow his sword and built momentum that he delivered with a loud smack to my ribs. The force drove me to one knee.

"Yer dead," he muttered, but there was no satisfaction in the statement. "Less'n?"

I winced when I bent to pick up my sword, then straightened, trying my best to keep the pain from my face. "Don't get distracted."

He nodded at first, then shook his head. "Aye, 'at's yer less'n. Mine is dif'rent, tho'." He eyed me appraisingly up and down. "Ya got yer momma's French blood in ya. More'n 'at brute does." He tilted his head to Stewart, who had stopped sparring with Gerald to watch my lesson.

His scowl deepened as he assessed me silently. Then, with a speed I didn't think possible, he drew a dagger from a sheath at his hip and sent it flying at me.

"Close yer mouth, Lad." I snapped my jaw shut as I looked down at the hilt of the knife protruding from the dirt between my feet. "Pick it up," Grimm said impatiently.

I bent down and felt for the hilt, never taking my eyes off Grimm, fully expecting another attack. None came, though.

"Yu'll never be big 'nuff to wield a broadsword. A long sword from horseback—maybe." He nodded, sure of his decision. "Maybe, but yer clever and quick. More suited for slippin' a misericorde or a 'talian stiletto between plate armor."

I was appalled. "You mean a sneak attack?"

Grimm snorted, but the flush in his neck showed his anger. "I mean a killer. 'At's what yer to learn here." He spread his hands to indicate the training ground. "Don't matter if'n ya slice his head clean off wi' a two-handed broadsword or slip a rondel 'tween his ribs from behind. Either way, he's dead. An' yer not." He pointed at the knife in my hand. "Carry 'at seax wi' ya' ever'where. Feel the weight of it, its balance. Sleep wi' it, for God'sake. When ya' can flip it over three times in th' air without cuttin' yerself and toss it hand-ta-hand without lookin', I'll teach ya how to throw it through a knight's visor."

He looked over at Stewart and Gerald to make his point. It took me a moment to realize he was telling me I could kill one such as them, despite my diminutive size. When he saw that I understood that lesson, he nodded.

"Now, git yerself back ta 'em horses, Boy."

Thus, I set out on the course the rest of my long life would take.

In short order, I moved from the stables, where I had learned to care for the horses and their tack and had become fluent in French as well, to the armory. There, I learned to sharpen and polish blades of all sizes and shapes. I memorized the many pieces of armor which enveloped a knight, and all the straps and buckles needed to hold them together. My training in the use of the smaller of those weapons also began.

Master Grimm showed me the various grips needed for thrusts and parries. Being small of frame, I developed a fondness for the smaller, more maneuverable, and more secretive blades such as the old seax Grimm gave me so deftly, the arming sword, and the misericorde, a thin, circular blade meant to deliver a merciful death to a wounded knight. My deftness at feinting and wielding the smaller blades did not go unnoticed, and soon I was given the nickname Sinister.

Somehow, even at thirteen years of age, Grimm had seen that I would not have the fair looks and silver tongue of Gerald, nor the physical presence and prowess at arms of Stewart. Instead, he knew instinctively that I would have to rely on my wit, speed, and stealth if I were to flourish, or even survive the role in life that I would be expected to play.

Being the second son of a baron's brother, I was well removed from any possible inheritance. Being noble born though, regardless of how distaff, I was expected to serve my lord in some capacity. The choices of that service were few and usually involved some form of combat. Knowing that my prospects for leading men into battle were small, like my stature, I hoped to prove my worth more as a counsellor, an ambassador, an agent secret, or even an agent provocateur. These hopes were no more than fantasies, or so I thought, because my lord uncle had no need for such ministers. Rather, whenever our King Henry called up men-at-arms to go to war, Uncle Geoffrey was duty-bound to provide footmen, sergeants, and knights, not ambassadors or spies.

Those footmen and sergeants needed training as well, so there was a constant flow of young men, serfs mostly, through Grimm's training ground. I spent a good deal of my training time as a sergeant-in-training, learning how to organize these amateur soldiers into a platoon to support, protect, and follow a knight like Stewart in battle.

So, my life's path was plain to see—long years of training on horseback and on foot aimed at keeping me alive in the melee of battle at Stewart's side. Defensive moves involving blocking and parrying, followed by the surprise thrust of a hidden blade, became my main technique. It proved surprisingly effective during our daily exercises.

Frustrating my opponent to the point of rashness, as I often did with Gerald, though much less so with Stewart, then taking advantage of his hot head won me many sparring matches, though not many friends among the other trainees. It did catch the appreciative eye of Master Grimm, however, which of course won me even fewer friends and several knocks on the head from my larger, but dimmer, opponents.

When Uncle Geoffrey's armorer outfitted Stewart and Gerald with their plate armor, I was given a suit of light chain mail. Speed and maneuverability being my primary means of both defense and offense.

Chapter 6

England, 1182 A.D.

I t seems now that the years of training passed quickly, though at the time the days were long and the work hard. Stewart became well known for his prowess with sword and lance, while my cousin's reputation was based more on his prowess with a different kind of "sword". Uncle Geoffrey railed against Gerald's licentious ways, but did little to stop his nighttime forays into town to drink and sow his wild oats. Those wild, bastardly oats were what Uncle feared most, lest an unwanted heir should be born.

Instead of confronting his son directly, though, he enlisted Stewart to be our cousin's keeper. Sober, hard-working Stewart became the counter-balance to drunken, hard-screwing Gerald. This arrangement seemed to work, as it kept Gerald out of serious trouble while allowing him to make a considerable amount of minor trouble.

As the day when Gerald and Stewart were to be knighted approached, however, Gerald's attitude seemed to change. His carousing lessened and his religious devotion increased, as did his training efforts. Perhaps it was Stewart's influence, or perhaps it was simply his fear of being embarrassed on the most important day of his young life.

Knighting ceremonies for those who were noble born were typically a three-day festival, with a series of tests for the candidates. The ceremony for Gerald and Stewart followed this pattern, and Uncle Geoffrey spared no expense, as befitted his pride in his only son.

He invited the local bishop to officiate. The day before the festivities began, Bishop Rose arrived with an entourage that included two escorts from the Order of the Poor Knights of Christ and the Temple of Solomon. These "Knights Templar", as they were commonly called, were most impressive in their simple tunics overlaid with pure white mantles emblazoned with an instantly recognizable blood-red cross. Their military bearing, combined with their humility, evoked both fear and admiration among the gathered knights.

Privately, Gerald scoffed at the Templars. "Why would a knight of noble blood dedicate himself to a life of poverty, chastity, prayer, and war?" I overhead him asking Stewart. In his typically stoic manner, Stewart merely shrugged. That didn't dissuade Gerald. "These two are French," he sneered. "Perhaps that explains it."

To Gerald, anything he couldn't understand, he attributed to being foreign, as if all Englishmen thought like him and all foreigners, especially the French, behaved unnaturally. Stewart and I exchange glances, but as always, remained silent despite Gerald's unthinking slander of our own heritage.

Stewart, by contrast, was quite impressed with the Templars, and I saw him huddled with one or both of the French knights frequently.

The first of the three days of festivities was a tournament day, during which the two young candidates being tested, along with the Baron's knights, and other knights from the region competed in a series of contests. Their ability to wield both long and short swords was measured against other knights in melees that ranged over hill and dale. Knights in full armor, aboard their armored steeds, battled furiously until one or another was knocked from his horse and forced to yield. Thus captured, they owed a ransom—sometimes as much as the very horse they had ridden into battle—to their vanquisher.

Over and over again, Stewart emerged victorious, amassing quite the hoard of ransom. With each capture, I festooned his banner with many of the ladies' brightly colored favors. If his temperament had been similar to Gerald's, he could have spread his wild oats far and wide that evening, indeed.

On the second day, their horsemanship skills and the command of their mounts were tested in races and obstacle courses. The day culminated with the final contest, the traditional mounted joust using blunted oaken lances. The candidates for knighthood were not expected to win, or even come close to winning, any of these contests. Rather, the trials were meant to prove their worthiness to be called knights and to be address as "Sir".

Gerald fulfilled these expectations, scoring well in the combat tests, though less so with his horsemanship. Stewart, on the other hand exceeded everyone's expectations—everyone except Master Grimm's and mine. He scored highest among all knights during the melees, and close to the top in horsemanship. It was in the joust, the most anticipated contest, that Stewart really proved his mettle.

He easily defeated many of the much more seasoned knights in the preliminary rounds. So many, in fact, that he exhausted his allotment of lances. As the final round approached, I, as Stewart's squire, had to borrow a lance from Gerald. Gerald had been eliminated from the competition after only the second round, so he still had several unused ones. But when I asked for one, I could see the jealousy in his eyes. Stewart was being cheered on by peasants and knights alike, overshadowing Gerald on what should have been his day of glory. So, I was surprised when he readily agreed to let his "beloved cousin" use his "best" lance.

His turn of phrase confused me, since I sought a fresh, unused lance, but my trained eye could see that the lance he pressed upon me was the one he had used when he was unseated during an early round. Being suspicious, I turned the lance in my hands as I walked to Stewart's end of the trace, covertly inspecting it. Alas, I found what I had feared, yet had also expected.

A fine fracture line mixed in with the grain of the oak meant the lance was dangerously cracked and would not withstand even a glancing blow, let alone a full strike to Stewart's opponent. As I lifted the lance to Stewart who sat astride his mount, I gripped it so my thumb and forefinger pointed to the crack.

Holding the lance high above my head, but out of Stewart's reach, I proclaimed in a loud voice, "Behold, Dear Brother, what our beloved cousin has so graciously donated to your cause."

As the crowd cheered, I lowered the lance enough to make Stewart bend to take it and whispered, "Beware, Brother, don't let the strength of this lance betray your own."

Surprised, but with an understanding of my cryptic words that can only be shared between brothers, he gave me a knowing look, took the lance from my hands, and held it at the ready.

Turning to the dais where Gerald sat with our family, and taking his cue from my hint, Stewart proclaimed, "Thanks be to you, Dear Cousin. I know the strength of this oak will reflect your own."

As the crowd cheered again, Stewart spun the lance a half-turn so that when it split along the crack, as we both knew it would, the splinters would fly harmlessly to the ground.

Stewart and his opponent, one of the greatest and most heralded knights of the age, Sir William Marshal, took their positions at opposite ends and opposing sides of the trace rail. With lances raised, they awaited the signal. Our mother's favor sailed from the grandstand and the crowd held its collective breath while it fluttered to the ground. When it landed, both knights dropped their lances into position and spurred their mounts forward.

The result of this pass being a foregone conclusion, I looked about for another source of stouter lances. It was for naught however, because when the jousters charged each other and his lance shattered as expected, Stewart was unseated by what appeared to be a barely glancing blow to his shield.

He landed with a crash and rolled over twice before stopping face-down on the grass. As I ran onto the trace with my bag of bandages and armor tools, the crowd grew silent. When I reached him, Stewart and I exchanged another knowing look. Then he slowly climbed to his feet, lifted his visor, and raised an arm in salute to Sir William.

The crowd, still hushed, erupted into cheers and bellows of "Huzzah!" as if he had won. Sir William dismounted out of respect and met Stewart at the trace rail, where they grasped each other's forearms in the traditional way. While the crowd's cheers celebrated William Marshal's victory and Stewart's stalwart efforts, the knight and knight-to-be shared private words which I barely overheard as I gathered Stewart's horse and his discarded gauntlets and helm.

"We caught each other with but glancing blows. Yet, your lance shattered, and it unseated you. How can this be?" Sir William asked, somewhat accusingly.

"It has been a long day, and some among us have tired of my success. It is better to end the joust than to end a friendship."

Understanding dawned on the famous knight's face, and he smiled ruefully. "It seems the most formidable knight today is also the wisest."

Chapter 7

England, 1182 A.D.

Having proven their mettle in the arts of combat, Gerald and Stewart faced a completely different kind of test on the evening of the first day. In order to demonstrate their humility and sobriety, although the feast was in their honor, they could not take part. Instead of sharing the feast in a place of honor at the high table, they sat on simple kitchen chairs on a platform to the side of the castle's great hall.

While the Baron's court, the visiting knights, the bishop, prominent merchants, and their families feasted on wild boar, venison, fowl, sweetmeats, candied fruits, and much wine and beer, Stewart and Gerald sat stoically alone. To share his joy with the townsfolk, the Baron ordered that a larger feast of somewhat simpler fare be laid out in the castle's forecourt, to which all were welcome, regardless of their station.

Following the meal, their chairs were removed, and the candidates stood while a steady flow of knights, merchants, freemen, and their families approached Gerald and Stewart at their humble position.

"Good evening, young man," one merchant from the town said as he shook Gerald's hand. "I am Thomas

Bridgeton, an importer of fine wines and spirits. We were most impressed by your…efforts during the melees today."

"Thank you, Kind Sir. And who might these lovely young ladies be? Your daughters?" Gerald's smile beamed at the two women accompanying the merchant. His eyes flicked over the younger of the two, who scowled a bit. But he held the elder woman's gaze, and she returned it with a broad smile of her own.

"Daughters? Oh, no—that is—well, one is," the merchant stammered, then sipped from the cup he carried. "May I present my wife, Martha, and our daughter, Emily. Emily just turned fourteen last month." He said the last with a bit of a leer, but Gerald barely nodded to Emily before returning his attention to Martha.

He took Martha's offered hand, leaned over and kissed it, his lips lingering on her knuckles long enough for her to press a note into his hand. Straightening, he gave Martha's hand a squeeze, then slipped the note into the pocket of his tunic. It was not alone in there.

"Enchante, My Lady." The twinkle in his eye told her he received the message.

Oblivious to this exchange, Bridgeton turned to Stewart. "And you, sir. Your prowess with both long and short sword was simply awe-inspiring. Congratulations on your much-deserved win."

Stewart, having witnessed Gerald beginning the cuckolding of the man, simply muttered his thanks. Similarly, young Emily's flirtatious smile and posturing, prompted by Martha's poke in her ribs, was lost on my brother.

The line of guests seemed to go on for hours and similar exchanges were repeated again and again. After introducing themselves and the members of their families, with special introductions for their eligible daughters, the merchants, knights, and nobles heaped praise on the young men for their rank, their looks, their physical prowess, and anything else they could think of. In response, Gerald returned the praise, concentrating on the beauty of the women whether they be marriageable daughters, wives, or grandmothers. Stewart, on the other hand, mumbled his thanks and promised to fulfill his title by being a good steward and protector of the community.

All this I witnessed from my seat at the end of the family table. By the end of the evening, Gerald's pockets fairly bulged with notes. Into his righthand pocket he deposited those surreptitiously given him by wives of middling or better attractiveness. In his left went the daughters' and wives' to whom time and childbirth had not been kind.

During a lull in the receiving line, I brought the cousins goblets of water and chunks of the hearty bread—the only food they were allowed. Gerald leaned toward Stewart and patted his righthand pocket.

"A bastard born of a wife can be claimed as their own, but the swelling of a daughter's belly will ruin her prospects for a fine marriage. So, I'm actually doing them a favor." He said the last with a chuckle. Stewart simply gave him a sideways look and shook his head.

When the final visitor had rejoined the now wild and drunken festivities, the Templars escorted the two candidates to a small room with just two straw mats on the stone floor. Sealing them in, the Templars retired themselves. I, being their squire, had been bringing my brother and cousin bread and water throughout the evening, when not chatting with Cece. But, when they led their charges away, the Templars forbade me from accompanying them. Intrigued, I quietly slipped from the hall and secretly followed them through the castle to the stone cell where Gerald and Stewart would spend the night.

From the dark shadows of a deep doorway, I watched as one Templar bolted the cell door from the outside while the other pressed a wax seal across the bolt. Thinking I was perfectly concealed, I held my breath as the knights strode past my hiding place on the way to their own room. However, as they drew abreast of my position, I clearly saw the eyes of the knight closest to me flick in my direction and his head nod ever so slightly. Apparently, I had not been as clever as I had thought.

The following day, the second of three days of celebration, was a festival and market day, open to the common people, during which the candidates were celebrated with a parade, in song by travelling minstrels, and by an acting troupe who performed their stock morality plays, but with either Gerald or Stewart as the heroes.

I noticed late in the morning that after releasing Gerald and Stewart from their confinement at dawn, the Templars had been absent from the day's festivities. After sharing the noon meal with Aunt Margaret, Mother, and Cecelia, I went looking for Stewart, who had been absent most of the morning, also. Taking my leave of the ladies, reluctantly so in the case of Cecelia, I found Gerald in the chapel at prayer with the Templars. I joined them until our prayers were complete, when the Templars rose silently and led us to the armory.

We spent the afternoon training in a way we never had before. The Templars explained their way of fighting as a unit composed of a knight, one or more sergeants, and a group of foot soldiers—pikemen, lancers, and swordsmen. The knight directed their movements and led the attack and the sergeants provided close support of the knight and positioned the foot soldiers for maximum effect.

They stressed again and again that as long as the Templars' battle flag was raised, they could not abandon the field, even if it meant certain defeat and death.

Stewart and I absorbed their teaching like a dry field accepts a spring rain, and I could see a look of zeal in Stewart's eyes. It was a look I had never seen before, even in the heat of training battles. We trained thus throughout the afternoon.

That evening was another feast, this time more sedate but with music and dancing. The guests were limited to just those staying within the castle. Gerald and Stewart were allowed to participate this time, for which I was very grateful since I did not have to attend them and could then dance with Cece.

Again, as they had at the end of the previous evening, the Templars escorted Gerald and Stewart from the hall. This time, though, they were accompanied by all of the knights present. They silently marched to the chapel where the candidates prostrated themselves before the altar. The gathered knights sat on benches, intending to sit vigil with them through the whole night. Though charged with staying awake until dawn, within the time it took for the moon to cross its width, all but Stewart and Gerald were sprawled on the floor and a chorus of snores echoed throughout the nave.

For me, this was a wonderful break, because it meant Cece and I could spend the evening together. Our mothers, smiling with approval, left us alone to hold hands and whisper words of young love to each other. When it was time to retire, I asked Aunt Margaret most gallantly if I could escort Cecelia to her chamber. Our mothers looked at each other, laughed, and granted my request.

"You may escort my daughter, Young Master. But after you have ensured her safe arrival, I expect you to return forthwith."

I bowed deeply and replied, "Of course, My Lady."

With that, Cece and I hurried from the main hall and, once out of eyesight or our mothers, we strolled hand-in-hand through the hallways of the castle to her chamber door. After much hand-play and cooing, I knew our mothers would be getting restive. So, I bid Cece good night and leaned in to kiss her cheek. I was transported with delight when, instead of offering her cheek, she tilted her head back and met my lips with hers.

Unlike the snoring knights in the chapel, I slept very little that night.

Chapter 8

England, 1182 A.D.

The knighting ceremony itself was surprisingly short, probably because it was held right after matins, the pre-dawn prayers, which ended the night-long vigil. Mass followed, officiated by the bishop, who, like the rest of us, had a bed to sleep in the previous night. He studiously ignored the nodding heads among those who had not.

After the mass, an honor guard of knights escorted Gerald and Stewart to the altar through an honor guard of knights. They knelt before the bishop and Uncle Geoffrey and swore oaths to protect the Church, protect the innocent, respond promptly to calls to arms by their lords, and strangely enough, to fight fairly and courteously with other knights. To the ears of someone like me, who was being schooled in the attack sinister, this seemed very odd indeed.

Once the oaths were administered, and with the blessing of the bishop, Uncle Geoffrey touched the shoulders of first Gerald, then Stewart with his ceremonial sword and bestowed upon them the title of "Sir". As Sir Gerald and Sir Stewart arose and turned to face the congregation, the knights stood their straightest, raised their swords over their heads, and bellowed out three roars of "Huzzah!"

I felt my heart nearly burst with pride, and I imagined myself someday to be in Stewart's place at the head of the procession of noble knights as they filed out of the chapel into the new day.

After a hearty breakfast, they again opened the castle gates to the townsfolk, where meats, cheeses, sweetmeats, and many other diverse foods and drink were served throughout the day. The market stalls opened again, and games of skill, games of chance, and foot races of all kinds were held in the fields.

About midmorning, seeing that Gerald was the center of attention, especially among the ladies young and old, I realized I had not seen Stewart or the Templars for quite some time. Assuming they were again praying in the chapel, or training in the armory, I set out to find them.

As had become my habit, I proceeded as stealthily as possible, first to the chapel, which stood empty, then to the armory. I found them there, but not training as I had suspected. Instead, they were sitting knee-to-knee with heads bowed, as if in prayer. As they sat thus, I crept closer until I was within earshot when they raised their heads.

I clearly heard one of the Templars say, "You have now received the first secret of our Order. Will you guard it with your heart, your will, and your life if necessary?"

In a clear voice, Stewart responded, "I will."

"Then you have begun your journey on God's path, consecrated by the Rule of our Order. Stand."

Stewart and the two Templars stood and the one who had not yet spoken drew from beneath his mantel a coarse rope of about two arm spans. He looped the rope around Stewart's waist and tied it in a knot I had never seen before.

When he finished, he said, "Sir Stewart of Sowich, you are bound to the Order of the Poor Knights of Christ and the

Temple of Solomon with this symbolic rope and knot, as we are."

Both Templars then lifted their mantels to reveal the same knotted rope about their own waists.

"Do you pledge your life and your fortune to the Order until death or until such time that you are honorably released by our Master in London or our Grand Master now in the Levant?"

Again, Stewart answered clearly, "I do."

With broad smiles, which I had never before seen on their faces, both Templars embraced Stewart as a brother.

Confusion, fear, and jealousy surged inside and overwhelmed me. Could I be losing my beloved brother on this great day?

Perhaps my shock caused me to gasp, or simply shift my weight enough to reveal my presence. Or, as I now think more likely, my stealth had not been as concealing as I had thought it to be. Regardless, the first Templar to speak turned and looked directly at my hiding place.

Calmly he said, "Come out of hiding Little Man. Your talents for skulking and deception are excellent for one so young, but not what they need to be to fool us."

The Templars were smiling at me as I rose from my hiding place, but in a kindly and indulgent way. Stewart was not surprised by my presence either, as he had long ago become used to me appearing seemingly out of nowhere. Instead, His face revealed a guilty look.

Playing on his guilt, and letting my feelings overtake me I strode up to him. Ignoring the Templars, I sharply rebuked him in a voice trembling with anger and sadness.

"When were you going to tell me? As you were riding away with them tomorrow?"

My verbal blow struck home, and I could see Stewart's eyes brimming with tears. Before he could stammer a reply, however, the second Templar, whose name I had learned was Jean de Payans, spoke to me in French.

"Go easy, Little Man. This day can be one of joining instead of separating for you, also."

The switch to the French gave me pause as I wondered how he knew I could speak the language. As I turned to ask him what he meant, he again spoke in his native tongue.

"We have been very impressed with both your brother and with you. Although you are not yet a knight, our Order has many ranks you could aspire to, and there are many roles to fill in the Holy Land."

This statement, astounding as it was, gave me pause, and I noticed Stewart looking at the Templar and me with confusion. So, despite my anger at him, or perhaps because of it, I replied in our native tongue – the one I knew to be the only one Stewart understood.

"Are you inviting me to join your Order, also? To leave my home and family?" And Cecelia, I thought. Leaving her and what I hoped was our blossoming love would be the hardest of all. Before the Templar could answer, however, my own question raised another in my mind.

"But this is not our home," I said as I turned to Stewart. "What of our father's estate now being held by Sir Robert Enderhite? I thought when you became a knight, you would reclaim it."

Stewart bowed his head and, in a voice that was almost a whisper, said, "I no longer have that ambition." He raised his head again and looked me directly in the eye. "I feel the pull of God deep in my very soul." His voice regained the strength I knew so well. "His Church and his righteous servants in the Holy Land need my strength. And I need to give it to Him."

Gone from his face were the guilt and confusion I had sown there. A burning zeal replaced them—the same zeal that I had seen in his eyes as we trained with the Templars the previous day, yet intensified even more.

My decision was obvious to me. I would follow wherever my brother and these formidable knights led.

I turned back to the Templars and said simply, "What role am I to play in this journey?"

They smiled, and the first replied, "I can only tell you the first one. Beyond that, it is up to you. I have no doubt, however, that it will be an important one."

Chapter 9

England, 1182 A.D.

My uncle was first to notice the rope around Stewart's waist as we returned to the festival field. Uncle Geoffrey, the bishop, Aunt Margaret, Mother, and Cecelia were all seated on the covered dais watching the festivities. He leaped to his feet and glowered at us as we—the Templars, Stewart, and I—approached the dais.

"What is the meaning of this?" Turning his fury on the Sir Jean, who stood straight and met his eye directly, Geoffrey bellowed, "Do you mean to steal my best from me on his first day of knighthood?"

Sir Jean drew a breath to answer, but Stewart responded first. In a clear, resonant voice, he declared his intentions.

"I make this choice of my own free will. The call to serve Our Lord rings in my heart clearer and louder than your chapel bell."

Since this was probably the longest statement Uncle had ever heard Stewart utter, his mouth hung open. Stewart continued over Uncle Geoffrey's renewed objections.

"The deed is done. I've sworn my oath and pledged my life and immortal soul to this most noble Order. I also petition you to pledge my worldly possessions, including those you hold in trust."

All Uncle Geoffrey could do now was stand red-faced and bluster. It was completely within Stewart's rights, now that he was a knight and therefore an adult, to demand the return of our father's holdings. And then to do with them as he wished.

While Uncle's face grew even more crimson, by contrast, the bishop was beaming. He raised a hand, attempting to calm my uncle. "It is customary that when entering holy orders, knights donate the major portion of their estates to that Order." He turned to my mother, who was also in a state of shock. "Of course, you would not leave your mother," he seemed to notice me for the first time, "or your young brother, destitute, would you?"

Caught off guard, Stewart's air of confidence wavered. "Uh, of course not…"

In the most adult voice I could muster, I came to his rescue. "While our loving Mother should keep enough income to repay our beloved Uncle for his hospitality throughout her remaining years—pray that they are long—have no concern for my welfare. I have this day also pledged my service to these noble knights and their Holy Order."

The bishop's smile broadened even more while Uncle stood completely flummoxed. Cecelia realized what my declaration—the first public speech I had ever made—meant.

"Nooo!" she screamed, her hands fluttering about her mouth.

Her exclamation broke Mother out of her shock. With tears streaming down her face, she knew, as a woman and his mother, she had no right to try to dissuade Stewart from his decision. Instead, I suspect she was proud of him. But my age put me firmly under her control. So, she directed her anger and disappointment at me.

"So, you mean to always be your brother's shadow?"

The venom in her voice pierced my heart like an arrow, and my conviction wavered. But I quickly recovered and, drawing myself up to my full, yet still diminutive height, I remained silently steadfast.

By this time, our announcement drew the attention of the revelers across the field. Gerald, now Sir Gerald, having reluctantly disengaged from the flock of young ladies who surrounded him, strode up to our position.

"What is the ruckus all about?"

His smiling and joking manner disappeared when he saw Uncle Geoffrey's countenance. Receiving no reply from those on the dais, he turned to Stewart. Stewart looked him straight in the eye.

"I…we," he nodded in my direction, "have joined the Order of these noble knights." He lifted the ends of the rope around his waist. "I am pledged…" his voice faltered, but he recovered quickly. "I have pledged my life and my worldly possessions to furthering their cause."

Knowing Gerald's temperament, I expected an explosion of temper, which he duly provided.

"How dare you! How dare you do this on my most important day?"

It seems Gerald was more concerned with losing people's attention than he was with the prospect of Stewart—or me—leaving. Perhaps realizing how petty his reaction seemed, he switched tactics.

"You can't leave. You are bound to this family—to my father. I won't let you break that obligation."

The blood rose in Stewart's neck as his ire rose at the insult.

"I am a freeman, as my father was. I have sworn no oath of fealty to you or your father. Indeed, if I had waited even a day to make my decision, you both would have pressured me to swear such an oath. Instead, I have sworn an oath to God and his Holy Son."

The Baron finally found his voice. "This is how you repay me for my hospitality, and for your training these many years?"

Years of frustration and resentment broke free from stoic Stewart. "I've repaid you many times over. Without my help, your son, 'Gerald the Fair'," he sneered, and his voice dripped with sarcasm, "would never have completed his training. And if I had not held back to avoid embarrassing him, I would have been a knight long before now."

Gerald's hand flew to his sword, but before he could draw it, Sir Jean stepped between the cousins and spoke calmly to Gerald.

"Take care what you start. Always see your way to a successful conclusion before you engage in battle."

The calm words gave Gerald pause, and although he still gripped the hilt, his sword remained in the scabbard.

Turning to the baron, Sir Jean spoke with authority.

"The die is cast. I am sure your nephews would have preferred a more joyous sendoff, but the knot that binds Stewart—and Liam—to us cannot be undone by a man such as you. We will take our leave once Stewart and Liam have made their preparations. I trust you, both" at this he looked at Gerald pointedly, "will not make the parting any more difficult than necessary.

"I will also send a missive, signed by Sir Stewart and witnessed by the bishop, to our Master here in England that details Sir Stewart's wishes with regard to the disposition of his inheritance."

With that, the Templars turned on their heels and the four of us marched to the castle.

Chapter 10

England, 1182 A.D.

Although the bishop was eager to leave after the festivities, the Templars granted Stewart and me a day to prepare. Much of that time, I spent saying goodbye to Mother and Cecelia. The parting was hard, and I cannot honestly say that I did not doubt my decision during it. Especially so when I tried to comfort Mother or dry Cece's tears. But, if there was one lesson I had learned living amongst knights and soldiers my entire life, it was that once a decision is made, questioning the wisdom of it only serves to weaken it. So, I remained steadfast despite the unspoken understanding that I would probably never see Mother or my lovely Cecelia again.

When the time came to leave, I saddled two horses, one for Stewart and one for myself, and loaded our belongings, including Stewart's armor and weapons, onto a third pack horse. We rode for two days to escort the bishop back to his Abbey, then two more days to London. Most of the trip we rode in silence, though the bishop found the jostling of his carriage tedious and insisted on repeatedly telling us so. But between us—the four Templars—there seemed to be a mutual desire for solitude with our thoughts.

During the last day before arriving in London, however, the Templars broke the long silence. They explained more about the order, its Rule, and its traditions.

"Our Order was founded by my distant cousin, Hugh de Payens and our patron, Saint Bernard of Clairvaux, nearly seventy years ago," Sir Jean explained. "In 1119, Bernard commissioned nine knights, many of them his kith and kin, to go to the Holy Land and protect the many Christians on pilgrimage there. You see, bandits, especially the Muslim scum, took the lives and fortunes of many of those righteous travelers. As holy warrior-monks, we fight, not for Earthly gain, but to protect the righteous."

"Only nine knights?" I asked. Knowing the reach and wealth of the Templars, I was quite skeptical.

"Aye, only nine. They labored there for nine years while Saint Bernard wrote the Rule of the Poor Fellow-Soldiers of Christ and of the Temple of Solomon, our rule which governs both our everyday lives and our holy purpose. He also petitioned the Holy Father directly to recognize the order, which Innocent II did in the year of our Lord 1129. Since then, our Order has grown throughout Christendom, establishing commanderies in every major town, and building castles and forts to protect pilgrims throughout the Levant."

Stewart listened with rapt attention while I tried to analyze this history lesson.

"How did the Order grow so fast?"

Sir Jean eyed me speculatively. "Our Order keeps secrets. Our order of battle, our rites, secrets of kings, and even of Popes. You have learned but the most minor ones during your initiation and at this stage of your training. There are many, many more. Only the Grand Master and his seneschals know them all, if even they do."

"Like how you hold pilgrims' property in trust while they travel?" The little I had learned of the Templars financial systems fascinated me.

"Indeed, and how they can safely carry the essence of their fortune with them and redeem it when they arrive."

I nodded, intrigued. "Secret coded receipts."

The two older knights exchanged knowing glances, then Sir Jean put a finger to his lips. "Secrets are only secret if they remain unspoken."

Abashed, I held my tongue. It was a lesson well-learned and well-used throughout the rest of this long life. Some secret, perhaps the deepest the Order possessed, caused—or forced—Pope Innocent II to grant them extraordinary powers. Unlike any other army, the Templars could cross borders between kingdoms unmolested and establish churches, estates, and abbeys wherever they saw fit. They ordained their own priests, using secret rites and rituals.

The tradition of landholders donating their estates upon entering the Order provided it with vast wealth and huge incomes that were used to carry out its primary mission, the protection of Christians in the Holy Land. Templars were the first Holy Order of knights and soldiers, and were hence doubly armored, their bodies sheathed with steel and their souls with righteousness.

Based on the Rule of the Benedictines, but much stricter and with strong marshal leanings, Saint Bernard's Rule for this order of 'warrior monks' prescribed both the monastic life and constant military training. Through their dedication, obedience, and certitude of salvation, they had become the best and most feared fighting force since the legionnaires of Rome.

As I was not yet a knight, I was not yet eligible to join the order as one of these warrior monks. However, I could serve as a layman squire and train to be first a sergeant, and ultimately a knight. The piety, bearing, and confidence of these knights made me proud, at the time as a naïve teenager, to be counted among them, even if it was in a minor rank.

55

Chapter 11

London and France, 1182-1183 A.D.

I n London, we lived at the Templars' English headquarters, and throughout that summer and most of the following autumn, we continued our training. Stewart fell into the ways of the Templar rule quite comfortably, while I enjoyed a high level of respect and responsibility for one so young.

One bright sunny, but cool day, as Christmastide approached, our Master declared we had completed our training. We were ready to begin our mission in the service of the King of Jerusalem, protecting pilgrims traveling to the Holy Land.

To our surprise, the two Templars whom we had first met, Sir Jean and his stalwart companion Sir Hughes, accompanied us on our journey. At the docks in London, we boarded one of a fleet of Templar ships and set sail with the ebbing tide.

Our route, planned by Sir Jean and our ship's captain—himself a Templar as were his crew—was to take us around Iberia to the Templar castle outside Barcelona. The long sea route, rather than one that would take us overland through France, was necessary as England and France were again at war. Though every Templars' loyalty lay solely with the Order, it was inadvisable to march our party of several hundred through the middle of a secular war. Our enemy lay to the east and south.

In London town, ships set sail in accordance with the rise and fall of the River Thames. Its height and direction of flow this close to the sea follows the rhythm of the tides. So it was that before dawn on a Spring morning, thirteen ships cast off from the piers along the river's edge and raised white sails emblazoned with the blood-red Templar cross. No cheering crowds, nor wives and daughters waving kerchiefs marked our departure. No, this band of warriors had long since left their loved ones behind all across the fair hills of England.

The winds and sea fought us from the moment we left the confines of the river and entered the waters separating England from France. Waters that had seen nearly constant conflict between two peoples so close in heritage, yet so hated by the other. King Henry had conquered and held the northwestern regions of France for most of his reign, so we were secure from attack, leastwise because of the bold announcement our sails made of our papal protection.

We were not secure from the weather, however. Southwesterly winds howled through the channel between England and France, forcing our flotilla to spread out across a wide expanse of the narrow passage to allow for the wide, tacking turns necessary to make even the slightest of forward progress. All day our vessel, the Triumph of the Faithful, fought the wind, but it was the waves that overcame even the most hearty of us land-warriors. The rolling and pitching of the ship, as the captain and his crew battled the elements, brought their passengers—our contingent of knights, sergeants, and foot soldiers—to our knees, retching and miserable. The decks became slick with our sea sickness.

A full day's struggle brought us only to the point of land known as Pointe des Groins. As night fell, so did the rain.

The storm that we could see hovering and threatening to our south throughout the day came at us with full force as the daylight waned, darkening the day and blackening the night so the ship's lanterns of but two of our companion vessels were visible.

At first, the rain seemed a blessing. It washed the decks clean of our gorge and refreshed us with its coolness. But our relief was short-lived, as the rain quickly became a deluge, the winds became a gale, then a tempest. Our ship, sturdy though it was, heaved and groaned as it hung precariously at the crest of a wave, then dove precipitously into the trough, bringing with each fall a wall of water breaking over the prow. With lengths of heavy rope, we lashed ourselves to each other and each end to the strongest beams we could reach.

We offered many shouted prayers to God, His angels, and saints. Their mingling with the incessant howling of the wind, the crashing of wave upon wave, the captain's shouted orders to his crew, and the pitiful whinnying of the terrified horses in the hold resulted in a cacophony of terror that none who survived that night could ever forget.

How we survived was a topic of debate for several weeks. Some claimed it was through the miraculous intervention of Our Lord and his minions. Those making that argument believed themselves to be more righteous and their prayers to be more heartfelt than our brothers, who were lost that night. It struck me then, and I believe even more strongly now, that it was simply the skill of the captain and his faithful crew that delivered us, not to Paradise, but to the western shore of France.

When, at last, the storm broke with the coming of dawn, we were but three ships out of our original complement of thirteen, in various states of disrepair, huddled in the shelter of a rocky cove. We later learned that six other vessels made landfall further down the coast, but four shiploads of our brethren were blown westward out into the vast ocean, never to be seen again.

The Triumph lay, listing heavily, on the shallow bottom of our makeshift harbor. A grazing blow against a rocky reef at the entrance to the cove had rent a gash in her hull just at the waterline. With daring born of experience and skill, the captain drove the ship almost onto the beach of pebbles, running aground less than a hundred yards out. Thus, he saved the ship, us, her helpless passengers, and most importantly, our horses, armor, and weaponry stowed in the hold.

There was water only up to our thighs below decks, the tide having run out as the storm abated. As soon as we came to rest, the captain ordered us to offload as much cargo as we could before the tide rose again. While the knights and sergeants led our terrified steeds to the beach and up into the hills beyond, the foot soldiers made many trips wading through the rising water laden with armor, swords, pikes, and all the weaponry they could carry. Alas, the seawater fouled most of our provisions of food and drink.

In the meantime, the crew set about quickly patching the hull to make the Triumph, if not seaworthy, at least able to stay afloat. We each then took turns at the pumps to empty the bilge.

Of our two companion vessels, one lay foundered on the very reef that we had almost avoided, while the other floated at anchor just outside the cove. The wind and waves had sheared off its main mast at its midpoint. As the water was deeper at the reef, and the pounding of the surf against the rocks was treacherous, very little cargo and none of the horses could be saved from the foundered ship. We stood, helpless and aghast, as the rising tide lifted her just enough that she slid off the reef and slipped under the surface. The neighs and whinnies of the drowning horses brought tears to the eyes of even the most hard-hearted among us.

Our remaining ships needed extensive repairs and could not continue the voyage. Leaving our seafaring brothers to repair their beloved and sturdy ships, we set off overland through hostile France. With Sir Jean and Sir Hughes to guide us, and with Stewart and the rest of the English recruits silent—my French was sufficient only to pass for a native of northern France—we marched from one Templar castle, estate, or commandery to the next across the face of southern France.

After several weeks, during which we maintained our regimen of prayer and training, we finally arrived in Marseille. From there we returned to the sea, this time in the more placid Mediterranean, and completed our journey quite pleasantly. It would prove to be the most comfortable two months of our service.

Chapter 12

The Mediterranean, 1183-1184 A.D.

T o me, a boy from cool, damp England, the Mediterranean Sea and its climate was a wonder. Our journey around this great sea took us most of the winter, though to us the weather felt like high summer. For the first several weeks, we were rarely out of sight of land, and never under sail for more than a few days at a time. By hugging the coastline, we were able to dock in the ports of France, Italy, and Greece to take on provisions and make necessary repairs. While the seamen who hailed from each of the lands we visited tended the ship, I convinced them to tutor me in their native tongues. While in port, the captain traded with the local merchants for basic provisions for us and his crew, but also for our brethren in the Levant.

I and the knights took advantage of the opportunity to get free of the ship and stretch our legs in these coastal towns. My pious companions wished to attend mass and visit local shrines. For me, though, I enjoyed the chance to experience the lives of these people who were so different from my English brethren.

After doing our duty at the local church and paying homage to the towns' saintly relics, I often made my way to the local market, at first under the protection of Stewart or one of the other knights. After the first few times, however, these warriors grew weary of me sampling all the strange fruits, vegetables, meats, and sweets. Soon, they left me to my own devices with the stern warning to stay out of trouble and be onboard before the tide began its run out of the harbor.

Besides the edible wares of the townsfolk, I also delighted in learning the local versions of their French, Italian, and Greek languages, noting the difference in dialects spoken by those separated by but a single day's sail. More than once, I was so engrossed in conversation with the locals that I lost track of time and had to race through the town and leap onto our ship as the crew was casting off from the dock.

While at sea, we trained constantly to avoid the boredom of long, hot, sunny days. The confines of our ship, however, which was a mere ten paces wide at amidships and fewer than fifty paces from bow to stern, limited our battle training to close-order, hand-to-hand fighting.

I also had a special assignment. As Sir Jean had seen my penchant for stealth, he and Sir Hughes encouraged me to secretly gather gossip from the crew and report back to them. Although the first few of these missions ended with me being discovered and duly whacked over the head, once I learned the secrets of our ship—which deck planks squeaked, and which door hinges squealed—I could eavesdrop with impunity. This was a skill that served me well in the years that followed during my service in the Templars and the many decades since.

Our boredom reached its height after we left Athens bound for Cyprus. I learned from my clandestine listening that the Templars and the Byzantine Christian leaders were at odds over claims made by each over coastal castles and fortifications. The dispute kept us from making landfall anywhere within Byzantium, forcing the captain to navigate the open sea directly from Greece to the Templar stronghold at Nicosia on the island of Cyprus.

Our ship was loaded to the gunwales with casks of water and wine, crates and sacks of provisions and trade goods of all sorts. Despite the heavy load of provisions, we were restricted to short rations of salted meat and increasingly brackish water. Rather than feeding us, our cargo was intended to help provision our isolated Templar brothers on the island. The trade goods we carried would also allow them to barter with the nearby townsfolk for other necessities. Luxuries and comforts of any kind were contrary to the Templar way.

Once safely in Cyprus, we stayed only a day and a night at the Templar castle at Templos, just long enough to unload a portion of our cargo and take on fresh water and more salted meat. We set sail with the tide, rounded the western side of the island, and made the crossing of a few days without incident to Acre on the coast of The Levant.

At long last, we had reached the Holy Land.

PART II

The Endless Mountains
Present Day

The Endless Mountains aren't, really. They can seem to be, though, if you have to travel from Scranton to Towanda on Route 6. They can hardly even be called mountains when compared to the Rockies out West, or even the Adirondacks in New York. Being more ancient than either, though, they have a presence you can feel in your bones. The eons have worn them down to nubs, smoothed their rough edges and scraped them with mile-thick glaciers time and time again. Even so, they command the sky and bend even the artifice of men to their will.

Dressed in oaks, beech, and maples that have silently watched the centuries pass, they are cut by deep gorges through which crystal-clear streams run. Streams that grow from step-wide creeks into rivers with names like Susquehanna, Lehigh, and Delaware. Sheathed in laurel and huckleberry so thick that only the whitetail deer, porcupines, and mountain lions can pass. They are dotted with deep glacial lakes and beaver dams. They define the northern tier of eastern Pennsylvania—known to the natives simply as God's Country.

To the locals, most of whom have lived there for generations, the mountains define a life on the blade's edge between jubilation and desperation. Hard working and hard drinking, they build things during the week, and kill things on the weekend. Their way of life keeps their lives short but intense.

Into this world was born Daniel Koprowicz, the last of seven children and fourth son of Joseph and Elizabeth. Daniel's father was a machinist, as were each of his three brothers. Starting with plain bars of steel, they created precision instruments of death. Expensive by local standards, their deer rifles were nonetheless back-ordered for years. Delivery of one to a customer was an event of celebration and ceremony.

Dan took his first deer when he was twelve, the year he got his license. For most fathers, that would have been a very proud moment. For Joseph, it was just a fulfillment of expectations. He had taught Dan to disassemble, clean, reassemble, sight-in and shoot rifles when he was six. Dan had made the rifle he used to bring down the deer himself. Joseph and Dan's brothers welcomed another killer into the Koprowicz family.

Chapter 13

"The U" Late September, Present Day

Dan sat at his desk grading the latest batch of test papers when a knock came from the office door and a voice said, "Father Dan, time for Mass." He glimpsed Evelyn, the Languages Department's admin. She hated her "old-fashioned" name, and insisted on being called Eve, though Father Dan thought "Evelyn" had a nicer rhythm to it. He leaned back in his desk chair to watch her walk down the hall.

He stood up, stretched, and reached for his coat. His office was little more than a closet, and what little floor space it had was stacked with books, journals, and student papers. Even the oak guest chair, its straight back and hard seat worn smooth as glass from decades of use, had to be cleared of academic detritus whenever he held office hours.

As he headed for the door, he stuck his fingers inside his stiff clerical collar to button the shirt beneath. Striding down the hall, he almost collided with Jessica Simms, Latin scholar and head of the department, as she darted out of her own office. Many people almost collided with Jessica on any given day. She presented a pretty large target but moved through the University hallways like a whirlwind.

"You know, sometimes I think you wait for me to walk by and actually try to have me run you down," Dan said as he dodged around her. His smile told her what she already knew—that he was just kidding.

It was a frequent comment, which was met with an equally frequent response. "You ran into me—well, almost ran into me. I think you lurk outside my door until you hear me coming."

The smiles they exchanged were sincere, even if the barbs weren't.

"Off to Mass this morning?" She knew that was where he was going.

"It's Thursday, isn't it?" His tone was a little harsher and a little more frustrated than he had intended, and Jessica picked up on it.

"Is that collar feeling a little tight this morning? You know if you ever want to take it off for the evening, there's a new brewpub that opened up downtown. They say it's pretty nice. Good music and cold beer… At least that's what I've heard." Her flirtations were not at all uncommon.

Dan looked sideways at her, and she batted her eyelashes comically.

"Why do pretty young women always flirt with us priests?"

"I guess it's the challenge…wait, did you just call me pretty—and young?" Not only was Jessica a large woman, she was also about his mother's age.

As he turned right down an adjoining hallway, he raised his hand and waved. "I did indeed! Both!"
Jessica let out a snorting laugh, but he knew he had just made her day.

Chapter 14

The U, Late September

D anny Boy, have some pie. If you don't, I'll feel
guilty."

Father Charlie Janowski liked his pie, and Dan knew
he wouldn't feel guilty at all.

"No, thanks. What's the point of spending an hour at
the gym if I just blow all that work on pie?"

Father Janowski chuckled. He had given up the gym
for pie, cake, and any other sweets he could find years ago
when he realized he was more interested in the coeds' leotards
than in pumping iron. He had decided it was better to switch
from temptations that could cost him his soul to ones that
would only cost him his physique—and maybe a few years off
his life.

As usual, his voice took on his "fatherly Father" tone.
"Just be sure you keep your thoughts on your workout, and
not on anybody else's."

"Charlie, I go there at 6:00 A.M.. Do you think there
are any coeds that are even up at that hour? Half of them
probably haven't gotten home yet." Dan knew Father
Charlie's attitude toward the morals of America's youth.
"Believe me, I have the whole gym to myself at that hour."
Dan gave him a sidelong glance. "Maybe you should join me
sometime."

Charlie grunted and pointedly stuck another forkful of pie in his mouth. Speaking around it, he mumbled, "Mind your manners around your elders."

Father Charlie had "retired" a few years before to the Jesuit Residence at the University. Jesuit priests never really retire, though, and soon he was taking computer classes, which led to a part-time programming job in the Computer Center. He figured he was saving The U a chunk of salary money, and it gave him a reason to get up and out the door in the morning.

The two priests sat silently for a minute or two until Dan spoke up in a more serious tone.

"Something very odd happened at Mass this morning."

"Did the Widow Bryant talk to her dead husband in the chapel again?" Charlie hadn't caught Dan's change in tone yet.

"No, it happened during communion." This time, it was obvious that Dan was serious. Charlie looked at him and raised an eyebrow as he continued. "It actually started two days ago. I was reading Paul when I felt like I was being watched."

The irony of this was not lost on Father Charlie. Early morning weekday Mass was typically attended by widows trying to prove to their dead husbands how pious they were, and by university students who had sown their wild oats the night before and came to Mass to pray for crop failure. They kept their eyes down, sometimes cried, and left before communion.

"When I finished the reading, I looked up and saw a young man sitting in the back pew, staring at me." Dan shifted uncomfortably in his chair. "He was too far back for me to see him very well, which I guess made the feeling of being watched even creepier."

Charlie leaned forward in his chair, which took an effort, to signal his growing interest. "Had he ever been to Mass before?"

"Not that I remember. And I probably would remember him. Not because of his 'Stare.'" Dan made air-quotes then continued, "But because he looked so out of place. He was dressed in a suit and tie and there wasn't a hair out of place."

"It sounds like you got a good look at him."

"Like I said, he made an impression."

"Maybe he was a salesman trying to wash away the stink of Len's."

Len's Blue Room was an infamous "gentlemen's club" where the men were anything but gentlemen, and the women let anyone join their club.

"I don't think so, because this was Monday." They both knew Len's wasn't open on Sundays. "I forgot about it, but yesterday he was there again. Navy blue suit, red striped tie. This time he sat about half-way back."

Dan said Mass on Mondays, Wednesdays, and Thursdays. This was Thursday, so Charlie knew what was coming next.

"Let me guess, he was there again today."

"Right! He was there again today. And I asked Joey if he had been there on Tuesday." Father Joseph Jones said Mass Tuesdays, Fridays, and every other Sunday. "But Joey said he wasn't."

"Where did he sit this time?"

"Right down front. On Monday, he just seemed to sit there staring. On Wednesday, he was saying all the prayers and responses, but he left at the start of communion."

Dan paused, waiting for a reaction, but Charlie's wasn't what he expected. "It just sounds like someone who is trying to reconnect with his faith. He's probably got some issues, and he's reaching out to the Church to help him through. I'm not surprised he came back to you. You touch people, you know."

Charlie's praise was genuine, and it warmed Dan's heart. Maybe it even made him feel a little embarrassed. But he definitely thought it was misplaced. He didn't believe he could inspire faith in others when he had always doubted his own. He had gone to Seminary because it was free, and his father, a hard man who could turn a block of steel into a high-powered rifle, refused to pay for turning his son into a "sissy college boy."

"I'd love to think that—without getting too prideful—but today he stayed for communion." Dan wasn't sure how to explain what happened next, and Charlie leaned farther forward in anticipation. "Like I said, he was in the front pew, and when he approached to receive the sacrament, we made eye contact. They were the deepest blue I've ever seen…" Dan caught himself drifting back in memory. "Ah, I mean they were very dark blue—like his suit—but also deep, depth-wise."

Charlie made a face. "OK, so he had strange eyes." He wasn't completely comfortable with the direction the story was going.

"Yeah, strange. But not as strange as what happened next. He opened his mouth to take the Host in the old style, and his tongue looked like it was branded."

"You mean like from a branding iron?" Charlie's tone became very tense, and his furrowed brow showed how wary he was.

"Yes. His tongue had some symbol burned into it. It was so out-of-place, since he seemed so straight-laced in his suit and all."

Dan had been expecting Charlie to react with revulsion, or at least disgust, with what the youth of America had come to. Instead, he reached out and grabbed Dan's upper arm. His grip was much stronger than Dan would have guessed he was capable of. That and the intensity in Charlie's eyes made Dan flinch. When Charlie spoke, his tone was a mix of suspicion and apprehension.

"What did this brand look like?"

"Well, I'm not totally sure. When I saw it, I did a double-take and just kind of shoved the wafer into his mouth. I'm not even sure I said the 'Body'…"

Charlie waved his left hand while still holding Dan's arm with his right. His voice was commanding, "Draw what you saw."

Next to the Dining Room where the two priests were sitting was a formal parlor. Dan went to a writing desk in the corner and returned with a pen and paper. His eyes unfocused as he thought back to standing before the altar, looking the young man in the eye. Then he started to draw.

It took him a couple of tries, but he finally drew what looked like a Gothic letter 'H' with a small bar at the base. He spun the paper around for Charlie to see.

Charlie had been watching Dan work with a look of growing concern. The artery in his neck pulsed with his quickening heart. By the time Dan flipped the paper around to show him, Charlie looked like his heart was going to leap out of his mouth onto the table. He had to swallow three times before his voice would work.

"You must never serve that person the Sacrament of The Eucharist ever again."

Dan's mouth dropped open. "What? Why not?"

"He has been deemed unworthy to receive The Lord." Charlie was red-faced and sweating. Dan shook his head, bewildered.

"How can you know that?"

Charlie took a couple of deep breaths to slow his pounding heart. He stabbed the paper with his forefinger.

"This is the sign of an unrepentant heretic. They commuted his sentence of being burned at the stake to being marked for all time as one of the damned."

Dan's confusion turned to shock. He knew The Church had used such brutal practices in past centuries, and his Order had been at the forefront, but he couldn't believe it still practiced such punishments.

"Excuse me? You're saying that The Church is still branding people for heresy? I don't believe it."

"I wouldn't have believed it either, until now. But there are still backwaters of extremism hidden away, even in this modern world."

"No, it had to have been some ridiculous fraternity initiation, or something."

Dan had spent his entire adult life in academia, but Charlie had served his Order as a missionary, out in the far-flung reaches of The Church's evangelism.

"I'm telling you this is the mark of a heretic who refused to recant his foul beliefs. He must have been a terror to warrant such a mark. You need to stay away from him."

Father Dan sat back in his chair, mouth open, staring. Charlie stood and began pacing the length of the dining room. Back and forth, back and forth, while gathering his thoughts.

"I know this sounds ludicrous in this day and age. But you know there are the devout out there who still flagellate themselves and crawl on their bellies for miles to visit shrines of obscure saints. Is it so hard to believe that some of those fan…uh…believers would keep other ancient traditions alive?"

"I suppose." Dan wasn't buying it, though, at least not yet. "How do we even know that the brand is 'official'? It could have been some stupid stunt? And, even if it is The Church's work," a shiver ran down Dan's spine at the thought, "how do we know he isn't repentant?"

"Did he say confession?" Charlie's voice was muted, confident of his authority in this matter. As Dan started to respond, Charlie continued, "I mean a personal confession, not the Penitential Rite. Most just mouth those words by rote." He still loved the old ways of The Church.

Dan knew Charlie was right, at least in The Church's eyes. It didn't feel right to him, though.

"No, no he didn't make contrition, at least not to me."

"Then you must respect the mark he has been given. That's your only choice."

Chapter 15

Scranton, Late September

Dan stewed over the dilemma posed by "Mr. Suit"—
he had a tendency to give people and things mental
nicknames, often in one of the several ancient languages he
knew. He checked with Father Joey after Friday's Mass, but
as expected, Mr. Suit had not attended.

Saturday brought a welcome distraction, though. After
a workout at The U's gym, Dan headed out to a local parish's
annual picnic. The University administration encouraged the
resident priests to take part in local church events. Most of the
Jesuits saw it as a chore and resisted, finding any excuse they
could come up with to skip them.

Dan, on the other hand, practically grew up at parish
picnics and fire company bazaars. He shared his first beer and
his first kiss at one. Besides, that day's extravaganza was
sponsored by Saint Theresa's, the parish that had sort of
adopted Dan when he was attending The U as a student.

After parking his car in a field that served as the picnic
grove's parking lot, Dan walked along the path through the
woods toward the source of the delicious aromas of halupki,
pierogies, and sausage. His first stop was the beer tent, of
course, even though it was still early afternoon. Dan would
have felt naked walking around the grounds without a plastic

cup in his hand. He recognized the beer tender as Joe Slawicki, one of the regular scripture readers at Saint Theresa's.

"Father Dan! Great to see you again." After a warm handshake, Joe continued, "What can I getcha?"

"A Lager, please."

"One Vitamin Y coming up." As Joe let the Yuengling run down the inside of the red Solo cup, he gave Dan a knowing smile.

"Feels good to get back to your roots, doesn't it? At least your adopted roots."

"It does. You know I grew up outside Tunkhannock, so I do feel right at home." Joe finished topping off the beer and exchanged it for Dan's dollar.

"In fact, I'm probably a little too comfortable with one of these in my hand," he said as he raised his beer, first in salute, then to his mouth.

"Stop back."

"Oh, I'm sure I will."

Not having had any lunch yet after his workout, Dan was hungry, and he knew the savory smells surrounding him would have his stomach growling soon enough. He strolled through the crowds past the food tents, the ring toss game, and the big wheel where elderly widows gossiped and put their quarters on their favorite numbers, waiting for the next round of bingo to start. Dan mockingly wagged his finger at them as he passed, and all but one gave him back a hearty laugh. The quiet one crossed herself instead as the wheel slowed. I'll have to say a prayer for that one, Dan thought as he walked away.

He spotted Saint Theresa's pastor, Father Pat Moran, sitting at a picnic table under the pavilion. With cheeks perennially red, he was sharing a story and a beer with someone sitting across the table.

As Dan approached, Father Moran paused, listened to his companion's response, then let out a loud burst of laughter. Leaning back, he noticed Dan approaching him and waved him over.

"Father Danny, thanks for coming to our little soiree." Father Pat's handshake came with a whack on the shoulder.

"Let me introduce you to someone."

The priest's drinking partner had risen to his feet as well. Until that point, he had his back to Dan, but as he turned around, Dan's heart skipped. Standing before him was Mr. Suit himself.

"Father Dan Koprowicz, this is Mr. John…ah…"

"John Haviland. It's my pleasure to meet you, Father." John Haviland, though dressed appropriately for a beer party in the woods, still looked like he had just stepped out of GQ or Esquire.

"Likewise, Mr. Haviland. I've seen you at my Mass a time or two, haven't I?"

Dan tried not to stare at John's mouth, though he secretly hoped he would get a glimpse of his tongue again.

"Yes, I've been in town for a couple of days." He sat down on the picnic bench and Dan sat across the table.

Father Moran remained standing, downed the rest of his beer, and started for the beer tent. After a step, he remembered his manners and spun on his heel.

"I'm off for a refill. Can I get you gents one, too?"

"No thanks, I'm good."

"I'm good, too, thanks."

With that, Father Pat strode off, perhaps a little too eager to get away, Dan thought.

"So, Mr. Haviland, what brings you to Scranton?"

"Call me John, please." Dan nodded. "I'm on a bit of a recruiting trip, actually."

Dan, who was by now fluent in several languages and could at least get by in several others, found John's slight accent hard to place.

"Where do you call home?"

A slow smile crossed John's lips. "Well, that's a good question. I feel at home wherever I'm standing. I currently live outside of Philadelphia, but I've lain my head in many different places."

"That's pretty enigmatic." Dan's wariness was becoming quite apparent in his voice. "Army brat?"

"More like an Army rat, I guess." John chuckled, almost to himself. Dan was silent. "I've done my duty, you could say."

Dan studied John's face, but he couldn't find a wrinkle. He looked down at John's hands, which were palms down on the table. The skin was smooth and tight. Physically, John looked no older than his mid-twenties. His bearing, though, suggested someone mature well beyond his apparent age.

John patiently waited out Dan's obvious examination. When it became apparent to Dan that John was comfortable in silence, he broke the conversational lull.

"What kind of position are you trying to fill?"

"Beg pardon? Oh, you mean my recruiting trip? It's a very specific job, really. I need someone with uncommon skills with languages. Exceptional, one-of-kind skills, in fact."

"Really?" Dan was pleasantly surprised and curious, in spite of himself. "I teach languages at The University."

John smiled and asked in Latin, "Are you applying for the job?"

Now Dan smiled, too, when he responded in kind, "But I already have a lifetime contract."

John gave out a short laugh. Without breaking cadence, he switched to Medieval Greek, "Vows are not contracts. One can be released from one's Vows."

Caught up in it, and loving the challenge, Dan pushed back with ancient Greek, "Not my vows."

Then, without missing a beat, he was speaking Hebrew, "But thank-you for the chance to stretch my memory."

"You are quite welcome."

Dan was stunned—shocked, almost. It took him a beat or two to recognize…Aramaic! His answer was not very fluid, and he was sure he wasn't getting it quite right.

"I've never heard Aramaic spoken or tried to speak it myself, for that matter."

Switching to Arabic, he said, "I have never met anyone else…like me."

With a satisfied smile, John put up his hand.

"Very impressive!", he responded in English, leaving Dan with the distinct impression that he had understood the Arabic, also, but refused to speak it.

Completely changing the subject, John said, "I feel like stretching my legs. Would you join me?"

They stood in unison. "Of course. Have you eaten?"

John shook his head and Dan continued, "Good, I recommend the kielbasa." He pronounced it as if the word ended with a 'y'. "That stand over there has it on a roll."

Dan nodded to a food stand from which savory smells emanated.

"With sauerkraut?" John asked.

Dan barked a laugh. "That might be a bit sloppy, but sure. I like it with mustard and horseradish."

John started toward the indicated stand. "Ah, sounds good. With another beer, of course."

Dan fell in step alongside. "Of course."

After ordering their sandwiches and slathering them with Dan's spicy mixture, they ate them while walking through the picnic grove. The kielbasa was more than enough to satisfy their appetite, and the various games of chance didn't interest them, so they naturally circled back toward the parking lot. As they walked through the woods, sipping the last of their beers, acorns crunched loudly under their feet.

In response to their noisy passage, John said, "Sounds like it will be a hard winter this year."

Dan looked sidelong at John. This was the first indication of any kind that John had given about his background. A hunter would know that oak trees produce an abundance of acorns in the fall before a winter with lots of snow—to feed the deer, squirrels, and other creatures of the woods. At least that's what the old-timers had always told him. Dan had never believed in the cause-effect relationship, but from the experience earned from a lifetime of autumns spent in the woods, he knew the correlation was real.

"Yeah, the Wooly Bears are almost all black."

John chuckled. "Ah, yes, pyrractia isabella. You think they can really predict the weather?"

Dan scanned the ground in front of him, then up at the towering oaks, maples, and beeches. A look of pure contentment crossed his features.

"Who's to say a lowly caterpillar can't feel the oncoming winter? You seem to think the oak tree can. The works of the Lord are wondrous to behold."

John chuckled again. "More wondrous than you—we—know."

"More than we can know."

John's only response was a slight tilt of his head.

They strolled along in silence, comfortable in their companionship. When they reached the parking lot, their parting was cordial. With a brief handshake, John climbed into his SUV and waved goodbye. Somehow, Dan knew that their separation would be short. He felt a connection to John that seemed collegial, yet somehow deeper. To Dan, they seemed of a common mind. He could sense in his heart that they would meet again. Just how quickly, though, he had no inkling.

Chapter 16

The U, Late September

I t wasn't until ater the parish picnic later in the evening that Dan realized he had forgotten to ask the one question which had been at the top of his mind for days, namely how John's tongue had been scarred so. He wondered how he could have forgotten, but somehow that didn't surprise him. John's demeanor was that of an old soul of tender years. He was so captivating that the whole encounter felt like a dream. It was no wonder that Dan was half-mesmerized by him.

The next several days passed without John Haviland far from Dan's thoughts. But it was only in his imagination that Dan asked John all the questions that filled his mind. Monday Mass passed with no sign of him, as did Wednesday's.

On Thursday, Dan returned to the rectory after hosting open office hours. He was giving tests to three different classes on Friday, so the line for help had been down the hall. He hadn't forgotten about John, but getting home well into the evening, all he was thinking about was dinner and a glass of wine.

As soon as he came in through the front door, even before he had hung up his jacket and exited the vestibule, he heard Father Charlie calling to him from the parlor.

"Don't get comfortable. Monsignor Jeffries wants to see you in his office." Monsignor Jeffries was the University President.

"The Monsignor?" Dan's tone was a mixture of excitement and nervousness. "Do you think the Vatican finally granted me access?" he asked as he shrugged his jacket back on.

"How should I know? All I know is Martha called about ten minutes ago and asked you to come to the office." Charlie heard the door slam before he finished.

Since he arrived at The U three years ago, Dan had been petitioning The Vatican to grant him access to their Archives. He wanted to compare the handwriting of manuscripts dating back through the centuries. His research had convinced him he could identify individual medieval scribes by their handwriting idiosyncrasies and how they were influenced by their teachers. He thought he could build a kind of genealogy of scribes and trace the spread of knowledge throughout Europe during the Middle Ages. It was an ambitious project, and he had made good progress with the resources he had available through academic libraries around the world. But the Vatican Archives was the motherlode of medieval manuscripts.

Each of his requests so far met with a curt rejection. Afterward, he would brood for a few weeks, then try to think of a new justification for access. When he had what he believed was a valid argument, he composed another petition and resubmitted it. His fourth and current request had been outstanding for almost three months.

So far, all the rejections had come directly to him through the mail, so perhaps this summons meant he was finally accepted. Either that, or Monsignor Jeffries, a stodgy old guard priest, was going to tell him to forget the whole thing.

Martha, Monsignor Jeffries' administrative assistant, had left for the day when Dan arrived at the Monsignor's office. He hung up his jacket and gently knocked on the oaken door to the President's inner sanctum.

From behind the door he heard, "Come in, Father Koprowicz."

Clad in dark raised panels, with a coffered ceiling above, Monsignor Jeffries' office always seemed rather ostentatious to Dan. The highly polished hardwood floor wore a thick oriental carpet. Tall floor lamps cast indirect light from the corners of the spacious room where furniture—club chairs and small tables—were arranged in small conversation groups. An imposing desk, of dark red mahogany, faced out into the room from the back wall. Above it was a crucifix showing Christ's agony.

Shadow cloaked that part of the, though, as the desk lamp and the floor lamp behind it were turned off. All in all, the room, which could have easily been imposing, instead invited you into the lighted corners. If Dan wasn't so anxious, it might have even felt cozy.

President Jeffries met Dan a few feet into the room with his hand outstretched.

"Thank you for coming so quickly after your office hours. I suppose you missed dinner."

Dan had missed dinner, of course, but when it became apparent that there would be no offer of refreshments, Dan smiled and said, "I don't mind, Monsignor. I had a rather large lunch."

Dan looked for a sign in the old priest's demeanor to show whether this was a good news or bad news meeting.

Seeing the scowl on his face and feeling his slightly clammy palm as they shook hands, Dan's heart sank.

Monsignor Jeffries motioned with an extended hand to the corner of the room behind Dan's left shoulder and a cluster of overstuffed chairs.

"Well, we won't keep you long."

We, Dan wondered as he turned to the offered chair. It was only then that he realized that Monsignor Jeffries and he were not alone. To Dan's surprise, rising out of a high leather wingback was John Haviland, dressed collegially in a button-down Oxford shirt, tie, V-neck sweater, brown tweed jacket, tan light wool slacks, and cordovan loafers. He, too, extended his hand in greeting.

"Good evening, Father Dan," John said with a pleasant smile.

"Ah, yes, I understand you and Mr. Haviland have already met," the Monsignor said.

The scowl on his face and his gruff tone made it quite apparent that Monsignor Jeffries was not happy about this *tete-a-tete*.

Despite his nervousness, Dan smiled back at John, shook his hand, then turned to the Monsignor, "Yes, we chatted at St. Theresa's picnic on Saturday." He turned back to John. "I haven't seen you in Mass this week," he said. A wry smile softened his accusing tone.

Before John could respond with his own banter, the older priest interrupted. "OK, then I won't keep either of you longer than necessary."

The University president sat in the largest of the three chairs surrounding a small coffee table. John resumed his own seat, and Dan settled into the third.

As Dan sat, his eyes lowered to the surface of the coffee table, and he saw an official-looking document that bore what appeared to be a Papal seal. His heart leapt and his hopes for access to the Vatican Archives, which he had briefly forgotten when he John's presence took him by surprise, soared.

Before Dan could get a good look at it, though, Monsignor Jeffries picked up the document and held it close to his chest.

"Mr. Haviland, here, is visiting us on a—what did you call it? A recruiting trip?" Dan nodded slowly, as he had already been told this by John. "He is looking for someone with a very specialized set of skills and talents." Dan nodded again, a little more enthusiastically this time. "He seems to think that you fit the bill."

Dan couldn't help himself, and a smile lit his face. But Monsignor Jeffries held up his hand.

"Wait, it's not what you may be expecting or hoping for." Dan's smile faded. "Trust me, it's not."

John, who had been sitting patiently watching Dan during this introduction, turned first to the Monsignor with a scowl, then back to Dan.

"No, it's not exactly the opportunity you were expecting." A smile formed on his lips. "But I believe you'll be pleased with the alternative."

"I don't understand." Dan's enthusiasm, as quickly as it had grown, now turned to confusion.

John looked back at Monsignor Jeffries. "Perhaps you should let him read his letter first, as I suggested."

His tone had an edge to it, and the social temperature of the meeting changed abruptly. It seemed now that John Haviland, this outsider, was in control of the meeting, and the Monsignor was reduced to a minor role in the meeting. Monsignor Jeffries reached into the inner pocket of his jacket.

"Yes, of course, you were right. We should have started with this."

He pulled from his pocket another document and handed it across to Dan. This one was a folded letter addressed to Dan, and as he scanned it, he recognized the text that he had read several times before. His request for access was denied again. But since Dan knew the previous letters' text by heart—they had always been the same, short and to the point—something clicked that made him go back and reread the letter more carefully.

"…your request for direct access to the Vatican Archives is denied."

He looked up from the paper at Monsignor Jeffries and saw his blank face. Some instinct told him that John Haviland was the Alpha male in the room and was now in charge. Without conscious thought, he turned his head and shoulders to John, further diminishing the Monsignor's role.

"This says I'm denied 'direct access' to the Archives. All the other letters just said 'access.'"

The implication was that Dan was being granted indirect access, without it being explicitly stated that way.

John smiled a little as he looked Dan in the eye. "Good memory, Father. Further evidence that I've made the right choice." After a pause, he continued, "Go ahead, ask your question."

Dan knew what question to ask, and he knew John was expecting it. "So, does this mean I'm being granted *indirect* access?" John's smile broadened, but Dan continued, "And if it does, what exactly does that mean? The Vatican Archives are vaulted and highly secure."

John nodded. "That is an excellent question. The answer to your first question is, 'yes', you are being granted indirect, though still highly secure, access to certain assets within the Vatican Archives."

Dan sat back in his chair, stunned. This meeting was becoming an emotional roller coaster—and he suspected the big drop was yet to come.

John continued, "The answer your second question will take some explaining." He turned to Monsignor Jeffries and held out his hand, but the old priest simply sat as if in a daze. "Monsignor. May I have the document, please?"

Monsignor Jeffries looked at the outstretched hand for a moment, then started from his apparent reverie. "Oh, yes, of course."

He handed the officially sealed document to John.

John took the paper and said, "Thank-you, Monsignor, and thank you for your full cooperation in this matter." John's words seemed to take on a physical substance as the priest's eyes glazed over again.

Rather than handing the papers to Dan, he held them face-down in his lap. "Before you can fully understand this Papal order, you need a little background information. I am indeed here on a recruiting trip, but it's not a fishing expedition. Rather, it has been more of an interview process. I came here to Scranton specifically to meet you and to take your measure."

"Excuse me? Why am I being 'measured?'" Dan wasn't sure he liked the direction this conversation was going.

John gave him a rueful smile. "Don't be offended. I simply meant that I wanted to assess your academic qualifications, to be sure they were as compelling as they were reported to be. You see, your petitions to the Vatican have not gone unnoticed. Word of your interests and your talents found their way to ears that knew we had a similar position to fill."

Dan started to interrupt again, wanting to know who "we" were, but John lifted his hand from his lap and Dan stopped with his mouth open.

"Let me start, not at the beginning, but far enough back to explain. I represent an order of lay brothers and sisters who have served the Church of Rome for many centuries. We are an enclave of scholars, whose official *raison d'etre* is the 'accumulation and preservation of worldly knowledge' as outlined in the Papal Bull that recognized and sanctioned our charter."

Switching to Hebrew, John continued, "My organization has gathered and cataloged much of the content of the Vatican Archives over the centuries. We continue to gather, translate, and interpret old and new documents from around the world. Those documents, along with our analyses, are fed into those ever-growing Archives. Our own library, and the other libraries around the world which we have access to—including major portions of the Vatican Archives, itself— represent the greatest store of knowledge in history."

Dan glanced at Monsignor Jeffries, who seemed oblivious to the language switch and, in fact, to the entire conversation.

This time, John switched to Aramaic. "Old knowledge, however, is not nearly as useful as new knowledge."

He switched back to English. "Our group's—the Enclave's—charter specifies that The Vatican assign to minister to our members, and to assist the Order in the conduct of its work. This decree," he held the Papal document out to Dan, "signed and sealed by the Holy Father himself, officially assigns you to be our 'Priest in Residence.'"

Dan took the document and read the Latin. After reading it end-to-end once, then re-reading parts again, he met

John's eyes, which flicked to Monsignor Jeffries and back to Dan.

Realizing for the first time that the University President sat in a kind of stupor, Dan understood that the bottomless well of questions which had sprung into his mind would have to wait for a more private conversation. Instead, remembering his vow of obedience to The Church, he simply stated the obvious. "So, I'll be leaving the University. Where and when?"

John smiled at how quickly Dan had grasped the subtleties of this meeting. He turned to the Monsignor. "Monsignor," the man started, as if waking from a doze, and his eyes refocused. "I am authorized to accept Father Koprowicz's assignment immediately. Of course, I can give you and Father," he glanced back at Dan to soften what would come next, "a couple of days to put his affairs here at the University in order." He turned back to Dan. "I'll be back on Sunday to move you to the Enclave."

Dan nodded. He would have time to visit his family and say his goodbyes, at least. Although he had no idea what exactly this whole turn of events meant, he had a feeling that it would be quite a while before he had the chance to see them again, especially since he had no idea where this "Enclave" was.

Turning to the Monsignor he said, "Mrs. Simms can cover my classes until the end of the semester. She's not great at Hebrew but can handle the Latin and Greek. I only have two Hebrew students this semester, anyway."

Back to John, he said, "So, where is this Enclave of yours?"

Dan meant to say it lightly, but it came out a little sarcastic. John didn't seem to mind, though, and answered pleasantly.

"Only a couple of hours away, outside of Philadelphia."

"Really, that close? I expected you to be in Europe, if not in Rome itself."

"You have a lot to learn about us. And, by the way, it is now officially 'our' Enclave. I hope you will soon come to view it that way, as well."

Dan was certain the first part was true, but he wasn't so sure about the second.

Turning to Monsignor Jeffries, John continued, "Monsignor, could you please give Dan your final instructions for him, as specified in *your* letter?"

Clearly dissatisfied with the entire situation, Monsignor Jeffries harrumphed and drew from his other pocket another letter. Rather than reading it, though, he simply cast it on the table.

"This one says I'm to tell you that any conversations you have with Mr. Haviland, including this one, and any other members of his Order, as well as anything you learn while working with his Order must be held under the seal of the confessional."

Dan started visibly, quite taken aback by these words. "I am also bound by this same order," the Monsignor continued, scowling at John. "If asked, we are to simply reply that you are being reassigned to continue your studies. Understood?"

"Ah, no, I don't really understand, but I will certainly obey his Holy Father, as we have both vowed to." John couldn't help smiling a little at Dan's parting jab.

Chapter 17

Northeastern Pennsylvania, Late September

The house Dan grew up in was dark when he pulled into the driveway. Only the flickering glow of a television lit the inside. He let himself in through the back porch door, which was never locked, as far as he could remember. The home of a gunsmith has no need for locks or a security system.

"Hello. Anybody home?" he called as he flicked on the kitchen light. The house smelled of the pine and lemon cleaning products Mrs. Erb used every week. The single pizza box on the counter told him she had been there only a day ago.

"Hey, you awake?" he called again.

This time he heard a grunt from the parlor and the click and rattle of the old recliner's mechanism being released.

"Yeah, yeah, I'm awake." Dan's father grumbled as he came down the center hall. He stopped at the kitchen threshold. "What brings the Holy Father back to his humble roots?"

"Dad—"

Joseph Koprowicz held up both hands placatingly. That simple gesture was both an apology and a sign that Joe was in no mood to argue. Neither was Dan, though the volatility of their relationship was like a pot on a hot stove, ready to boil over at any minute.

"—Good to see you, too," Dan finished, a rueful smile on his face.

The men each took two steps to close the gap between them and embraced.

"'djeat?"

"No, 'djou?"

They both chuckled at the old joke.

"There's some pizza left." Joe nodded to the box on the counter. "From yesterday," he added a little sheepishly.

"Ah, I think I'll pass."

"Probably a good idea. Beer?"

Without waiting for an answer, Joe opened the ancient refrigerator and pulled out two bottles. They sat across the kitchen table from each other.

Dan accepted his with a nod. "Thanks."

After a long pull from his, Joe asked, "So what brings you here to visit your Old Man?"

Dan grinned. His father used to hate it when anyone called him 'Old Man.' Looking at him in his tattered bathrobe, Dan realized the moniker now fit.

Instinctively, Dan knew they had to dance through the minefield of old squabbles before he could deliver his news. "How's the shop?"

Joe grunted, also seeming to understand the need to clear away the old disputes. "I only go in about once or twice a week now, mainly to do the books. *Your brothers* are doing a fine job running the business."

In his day, Joe Koprowicz was a master machinist who could take a steel bar and a block of walnut and fashion a deer rifle so beautiful and accurate that hunters across the state waited years for theirs. Pictures, sent by happy customers, of the trophies taken with their 'Kops' covered the walls of the family forge. Some even showed the Expert marksmanship badges earned with military-spec Kops.

Joe passed his weapon-making prowess down to two of his three sons. The fact that Dan chose books and the Church over the forge and lathe was the root of their fraught relationship.

"So, they finally kicked you out?" Dan kept his tone lighthearted.

"Nobody kicks me out of my own shop." Joe's response was gruff but accompanied by a smile. "No, after your mother passed…"

Dan nodded. "It wasn't the same," he finished for his dad.

Joe just shrugged, but then looked Dan straight in the eye. "So, what'd ya come here to tell me?"

The flippant, "Can't I just visit my dad?" answer died unspoken. Instead, he met his father's gaze.

"I've been reassigned."

"Oh. To Rome?"

Dan frowned and dropped his eyes. "No, to someplace outside Philly. I'll have access—" He stopped himself, not sure how much he was allowed to say, based on the admonitions of the papal decree. "I'll be able to continue my research a lot better there."

"So, they finally got tired of you poking the bear, eh?"

He realized that, to his father and maybe to his own ears, this sounded like a demotion.

"Maybe. Either that or I finally poked it where it counts."

Joe's guffaw was unexpected. He reached across the table and flicked a finger against Dan's collar. "At least ya poked something 'where it counts.'" Dan let out his own laugh, despite himself. "I'm sure you'll make the most of it,"

Joe said. "You always have." He got serious for a moment, looking over Dan's head into the middle distance, then met his eyes again. "Your mother would be proud. She always was."

They raised their beers in a salute and clinked them together, which was as heartfelt a tribute as either of them could muster.

More difficult than his goodbyes with his father or his brief chat with his brothers at the shop, was his visit with Mrs. Simms on Friday. It seems the President had not yet notified her of her added course load, and she was not happy about it. At least that is what she said. Dan was pretty sure, though, that what really upset her was the fact that he was going away. They had become quite good friends over the past couple of years. She mellowed after a few words of consolation from Dan, and they parted with a hug and best wishes.

Most traumatic of all, however, was the weekend-long rant by Dan's housemate Father Charlie. Not wanting to be seen as disobedient to the Church, let alone the Pope himself, Charlie kept his comments to Dan private, but they were no less vehement than if he had screamed them from the rooftop.

By Saturday evening, Charlie was fuming. "I'm telling you, there is something fishy going on here. How can you be sure that this supposed Papal decree is legitimate?"

"I've seen the document myself." Dan was getting very exasperated by Charlie's baseless objections. "It's the Holy Father's signature and the Papal Seal. How much more legitimate could it be?"

"Both of those could be forged with today's technologies."

To Dan, this sounded pretty desperate. He had enough. "It came by courier directly from Rome." This visibly deflated

Charlie. Dan continued, "Whatever this new assignment is, the Vatican blessed and sanctioned it. Besides, it can't be that important if I'll be staying here in Pennsylvania. Plus, I'm—we're both—sworn to obey."

"You have a point about it being located over here. I would think if it was very important, it would be closer to Rome." Dan shrugged and felt a little offended by the remark. Unnoticing, Charlie continued, "But why all the secrecy?"

The decree had explicitly stated that Father Dan was to treat anything he learned about The Enclave—its workings, organization, personnel, and the information it gathered—as if it was disclosed "under the seal of the confessional", and Charlie clearly wasn't buying the "continuing his research" cover story. True to his vows, of course, Dan would tell no one anything about The Order, and knew he would take such knowledge to his grave.

Such a level of secrecy did bother him, but it also was a little thrilling. To become part of a secret society, legitimately and with the blessing of the Pope, teased him with a sense of belonging and not a little pride. Still, he couldn't suppress his suspicions that such extreme secrecy was a hold-over from more dangerous times, times when gathering "worldly knowledge" could get you burned at the stake.

Now, though, in the days of the Internet and instant social media posts, it made much less sense. Instead of discussing his suspicions, though, he sidestepped any debate with Father Charlie. It had become too exhausting.

"Look, I don't know much of anything yet, but I can only assume they have a good reason." Dan couldn't keep the exasperation out of his voice.

He and the old priest had become very close, and Dan knew Charlie thought of him as more than just a fellow priest. Perhaps not quite as a son, but more like a little brother. Dan reciprocated those feelings, so when he placed his hand on Charlie's forearm, the warmth both men felt for each other softened their faces, the set of their shoulders, and their voices.

"Don't worry. I'll be careful." Both knew Dan was referring to his soul. "This is a step in the right direction for my studies. I don't know how extensive my access to the Archives will be, but at least I'll have *some*."

With a sigh, Charlie had his final say. Thoughts that he had harbored for a long time but had never vocalized before. "I know you came to the priesthood a roundabout way. Not as a calling so much as a way out of your prior life." He put his hands on Dan's shoulders. "I don't doubt your faith or your sincerity, or your respect for your vows, obviously. But if your faith isn't rock-solid, I fear this 'assignment' will test it beyond its limits."

Charlie's warning almost moved Dan to tears. His voice softened and dropped to barely a whisper. "I promise I'll be steadfast whatever I face," his eyes took on a mischievous glint, "out there in the wilds of Pennsylvania."

Charlie chuckled and knew he could do no more, so he raised his right hand with two fingers extended and made the sign of the cross. "In the name of The Father, The Son, and the Holy Spirit. The blessings of Our Lord be with you."

When he was done, Dan took both of Charlie's hands in his. "Amen. Thank you, Father. May God's blessing be with you, also." Somehow, they both knew they would never see each other again.

Chapter 18

Northeastern Pennsylvania, Late September

After Mass on Sunday, Father Dan was stowing his few personal belongings into the trunk of his car when a light blue Chevy mid-size SUV pulled into the driveway of the Priests' Residence. He had been half expecting a giant black Escalade with heavily tinted windows. Instead, the car from which John Haviland and another man emerged could have been driven by any soccer mom.

John greeted Dan with an extended hand.

"Good morning, Father. I'd like you to meet Bill Jones." Dan shook Bill's hand, as well. "If you don't mind, I'd like you to ride with me. Bill can follow in your car."

"Ah, OK, I guess. I do have a lot of questions for you. And you've got a nicer ride." He tossed Bill his keys. John chuckled, but Bill just turned to Dan's old Camry with a scowl.

"I'm sure you do. I promise you I will either answer any question you have truthfully, or I won't answer it at all." John turned to Bill for assurance that he was ready. Bill nodded and climbed into the Camry.

"That is one of our founding principles, and a principle we live by every day. Information we exchange is both timely and truthful. I will never lie to you, but if I don't think you are prepared for your question to be answered, I will simply tell you that. Fair enough?"

Dan considered this for a moment. "I guess it couldn't be more fair. Although I may think I'm 'prepared' when you don't."

John nodded again. "Oh, believe me, that will happen a lot."

The ride through Scranton and out onto the Pennsylvania Turnpike's Northeast Extension passed mostly in silence with the occasional exchange of pleasantries about the weather, the coming winter, and the Eagles game later that day.

Dan had spent a restless Saturday night, tossing and turning, while he composed a long list of questions in his mind. He wanted to be sure that he asked everything he could during the couple of hours they would be on the road. So, when they were safely cruising along on the Turnpike, he launched into them.

"Can I ask you some things?"

"I'm surprised it has taken you this long. As I said, you can ask me anything, and I will answer you truthfully or not at all."

"OK." Dan mentally sorted his list and started with the one question he had forgotten to ask during their first conversation. "So, how did you get the scar on your tongue?"

Genuinely surprised, John barked a laugh. "Not the first question I was expecting!" He looked sidelong at Dan from the driver's seat. "Let's just say it's the result of a youthful indiscretion."

Not letting it lie, Dan pressed on. "You mean like a fraternity ritual? That's what I thought, but Father Charlie—he's another priest at The U—says it's the mark of an unrepentant heretic."

Dan looked for some revealing reaction from John, but he just nodded.

"I suppose it was at one time, but The Church hasn't sanctioned that method of punishment for three hundred years."

"Perhaps not officially, but I've heard it's still practiced in some places."

John nodded again, but kept his eyes on the road. "Then I'm glad I've never been to those places. Next question?"

Dan wasn't satisfied, and his face and voice showed it. "But you didn't answer the question. 'Youthful indiscretion?' Really? That's a pretty serious fraternity prank."

"Consider this the first time, probably of many times, when I have to say you're not ready to hear the answer."

Dan fell back into silence. He wasn't at all certain that any of his questions would be answered now. After a few minutes of tense silence, John broke the ice.

"Is that it? I have to say I'm a little disappointed." His tone was light, hoping to cut the tension.

Dan wasn't ready to be soothed, though. "No, that's not it. I have many questions, but I'm not sure you'll answer any of them." He even sounded petulant to himself, so he leaned back in his seat and tried to relax. "Sorry. This is happening so fast, and I guess I'm not very good at adapting to change."

"Embracing new situations is a learned skill, just like anything else. The more it happens, the better we get at it. Becoming a priest seems like it would be a pretty big leap. You managed that okay. Right?"

"Oh, yeah, about that. My dad's a hard man who never believed in the value of any skill or knowledge that didn't help you build things. I had no interest in following in his footsteps and working in his machine shop like my brothers. I desperately wanted to go to college, but I knew he would never help me pay for it.

"When I told Father Kelly, our parish priest, he planted the seed of having the Church pay for my schooling by becoming a priest. I admit, I was skeptical at first and stewed on it for quite a while. But as the admission deadlines approached, the idea looked better and better."

John turned to look at Dan, whose gaze was lost in his memories. "So, you didn't have a 'calling' to be a priest?"

Dan came back to the present and smiled. "No, not really. I just wanted to learn all about history and languages and…the Jesuits seemed to be my only path toward that goal." Dan was thoughtful for a moment, then said, "The funny thing is that I really enjoy the social aspect of being a priest. Teaching and ministering to folks. I've thought a lot about this new assignment over the last couple of days, and I'm actually excited to have my own parish, besides the access to the Archives, of course."

John looked pleased. "I'm sure the faithful among the Enclave residents will be thrilled to have you."

"Not everyone is Catholic?"

"Oh, no, we are a very diverse group."

Dan looked out his side window as the trees and the mountain laurel, now burnishing to reds and golds, flowed past. His face, reflected in the window glass, showed his nervousness.

John picked up the thread of his question. "You applied to go to the Vatican. That would have been much more drastic than joining our little group." John hoped a little teasing would lighten Dan's mood. It was apparent he really wanted Dan to accept being a part of the Order.

Dan turned back to gaze out the windshield. "Yes, it would have been a long way from home, both distance and culture-wise, but it still would have been in the bosom of the Church. Plus…" Dan paused long enough that John was ready to interrupt, but then Dan continued quietly, "Well, I guess I never really expected to be accepted."

John nodded. "My experience has been that the Church rarely appreciates the individual talents of their priests." The sarcasm didn't exactly drip from his words, but they kind of sloshed in it.

This drew a sharp look from Dan. "Do you really have that much experience with the Church?" His skepticism that such a young man could have such an opinion was evident in his tone. "No offense, but how much 'experience' could you have at your age?" He found John's attitude toward his Mother Church offensive, and his pique came through in his tone.

"Don't let your eyes deceive you. Use every meeting we've had, every discussion, every step I've taken, every word I've said and how I've said them to form your opinion of me." John looked straight ahead at the Turnpike asphalt.

Dan felt like John's words were a slap to the back of his head, like those his father or brothers would give him when he said something stupid. They had the same effect, too. His building anger evaporated, and he felt a new clarity of thought. Reflecting on the two meetings they had before this trip, he almost felt as if he was being guided, if not being led by the nose. In his memory, he focused first on John's diction. He listened to his voice, his tone. Then his language skills. Replaying how he chose his words, how he never hesitated, how his arguments were so well thought out.

Then he considered his physical presence, how he moved. How he never took a misstep, and how his movements flowed smoothly from one into the next. Understanding clicked and Dan blinked several times.

He turned to John, who was still calmly driving along the near-deserted highway.

"You're older than you look. I'd say much older."

The smile that crossed John's face looked very satisfied. "Very good. We can glean more useful information through observation of the whole *gestalt* than the words thrown at us."

"So, how old are you?" When John remained silent, Dan continued, "And why do you look so young?"

Choosing to answer the second question only, "Maybe it's good genes. Maybe it's healthy living. Maybe I was kissed by an angel—or maybe I sold my soul to the Devil."

John wasn't smiling, and Dan didn't take a statement like that as a joke. Looking at John, he said, "Am I to be tested that way?" He turned back to the windshield. "If so, I can tell you I'll never bend to his—" he turned back to John, "—or your temptations."

John said simply, "I believe you." He continued after a pause, "I didn't choose you simply because of your language skills—although they are exemplary. I know you read the papal letter that assigned you to our Order, so we both know that you are bound by the seal of the confessional."

"Yes, I'm very curious about that." Dan tried to catch John's eyes, but they remained fixed on the roadway.

"I imagine you are. You need to understand that your letter is the latest in a very long line of such decrees. Indeed, the text itself hasn't changed in centuries. And there are still excellent reasons for that—even more so these days."

Dan had long worried about the intrusiveness of technology, so he understood the general need for security, but such a level of secrecy was disturbing. It was also very exciting, though.

"The workings of your Order are obviously secret, and very important to the Church." Dan's heart rate picked up as he contemplated what he might be getting into.

John knew that for his mission to be successful, Dan would have to embrace the Order as his own. Even this early on, though, he could see Dan was holding himself at arm's length. He needed to change the young priest's way of thinking.

"You're correct, but your pronoun is wrong."

Dan's face screwed up at the apparent *non sequitur*. "My pronoun?" He thought back and parsed his last statement. "'Your'?" But he refused to let John manipulate him. "Ah, I'm not sure the Order is *my* Order, yet."

Trying a more direct tack, John responded, "You've got that backwards, too. You've sworn an oath of obedience. The Holy Father himself has given you this mission. You don't have to be sure." He let the verbal slap sink in for a moment. "And besides, the Order is not yours, nor is it mine. I, and now you, belong to it, not the other way around."

This dose of reality brought on several minutes of tense silence as the SUV slid through the Pocono Mountains. John hummed tunelessly to himself while Dan watched the beeches, birches, and aspens pass by the side window. As they climbed higher in elevation, the trees and even the low-lying mountain laurel exploded into flaming reds, brilliant yellows, and somber oranges.

They passed a turnout where several vehicles, mostly pickup trucks, were parked and empty. The hunters they had carried here into the mountains were now deep in the woods, up in their tree stands or huddled in their blinds. The sight made Dan suddenly deeply homesick. Even though he hadn't hunted with his father and brothers since becoming a priest, he now realized those days—and his previous life—were probably gone forever. He was leaving them behind at highway speed.

Chapter 19

Southeastern Pennsylvania, Late September

B ecoming aware that the mountain forests and river gorges had given way to houses and farms, Dan realized he must have fallen asleep. Quite embarrassed, he yawned and sat up straight in the passenger seat.

"Excuse me. I guess I dozed off." He squinted into the bright sun. "I'm not making for very good company."

"Don't worry about it. I've got a lot of things I have to sort out, so a little quiet time did me good." The earlier tension seemed to have evaporated. "I imagine you have more questions?"

Dan nodded. "Indeed, I do. Let's see, where to begin? OK, can you explain to me what exactly the Order is, and what you—what *we* do?"

John smiled at the corrected pronoun. "Think of our Order, which, by the way, is known to the outside world as 'The Enclave', as the eyes and ears of The Vatican. The Church has always known that there is a world outside its purview. In the early days, and for centuries after its founding, the Catholic Church was the center of people's lives—at least in Europe and western Asia. Of course, it isn't anymore. The spiritual world and the secular world have been drifting apart for centuries. Our official mission is to 'grow the Church's store of worldly knowledge,' so the Church can stay relevant in the secular world."

"'Worldly knowledge' is a pretty broad term."

"You're right. Initially, that meant discovering, or re-discovering, what existed outside the Church's influence, both geographically and historically. We travelled the world, not as clergy or representatives of the Church, but as regular, normal people. Explorers, merchants, physicians, cooks—you name it."

John paused for a reaction, but Dan sat quietly, apparently enjoying the history lesson, as the farms and tract houses of this part of Pennsylvania flowed past.

John continued, "We also travelled back in time, if you will." This time he got more of a reaction as Dan turned his head and raised his eyebrows, "by collecting writings and stories from different cultures. We've preserved many traditional songs, legends, and even entire languages that would otherwise have been lost even to their own cultures. In many cases, the cultures themselves are long gone, or so transformed that today they are unrecognizable."

"This is the archives you hinted at?" Dan was beginning to see how his recruitment may have come about.

"That was the origin of it, yes. But it is much, much broader in scope now. As the centuries have passed, the split between the spiritual and the secular has grown wider and wider. The central role in people's lives that the Church played early on has become more and more marginalized as the influence of governments and of science and technology has grown. The need for information that we would call today 'near real-time' has grown correspondingly. 'Worldly knowledge' now means more than geography and history. A lot more."

Dan began nodding while John spoke. "So, we are an order of spies?" Dan's tone was light, but from his intent look, John knew he was serious.

John chuckled, not just at the generalization, but also at the fact that Dan got his pronoun correct on the first try this time. "That's a bit of a generalization and an over-simplification." He paused. "Though there is a kernel of truth there. We monitor, as best we can, the actions of governments and corporations and other significant groups. Mostly, though, we do that through public media and the Internet."

"You just monitor? It seems like anyone could do that." They had reached the Quakertown exit of the Turnpike, where John turned off. The conversation resumed after they negotiated the exit ramp and the tollbooth and were headed south on PA Route 663.

"If they had the resources we've built up over a very long time, others probably could do what we do. Of course, there are other groups with similar missions. Most are governmental or government-sponsored. But to answer your question, no, we don't just monitor. Initially, that was our mission. To simply gather knowledge for the Church to use how they saw fit. It became apparent, though, that simply gathering information wasn't enough. So, we started analyzing the tidbits of seemingly unrelated information, and putting them together like a giant jigsaw puzzle."

Dan, who had naturally been relating John's story to his world view from inside the Church, interrupted. "How does The Vatican use your analyses?"

John's reaction was exasperation. "Not at all!" He exhaled to calm himself, then glanced at Dan with a half-smile. "At first, they didn't want lay people telling them how to deal with kings. But, after a series of disasters that we had warned them against, it became apparent to us, though not yet to those inside The Vatican's walls, that to understand how to put the pieces together into the big picture, one must use first-hand knowledge and intuition gained from living in the real world. We also realized that decision making within the Church, or any large organization, is a glacial process." John glanced sideways at Dan. "As I'm sure you know."

Dan nodded again. His many Vatican Archives requests, and their slow responses, had taught him that. "So, the Order took on a more 'active' role?"

"Not in the way you are probably thinking." John was surprised, but pleased by how quickly Dan was catching on, and by his own willingness to divulge so much. "Are you familiar with the concept of a Tipping Point?"

It took a moment for Dan to adjust to the change in conversational direction. "I think there was a book by that name not too long ago. Something about how a minor event, given the right conditions, can cause a cascading effect."

John nodded firmly and his voice rose as he spoke. "Exactly right. We came to realize that the right word, spoken into the correct ear, at just the key moment, could have a huge effect. It could, in fact, change the course of history. The next logical step, of course, was to find the right word, get close to the correct ear, and create that key situation to build up to that tipping point."

"So, we are spies." Dan's tone was matter-of-fact. "And *agents provocateurs*." Dan had just proven that John's assessment of the priest was spot on.

John's response tried to dissuade Dan from having the wrong impression of the Order. "Perhaps more so in the past. But nowadays, that is a very small part of what we do. And I must warn you, knowledge of our operational activities is a closely held secret even within the Order. The vast majority of our members do research and write reports or keep the Enclave running smoothly."

Dan nodded his understanding. "What other kinds of research do we do besides geopolitical?"

"We try to keep abreast of developments in all fields of science, as well as emerging technologies. We then correlate the various trends in scientific and technological research with societal trends."

"Sounds like what investment bankers do." Suspicion tinged Dan's tone. He firmly believed the old proverb that, *The love of money is the root of all evil.* In his worldview, primarily because of his upbringing, bankers and Wall Street types were therefore the embodiment of evil.

"Well, we have to eat." John meant it as a joke, but it had the opposite effect.

The young priest didn't even try to hide his distaste. "Is that how you fund the Order?"

John made no attempt to smooth Dan's feathers. "Over the centuries, the Enclave has built an endowment that contains a very robust investment portfolio. So yes, in part, this is how we are funded. We take no funding from anyone or any group outside the Order—including The Vatican. Even though, if you remember, besides being the spiritual center of Christianity, The Vatican is also an international bank."

John waited for a further reaction, but apparently he had made his point, because Dan remained silent. Then he continued after a minute or so. "You'll find the notion of self-sufficiency to be at the core of the Enclave's nature. Not just financially, but in everything we do. From the basics of food, water, and shelter, to the most advanced medical care and even power generation."

Dan's curiosity was back, but his tone was distant. "How can you be so isolated from the world, given your mission?"

John noticed the wrong pronouns were back, but ignored them. "I didn't say 'isolated.' I said self-sufficient. It's the classic Observer's Dilemma. How do we observe systems—science, technology, politics, or financial markets—without disturbing them? Our solution is to be *in* the system, but not to be *a part* of the system." John paused a moment. "But it's a delicate balancing act."

Dan still had questions and doubts about this aspect of things, but he kept them to himself. Sure, don't disturb the system—unless you can profit from it. Skepticism was unusual for him, but perhaps he was adapting to his new reality. Unconsciously, he knew he would have to.

Chapter 20

Southeastern Pennsylvania, Late September

They continued south down Route 663 for several miles in silence, through Pennsburg, New Hanover, and Limerick, then along a series of country roads through a succession of quaint towns and villages. Dan watched the scenery stream by.

Two-hundred-year-old farms adjoined tract housing developments, which were across the street from cul-de-sacs lined with overly ostentatious McMansions. Rolling hills, separated by meandering creeks and streams, wearing a patchwork of corn, hay, alfalfa, and soybeans, were all dry and brown now that Autumn had set in. Those fields were interspersed with pockets of forest.

Around every bend and over every hill, the view changed. Dan was a little surprised to find that the landscape felt comfortable to him. The hills weren't as steep or the woods as thick as back home, but he could see the same forces of nature at work there.

Coming out of another reverie as if coming awake, although he was conscious the whole time, Dan realized John was playing tour guide.

"Much of this area was settled in the late seventeenth and early eighteenth centuries. A little way that way," John pointed off to the west, "Daniel Boone settled for a while. You can visit his homestead. There's even a school district named after him." He shook his head slightly and chuckled to himself, as at a private joke.

Dan didn't know what was humorous about that, but he let it go. Instead, he asked, "How far are we from the Enclave?"

"Our border is about another ten miles from here, but on these roads, that'll take us at least twenty minutes."

Almost to make his point, John swung onto an even narrower road whose shoulders were crowded with overhanging trees.

Dan was struck by John's choice of words. "Your 'border'? How big is the Enclave?"

"Ah, good question. We're a small municipality as far as the state of Pennsylvania is concerned. We have about ten thousand acres all together."

Dan was shocked. He was thinking of the three-to-four-hundred-acre farms he knew from upstate. "Ten thousand acres? Wow, how many people live there?"

"Well, remember that we're very self-sufficient, so most of that is farmland and old growth habitat. Did you pack your rifle?" John smiled and glanced over at Dan.

"Actually, I did, but I haven't fired it in a long time." Dan was a little embarrassed to admit that. "So, you hunt?"

John nodded. "Certainly, but we try to use every part of what we take. It would dishonor the game if we didn't."

It was Dan's turn to nod. "That's what Dad always said." After a pause, he continued, "So, you didn't answer. How many people does ten thousand acres support?"

"We have about two thousand residents. Not all are members of the Order. Some are employees, and some are children. We could support many more, but we don't need to."

The scenery changed into expansive horse farms dotted with old stone barns and newer, large country-style houses. Although the road wound deeper into the woods, around blind curves and along a rushing creek, John picked up his speed. Perhaps he anticipated getting home.

"So, where are we, exactly? If someone asks, where do I tell them I live?" Dan tensed as John whipped them around a sharp curve and then had to brake hard to for a small herd of deer—a doe, a yearling, and two fawns just losing their spots.

Blowing out a deep breath, John let his annoyance show. "That's always a hazard on these roads. The houses they plop onto the old farms around here force the deer to forage further afield. A lot of them end up dead on the side of the road." He sighed. "It's a waste."

Keeping his eyes on the road, he continued, "Anyway, the Enclave is a separate municipality. From the Commonwealth of Pennsylvania's perspective, we're incorporated as Enclave Borough, but that's just a technicality. The Enclave has the same sort of autonomy that a Native American reservation does, so we're not really even part of Pennsylvania."

Dan was confused. "How can that be? Do you have a large Native American population?"

John thought a moment. "Hmm, I don't think we have any. Although maybe Jenny… Anyway, we're not an Indian reservation. The English king Charles I granted our property to the Order in 1630, well before his son Charles II gave what was to become Pennsylvania and Delaware to William Penn."

"You've been here since 1630?" Dan didn't know the settlement of Pennsylvania went back that far.

"Me, personally?" John laughed and Dan had to chuckle a little. "It took us a year or two to prepare for the move. We broke ground on the first buildings in 1632." He had noticed that Dan was still using the wrong pronouns, and decided he needed to be reminded again. "I hope, actually I expect, that you'll soon think of the Enclave as your home, too, and that you are a part of it." He paused, but before Dan could respond continued, "You'll be a lot more comfortable if you do. Our folks are not overly fond of outsiders. We're very accepting of new members, but only if that acceptance is reciprocated. You can do your priestly duties as…well, as an employee, and everyone will treat you with respect. But you won't get to know your flock very well that way. And you strike me as the kind of priest who wants to be a part of his parishioners' lives."

John glanced at Dan and smiled a little to soften the rebuke.

Dan was silent for a few moments before responding. "I take your point, and you are right, of course. This is a monumental change in my life, and it has come on so quickly that I'm still in shock a little." After a pause, he continued, "I guess I'm also a little scared. Although I've assisted with different parishes over the years, I've never had one of my own. I've been thinking about what a responsibility that is. I'm certainly looking forward to it—which is a little surprising to me since I never expected to be a parish priest. But it's all pretty daunting."

John nodded at Dan's sincerity. "Yes, of course it is. I'll try not to push too hard. I've searched for someone with your talents for a very long time. The fact that you're a priest as well is, frankly, a bonus. We've always had a resident priest. A lot of them, most actually, never fit in. I think most became pretty miserable and constantly petitioned to be released. But none of them ever had your facility with languages or your knowledge and appreciation of history. I think your hobbies…" Dan bristled, which John noticed. "No, you're right. I can see your interests go well beyond a hobby."

Relaxing a little, Dan said, "Being a priest doesn't allow me to have too many passions outside of my faith." John chuckled a little at the unintended pun, and Dan smiled wryly. "Understanding how people have accumulated and shared knowledge throughout history is fascinating to me. Given the pace of technological and scientific advancement today, the notion that entire cultures dating from the fall of Rome to the Renaissance could remain relatively constant, socially and technologically, is amazing to me. And when you think about how flat out wrong a lot of their understanding of nature and the world was, you have to wonder why no one stood up and said, 'This is just wrong.'"

He paused to catch his breath, and John jumped in, "Well, no offense, but you don't have to look very far to know why all of Europe was stagnant for a thousand years."

Dan looked at him questioningly, so he continued, getting increasingly passionate. "Anybody who stood up and questioned the Church's 'official' view of the world was labelled a heretic. The Church, *your* Church, suppressed any notion of free thought or scientific advancement. Any idea or discovery that contradicted their official doctrine, which was based on superstition not observation and logic, was deemed evil and they tortured adherents until they recanted."

He took a breath to calm down, so Dan stepped in. "I know the Church was pretty reactionary, but you certainly can't blame it for the Dark Ages." He was partly joking, and he expected a jest in response, but the heat of John's reply shocked him.

"In our library, we have the only surviving copies of codices that propose a heliocentric view of the universe centuries before Copernicus. Others discuss, and even promote, individual freedoms and equality of the sexes at a time when outspoken women were burned as witches. Do you know why we have the only surviving copies?" He didn't wait for Dan to respond this time. "Because after we brought them to their attention, the Church burned all the other copies—along with their authors. Why? Because the Church had painted itself into a corner. If their doctrine was a direct communique from God, then any evidence or even thoughts to the contrary must therefore be the Devil's."

Dan was thoughtful while John fell silent. After a minute of watching the rolling farmland pass by, though, he spoke. "And yet the Order was formed to learn about the secular world. How could it have come into being under the auspices of such a repressive regime?"

John nodded slowly while he framed his answer. "Two things converged. An enlightened man, well ahead of his time, became Pope. Who, alas, didn't serve for very long." He fell silent, reluctant to continue, but he knew Dan would not let the matter lie.

"That's one. What's the other one?"

John held his breath for a beat because he knew Dan was holding his. Then he said simply, "Leverage."

Before Dan could ask any more questions, John yanked the wheel hard to the right and made a sharp turn between two trees, straight into the surrounding woods. The turn threw Dan against the center console, and he had to grab the handle above his door for support.

"Whoa! What the—" Then he saw they had entered a lane that had been invisible from the road and was still nearly so even as they followed it.

John negotiated a sharp right turn that doubled them back parallel to the way they had come, but in the opposite direction. Looking out his window, Dan could barely see the road through the trees and thick underbrush, and he knew they were probably not visible from the road either, even though it was only a few yards away.

Two more left turns brought them back to their original direction, then a sharp right took them deeper into the woods. The overhanging canopy of branches darkened the otherwise bright day. Abruptly, John stopped the SUV at a simple metal gate.

Powering his window down, he looked into the underbrush and spoke, seemingly to no one, "John Haviland. I have Father Dan Koprowicz with me."

From nowhere, a voice responded, "Of course you do. Identity confirmed. I thought you'd be bringing him in the front." The voice from the woods sounded a little disapproving.

John responded with authority. "Just trying to keep it informal."

"OK, then." Although unsaid, the missing "you're the boss" was clearly implied. The gate blocking the lane slid quickly and silently to the side, then back into place after John drove through.

Around another bend in the lane, they crossed a metal bridge that looked sturdy enough to carry M1 tanks, though it was barely wide enough to admit the SUV. Beneath the bridge, Dan saw a rushing creek. The bridge was buttressed by what appeared to be hydraulic cylinders.

To his practiced eye, which had spent years roaming the woods and streams back home, though, something about the creek seemed odd. He couldn't put his finger on it until the sun glinted off the creek bed. At first, Dan thought it might be the shine off a brook trout lying in a shallow pool, but as they crossed back onto land, Dan looked back and saw another and another and another spaced at regular intervals. He didn't yet know what they were, but he knew they were manmade.

The hidden entrance, the switchbacks, electric gate, drawbridge, and what were probably metal barriers buried in the creek bed led to only one conclusion. The Enclave was very well fortified.

He quickly forgot that oddity, however, when their SUV emerged from the heavy cover of the trees into a spreading meadow that covered several dozen acres of hillside. The forest track they had been following became an access road that traced the edge of the forest up and over the hill a couple hundred yards away.

Looking out his window, Dan could see evidence of what must have been a sizable deer population. He saw bark rubbed off trees where bucks had scratched off the velvet covering their antlers. He also saw disturbed ground where the does had piled leaves for their beds. His experienced eye could follow their trails as they disappeared into the woods.

John noticed Dan's interest and smiled. "Now, aren't you glad you brought your rifle?"
Turning from the window, with his own smile, Dan nodded. His smile turned to a grin as he realized he felt like he had just come home.

PART III

The Levant
1184 A.D

The first few years of my time in the Holy Land comprised constant training, skirmishes with bandits, prayer, silent meals, and spying. While the first taught me the art of warfare, the last taught me much about the politics of power and the egos of those who have it and should not.

Chapter 21

Acre, 1184-1186 A.D.

The great walled city of Acre embraced the sea with an excellent, well-protected harbor. It served as the port of entry and departure for Christians on pilgrimage to the Holy Land. Templar knights escorted groups of pilgrims every few weeks as they toured the holy sites. From Acre, they crossed eastward to the stronghold of Safed in Galilee, south through Jesus's homeland to La Feve, then back to the coast at Chateau Pelerin. They walked between Templar castles, making their way to the ultimate destination, Jerusalem. As these were each one-day journeys, and since the land was open and under control of various Christian Orders and secular lords, the caravans of pilgrims and merchants travelled in relative safety.

Because of the low risk, newly arriving Templars, like us, who had not yet been fully trained in the method of battle employed by the Order, patrolled these early legs on the pilgrimage route. From Chateau Pelerin, more seasoned knights and their sergeants, squires, and other attendants protected the pilgrims as they continued south to Caesarea, Bethlehem, and Jerusalem. After being relieved of our charges at Chateau Pelerin, we trainees followed the coast northwards back to Acre.

This loop, Acre to Safed to La Feve to Pelerin and back to Acre, took up to a month, depending on the size of the caravan and the timing of the many religious festivals along the way. As I had done on our sea journey, I explored each of the towns on the route, learning their customs and the patterns of Arabic, Hebrew, and Aramaic spoken.

It was during this time that our Order began a system of money handling designed to protect our pilgrims and their wealth. I noticed, while watching a cockfight in Safed, that many of those cheering for their champion were waving bits of paper in the air. When the fight ended, half of those with these slips of paper tossed theirs away in disgust, while the others rushed to a man with heavily armed guards. These winners exchanged their slips of paper for money. Before the next fight started, the opposite exchanges happened. I soon realized they were bettors exchanging their coins for one of the pieces of paper that the money changer scribbled on. Curious, I picked up one of the discarded papers, only to find characters scribbled in some language I could not decipher.

Collecting several of the slips, I discerned a pattern and realized they were coded records of how much was bet on which cock. I realized the same method could hold in trust the pilgrims' wealth while traveling, allowing them to carry only the encoded record of their deposit, rather than the coin and jewels that made them targets for bandits. Upon arriving at their destination, they could then present their encoded deposit record at the local Templar commandery and exchange it for some or all of the equivalent value in local coin.

When I discussed such a system with my training knights, they simply smiled condescendingly but otherwise ignored my suggestion. But, soon after the Master of the commandery at Acre overheard my insistent discussion of the idea, the first outposts of what became a banking system for travelers spread across Europe.

While in garrison at Acre, our training masters, who were grizzled veterans of many battles with the Muslim hordes, drilled us relentlessly. Despite their scarred and maimed bodies, or because of them, they taught us to respect the tactics and fighting spirit of our enemy, who invariably attacked with swiftness out of either the rising or setting sun. Small bands of raiders routinely attacked the pilgrim caravans during the long march across the desert and through the mountains on the last leg of their journey to Jerusalem.

The raids were much rarer on the circuit that we patrolled, but when the ever-watchful Muslim horseman believed they saw an opportunity, for example, when the caravan was stretched too thin, they swept down from the hills at full gallop. Their goal was to capture horses or camels loaded with valuables. The experienced knights who were able-bodied enough to accompany us used these lightning attacks as training exercises, exhorting us with shouted orders, signaling flags, and blasts of battle horns.

Forming into the battle order that Templars were known for throughout the world, I and the other sergeants-in-training served and protected our brother knights as they met and deflected the raiders' thrusts.

We did not yet counterattack, not for a lack of training, but rather to avoid being drawn away by a feint and leaving our charges vulnerable to a flanking second wave. Only a larger force than ours could be split safely to pursue the raiders as they fled, and only then if the land was open enough to avoid entrapment and ambush.

My particular training regime also included further lessons in stealth, observing the deployment of troops and weaponry from hiding, and learning the natives' Arabic tongue. In short, the art of spying. I must confess that to hone my skills, I spent as much time spying on our trainers and the Templar councils as I did on the local Muslim tribes.

As my skills improved, I often ventured ahead of our column of pilgrims in search of bandits lying in wait. After a mission that revealed their hiding places and allowed us to encircle and rout them, I was perusing the locals' wares in the market and practicing my language skills by chatting with the various merchants.

While thumping melons to test their ripeness, a young boy, probably the son of the merchant keeping a close eye on my hands, spoke just above a whisper in the local dialect to his father.

"The *alshayatin* with the red crosses killed your cousin Mustafa yesterday."

The boy looked at me sideways with hatred in his eyes, but I gave no sign I understood him. His father just snorted derisively.

"They are not devils, *Abn*. They are men just like us...well maybe not like you—yet."

He chuckled at his own joke, but the boy would have none of it.

"If not devils, then how do they find our raiders when they are so well-hidden?"

The father lowered his voice, and I moved to a basket of dates, but still within earshot.

"It is said that one among them can move without being seen or heard and with leaving no trace of his passing."

"A *shabah*, then?"

The older man shook his head. "A man, not a true ghost. A *Shabah Tamblar*."

I covered my gasp with a fake cough. *A "Templar Ghost" who can see raiders wherever they hide,* I thought.

Although my Templar demeanor would never allow me to show pride at hearing them talk so, inwardly I embraced the moniker and began to think of myself as this Templar Ghost.

Lifting two melons and a basket of dates, I drew back my dusty cloak, revealing my white mantel emblazoned with its crimson cross and asked the merchant, "*Kam althaman*"— "How much" in perfect Arabic.

The boy blanched as white as my mantel, and the merchant just waved his hand and said, "My gift to you and your brothers."

I smiled. "*Shukran lak,*" I said and tucked the produce into the sack slung over my shoulder.

Chapter 22

Jerusalem, 1186-1187 A.D.

T he training and missions in Acre became routine—as routine as any armed conflicts can be. At last, after having proven our worth escorting pilgrims to the satisfaction of our training masters, Stewart and I were transferred to the Templar garrison in Jerusalem. Over the next two years, we met our Muslim foes, the *Ayyubid,* in many skirmishes and battles. The truce that had existed between Christian and Ayyubid forces dissolved as a new leader of the Ayyubid armies asserted control.

Salah ad-Din Yusuf ibn Ayyub, known to us simply as Saladin, rose to prominence among the various enemy factions. His military brilliance, along with his charisma, united the fractious tribal leaders as lieutenants under his command, and he became the first Sultan of Egypt and Syria. With an army of over ten thousand seasoned veterans, Saladin set about weakening the Christian hold on the holy places. These were locations that were equally sacred to Muslims and Jews, as well as Christians.

Our first meeting with Saladin's troops on the field south of Jerusalem in Gaza was a shock to Templars and secular lords alike. Stewart, now a captain in command of some twenty knights and their sergeants, as well as eighty or so foot soldiers, led his mounted knights and sergeants in the vanguard of a spear point attack into the heart of the enemy's line of battle. At first, the tide certainly seemed to be in our favor as we made steady progress, gaining more and more ground into the enemy's belly.

The satisfaction I felt at our steady progress evaporated, however, when I, as Stewart's first sergeant defending his off-hand left side, realized the enemy was fighting backwards. I mean, they were falling back without being forced to do so.

"Brother, this is too easy," I yelled to Stewart.

Through the slot in his visor, I saw the same realization come to his eyes.

"Halt the advance," he called to his lieutenant knights. Faithful as ever, they followed his command, recognition coming to some of them. "Form up in defense of our flanks."

Our well-trained cohort obeyed his orders immediately, and they did so just in time, as no sooner were we deployed thus, than the counter-attack came at us from both sides. Having thus prepared for the onrush of attackers, and with the support of the foot soldiers who came up behind us at a dead run, we repelled both flanking maneuvers. Seeing that his feint and parry had failed, Saladin sounded the signal to withdraw to defensive positions. With the enemy setting a defensive posture, Stewart likewise signaled a withdrawal back to the main body of our army.

When Stewart delivered his after-action report, I was positioned in the hidey hole I had previously discovered while practicing my skills at stealth and subterfuge. In that hiding place, I routinely spied on the Templar leadership—Master Gerard and his seneschals. I was thus positioned when Stewart delivered his after-action report. Expecting at least a warm, if not celebratory, welcome for anticipating and mitigating

Saladin's stratagem, I was shocked when our Grand Master, Gerard de Ridefort, berated Stewart for his lack of initiative.

"Your actions—or rather lack of action—today was unacceptable," Gerard stormed. "Your failure to press your advantage with the enemy in full flight—"

"They were not running away," Stewart interrupted, to the amazement of the other knights present. "They were laying—"

"Enough! Your lack of initiative was tantamount to cowardice."

"But—"

"Silence!" Gerard de Ridefort's face fairly glowed red in his anger as spittle flew from his mouth and splattered on Stewart's beard.

"Master Gerard," one of Gerard's own lieutenants, Robert of Mont Charmont, calmly interrupted Gerard's rant. "We have seen Saladin employ this ambushing tactic before. Remember, if you will, the losses we suffered just last month at his hand."

The skirmish Sir Robert referred to cost the Templars seven good knights and most of their supporting sergeants and footmen, a complement led by none other than Master Gerard himself. Abashed at this reminder of his incompetence, Gerard halted his fuming, but never acknowledged that Stewart's actions had not only been prudent, but had probably saved the lives of his entire command. Instead, he simply dismissed Stewart and the other members of the Council with a wave of his hand. This was just the first of many times that Gerard acted out of jealousy of Stewart's tactical and strategic superiority.

Though visibly furious, Stewart silently spun on his heal and strode from the chamber. The look in his eyes, however, was clear to everyone present that any respect

Stewart held for Gerard's ability as a military commander was gone like morning mist before the rising sun.

He was not alone in feeling betrayed, either. Most of our company, whose lives Stewart had undoubtedly saved that day, could be heard muttering and whispering amongst themselves for many days. Even some of Gerard's inner circle seemed to be embarrassed by the outburst and privately showed their support for Stewart with an occasional simple clasp of his shoulder. No words needed to be exchanged, or in fact, could be without violating our oath of obedience.

Over the next year, despite our best efforts, and largely because of Gerard's incompetence, Saladin's forces steadily gained ground, taking one castle and fort after another. His continued study of Saladin's strategy and tactics led to advice and recommendations which, when followed by other commanders—never by Gerard himself—stopped Saladin's advances cold. Only when we were in the field and Stewart could not be consulted, or when Gerard simply ignored his recommendations, were Saladin's armies victorious.

His leadership and insights did not go unnoticed by the secular lords and their commander knights, however. Eventually, Stewart, despite Gerard's lack of support, was advanced to membership on the wider War Council.

The War Council, composed of Templar leaders and the local secular lords and their commanders, reported to Guy, King of Jerusalem. Guy had succeeded his young nephew, Baldwin V, after his death two years before. The many twists and turns of politics in the Holy Land led only to weakness due to in-fighting and insubordination among the various lords who believed they had better claims to the throne.

When the council met, Stewart often voiced the need for reinforcements to be recruited from the Frankish, English, and German nobility—effectively another Crusade. Gerard scoffed at the need for a third crusade. The lords, including Guy, whose military expertise was always suspect, however, took notice and agreed, sending an appeal to Pope Urban III. It was not until too late, though, that a Holy Father heeded their appeal.

Chapter 23

Jerusalem, Winter 1187 A.D.

The Seljuk Saladin and his armies had captured all the Christian towns, forts, and castles—including several Templar strongholds—from Aleppo in the north, to Damascus in the west, and even the Fatimid states to the south. The Kingdom of Jerusalem, the County of Tripoli, and the Principality of Antioch, stretching along the coast of the Mediterranean Sea, were effectively surrounded by Saladin's united Muslim forces.

I was training sergeant-candidates when Stewart signaled to me from the edge of the training grounds.

"Yes, Brother?" I asked as I reined in my horse next to his.

"Your presence has been requested by Grand Master de Ridefort," he replied. His demeanor, stoic as always, gave away nothing.

"Of course." I nodded and called to my fellow trainers to oversee my group until I returned. We then walked our horses in silence for a few yards until we were clear of the training grounds outside the city walls in the Valley of Jehoshaphat. I was surprised when Stewart turned east toward the Mount Sion Gate, rather than north to the Golden Gate, closest to the Templars' quarters. My curiosity got the better of me.

"Can you tell me, Brother, why I've been summoned?"

Stewart shook his head, but kept his eyes forward. "I was not told." He sighed. "What trouble have you brewed this time, Little Brother?"

Early on, while still awkward in my clandestine ways, before I achieved the Templar Ghost moniker, I was caught a few times spying on council meetings and battle plans. Each time Master de Ridefort derided my talents and assigned me the most humiliating punishments. It had been several months, and many secretly observed meetings, including personal audiences with King Guy, since I had been discovered, however.

"I'm not aware of any known indiscretions on my part," I replied coyly.

This time, Stewart turned to look my way. "*Known* indiscretions?"

I shrugged. "It seems my worth to the Order, and to King Guy, goes beyond being a simple sergeant."

My mention of the King raised his eyebrow, but that was all.

"There is nothing simple about being my sergeant." Before I could protest, he continued, "But I understand how important your *other* skills may be when called upon."

Understanding dawned on me then. "Do you think my skills are being called upon now?"

It was Stewart's turn to shrug. "Understanding our Grand Master's thinking has proven to be beyond my ken."

We both chuckled as we rode through the gate in the southern wall.

The city's citadel stood against the eastern city wall, which presented an impregnable barrier to invaders. Its inward-facing side, however, shared a broad courtyard with the King's palace off to the left. The square bustled with activity as scribes hurried to attend the many political and governmental offices surrounding the source of power in the kingdom. I caught snatches of conversation in French, Italian, English, and even Arabic as ambassadors, functionaries, and merchants conducted their business.

A small market was even set up to cater to the wealthy residents of that quarter with luxury items—robes, scarves, honey-laden pastries, and even delicacies from as far away as Greece and Turkey. The calls of the sellers and the pungent smells of spices, roasting meats, and baking of the local flat bread that wafted from the stalls marked Jerusalem as the most cosmopolitan city in the region.

We dismounted and handed off our mounts to grooms at the base of the broad steps that climbed to the citadel's massive doors. Inside, two of the king's guard met us at the entrance and escorted us up flights of stairs and through twisting passages to a large chamber high in the keep. Large windows, with their heavy tapestry draperies drawn back, overlooked the courtyard we had just traversed. Indistinct voices and the strongest of the smells drifted in from below.

King Guy, Grand Master de Ridefort, several of the noble lords, both local nobility and those on pilgrimage themselves, stood around a large table in the center of the room. Their seneschals and lieutenants hovered around the edges of the room, ready to provide advice or run errands as needed.

Stewart and I approached, and the lesser nobles drew back to make space for us at the table. I admit my hands shook a little with nervousness at the political and military power gathered there. A glance at Stewart's calm and assured demeanor, however, strengthened my own resolve to face whatever mission—or punishment—was forthcoming.

Spread across the table was a map of the region with colored stones marking the boundaries of the three remaining Christian territories. Tiny carved figures of knights, horsemen, and foot soldiers—the King's and his nobles' personal chess pieces—huddled within the confines of those territories. Roughly carved figures bearing the long, curved swords, lances, and maces of our Ayyubid enemies surrounded them all.

When we reached the table, Stewart and I bowed to King Guy and offered a smart salute to our Grand Master. Guy nodded in return, though de Ridefort simply sniffed and pretended to ignore us.

"I have brought my Sergeant Brother as requested," Stewart said.

We both stood rigidly, awaiting the purpose of my summons. King Guy glanced at de Ridefort, as if expecting him to deliver the expected explanation. But rather than addressing us, de Ridefort turned to the king.

"Your Grace, I must insist that we abandon this foolhardy idea—"

"Enough." King Guy cut off the Grand Master. "We have discussed this to death. You have made your arguments over and over without convincing a single other member of this Council. Deliver your orders to your sergeant."

De Ridefort scowled, but finally turned to face me. "It seems your previous attempts at underhandedly spying on myself and my seneschals, and your pitiful attempts at clandestine observation, even his Grace's War Council, have somehow impressed these secular lords."

He paused to push down the anger showing on his face, so I, swallowing my fear, asked, "My *previous* attempts, Grand Master?"

Taken aback by my impertinence, de Ridefort sputtered. "You wisely abandoned your foolish practice months ago, have you not?"

I fought hard to keep the smirk from my face, but I admit I could not keep it completely from my tone. "I abandoned my foolish practice of getting *caught* is all, Grand Master."

Somehow, I felt Stewart stiffen even more while I could hear snickers throughout the room.

De Ridefort fairly shouted his response. "The guards and watchers I deployed against you have neither caught, nor even observed you spying for—"

The laughter that burst from the king and his nobles cut de Ridefort off mid-sentence.

"I think what the sergeant is trying to tell you, Grand Master, is that his skills have improved to where he has escaped detection, despite your specific efforts at that detection." King Guy smiled at me. "Is that not so, Sergeant?"

Keeping my eyes firmly on the king, I nodded. "Aye, Your Grace."

"Liar!" de Ridefort barked. "I'll have your—"

This time, I interrupted him. "Should I tell these nobles about your latest plans with Seneschal Hurson to evacuate our Order's forces to Acre?"

"That is simply contingency planning," Hurson spoke up from his position behind de Ridefort.

"That is certainly reasonable," King Guy said. "When did you last discuss these plans?"

De Ridefort glared at me while he responded, "Last evening. In my quarters."

The king turned to me. "And the specifics of these plans?"

"Sir Edward of Glaston's contingent will be the first to march, followed by *Monsieur Francois*—"

"Enough," the Grand Master interrupted. He looked at King Guy. "It seems I have…underestimated the *Sergeant's* abilities, Your Grace."

"I agree." King Guy turned to me. "Undress, Young Man."

I blinked. "Excuse me, Your Grace?"

"Remove your clothes."

Understanding that no further explanation would be forthcoming, I slowly stripped off my black sergeant's mantel, tunic, sword, chain mail, leggings, and undershirt. These I handed to Stewart, who passed them to a servant. Shortly, I stood before these noble gentlemen wearing only my braies about my privates.

One of the King's ministers pointed at me and said, "As we suspected, Your Grace. He needs time in the sun unclothed."

I looked down at myself. My forearms were tanned a deep brown, as I suspect my face and neck were based on those of my brethren I saw around me every day. But the rest of my body still bore the complexion I inherited from my mother, that of a native of southern France. The discrepancy was obvious, as was their intended assignment.

"If he is to pass for an infidel, Your Grace, he must be baked to an even degree."

The King nodded to de Ridefort to issue the orders. Without looking at me, he turned to Seneschal Hurson, who handed him a parchment from which he read.

"Sergeant, you are relieved of your current training duties and assigned to…the roof of your quarters, where you will bake in the sun throughout the day. You will be examined thus," he waved his hand at my near nakedness, "daily, until you can pass for a member of the local race. At such time, you will be escorted to the western border, where you will pass secretly into the Seljuk territory for a period of one week, gathering whatever information your *skills* afford you regarding the disposition of the enemy's forces and their preparedness for battle." de Ridefort looked up from the parchment and glared at me. "Do you understand these orders, *Sergeant*?"

My heart thudded in my chest. At last, I could put the craft of stealth that I had been honing for years to good purpose. "I do, Grand Master."

He dismissed me with a wave of his hand.

Gathering my kit from the servant, Stewart and I left the chamber. While I dressed in the hallway, Stewart whispered, "Be careful, Brother. You made a powerful enemy today."

I nodded, but looked at him with a sly grin. "A shared enemy, eh?"

Stewart chuckled and handed me my sword. "Aye, but that does not make him any less dangerous."

I laughed and buckled my sword belt as we walked down the hall. "At least I get a few days of respite baking in the sun."

Stewart, whose Norman paleness lent him a constant sunburn, simply said, "Better you than me, Little Brother."

Chapter 24

Jerusalem, Spring 1187 A.D.

Jerusalem, home to holy sites and shrines of three religions, was a truly cosmopolitan city. Although most Jews were expelled when the Christians conquered the city in 1099, some Jewish merchants remained. Thousands of Muslims and Christians shared the city side by side, however, leading to many intrigues and persecutions.

After my success in the desert, and with the reluctant agreement of Grand Master de Ridefort, I was ordered to use my skills at stealth to ferret out plots and plans targeted at our Christian forces. I quickly learned, however, that there were as many subterfuges among the secular lords for control of each other's castles and forts than were planned by the city dwellers, who, mostly, just wanted to live in peace.

I was soon to discover, though, that there was another group of players in this drama, of which we were completely ignorant until it was almost too late. In the mountains north of Jerusalem, there lived several tribes known as the Hashashim. Although ostensibly Muslim, they followed the Shi'ite form of Islam, rather than the prevailing Sunni form practiced by the Ayyubid rulers, Saladin chief among them. They were therefore considered tainted outcasts by their more self-righteous brethren. But despite his disdain for them, Saladin and his lieutenants found the Hashashim very useful. Trained from birth in the arts of stealth and silent killing, these Assassins, as they came to be called by western Crusaders, were employed by our enemy to eliminate our leaders and best fighters.

Because of the Templars' individual fighting prowess, and our constant vigilance of posting guards even when garrisoned, these Assassins mostly left my brothers alone. Rather, they targeted the less disciplined secular knights. A single assassin, moving like a ghost, would slip into the camps and barracks of the noble Lords' armies. While all slept, he would slit the throats of their captains, easily identified by their ornate tents and banners, and then slink away undetected.

It was on a moonless night, as I was returning to my cot after one of my nightly spying forays, when I, the so-called "Templar Ghost," encountered one of these spectral assassins. At first, all I saw was a shadow, caused not by the absent moon, but rather by the purest chance. As my soon-to-be quarry slipped along between two houses, the resident of one of them threw open his window shutters to let in the cooler night air. The light of the single candle within caught the stalker darting down the alley.

If he had frozen in place instead of running, I would not have noticed the faint shadow he cast into the street. Rather, it was the movement of that shadow, a clear outline of a hunched figure that caught my weary eye. I set off in search of this late-night interloper, expecting him to simply be a husband sneaking home from the town's brothels.

I quickly realized, however, that this was no stumbling adulterer, but rather one even more skilled at stealth than I. I am sure that the only reason I was not detected following behind was that he never suspected that he would be followed. Certain in his mind that he was the hunter, not the prey, it was easy for me to anticipate his few backward glances and freeze in my hiding places deep within the shadows. Even with this advantage, however, more than once he paused and peered in my direction, and I was sure he had somehow detected my presence, despite me employing all my skills at stealth.

Only the fact that we were slipping between homes, among the snoring, farting, and screwing populace, kept the slight crunch of sand beneath my feet from drawing his attention.

He continued on in the general direction of the city citadel, and two frightening realizations dawned on me. First, this must be one of the dreaded Assassins that our men feared. I envisioned him sneaking between tents as he now snuck between houses, then slipping undetected into a captain's quarters and silently sending him to heaven.

But we were not sneaking through the tents of the garrisoned armies. We were making our way through the heart of the city towards King Guy's palace. When this second realization hit me, I must have let out a small gasp, because my prey—which is how I now thought of him—stopped his advance, remaining hidden within the shadow of the doorway two houses in front of me and across the street.

For long moments, which seemed like minutes, then like hours, I held my breath and locked my muscles so not even a change in the slight breeze would betray my presence.

When I knew I would have to let out the spent air burning my lungs, a sleepy voice emerged from an open window between us.

In Arabic, a woman said, "Get off of me, you drunken sot."

I heard the Assassin's exhalation of his own held breath and saw first his shadow, then his figure dart to the side of the next house.

As he moved, I moved. When he froze, I froze and searched for my next hiding place. Despite my care, he must have felt my presence, even though I was sure I had not betrayed myself with either movement or sound. His pace quickened, his shadowy pauses lengthened, and his backward glances became even more frequent.

Almost at a run now, we made our way toward the palace. My mind raced along with my body, trying to plan how to stop him. If I ran even faster to catch up, he would surely hear me, and I would lose the element of surprise. He would then have the advantage and could ambush me from any of the many darkened doorways or alleys.

Not surprisingly, we were not approaching the palace from the front, which would have been suicide. Before the main gate, which was heavily guarded, lay an open plaza, perhaps two hundred paces across. He could not possibly cross that expanse undetected.

The sides of the walled royal compound, however, were not set off so much from the rest of the city. A single wide street separated the houses from the high walls that towered as high as six or seven men standing on shoulders.

As with the rest of society, the houses that lined this street were stratified by proximity to power. Lining the palace entry plaza were the walled compounds of the wealthiest lords. Those houses, with their armed guards, were themselves palatial.

As the distance from the grand plaza increased however, both along the sides of the palace and block by block outwards, the buildings diminished in size from the large single houses of minor lords, to spacious townhouses of wealthy merchants, down to common houses and tenements for craftsmen and servants.

Within the palace, where I had been only a few times before serving as Stewart's aide, a similar pride-of-place hierarchy existed. Surrounding the royal apartments, courtiers vied for proximity and access. In decreasing precedence and increasing distance were councilors, scribes, cooks, maids, and private body servants. At the very back of the palace compound, where the walls were highest and nearly windowless, were the lesser servants' quarters and the common privies.

Each of these privies could be identified by its narrow window and the slot in the wall directly below. The lower opening served as the mouth of a sluice that deposited the occupant's efforts into an open pit that spanned much of the palace's back wall. The window, intended to provide light and at least some fresh air, more often simply allowed in the stench that arose from the pit.

That smell was overpowering, and my prey was leading me right to it. He had planned this attack well. The obnoxious stench and the protection of a moat of filth meant that this section of the palace wall was left unguarded except for an infrequent patrol. When a guard did pass, he did so as quickly as possible, usually with his face covered and his eyes watering.

No one with any financial resources would live in this section of town either, so the residents were surely lowly peasants and servants with no love of their Christian occupiers. In this part of town, the Assassin relaxed his stealth, and moved more openly, not fearing that anyone would raise an alarm. Dressed all in black and, as I could now see because he walked more openly, with some bundle strapped to his back, he was clearly up to no good, but it was more likely he would be aided, not betrayed, if discovered.

I, on the other hand, faced the opposite situation. The danger to me had risen as his had declined. If discovered, I was likely to face a very unpleasant death. And, if it became known that I was more than a foot soldier among the Templars, probably a prolonged, very painful one. So, I increased my vigilance, which slowed me down. The separation between us grew.

As a result, my prey reached the edge of the pit well before me. After losing precious minutes skulking from shadow to shadow, I found a hiding place only two hovels from where I thought he had stopped. This place was directly across the moat from one of the privy windows.

My heart raced as I searched in vain for his shadow or silhouette. The fumes from the pit compounded the difficulty by making my eyes run like a rain gutter. Unable to locate the Assassin, and unable to even see my own outstretched hand effectively, I tilted my head to clear the tears from my eyes. By doing this, the pit and its filth revealed my prey to me.

Looking up and blinking the tears from my eyes, I saw him standing on the roof of a mud-brick house. Thinking in three dimensions instead of just our earthbound two was a lesson I learned well that night and which has served me well many times since.

I could see the man had unstrapped his bundle and was preparing to throw it, javelin like, across the pit. Holding the bundle above his head, he backed up to the far side of the roof and prepared for his run and throw. I could see a thin cord, one end tied at the end of the bundle and the other tied around his waist.

This brought to my mind the sailors I watched on our journey from home. They often threw a small, weighted string tied to a larger mooring rope from ship to dock or ship to ship.

The string was then used to haul the mooring rope across the gap.

The Assassin's bundle reminded me of this operation, but what he planned must somehow be different. I understood the difference when I saw the bundle more clearly as it sailed through the air, though. It appeared to be a javelin, as I had thought, but one that was wrapped front to back with layers of thin rope. Trailing behind it was the cord leading back to his waist.

My prey's throw was true, and the rope and javelin sailed cleanly through the privy window opposite, making only the slightest thump as it landed inside the palace. I watched, fascinated, as the ingenuity of the Assassin was revealed to me. Pulling the cord taut, he tugged on it a few times until it again went a little slack.

These tugs must have slid the other end of the cord, which was grafted to the larger rope, off the end of the javelin. He then hauled first the cord, then the rope hand over hand from the window to his rooftop perch. I heard a slight rattling from the privy window, and I pictured in my mind the javelin wedged across the window, serving as an anchor for the rope, which was tied at its midpoint.

My fascination turned to horror as understanding of the rest of his plan came to me. He intended to swing across the moat, climb the rope, and slip through the window into the palace. With no guards in sight, he would be inside amongst his servant brethren before I could even raise the alarm. I knew it was up to me to stop him in the next few moments.

Again, he backed up, but this time only a few steps, as he readied himself for a leaping swing. How could I stop him, or at least slow him down long enough for me to call forth the guards?

Without a plan in mind, I reached for my belt. I had come lightly armed with just two daggers, a stiletto and a baselard given to me by a drunken Teutonic Knight after I had helped him back to his barracks on another of my late-night excursions.

The pommel of my stiletto, which in my mind I had secretly named Luisa, fit my hand perfectly and was instantly drawn from her sheath without a conscious thought on my part. My Luisa was named after a local brothel owner, who the secular knights claimed would slit your purse strings and perhaps your throat if you fell asleep in her house.

As I drew Luisa from her leather sheath, I flipped her point-down between my fingers and thumb. I had been practicing my throwing skills recently, though this throw, at a moving, swinging target anywhere from ten to thirty yards away, was by far the most challenging throw I had yet tried.

I stepped from the shadows into the street as the Assassin took two running steps and leapt. If I had had time to think through this attack and anticipate his actions, I might have expected him to do what he did as he launched himself into the air. He immediately started climbing hand-over-hand, even as he swung toward the palace wall.

I fixed my eyes on the center of his back, the widest target, as he began his swing. My aim was excellent, and Luisa flew true. But the swinging motion and the Assassin's quick, monkey-like climb combined to raise him most of a yard higher than my aim allowed for. As a result, rather than delivering a death blow, Luisa buried herself in the back of his left thigh.

Though not mortal, the wound was certainly debilitating. The Assassin's grip loosened, and he slid down the rope toward the moat. Mere feet above the poisonous filth, though, he regained his grip on the rope, arresting his descent.

Without a single cry or even a moan escaping his lips, he began slowly climbing toward the window while his blood, streaming from around Luisa, dripped into the moat.

Knowing he was far from finished, I turned and ran for the side gate of the palace, yelling for the guards to raise the alarm. Bellowing in both French and English, I ordered the guards to open the gate. When they did, however, I faced a phalanx of drawn swords. Disguised in Arab garb, I must have seemed like a madman proclaiming my name and Templar vows in every language—except Arabic—that I could summon.

Finally, after too many precious moments had passed, I flung off the typical striped Arab peasant tunic that I wore to show them the belted rope tied around my waist.

Faced with indisputable evidence of my loyalty, for only a Templar could tie the complicated knot that secured my simple badge, the captain of the guard admitted me and listened while I warned him that an Assassin may already be in the palace. Luckily, the captain was quick-witted and grasped the threat immediately. He and I, together with three or four of his men, set off at a dead run for his point of entry.

When we arrived at the privies, it was obvious which one interested us, but it was equally obvious that we had arrived too late. The javelin, which had supported the rope and the weight of the Assassin, still spanned the window, but the rope attached to it was slack. Thinking that he may have lost his grip and fallen into the moat, I rushed to the window, stood on the wooden seat, and leaned out into the night air. Without having to look down, though, I knew he had completed his climb to this room. My hands, which I placed on the windowsill, encountered the sticky wetness of his blood. It was a sensation that I knew all too well.

Calling to one guard carrying a torch, "You, there! Light this room." The torchlight revealed what I expected to see, a trail of darkness leading from the window across the small room and out into the hallway. Seeing the blood trail, the guard captain turned to run after our prey, but before he could take more than a step, I grabbed him by the collar to stop him.

Bending his ear down to my mouth, I whispered, "We require stealth, not force. Keep your men here and remain utterly silent."

Before he could protest, I melted into the shadow-shrouded passage. Hugging the wall, I proceeded slowly and silently, waiting for my eyes to readjust to the darkness. My prey had the advantage of position and initiative, but I had my own advantages. His wound was bleeding so profusely that I suspected he had withdrawn Luisa from his leg, allowing the blood to flow more freely. Although he now had Luisa to use against me, he was not familiar with her heft or how she would flip in the air.

Adding to my advantage was the fact that the alarm had been raised, and he could not expect sanctuary among his Muslim brethren. They would be in immediate mortal danger if we discovered the Assassin among them. I was confident the servants' quarters would now be closed to him.

With my eyes fully adjusted, I could see that the blood trail thickened where he had slowed and thinned out where he had rushed. At the intersection of my passage and another, a large pool had formed, and the drag marks leading down the side passage told me, as if they whispered in my ear, that his injured leg was nearly useless.

This observation gave me pause. If I was in his predicament, I knew I would find a place to make a last stand, intending to take with me as many of my enemies as I could to either heaven or hell, whichever our final destinations may be.

Including Luisa, I reckoned he was armed with at least three and possibly four knives or daggers. Unwinding the *kufiya* I wore to disguise my head and face, I gathered it into my hand and shook it into the opening of the side hallway. Before it had even fully unfurled, it flew backwards, nearly yanked out of my grasp. There, piercing the very center of it, was Luisa.

In Arabic, I whispered *sotto voce*, "Thank-you, *Sadiq*—friend, for returning my Luisa to me." When no response came, I continued, "I admire your fortitude in getting even this far. Your skills far surpass mine, but now I have the upper hand, and you face a singular choice. You know you have no escape. We can simply wait here and chat while your lifeblood drains from your body, or you can surrender to me. I can bind your wound with my *kufiya*, and you might live to see the morning light."

After a moment's silence, a single throwing knife, similar to my Luisa, clattered across the rough stones of the passage floor.

Knowing this was just a feint, I spoke aloud this time, "Ah, *Sadiq*, I know I would not come into the enemy's den with a single blade. I have seen many men die from wounds such as yours. It is not quick, and certainly not painless. But, of course, you know that as well."

Two more weapons skittered down the passageway, a good size dagger and a smaller stiletto. Without turning my head, I called for the guard captain to bring forward a torch.

He hurried forward, and I made another request of him. "Well done, Captain. Now I need two leather thongs from your tunic or belt."

Reluctantly, he stripped them free and held them out to me. I chose the shorter one and signaled for him to follow me around the corner.

Our prey, soon to be our prisoner, leaned against the stone wall of the passage, barely able to hold himself upright. In the torch's light, his normally swarthy complexion was pasty, and sweat stood out in beads on his forehead. He was obviously at death's door.

With Luisa in my right hand and my other blade in my left, I led the guard captain, with his own sword drawn, toward our quarry. As we approached him, his legs gave out, and he slid roughly down the wall.

"Lie face down and put your hands behind your back."

When he complied, I tied his hands and lifted his tunic, revealing his wounded leg. Blood flowed freely from the wound. Though it was not spurting as a severed blood vessel would—he would have been dead long before if it had been—the blood flow did pulse with the wild beating of his heart.

I tried to stanch the blood flow with my scarf pressed tightly to the wound, but the pulsing of his blood told me that, though it was not completely severed, some blood vessel had been partially sliced, and my scarf would do little to save his life. Hearing the clatter of the remaining guards as they approached, I addressed the captain.

"Hold your torch closer, Captain." As he did, I drew Luisa from her sheath, and seeing it, our prisoner tried to squirm away from my blade. I placed a hand on his back to steady him, thrust Luisa into the flame of the torch, and spoke in Arabic. "Calm yourself. My Luisa is your saving grace, not your pass to martyrdom."

Luisa's blade began to glow dull red in the dimness. When the leather pommel was nearly too hot to hold even with my hand wrapped with my scarf, I withdrew her from the flame and gently laid her back into the passage she had cut into his flesh. The would-be assassin stiffened, and a low growl escaped his lips. My captain drew back as if to strike with his sword.

"Hold!" I commanded. "I am saving his life for a reason."

The smell of burning flesh wafted in the air, and I lifted Luisa from his wound. The bleeding stopped, but the prisoner was unconscious, having passed out from the pain even though only a single moan had escaped his lips. With the second thong, I tied my scarf around his leg and stood.

"Captain, have your men carry him to a clean cell. It must be a clean cell and post a guard. If he still lives in the morning, I will come to tend to him."

A voice spoke from behind me, "Why, pray tell, is he still alive now?"

Recognizing the voice, I turned and dropped to one knee. Before me was King Guy.

"Your Majesty, this man could reveal many secrets of our enemies."

Guy considered this for a moment. "Aye, he may well indeed, though he is much too weak now to be interrogated harshly. I will send word to your captain. He is your brother, Sir Stewart, is he not?" I nodded. "You will tend this prisoner until he is strong enough for the rack."

Before I could protest that a gentler form of persuasion might work better than the rack, King Guy turned on his heel and strode out of sight, surrounded by his own guards. The captain of the house guard signaled to four of his men, who lifted our captive Assassin and carried him to his cell.

Chapter 25

Jerusalem, Spring 1187 A.D.

My captive's name was Yusef. His wounds healed without festering, probably because of Luisa's burning touch. But she left him lame. When he again could stand, Yusef dragged his stiffened leg as he paced ceaselessly around his cell. Either my cajoling, or his quite reasonable fear of the rack loosened his tongue, starting on the first morning of his captivity.

Yusef explained that his tribe, an offshoot of the Shi'ite Hashashim far to the north in Persia, practiced a form of Islam that Saladin's sect viewed as almost as blasphemous as our Christian beliefs. For generations, the main threads of Islam, the Shi'ite and the Sunni, reviled and hunted them. This persecution forced his people into a life of furtive hiding deep in the desolate mountains.

Generations of hardship and repression had served as a whetstone that sharpened their skills at stealth and fostered a violent way of life. From birth, they learned that surviving in such a harsh world meant knowing how to stalk, strike, and kill without a sound. The skills they learned and perfected while hunting the elusive desert animals easily translated to hunting enemies of the tribe.

With the supremacy of Christians in the Holy Land, an uneasy truce of sorts came to exist between them and the more numerous Shi'ite Muslims who lived in the more hospitable lowlands. They shared a common enemy, after all. Still, on the rare occasions when the Shi'ite caravans ventured into the mountains, they did so in large groups with many men under arms. To do otherwise would guarantee deadly nighttime raids by Yusef and his cousins, costing them their goods, horses, and lives. Usually, a lone survivor would be the only remnant of the devastated caravan. They would leave him alive to carry home stories of the horrors that befell his companions and kin.

Everything changed, though, when Saladin swept down from Mesopotamia, capturing the Shi'ite lands with his Sunni armies. After a few disastrous forays into the mountains—usually prompted by conquered Shi'ite advisors exacting petty revenge on their Sunni overlords—Saladin came to think of the offshoot Hashashim not as despised vermin, as the Shi'ite had, but as a valuable weapon to use against the even more hated Christian occupiers. It turned out that skills developed for hunting in the mountains, and later for defending themselves, could also be turned to driving out a threat to all Muslims.

This much Yusef explained to me as his wounds healed and he gained back his strength. When I pressed him for more timely information about Saladin's plans and strategies, however, he claimed ignorance, saying his people were just tools that Saladin used at his whim. The threat of the rack weighed heavily on his mind, however, and one day, when it was obvious he had grown strong enough to feel its relentless torture, he fell to his knees when I entered his cell.

"*Yutqin*, if I were not Hashashim, who are a proud people, I would beg you to forestall my torture at the hands of your fellow Christians. I know if the decision was yours to make, you would see my plight as a poor cripple with sympathetic eyes. I am surely an outcast among my own people now, both for being captured, but also as a cripple, a burden to the tribe, unable to feed myself and my family."

He looked up at me with eyes that seemed on the verge of weeping, and I admit his plea touched my heart for a moment. Then I remembered what his intent had been as he had climbed through the privy window, and my heart hardened.

"I care not for your standing with your tribe, Assassin." He winced when I used the Frankish bastardization of his sect's name. "We do, however, share a common purpose." With this, a light of hope shone in his eyes. "I had hoped you would provide us with valuable information about our mutual Sunni enemies. I've come to believe, however, that you speak the truth when you say you know nothing of Saladin's plans."

His head nodded slowly, warily as I continued, "And so, I am now inclined to end this wasted effort swiftly," I drew Luisa from her sheath, "and return to my brother Templars."

Yusef struggled to his feet, although more easily than I would have thought given his crippled state, and backed into the corner of his cell. His stance showed he was prepared to defend himself despite his stiff and weakened leg.

"No, no, *Yutqin*! Show some Christian compassion, please!"

His words and voice spoke of genuine fear, but his relaxed stance, protecting his wounded leg, and tensed arms poised for quick movements told me his pleas were but ploys. I was most uncomfortable being called "Master," especially by this highly skilled killer. Shifting my weight into fighting balance and Luisa into a neutral position between attack and defense, I told him more eloquently than words could express that I saw through his charade.

"So, tell me, Assassin, if you have no knowledge of Saladin's plans, what use are you to me?" I had my own idea, but I needed him to come to the same conclusion.

Without relaxing his stance any, and with his black eyes fixed on mine, I could see that his mind was racing as he sought an answer. When it came to him, his face softened, though his body did not, and his mouth curled into a small smile. It took him only a few moments to compose his argument, which we both knew his life depended upon.

"*Yutqin*, when you followed me through the city, you betrayed yourself three times. I admit that each time you remained completely hidden and silent, so much so that I believed you were simply a snore or a fart." His countenance showed that he meant no insult, and I almost laughed in spite of myself as he continued. "Your skills are exceptional, especially compared to your lumbering compatriots. Though good, they are not equal to mine, however. You admitted as much yourself when you first spoke to me that night that you gave me this."

He flexed his wounded leg and paused to let me think, but I already knew he had come to the same solution as me.

When I did not yet respond, he continued, "You still have much to learn…and I can teach you."

As I had expected, we now agreed on a course of action, though I was not yet ready to admit it.

"How can a cripple teach me the stealthy arts?"

At this, he chuckled. "Ah, the arrogance of the young! Why did you have to risk the loss of your precious Luisa that night?" He did not wait for an answer. "Because you had lost my trail. And why did you lose my trail?" Again, there was no pause. "Not because of the dark—you had followed me through much of the city—but because you betrayed yourself, and I darted away while you stood frozen in place."

I tried to hide the chagrin I felt, but I could not prevent the heat rising in my cheeks. With this, he smiled again.

"Do not be embarrassed, *Yutqin*. I have had many years of deadly nighttime encounters while you are but a boy. I ask you only this: why did you throw your only weapon when you could have picked up a rock from the street that would have broken my back or bashed in my head?"

I could have taken his question as a challenge and been even more chagrined, but instead I thought of it as, perhaps, my first lesson.

"Luisa is just a tool, and not the only one I wore that night. Though she is my favorite, if I had lost her, I would get another—and learn its weight and balance just as well."

That was the real reason, though I had not thought of it that the time. "I know Luisa as I know my own hand. To find a stone of enough heft to bring you down would have taken too long, and the chance that I would hit my target— you—on the first throw of such an unfamiliar missile was too small."

Yusef now smiled and relaxed his stance, knowing he had just won his life. "Of course, you did not think these things through at the time. You did not have the time. Instead, you reacted as your training has taught you. You made only two mistakes, although you were, I admit, ultimately successful."

"Two mistakes? I know of only one. I misjudged the effect of your swing and hit your leg instead of your spine."

"Yes, *Yutqin*, and I thank you for that!" We both laughed at that. "But you also forfeited one of your only two weapons to me, changing the balance of power between us."

Now I was genuinely confused. "What other choice did I have? You said yourself I did not have time to search for another weapon."

"Why, of course, you had no other choice. You did the only thing you could. And that was your second mistake."

My face revealed my bewilderment. Yusef smiled widely as he drove home his point. "Your second, or really your first, mistake was that you had not prepared for me, or for any other situation besides your amateurish spying mission."

Recognition of Yusef's true value came upon me instantly. Without another word, I turned on my heel and left him standing in his cell.

Over the next several months, Yusef remained in captivity in King Guy's palace, where I visited him for training whenever we were not fighting in the field. Grand Master de Ridefort refused to allow a potential assassin into his garrison, and in fact, being as shortsighted as he was, would have executed Yusef himself without a second thought. I managed to convince King Guy, however, that Yusef, if properly watched and guarded, could be of service to the kingdom. So it was that I learned subtleties of sinister and stealthy warfare that have proved invaluable many times in my long and eventful life.

Chapter 26

Emirate of Damascus, Spring 1187 A.D.

I felt naked. Not as I had for each of the four days I lazed about in the sun upon the roof of our barracks. Nor when, at the end of those days, one of the King's ministers examined me from head to toe. No, in this case I was fully clothed as an Arab peasant in a loose, rough spun *aba* robe and a separate *kufiya* wrapped over my head and face to protect me from the desert's sun and windblown sand. For that is where I hid myself—between the Jordan river and Damascus, deep inside Saladin's occupied lands.

My days in the sun had turned my skin as dark as a native of the desert, and my Arabic, though spoken with the accent of a Jerusalemite, rather than that of the Seljuk invaders, should gain me entry into their camp. I was betting my life on that "should."

Finding Saladin and his main force was easy. An army of thousands cannot pass through the land without leaving an obvious trail. For two days, I hid from patrolling soldiers among the rocks and sand in the hills overlooking their encampment, all the while watching and learning. I must admit that their discipline and general good order impressed me greatly. Their camps were orderly and the men pious, it seemed.

Of course, there were the usual camp followers—merchants supplying everything from water and food to livestock and women, though the contingent of whores was surprisingly small and housed in their own orderly compound. Perhaps it was the piety of the men, or at least their officers, and the Muslim prohibition against strong drink that kept them so orderly.

When I made my way into the camp, I did so as a water-bearer, circulating among the troops selling cool water flavored with fruit juice from a sheepskin bladder. The merchant who employed me was fastidious in his weighing out of the precious commodity and his collection of the small copper coins used for payment. More than once, he beat another of his water boys when the count of his coins was even one short. Since my goal was to collect information, not meager wages for a starving family, I made sure my returns sufficed to keep him happy.

With such a job that allowed me to wander freely throughout the encampment, and one I would employ to great effect later, I learned many things by simply listening between my calls of *ma', ma', miah alfakiha*—water, water, fruited water.

Slowly, making several roundtrips through the camp, I worked my way closer and closer to the commanders' tents at the center of the encampment. As I got closer to the source of the rumors I overheard further out, their veracity and meaning became clearer. While serving a tent full of lounging officers, I made myself practically invisible in a dark corner of the tent, emerging only when a raised cup needed filling. Though these wealthy officers' Syrian dialect was at first hard to decipher, I quickly realized I was in the presence of one of Saladin's nephews and three of his lieutenants. As with anyone privileged with wealth and power, they quickly ignored the insignificant servant with the waterskin huddling in the corner and spoke freely.

They argued about whether they could trust "the Infidel" or whether his offer of a truce was simply a lure to trap the Ayyubid armies. Their argument circled, not around the trustworthiness of the Crusader lord offering a truce as they found him to be more self-interested than righteous, but rather around whether they could trust the woman who had brokered the deal.

"She is *aniha sahira*, a she-witch," Saladin's nephew said.

"And *eahira*, a whore, Al-Muhammed Isa."

There were nods all around.

"Of course she is," the nephew replied. "She owns the brothel tents among the camp followers. I have seen her there myself." More nods. "But I can't tell my uncle that now, can I?"

Nods turned to snickers.

A third member of the group spoke up. "The truce with the infidel, Raymond of Tripoli, does offer us a very strategic advantage, Isa."

The fourth member scoffed, "She is a cancer that has infiltrated the mind of Yusuf ibn Ayyub ibn Shadi. He takes her advice to heart while challenging, and ignoring, that of his most trusted commanders."

"She has infiltrated more than his mind, I fear," Al-Muhammed Isa mumbled. A few chuckles were quickly cut off when he glared at his fellows. "We must cut this cancer out," he said in a low voice, which I would have missed if not for the raised cup that summoned me forward. "We must kill this *eahira* and return my uncle's mind back to its pious nature."

The three minions exchanged glances but held their tongues. They knew, I am sure, that such talk could lead to either increased influence within Saladin's court or an ignominious death. I watched as each did the political calculation.

"Aye," the first lieutenant, the one lounging to Isa's right, finally said. "We must make a plan."

The die of treachery having been cast, the other two nodded. They were guilty, if not by consent, at least by association.

"The she-devil must die," one said.

The last one nodded. "Aye."

The revelation of a traitorous truce between Raymond of Tripoli and Saladin to allow the Ayyubid forces safe passage across his lands convinced me to abandon my mission and return to Jerusalem with this critical information. As the contents of my waterskin had already been purchased in full, however, I remained until it was drained, listening to their plan to lie in wait for the woman they called Moira the She-Devil at her compound of brothel tents when she made her weekly inspection. They planned to dress as common soldiers and with knives secreted in their boots, as no weapons were allowed within the compound, dispatch her with a knife thrust to the chest from each.

I saw several flaws in their plan—I doubted she would go about unguarded, for example—but held my tongue, since the failure of their attempt might sew discord within the Ayyubid command.

At last, I squeezed out the last drops of fruited water and took my leave, promising to return, though I did not, of course. Instead, after paying my employer and refilling my skin, I snuck out of the camp and back into the hills, heading westward back to the Jordan river and the long trek to the Templar fortress at Safed.

Chapter 27

Springs of Cresson, April 1187 A.D.

Disagreements between our Templar Grand Master de Ridefort, King Guy, and his increasingly disaffected lords from the surrounding territories were becoming more frequent and heated. As either the cause or the effect of this strife, Saladin captured one town, fort, and castle after another, sweeping down from Syria in the north, taking all the territories to the east of the Jordan River, and even conquering the Muslim Fatimid kingdom to the south of Jerusalem. Stewart told me many times in confidence that he firmly believed Saladin's erosion of the hard-won territory captured in the First Crusade was caused as much by the political intrigues and in-fighting of the Christian nobles as by the Ayyubid fighters, though he held their prowess and bravery in high regard.

The worst rift came, I admit, when I reported the intelligence I had gathered while in Saladin's camp. The secret pact which the Count of Tripoli, Raymond III, made with Saladin, allowing safe passage of an Ayyubid force through Raymond's lands, was the tipping point.

I reported this news to Stewart, who conveyed it to our Grand Master, who then informed King Guy. Within an hour of my return, they summoned again me to the War Council in the Citadel. Stewart, de Ridefort, and his seneschal Hurson were already present, along with King Guy, his ministers, and representatives from the Prince of Antioch.

Without preamble, King Guy said, "Tell us, Sergeant, what news you have brought from your mission."

I told them of the rumor—I definitely couched it as such—of Raymond's truce with Saladin, allowing free passage through his lands.

De Ridefort seized Guy's attention before I had even finished. "He means to make himself King of Jerusalem, Your Grace. That has been his ambition all along."

It was true that Raymond did not support Guy's succession to the throne after the death of the child King Baldwin V. Heads nodded around the room at de Ridefort's assertion.

"Tell us how you gained this knowledge," Guy asked me.

I then related the hour I had spent in the tent with Saladin's nephew and his cronies.

Stewart's proud nod when I finished and de Ridefort's smug smile filled my heart with the sin of pride, and I vowed to do additional penance to cleanse my soul of it.

Guy nodded thoughtfully. "You have done well, Sergeant. I fear we will have occasion to use your skills extensively in the months to come."

Few in the room understood how prophetic those words were.

"Your Grace, we must punish the man. Strip him of his titles and land," de Ridefort said in a tone that made it clear how much he relished the idea.

Guy brightened, probably imagining Raymond prostrated before the throne, but Stewart stiffened and spoke up for the first time.

"Your Grace, while Raymond's actions are certainly heinous, our real enemy is Saladin and the Ayyubid." He turned to me. "Liam, what else did you learn regarding the reason for Raymond's agreement with Saladin?"

A little taken aback, because this other bit of information I had overheard during my mission was even more inflammatory.

"Your Grace, my Lords, I overheard rumors that Prince Reynald of Antioch attacked an Ayyubid caravan, despite your kingdom's truce with Saladin, Your Grace."

Reynald's ambassador, Godfrey, who had been silent previously, stiffened, and with all the hauteur he could manage, spoke up. "Prince Reynald of Chatillon, being absolute sovereign over the Principality of Antioch, does not acknowledge, nor is bound by any truce made by the King of Jerusalem, Your Grace."

The sound of steel being drawn echoed through the room, as did King Guy's voice.

"That is outrageous! I am sovereign over all four Christian states her in *Outremer*. As prescribed by His Holy Father in Rome."

There was an uncomfortable shuffling in the room before Godfrey spoke up. "May I remind Your Grace that only three Christian states remain here in the Levant, the County of Edessa, having fallen to the Ayyubid armies four decades ago. My Prince's lands are now almost totally surrounded by Muslim states, with only a narrow strip of land connecting us to our Christian brethren in Tripoli."

Stewart, who had been listening intently to Godfrey's argument, spoke up. "Why, then, do you provoke the Muslim Sultan by attacking his caravans?"

"That caravan was meant to supply the forces Saladin is gathering around Hamah to our south. We fear, rightly so, that he intends to push westward to the coast and cut our ever-threatened overland route to Tripoli and hence your kingdom, Your Grace.”

De Ridefort seized his chance to enter the argument. “Now it seems your *Prince's* calculations were wrong, though. Saladin intends to march those forces south, through Raymond’s lands, to extract his revenge from Your Grace’s lands and people.”

Godfrey looked smug but remained silent.

“Perhaps that is what the Prince intended all along,” King Guy muttered.

Heads nodded around the room, including Stewart’s.

Having decided, Guy turned to de Ridefort. “Grand Master, assemble a force of your knights and mine to sally forth to teach the traitorous Raymond his lesson.”

De Ridefort actually rubbed his hands together, so obvious was his glee. Stewart again opened his mouth to speak—I am certain to argue against internecine conflict—but de Ridefort’s glare reminded him of his vow of obedience, and he held his tongue. He confessed to me many times over that he regretted that act of obedient inaction.

King Guy’s order was, without a doubt, the singular decision that marked, if not the beginning of the end, at least the point of no return for the fall of Christian control of the Holy Land.

Stewart did point out, however, that our march would take us within a few miles of where it was reported that Saladin’s forces had passed. He suggested, rather more forcefully than was prudent, that the Ayyubids could easily be lying in wait to ambush us. As had happened many times in the past, Stewart was right.

～

Against Stewart's recommendations, de Ridefort rode out with only a relatively small force of less than two hundred knights and their sergeants, and only three hundred foot soldiers. Stewart commanded the rear guard, with me at his side.

When the vanguard, commanded by de Ridefort, encountered Saladin's force at the Springs of Cresson, the Ayyubid forces attacked half-heartedly, then retreated. Stewart and I recognized Saladin's oft-used opening feint, intended to lure the inexperienced into the trap set by the main bulk of his army. We in the rear ignored the gambit and prepared for the flanking maneuver that usually followed.

We were shocked, however, when we heard the Templar trumpets sound the rally call and saw our holy banner advancing. The main body of Templar knights and horsemen were chasing the retreating enemy, just as Saladin intended. They rushed straight into the trap, rapidly outrunning their supporting foot soldiers. Hoping to stop what promised to be a slaughter of our brothers, Stewart kicked his steed into a gallop and I and the dozen knights and their sergeants who made up the rear guard followed closely behind.

By the time our meager force approached the vanguard, however, the trap was already sprung. We could see Gerard de Ridefort, his seneschal, and a handful of knights huddled around the Templar banner fighting for their lives. The rest of the vanguard was nowhere to be found, and we feared the worst.

There was no time to think of our fallen brothers, however, as Stewart led us charging into the rear of the swarming Ayyubid attackers. Our purpose was clear—drive a wedge through our enemy's ranks and clear a lane for the few remaining survivors to escape. This we accomplished through the sheer will and skill of Stewart.

His blade flashed left and right, felling foot soldiers and cavalry alike. When Gerard saw us advancing through the enemies' ranks, he rallied his own force, and they slashed their way to meet us.

Our advance and subsequent, but necessary, retreat cost us dearly. We rescued our precious banner, with its relic of the true cross, but the cost was high indeed. Only a handful of the nearly two hundred knights returned to Jerusalem. Even fewer of the well-trained sergeants, such as I, survived and all of us bore wounds of some severity.

Templar and secular foot soldiers suffered as badly or worse. The day was a disaster on all accounts, and signaled, to Saladin if not yet to us, the beginning of the end of Christian rule in the Holy Land.

Chapter 28

Jerusalem, May 1187 A.D.

T he aftermath of the defeat at Cresson was nearly as terrible as the battle itself. We lost over three hundred knights, sergeants, and soldiers, many of whom were my brothers. We Templars grieved in silence, as was our nature, but the secular lords railed against the incompetence of Grand Master de Ridefort, especially against the backdrop of Stewart's previous recognition of Saladin's feinting tactic and our thwarting of it. Many voices were raised calling for de Ridefort's removal and Stewart's elevation to, if not Grand Master, at least the overall command of the Templar forces. Stewart remained stoic, neither defending nor supporting de Ridefort, but simply obeying orders, as he had vowed to do.

Shortly after a particularly contentious Council meeting, which I observed from behind an armorer's cabinet, I went to Yusef's cell for a training session.

"You are very distracted today," Yusef said as I rubbed my side where his blade would have disemboweled me if it was not blunted.

"Aye. There is much turmoil among our warlords."

He nodded. "This information is not news to me," he said. When I raised a questioning eyebrow, he shrugged, then pointed to the one narrow window high on the wall that provided all the cell's light and air. "Your King likes to take a goblet of wine onto his balcony at night when the breezes blow cooler. His mistress often joins him."

He shrugged, but said no more. So, even from the confines of a barren cell, Yusef was gathering intelligence. I tried to not look impressed by his admission, but after a heartbeat, my face broke out into a smile.

"And what else do you overhear during the night?" I asked with a wink.

Yusef simply wagged a finger and returned my smile. After a moment, his face took on a more serious countenance.

"Here is your lesson for today, Young Templar. Wives and mistresses, especially mistresses, are more dangerous to an army than the most well-trained enemy. They are often privy to the most secret information, and they have access to powerful men's ears when they are at their most suggestive and vulnerable."

The truth of Yusef's words was obvious to me, and I was proud that we Templars had sworn a vow of chastity, eschewing even the touch of a woman. When I said as much, Yusef scoffed.

"You simply store your desire up like grain against the winter. Eventually, it either overflows, or rots in the silo."

I thought for a moment, then shook my head. "Neither. It becomes a bloodlust on the battlefield. Many a warrior must wash his braies in private after a battle."

Yusef thought for a moment, then nodded. "Perhaps you have taught your teacher a lesson today. What may I teach you in return?"

"Does Saladin have a mistress? One that we could turn to our purposes, perhaps?"

Yusef smiled appreciatively. "I understand he does, indeed, have several playthings that he keeps close to hand." He paused and became serious. "But there is one in particular.

A true *anaha shaytan*, a she-devil whose beauty and prowess in the bedchamber have captivated The Sultan, by all accounts. They even say she is the architect of his success in battle, filling his head with all manner of stratagems from battles fought down through the ages. Some even think she is a *jinn*, saying her accounts of ancient battles are so vivid, she must have witnessed them first-hand. Whether human or *jinn*, her incomparable beauty and dagger-sharp intellect make for a most dangerous combination."

"Moira," I whispered.

Yusef's shocked look made me grin.

"How do you know her name, *Yutqin*?"

I related to him my foray into Saladin's camp. Afterward, he chuckled, and nodding said, "The *talib ealm*, the student, has become the teacher, I think."

"And how is it that you know of her and her name?" I asked. "Have you been to The Sultan's camp, also?"

Yusef shook his head. "I do not need to cross the desert myself. Words—rumors and reports—follow along with the caravans."

"So, you have a network of spies? Even in Saladin's army?"

"Spies? Such a negative word. No, merchants are in the business of selling their wares. Rumors and rumors of rumors are just a commodity that costs nothing but may be precious to the right ears."

I tried to tamp down my excitement. "How might I purchase such rumors?"

Yusef shrugged. "Many in the bazaar will take a copper for a whisper." He paused and looked me straight in the eye until I understood his thinking.

"But a rumor loses its truth the more it is echoed."

"Indeed."

"So how do I drink from the source of this spring?"

He chuckled. "So, the teacher has more to teach, eh?"

"And the student still has much to learn."

Two days later, a particular caravan arrived in Jerusalem. The merchants who made up its complement took their wares to their storehouses and market stalls. One in particular, an older man with more grey than black in his beard, carried his entire hoard to his house in a simple sack slung on his back. The next morning, he opened his stall in the bazaar arrayed with brass and copper pots and cooking utensils—nothing that local craftsmen couldn't produce.

A young man, dressed in a nondescript hooded robe, waited in the shadows for the merchant's first call of the day, then stepped forward. Clinking the copper coins held in his hand with a shake of the wrist, he inquired after *hamasat*, whispers. The merchant was happy to make his profit for the week at his first sale of the day. By tradition, once whispered, the *hamasat* the young man purchased was forgotten.

Without a word, the young man made his way to the next *hamasat* merchant on his list.

Chapter 29

Tur'an, July 3, 1187 A.D.

Stewart's warnings of Saladin being the real threat proved prophetic. The end, when it came, involved Raymond and another internal dispute. After the debacle at Cresson, Raymond traveled to Jerusalem and prostrated himself before Guy, begging forgiveness. Although he was inclined to strike him dead on the spot, Guy knew he needed Raymond and his loyal lords as allies, not enemies. So, he accepted Raymond's obeisance, but he tasked me with keeping a close eye on Saladin through my network of Hashashim spies.

Word came in June from these disaffected spies that Saladin had amassed a vast army east of the Sea of Galilee near the town of Tal Ashtarah. Assuming that Saladin would march south along the Yarmuk River into Guy's kingdom, he ordered the assembly of an army of every available warrior. Stewart, with King Guy's support, suggested that the rally point for the army should be just north of Jerusalem. Grand Master de Ridefort, perhaps simply to be obstinate in his opposition to Stewart's rising influence, suggested Acre as the assembly point instead, arguing that his Templars were based there.

Pointing to the maps laid out on the table, Stewart argued that three or four days of forced march all the way to

Acre, then across the desert eastward, was a much more difficult route than marching north along the Jordan River valley. Driving such a large force through the desert and mountains, with very few way points with water enough for such a large force, would leave the men exhausted. Traversing the river valley, on the other hand, was a much easier march that would provide all the water the men could drink.

The decision was made, though, not through reason or even stubbornness, but rather because of simple expediency. Raymond declared he could not bring his forces all the way south from Tripoli to Jerusalem, only to march them back north to meet Saladin. He had neither the stores to supply such a circuitous trip, not the means to supply them. Acre was the logical place, he argued, it being midway between the two centers of political power, neither of whom trusted the other.

Guy and Stewart had to concede this point and, coupled with the fact that supplies could be shipped by sea from Tripoli to Acre, both being on the coast, the decision was easily made.

Over the next few weeks, we marshaled the largest Christian army ever assembled in the Holy Land at Acre. The holy orders, including the Templars, numbered six hundred knights, fifteen hundred sergeants, and four thousand pikemen and foot soldiers. Raymond contributed about five thousand knights and men, while Guy's forces increased our strength to twenty thousand.

Late in June, word came from my spies that Saladin, after a foray north to gather more men, was indeed marching south into Christian territory. On the last day of that month, our army, which we believed to be invincible, marched southeast from Acre, expecting to meet Saladin's forces in Nazareth, the homeland of Our Lord and Savior Jesus Christ.

Most saw this as a sign from Providence that our mission would be blessed with a glorious victory.

With Raymond in the vanguard, the Templars, commanded by Stewart, in the rear, and Guy leading his army of twenty thousand in between, we set off for the Spring of Sephorie, two days' hard march southeast of Acre. The plan was to rest at Sephorie, whose spring could provide enough water for our army, even one which numbered twenty thousand.

Confusion reigned in the War Council, however, when I relayed a report that came from my men positioned along Saladin's expected route, that he had split his forces after crossing the Jordan. The bulk of his army turned north along the banks of the Sea of Galilee, while about one-fourth continued westward toward us.

"Their goal is obvious," Raymond insisted.

The War Council gathered in Guy's command tent. Stewart and I had ridden ahead of our men, who were still setting up camp, to meet with de Ridefort, who rode in Guy's company.

"The devil Saladin has laid siege to Tiberias," he continued.

Tiberias was the largest city on the shores of the Sea of Galilee and was the home of Raymond's wife, Eschiva II, Princess of Galilee. With Raymond's army deep in the desert, Tiberias was only lightly defended, and those gathered knew it could not hold out for many days.

Raymond's voice had a bit of a tremor to it. "We must rescue my wife, the Princess, and her subjects before they are laid waste by that devil." There were many nods of assent around the table. "And we must do so with all haste."

"Agreed," Guy said. "We will set out again at first light—"

"No!" Raymond's outburst snapped heads in his direction. "Your Grace, we must decamp *now*. The city cannot hold out for that long. I fear, in fact, that it may already have fallen."

"Surely we must allow our men to refresh themselves with water, a meal, and a night's sleep," Guy responded.

"My men are refreshed and ready to fight," Raymond insisted.

"Your men, being in the vanguard, arrived at the Springs hours ago," Stewart said. "My men have not even made camp yet."

"Then they can be ready to march even sooner," de Ridefort said, taking up Raymond's cause.

"But Grand Master—" Stewart tried to argue, but de Ridefort cut him off.

"Enough." de Ridefort silenced Stewart with a glare and a wave of his hand. "Do you deny that your brother Templars are the hardiest among us?"

His challenge afforded but one response.

"No, Grand Master. I will give the order," Stewart said through gritted teeth.

The grumbling of the Guy's men, who had drained their waterskins in anticipation of refilling them at the Springs, grew loud when the orders to break camp came. The Templars, given their oath of obedience, remained silent, though their tired and drawn faces could not hide their disappointment.

Tiberias was still two full days' march away through the harshest terrain when Raymond's troops left Sephorie in the noontime heat. Guy's army, intent on replenishing as much of their water supply as possible, trailed well behind the vanguard. Stewart's command, being the rear guard, was forced to leave the Springs with barely any refreshment.

We reached another oasis at Tur'an, about a half-day's march further, by late afternoon. It was on this leg of the journey that we first met Saladin's forces. The smaller of his two contingents launched a continuous series of harassing attacks against the southern flank of the army. The disordered way we left Sephorie meant our column was drawn out too long and thin. As a result, our losses to the constant attacks by the Ayyubid cavalry and archers were heavier than expected. While we were resting at Tur'an, however, word came from Tiberias that the Ayyubid engineers had undermined the citadel's walls and Eschiva had surrendered the garrison to the invaders.

King Guy, who had been first to slake his thirst at Tur'an's spring, called for a council of war. Stewart and I were tending our horses and making sure our men were getting their water rations when the messenger came summoning Stewart to the council tent. He left me to finish setting up camp and hurried off.

Luckily, our men were well-trained, and I could follow Stewart within a few minutes. I heard the raised, angry voices long before I reached the council tent.

Stewart's was the loudest. "This is madness! Our men are exhausted, and half of them have not even had their water rations yet. To continue on to Tiberias now instead of waiting until morning is mass suicide."

"You will follow orders!" Gerard de Ridefort was apoplectic. His face was bright red and the veins of his neck stood out like taut ship's rigging.

"Of course, I will follow orders. I'll follow you into heaven, which is surely where you will lead us."

Stewart's sarcasm was lost on de Ridefort, but not on the others, as reflected on Guy's and Raymond's shocked faces. Stewart continued, "But I must offer my opinion before this council. We have made less than half the distance to Tiberias and have only a few hours of light left this day. Saladin will have entrapments set for us all along the way, and when we are forced to stop, it will be somewhere without the water our men and horses require."

Despite Stewart's obedient assurance and seeing that Stewart's arguments were swaying both Guy and Raymond, our Grand Master sealed the fate of the Christian armies.

"If your lack of faith, or your cowardice, prevents you from seeing the righteousness of our cause and the inevitability of our holy victory, then you should not share in its glory. You will take ten knights and their sergeants back to Jerusalem as a garrison until we return with Saladin's head."

To argue with the Grand Master at this point would directly violate Stewart's oath and would simply prove Ridefort's point. In shock, Stewart stood stock still and slowly looked from Raymond to Guy, and then to all the assembled lords. None would meet his gaze. He bore the insult silently, though had it come from anyone other than his Supreme Commander, it would have earned a deathblow from his sword.

Instead, Stewart turned. I pulled open the tent's entry flap, and he strode through the opening with me at his heels. As we marched back to our men, Stewart was already in control and planning how to perform this new, humiliating assignment.

"Muster Alain, Robert ..." he named ten knights in total. "We will leave before these fools do. We will not slink out after them. We must prepare Jerusalem for the coming siege."

Chapter 30

Tur'an, July 3, 1187 A.D.

I did not know what to expect from our brothers and the other knights assembled during our departure. But, as we set out, Stewart told us all to hold our heads high and keep our eyes forward. He assured us we would be the last to defend the Holy City. Still, many of us rode out through the throng of armed men with trepidation.

Our brothers in arms through many battles did indeed react to our passing, but not as I had feared. The order to prepare to march had already come down to the men, many of whom had not yet received their ration of water from the spring.

Apparently, rumors of the conflict in the council tent had reached them as well. Being unquestionably loyal, no protest of the council's decision to set out again into the desolate desert would cross their lips. Their protest, instead, was completely silent, but no less meaningful.

I caught the first movement out of the corner of my eye off to our right. It moved like two waves through the sea. First, to a man, the entire army stopped their preparations for departure and turned to face our column of knights and sergeants led by Stewart.

Then, as if someone had given him a silent order, a pikeman far off to our left lowered himself to one knee. His neighbors in front, behind, and to the sides followed suit. Then their neighbors, then theirs. In the space of a few heartbeats, a wave of respect spread through the entire army as they knelt and saluted with clenched fists held to their hearts.

By the time we passed the council tent, the assembled twenty-thousand knelt in silence. Standing outside the tent entrance, the remaining council also watched our passing. Grand Master de Ridefort muttered an epithet about our filthy English blood and swept grandly back into the tent. Raymond of Tripoli and King Guy himself, however, watched us pass and touched their own hearts in farewell.

The road back to Jerusalem led us out of the valley of Tur'an through a gap in the low hills surrounding the spring. We rode in silence while the sun moved a hand span across the sky. We could hear the army behind us resume their clatter of preparations after we had passed out of the camp, though there was none of the nervous banter that was typical before a battle.

When we had passed behind the line of hills and were out of sight of the army, Stewart relaxed his rigid posture and turned to me.

"You must use your skills to follow those fools as they march to their doom. When you have witnessed their fate, observe Saladin's preparations, then hurry back to Jerusalem ahead of him to warn us of the Ayyubid advance."

"I could be many days in the desert." I was not arguing my assignment, nor asking for relief from it, simply stating my expectation.

Stewart understood and acknowledged me with a nod of his head. "If you do not return in ten days' time, I will pray for your soul."

Little did I know I would soon pray for his—more than once.

I thought at first that Stewart's grace period of ten days was quite short, but it turned out that I needed fewer than half before I had returned to Jerusalem. When I separated from our group of exiles and doubled back, my horse, whom I had named Almae, was heavily laden with water skins. I estimated that if I was careful, the water rations would last Almae and myself three days at most. We would need to find a source of fresh water after that, but for now, we could follow the Christian army from the safety of the surrounding mountains.

The folly of the Council's decision to march on Tiberias that same day became apparent as soon as our men broke camp. Ayyubid cavalry immediately began harassing the columns of our twenty thousand men. Our men fought gallantly in response, but without having refreshed themselves at Tur'an, they quickly became weakened by exhaustion, the heat, and thirst. How I wished I could ride down from my hiding place in the hills and share my water with them! But I stayed true to my mission, even though my heart seemed to slowly die in sympathy with my brothers.

Our own cavalry rode out to engage the harassers, of course, but each time they did, the Ayyubid cavalry retreated, and as our horsemen followed them, they were met with a hail of arrows from archers hidden in the hills. The skirmishing continued throughout the afternoon, costing many men their lives, and costing the king and his army many knights.

Tiberias was only nine miles from the springs at Tur'an, but a fully armed and refreshed army could barely make that distance through the desert in a full day. Attempting a forced march of tired and thirsty men through the heat of a summer afternoon in this desert was pure madness. With the added delays caused by the constant attacks, the army's pace slowed to a crawl.

From my hiding place in the hills slightly in front of the army, I could also see most of the remaining distance toward Tiberias. It was from this vantage point that I saw, to my horror, yet another force of Ayyubid horsemen flying Saladin's own banner, riding hard from Tiberias toward my brothers. I knew then that the city and citadel had fallen, and that this ill-conceived expedition had all been for naught.

As the afternoon faded to dusk, the Christian army was stretched out within a valley bordered by two rows of rugged, rock-strewn hills. It was within a protecting cluster of large boulders in these hills that I had hidden Almae and myself.

The oncoming Ayyubid horsemen rode at full gallop behind the line of hills in which I hid. Our army was within the confines of the valley and had no outriders scouting ahead, so the Ayyubid horsemen's advance was hidden from the Christians.

Once past the bulk of our army, they turned into the area of hills from which I had seen the harassing forays originate. Their strategy was now clear to me, and my heart sank even further when I realized what Saladin, who led these reinforcements himself, had planned.

Within an hour, several hundred Ayyubid horsemen rode down from the hills and concentrated their attack on the Christian rear guard, stopping it in its tracks. With the rear guard halted, it forced the entire army to halt to avoid a breach in their ranks. The Ayyubids swept around behind my brother Templars in the rear guard, forcing them to battle on three sides, and cutting off any chance of escape back to Tur'an. With the army stopped and with nightfall coming on fast, the Council had no choice but to sound the horns, signaling the army to consolidate, set their defenses, and encamp. To my utter horror, I saw they would need to spend the night in the middle of the desert with no water, no supplies, and no way to escape.

That night was sleepless for me and my comrades. I watched helplessly as the Ayyubid force repeatedly raided the least protected parts of the camp. When the night guard rushed to protect those under attack, the raiders melted away into the dark. Thus, a small force of perhaps a few hundred horsemen brought an army of twenty thousand to its knees.

These horsemen continued their assaults throughout the night while a more insidious plan was unfolding. Beyond the light of the Christian watch fires, our enemy made great piles of wood cut from the local creosote bushes. These soon-to-become bonfires were upwind of our captive army. In the dark hours before dawn, they set the pyres alight, and a thick, greasy smoke first wafted, then billowed down the valley.

Within the time that the crescent moon moved a hand span across the sky, the valley filled with an impenetrable screen of smoke. By first light, the smoke obscured even the Christian watch fires, so I broke camp and led Almae forward toward Tiberias. The smoke would hold the army in place for hours, and I had to determine why the Ayyubids needed to delay our exhausted and thirsty fighters even longer.

Chapter 31

Horns of Hattin, July 4, 1187 A.D.

I feared what I would see before I saw it, and my fears were confirmed. As dawn broke, a great cloud of dust rose against the horizon. Saladin's immense main army was marching from the east. I guessed it to be half again as large as Guy's twenty thousand. As the sun became visible through the gaps in the mountains, the great dust cloud became two.

A portion of his army, I estimated about one third or so, broke off toward the south. They headed to reinforce those who blocked our retreat to Tu'ran, while the remainder rushed to cut off the road to Tiberias.

To this day, I am proud of the gallant fight the knights and soldiers, both secular and holy, of the Christian army fought that day. And I am still disgusted and ashamed by the foolhardy decisions and ultimate cowardice of our leaders, Grand Master de Ridefort in particular.

The day did not go well. In fact, it was a total disaster. Fighting first on two sides, then three, and finally four, the valley became a death trap. Our army made three separate assaults, trying to break through the Ayyubid lines and escape toward Tiberias. Each time we pressed forward, and each time the Ayyubids absorbed the attack, then pushed our forces back.

By noon, the ground turned crimson from the blood of the dead and wounded who littered it. The desert sands could not absorb the blood that poured from the thousands of soldiers, knights, and horses who had fallen. The carnage on both sides was heartbreaking. I knew, as I'm sure everyone on both sides did, that a Christian victory was beyond our grasp. Another failed assault would end any hope of escape, let alone victory.

As afternoon approached, the armies rested, or at least our enemies did, since they could refresh themselves from their plentiful stores of water. My brothers in arms, however, had no respite from the heat and their unquenched thirst. While they collected and tended their wounded—the dead were left to bake in the sun—I slipped from my hiding place high in the hills and, leading Almae, crept toward the Ayyubid battle line.

I faced a crisis of conscience as I watched the battle unfold. My mission, as ordered by Stewart, my captain, was to observe and report back. My heart ached, however, for my friends and Templar brothers. Upon joining the Order, I had sworn to protect my fellow Christians here in the Holy Land. But I had also sworn to obey my superiors unquestioningly. I was torn between these now conflicting oaths.

As I fulfilled one oath and obeyed Stewart's order, I felt I was violating the other by passively watching my brothers in Christ die by the thousands. My heart struggled with this conflict throughout the morning until I finally hit on a solution.

I knew I could do nothing to turn the tide of this battle. My skills were not those of a warrior like Stewart, who could fell dozens himself and inspire his troops to slaughter hundreds more. Rather, my talents lay in more subtle pursuits. It was time for me to put those talents to use.

My plan was to sneak into the Ayyubid camp after dark. If my Christian brothers survived the day, I would determine the Ayyubid plan of battle for the following day. If they did not survive, which I feared would be the more likely result, perhaps I could help any captives. In either case, I would exploit any opportunity to use the skills of the Assassins that Yusef had taught me.

Knowing they could not spend another night camped in the open desert, the Christians began their final assault. I was making my way northward to a new hiding place below the line of the ridge when the charge began. Being out of sight of the valley, I did not observe their preparations. When I heard the horns signaling the advance, the battle cries of the men, and the subsequent clatter of steel on steel, I scrambled to the top of the hill I was skirting.

My eyes went first to my brother Templars, whom I expected to see in the rearguard position they had occupied up to that point. They were not there. Instead, a cadre of King Guy's knights and men protected the rear. I scanned the valley for my brothers, but they were nowhere to be found along any fighting front. Instead, as the army thrust forward, the Templars rode through the heart of the valley, separate from the four battle lines.

When the Ayyubid forces thinned their forces on our flanks to counter our assault up the valley, the Templars launched a second breakthrough attempt out of our left flank.

The breakthrough was successful, but instead of circling to the right to assist the main force as I had expected, they continued straight toward a pair of steep hills directly to my left. This formation, the remains of an extinct volcano, known as the Horns of Hattin, was prominently visible for miles around.

When the Templars had successfully established a safe corridor from the valley to the Horns' high ground, the battle trumpets sounded again and the army, led by King Guy and the Council, turned as one and poured through the hole in the Ayyubid lines.

It was a brilliant tactic and expertly executed, but ultimately the strategy behind it was flawed. While they were safe for the moment from imminent annihilation, the Christian army had simply exchanged one trap for another. Although they now held the advantage of high ground with less exposure to attack, they were still without water, food, or other basic supplies.

By contrast, Saladin appeared resolved to complete his victory before nightfall. He repositioned his army, preparing for an uphill assault on the Christian position. Three times, his men charged up the slopes. The first assault seemed easily repelled, and my hopes rose that disaster could be avoided. The second assault concentrated much more on the center of the Christian line and, though it was also repelled, the enemy penetrated much further into the heart of our position before being pushed back. Seeing how many troops Saladin still had in reserve, my hopes sank again.

Without a respite, Saladin immediately brought up more, better rested troops to attack the now weakened Christian center. From their command tents on the crest of the Horns, the Council ordered troops from the right and left sides of the defensive line to reinforce the center. What the Council could not see, but which I could, brought forth from me a cry of despair.

While Ayyubid foot soldiers ran up the hill attacking the center, cavalry on horseback swung to the right and attacked our depleted left flank. The frontal assaults had been feints, and once the cavalry broke through the left side of the

Christian defense, Saladin's remaining men crashed through the breach into the heart of our position.

Like a flooded river that flows over any obstacle on its way to the sea, so the Ayyubid army inundated the Christians on their way to the hilltop. When the Council tents crumbled and our standard, the Templars' holy banner fell, I knew my mission that night would be one of rescue and revenge.

Chapter 32

Saladin's Camp, July 4-5, 1187 A.D.

Darkness had fallen by the time I made my way into Saladin's camp. Using the ruse I had employed previously, I took up a waterskin and followed a wandering path through the Ayyubid camp. My goal was the officers' tents, of course, but I picked up snippets of gossip at my stops along the way.

"Her strategy worked," and "The she-devil's plan was brilliant," captured the sentiment that Moira was, indeed, the brains behind Saladin's winning plan. Not everyone was so sanguine about following a woman's advice, however.

When I reached the tent of Saladin's nephew, Al-Muhammed Isa, from whom I had first learned of this woman, Moira, I offered my fruited water to the guards stationed outside and, after being searched—I had left my Louisa with Almae—I slipped inside.

"Tonight, Isa. Will it be tonight?" one of Al-Muhammed Isa's lieutenants asked.

"Indeed," Isa replied. "My uncle will celebrate his victory with new playthings I have provided him. The she-witch will sleep alone."

The second of Isa's three companions snickered as I filled their goblets. "I have bribed the guards The Sultan provided for her protection, telling them your uncle made her available to us to celebrate, also."

Isa gave him a sharp look. "They believed this?"

The other man shrugged. "They believed the gold coins I placed in their palms." The others laughed. "They will send word when she has retired."

"Good." Isa sounded very self-satisfied when he raised his cup in a toast. "We won a glorious victory for the Faith today, and we will win an ever greater one tonight."

Feigning an empty waterskin, I slunk out of the tent.

I spent the rest of the night earning a heavy purse from both the Ayyubid and the captured Christian soldiers. The first celebrated their total victory, and the latter tried to slake their thirst and nervousness about their fate. My brother Templars, especially, had cause to be nervous.

At dawn, after the pious among the Muslims had bowed to the East and said their morning prayers, a throne was brought out of Saladin's tent, and he, along with his sons and nephews, including Al-Muhammed Isa, held court. Nephew Isa and his lieutenants laughed among themselves before trying to hide their smiles when Saladin took his seat. The Sultan did not even look in their direction.

Throughout the morning, King Guy and the secular lords and knights were brought before The Sultan and he passed judgement on them, ransoming most for what I thought were quite reasonable terms. If the captives produced the required ransom, he freed them, but stripped them of their arms and armor. If they did not have the means to pay, they were allowed a missive to be carried with the ransomed captives and were hustled off to cage wagons for their journey to Saladin's dungeons. It was understood that they would sell common sergeants and soldiers as slaves.

Saladin had special plans for my brother Templars, however. As the nobles pled their cases and received their ransom prices, Ayyubid soldiers circulated through the thousands of prisoners rounding up any who wore the mantle of a Templar knight, sergeant, or soldier. When Saladin had finished with the nobles, with no additional bloodshed, twenty of my brothers were herded out and made to kneel before him.

"Where is your Grand Master Gerard de Ridefort?" he called out in clear French.

My brethren glanced at each other and shook their heads. When no one answered, an Ayyubid swordsman stepped up behind each kneeling captive. Together, they raised their swords, prepared to strike. Before The Sultan could give them the signal, however, a voice barked, "Hold!" from inside Saladin's tent.

My mouth hung open, as did most of the onlookers', when the most beautiful woman I had ever seen strode from the tent to stand at Saladin's shoulder. Her long, flowing, raven-black hair, perfect features, and flawless skin marked her as Moira, the she-devil herself.

Gasps identified those who knew of, or had heard rumors of, Al-Muhammed Isa's murderous plan. I heard Isa, himself, exclaiming, "No! That's not possible."

Saladin finally turned in his direction, his gaze a mixture of rage and sorrow. By contrast, Moira's face carried no hint of sorrow, only indignant vengeance.

"And why do you think my Moira's appearance at these proceedings is 'impossible?'"

Isa, knowing his fate was sealed, spoke proudly. "Because we—I—killed this *jinn*, this *aniha sahira* last night.

The fact she now walks among us proves she is *Shaytan* himself."

Moira spoke. "So, you admit you thrust your blade into my chest?" She turned to Isa's first lieutenant standing behind him and to the left. "And you slit my throat?"

The man gulped, but nodded. "To the bone."

She looked at each of the others in turn. They each nodded and recounted how they had stabbed her again and again until her bed dripped with her blood.

"And yet I stand here at The Sultan's side. Perhaps I rose from my deathbed this morning." She pulled aside the scarf to reveal the pendant hanging against the unblemished skin of her neck. "Or, perhaps you *killed* a mere illusion, or some poor serving girl who thought she was being rewarded with a good night's sleep in a proper bed."

Isa shook his head. "No. It was you. We all saw that magical symbol you always wear at your throat."

Moira fingered her pendant and laughed. "This? This is just my name in the language of my birth."

"Enough!" Saladin barked.

He shifted uncomfortably in his chair, then nodded to the guards standing behind Isa and his co-conspirators. They forced the condemned to their knees.

"Al-Muhammed Isa, son of my beloved sister, I condemn you and your men to death for the sin of treason and treachery."

A flick of his wrist brought swords down on their necks. The thud of their heads on the ground and the gush of blood from the stumps of their necks were just the precursor to the bloodiest day the Templar Order ever suffered.

Turning back to my kneeling brothers, Moira raised her voice. "We ask you again, where is your cowardly Grand Master?"

Saladin, perhaps himself disturbed by the silent acquiescence of my brother Templars, added, "If you reveal where he is hiding, we will stop the slaying. If you do not, you may at least save yourself by renouncing the false prophet Jesus of Nazareth and swearing your love for God's true prophet Mohammed."

My heart nearly burst with pride and heartache when each of my brothers simply bowed their heads and began their final prayers. Saladin's hand signal cut them off as surely as it did their heads.

Over the next several hours, every Templar was paraded before the throne and made to kneel in the blood of their brothers before adding their own to the sodden ground. I could not bear witness to any more of the carnage and instead set out to answer the question Saladin kept asking. Thinking that producing de Ridefort and Hurston might put an end to the slaughter, I made my way with my waterskin through the pens holding the secular captives.

Chapter 33

Saladin's Camp, July 5, 1187 A.D.

Revenge was on my mind again, but it was not aimed at our enemies who had fought valiantly, but rather at those who had caused this devastation, and then had broken ranks and slunk away like rats. I knew, because I witnessed it with my own eyes, that de Ridefort and his seneschal Hurson were captured when our banner fell.

Against our vows and any respect they held for the Templar brothers who were being slaughtered by the score, the two cowards must be hiding like frightened children.

The Ayyubids held the captured Christians in several prisoner pens. In pen after pen, I joined the other water bearers who walked among them selling sips from their skins. I took the smallest payment I could without being noticed, knowing these men would need whatever they had left to ransom themselves. My purpose was not to slake the thirst of these poor souls, however. Rather, I was searching for the cloaks I knew so well, even without their white mantles. I was seeking those who had betrayed the Order.

I found them in the third pen I searched. They sat huddled together, hoods covering their bowed heads, despite the lingering heat. I stood behind them and offered them free water, but the seneschal, Hurson, waved a dismissive hand. Taking his hand in a debilitating, twisting grip that Yusef had taught me, I drew my knife and held it to his throat from behind.

"Tell me why I should not slit your throat to pay for your cowardice," I hissed into his ear.

De Ridefort, recognizing my voice and face, held up a hand to stay my blade. "Brother Liam, wait, please. We must return to Jerusalem before these filthy savages lay siege."

My voice was low, but fierce. "You ran from the field of battle! You left your brothers to die by the thousands."

"It is true. And we will answer for that when our day of reckoning arrives. But we did not flee to protect ourselves. We are trying to protect something much more precious."

I was incensed, but still I kept my voice low. "What could be more precious than our blessed banner and the sacred relic of the True Cross it bore?"

De Ridefort and Hurson looked at each other and Hurson whispered, "Master, he is just a boy. He cannot learn of the Secret."

de Ridefort held up his hand again, but this time to still his seneschal's objections.

"He may still be a boy, but here he stands free, blade at your throat, in the midst of the enemy horde. If Jerusalem should fall, and I have little doubt now that it will, we may well need his skills. Show him what you carry."

Slowly, with no sudden movements which could, even inadvertently, spill his life's blood from his throat, Hurson opened his cloak to reveal a bundle wrapped in white linen lashed to his left side. It ran down his body from his armpit to his knee.

Intrigued despite myself, I asked, "What is it that is more precious that the True Cross?"

Grand Master de Ridefort looked straight into my eyes. "That I cannot yet say, and I hope you never see this again."

Hurson closed his cloak while de Ridefort continued, "You must trust that what we carry is more important than our lives, or the lives of all our brothers who fell today, or even the lives of all Templars everywhere. Knowledge that it even exists is shared only among the Grand Masters and their most trusted seneschals. But I foresee a time soon to come when I will need to place this prize into your hands for safe keeping. But even then, I will not tell you its secret." His voice cracked and his pleading tone sent a chill through my heart. "Help us, Brother Liam. Help us escape and return it to Jerusalem."

If what de Ridefort said was true, their actions this day were fully justified. Could I believe them, though? I did not believe that I could afford not to. Withdrawing my knife, but still holding Hurson's wrist, I made my decision.

"I will take you to Jerusalem, but as my prisoners." I lifted the purse full of coins I had collected selling water. "This ought to buy your freedom—as my slaves." With that, I released Hurson and slipped away into the dark.

It seems the supply of Christian prisoners was so plentiful that I ransomed both de Ridefort and Hurson for a few dinars each. I had enough left to buy one of our wounded warhorses as well. The Ayyubids thought our heavily armored chargers were magnificent beasts, but they preferred their smaller, swifter Arabian ponies.

The horse had taken a lance thrust in the hindquarters and could never charge into battle again. But, stripped of its heavy armor plate, it could easily carry my prisoners back to Jerusalem. It reflected our enemy's respect for a good and faithful beast that it cost me more than both ransoms combined.

Pausing only to fill two water skins, I led de Ridefort, Hurson, and our newest companion, whom I named Vulcan, out of the Ayyubid camp into the hills where I had hidden Almae. By riding as fast as Vulcan could all night and all the next day, we arrived at the gates of Jerusalem at dusk. Stewart rushed out of Templar headquarters to greet us, and we embraced like the brothers we were.

When he recognized my companions, though, he stood dumbfounded.

"Grand Master, where are your mantle and your arms?"

"Ah, Brother Stewart, I stand before you, a broken man. I have lost every one of our brothers who did not return here with you."

De Ridefort and Hurson sank to their knees, clasped their hands in prayer, and the Grand Master called out, "Forgive me, Oh Lord! I have committed the grave sin of pride! My arrogance has brought the deaths of thousands and will soon bring the fall of your Holy City!"

His sobs echoed off the city walls. I rolled my eyes, as I had been listening to their relentless contrition for two days without pause.

Stewart listened to the seemingly sincere confession, but believed none of it. "Enough!"

De Ridefort stopped his sobbing as if his throat had been cut, which I feared was coming next. Stewart was incensed.

"Confess your sins in the privacy of the confessional. This city has not fallen yet."

My brother caught my eye and with the understanding of blood brothers, we left the penitent officers kneeling in the dirt. Arm in arm, we entered our headquarters to make plans for the coming siege.

For hours, I recounted what I had seen while Stewart and the other knights peppered me with questions. At first, they were simple—how many troops did I estimate Saladin still commanded? How many horsemen? Lancers? Archers?

After these obvious questions were asked and answered many times, in many ways, the queries became much subtler, and I had to relive the horrors in my memory to answer them.

"Which of Saladin's sons were among his lieutenants?"

"His sons? How would I know his sons?"

"By the pattern of the *smagh* on their heads, of course, and by who stood at his sides, and by who followed him into and out of his command tent."

I should have thought of those distinctions. I certainly understood the Arab customs of family and caste better than any other Templar. Closing my eyes, I tried to remember what I had seen but which my mind, consumed with the horrors surrounding me, had failed to notice. Slowly, a picture of the aftermath of the disaster in the desert formed in my mind.

"Three of his sons were with him. Two of about your age, Stewart. They were taller than Saladin by a full hand span. The other was younger than me, not much more than a boy."

I opened my eyes, pleased with myself for having recalled something that, moments before, I would have sworn I knew nothing of. But when I saw the look on the faces of Stewart and the other knights, I knew I had conveyed bad news.

"What?"

Stewart put a hand on my shoulder. "You have done excellent work, Liam. I am very proud to call you my brother."

The other knights murmured their approval.

"Thank you, Brother, but why is this bad news?"

Stewart looked grim. "Saladin brought five of his sons on this campaign. If only three were present to celebrate his greatest triumph, where were the other two?"

At first, I did not understand, although the answer to the question was obvious. "They must be elsewhere preparing for…" I halted as understanding dawned.

"Yes, and there is but one more thing they need to prepare for."

I nodded, fully understanding the import of my report.

"Jerusalem. A siege. With fresh armies."

All around, I saw other heads nodding.

PART IV

The Enclave
Present Day

In Kimberton, the French Creek makes an oxbow curve across nearly a mile of its course. Its wide, shallow waters teem with brook and brown trout, its pools harbor bass and perch. The bottomland within the bend is fertile, its soil rich with the remains of centuries of spring floods. The surrounding hills, planted with corn, soybeans, hay, or left for pasture, roll gently, gaining height as they climb away from the stream to an encircling ridge of forest strewn with boulder-sized ringing rocks. Together they form a natural border and barrier that keeps the outside world at bay. Nestled within this bosom of nature is The Enclave.

Chapter 34

The Enclave, Late September

Riding along the main road in the village, Dan could see a mixture of building styles ranging from timber frame to more contemporary. Slowing to a stop, John parked the SUV in front of a small but beautiful Gothic-style chapel. The building was made from native field stone hewn into blocks that fit so tightly no mortar was visible between them. The brown shades of the stones gave the impression that the chapel had grown out of the soil. The arched stained-glass windows and main doorway were perfectly proportioned, guiding the eye on a sweeping upward path to the equally well-proportioned steeple where, Dan was sure, an old iron bell waited to call the parish to Mass.

John climbed the wide steps leading to the entrance and opened the ten-foot-high double oaken doors, but Dan walked to the left down a side walkway and out into the church's graveyard to where he could take in the entire structure. He saw the bell tower was octagonal, which mimicked the elongated eight sides of the main building.

The three-sided portico that housed the entryway also covered a set of beautifully carved statues of the Holy Family. Following the path around to the back of the church, Dan caught his breath when he saw the three sides of the apse clad in two-story stained glass. Looking at the sun's position this late in the day, he knew it would shine directly through these South-facing windows, illuminating the interior with their colors all day.

The two long sides of the chapel also held their own share of smaller windows, depicting the Stations of the Cross, fitted between small buttresses.

Finishing his walk-around, he saw John waiting patiently, holding one door open. Crossing himself, Dan climbed the stone stairs to the portico and strode through the entrance into his new domain.

After passing through the narthex with a spiral staircase going up to his right and a more conventional one going down to his left, Dan's breath again caught in his throat. The nave of the sanctuary comprised most of the fifty-foot width of the church. Narrower aisles ran up either side, separated from the center nave by massive oaken pillars, mimicking much larger, centuries-old cathedrals.

The pillars tapered naturally, as they had when they stood proudly in the woods. At their tops sat the ends of the buttresses Dan had seen outside, and on top of those was a scheme of half-arches, the likes of which Dan had never seen before, supporting a sharply pitched roof.

The gothic arches over the nave soared to a height of thirty feet or more. Carved into the wood of the supporting pillars were bas-relief death masks, probably of those honored to be buried in the crypt below.

The item that had taken Dan's breath away, however, was the life-size crucifix hung in the apse behind the altar. The body of Jesus was gilded all over with pigmented gold leaf in natural colors—black for his hair and beard, brown for his deeply suntanned body, red for his bloody wounds, and brilliant white for his loincloth. The deep lines of his face, and the taut sinews of his arms, seemed to be in the act of relaxing as if the sculptor had caught the exact moment of his soul's release.

Rough iron spikes held the statue to an oaken cross. Around the base of the crucifix was a tableau of equally detailed witnesses: the two distraught Marys, Joseph of Arimathea, and cowering off to the side, a terrified Peter.

Strangely, though, the pride of place among the onlookers, which naturally drew the eye, was held by a Roman centurion. Longinus stood next to the cross with a lance in his hand, poised to plunge it into Christ's side.

The sun shone through the window directly behind Jesus, silhouetting him in an otherworldly glow. The rays refracting through the side windows illuminated the scene from the sides.

As Dan stood in awe gazing at the scene, the sun moved infinitesimally across the sky and its light, whose movement was magnified by the facets of the windows' cut glass, seemed to dance across Christ and his witnesses, animating them and bringing the entire scene to life.

"It's almost too beautiful, isn't it?" John whispered from behind.

Dan continued to take in the scene for a moment before replying. "It's beyond words."

"I'd say you get used to it, but I'd be lying. Welcome home."

Still nearly mesmerized by the otherworldliness of the tableau, Dan followed John as he gave a tour of the rest of the church—the sacristy and two side chapels in the transepts which completed the cruciform footprint of the sanctuary.

Although not as brightly illuminated as the main windows behind the altar, the side windows which opened between the buttresses also caught and refracted the sun's rays. When Dan examined them closely, he realized they were angled in their frames, rather than flush with the walls. This clever arrangement meant that they would always catch at least some of the sunlight on that side of the church and direct it into the interior.

There was also strange statuary adorning the top of each of the twelve buttresses, six per side, which separated the side windows. John didn't explain them, and Dan didn't ask about them, even though he noticed they were not the typical saints, popes, or religious personages. Instead, he caught glimpses of what looked to be a phoenix, tulips, barley, and some kind of tree.

Chapter 35

The Enclave, Late September

Dan's apartment was above the entrance narthex, and comprised a fairly spartan bedroom, a sitting room, a bathroom, and a small kitchen nook. It was certainly adequate for his needs, and more spacious than the single room he had occupied at The U.

John held out the key to Dan. "Feel free to make your meals here in your rooms if you wish. But you also have access to our communal meals in the dining hall."

"You eat communally?" Dan was surprised.

"Of course, we always have. Our chef is quite good, and there are two meals a day—breakfast between six and eight, and dinner at six—which are open to all. If you want a light supper later in the evening, or if you miss dinner, there are usually leftovers put out around eight."

Dan dropped the luggage he had retrieved from his old sedan, now parked next to the church, onto the floor of the sitting room. Bells began to chime from above them in the bell tower. Dan checked his watch, noting it was ten minutes to six. "Is that the dinner bell?"

"Indeed, it is. Shall we meet some of your flock?"

"I'd love to."

As they descended the portico steps and walked down the sidewalk leading away from the church, Dan saw people

206

streaming from various directions toward a large four-story building that looked like it could have been ten years old, or a hundred.

"I assume that is the dining hall?" Dan asked, pointing at the building as they approached.

"Among other things, yes. Obviously, the main kitchen is there, along with storerooms in the basement. Upper floors are dormitories for our unmarried members who don't want to live with Mom and Dad."

"Men and women?" Dan's tone was slightly disapproving, but John just chuckled.

"Yes. How else do you think the unmarried members become married members?" Dan looked sharply over at John but relaxed when he saw him smiling back. "We're not a monastery or a convent, Father." He emphasized the title. "We're a community, sharing our prosperity, and working with a common purpose."

"Like a commune?" Dan remembered stories he'd heard of similar experiments in the 1960s and '70s.

"Well," John sounded a little condescending, "maybe like hippie communes aspired to be. We've had a couple more centuries to work out the kinks."

Dan nodded, and John continued, "Not everyone who works here is a member of the Order. We have some day workers and part-timers who commute in and out. They're welcome to share our meals, though most go home to eat with their families. Also, our kids who are under eighteen aren't members yet either. They decide for themselves whether to commit to this life, usually after they've finished college."

"So, you have a school here, also?"

"Yes, up through high school. We strongly encourage our graduates to leave the Enclave for a while—college is the usual choice—before they decide whether to return. Membership is a commitment—ideally a lifelong one."

"Do most of them return?"

They were nearing the dining hall, and people were waving to John.

"A pretty high percentage, I'd say. Certainly, more than half. Many bring their new, or soon to be spouses with them."

Dan looked surprised.

"Yes, Father," this time the title came naturally, "your duties will include the occasional wedding." Dan realized that the idea pleased him a great deal.

They were among the first to arrive, and John led Dan to an otherwise empty table. Dan wondered how he was going to meet people if they were eating alone, but it soon became clear that they wouldn't be. Quickly, the table filled up around them and John introduced everyone to Dan, who tried, mostly unsuccessfully, to remember names and faces. What did impress him, however, was the cross-section of jobs held by their dinner companions: electrician, software engineer, nurse, teacher, and farmer.

John greeted everyone by name, including those who just stopped to say hello on their way to seats at other tables. Within a few minutes, the entire table was full except for the two seats directly across from John and Dan. Nobody took those seats until a man and woman came in together and sat down in what was obviously their designated places.

"Father Dan Koprowicz, I'd like you to meet two of our Borough commissioners, Mack Stewart, our Mayor, and Patricia La Croix, our Borough Manager."

They rose and shook hands. "Just Dan, or Father Dan, please."

"And I'm just Pat," the Borough Manager smiled as she shook Dan's hand. "Welcome to our little village, Father."

When they were all seated, John became serious and all business. "OK, what have you got for me?"

Their conversation covered all sorts of mundane topics about the day-to-day operations of the Enclave. Two things struck Dan about this meeting. First, John was clearly in charge, regardless of Mack and Pat's job titles; and second, they discussed details of issues facing the Enclave openly in front of the other members. And yet, after a few minutes, Dan and the others at the table drifted off into their own conversations.

While everyone chatted, steaming plates and bowls were delivered to the tables by teenage servers. Dennis, the farmer seated to Dan's right, pointed out that the vegetables were grown on the Enclave land, as was the beef. The growing clamor of conversation was replaced by the clatter of utensils and murmurs of appreciation as luscious smells pervaded the room.

Dan found that once he talked to the teacher, farmer, and electrician, he had no trouble remembering their names. Only the software engineer remained aloof. He chalked it up to the man's general nerdish awkwardness.

While Dan chatted with the others, the programmer leaned over and whispered to John, "He's using the wrong pronouns."

John nodded, but his response was confident. "Oh, he'll come around. I have no doubt."

Chapter 36

The Enclave, Late September

After dinner, John took Dan on a tour of more of the Enclave grounds, including the infirmary and nursing care facility where the priest would minister to the sick, injured, and elderly. It was a clear, cool fall evening, and their stroll took them past the main street's storefronts of shops and offices.

Turning down a side street, John showed Dan the school and the health club. Housing for the residents was a mixture of small cottages, townhouses, and apartments. John explained that both members of the Order, and non-member residents were provided with an apartment, or they could rent a townhouse or cottage as their families grew. There was no private ownership of property within the Enclave. Looping back out to Main Street, they ended their walk at a large stone building which held John's office.

They passed through an outer waiting area where John's administrative assistant held court during business hours. Beyond this space was John's private office, which was elegantly decorated with solidly built furniture including a large desk, bookcases, file cabinets, credenza, and a small conference table with chairs. There was also a cluster of upholstered club chairs to the left and a small dry bar to the right.

Though the furniture was well made from solid hardwoods and leather, it was not nearly as ostentatious as the university president's back in Scranton.

"So," John began after they had settled down at the conference table with cups of coffee. "It's been a long day, hasn't it?"

"It certainly feels like it. I'm kind of overwhelmed at this point." Dan sipped from his steaming mug.

"I imagine you are, but you'll settle in pretty quickly, I think." John sipped his own coffee before continuing. "You made a good impression at dinner. Everyone thinks you'll be a great asset."

Dan looked puzzled. "Really? Don't get me wrong, I appreciate the vote of confidence, but how could you know that? Most everyone just stopped by to say hello."

"That's true, but like I said before, we're a tight-knit community. We know each other so well we tend to communicate non-verbally, sometimes. I got lots of positive signals from everyone."

Dan wondered if he would get to know the Enclave's residents well enough to communicate that way. It surprised him a little that he wished he would.

"Well, I'm glad I made a good first impression. I hope they feel the same way after they get to know me better."

"I have no doubt about that," John reassured him. "There's one last thing I'd like to show you this evening, if you're up to it."

Dan looked at John in anticipation. "The library?"

"You got it. Are you ready?" John was just teasing, since he knew the answer.

"I am."

Dan practically jumped out of his chair, and John led him out through the anteroom into the hallway. A few steps to their right John opened another door and stepped through into a loft area furnished with comfortable chairs that overlooked a large room below. To both the left and right of the doorway on this level, ten rows of bookshelves reached out from the wall. Running in front of them was a walkway and banister forming a gallery at least twelve feet above the level below.

As they walked along these stacks, Dan noticed some classic works of both fiction and nonfiction. Halfway down the aisle, the gallery railing bulged out to reveal a spiral staircase leading down to the lower level. As they approached the stairs, John explained the layout of the library.

"Up here on this level are fiction and general nonfiction titles. This area is open to all residents. Think of it as the Enclave's public library. There is a checkout scanner and a return area by the door." He indicated the door they had entered through.

As he started down the spiral steps, he continued. "Down here on the lower level are older, more fragile items that we keep protected, and which have more restricted access." Dan could see glass and wood cabinets tucked under the stacks above. "And, of course, the main reading area."

With his outstretched arm, John swept the main floor, which was open to the beamed ceiling at least thirty feet above. One end of the room held large tables on which one could examine multiple books and documents at the same time. At the other end were the sort of study carrels found in a college library. In the center of the room were club chairs, floor lamps, and couches arranged around a massive fireplace centered on the long wall opposite the gallery.

The field stone fireplace extended a couple of feet into the room. It was open on three sides so that, in effect, the fire box sat in the center of the seating area beneath a cantilevered mantel and chimney that rose up the center of the long wall and out through the roof.

Although the reading room was a large open space, about sixty feet long by twenty feet wide and two stories high, to Dan it felt intimate, and with the fire burning, it was downright cozy.

After explaining the room's layout, John led Dan under the second-floor gallery to the locked, airtight cases beneath. The documents housed there stretched back several hundred years, and although the number and age were fairly impressive for a private collection, Dan couldn't help feeling disappointed. He had been hoping for something more on the scale of a major university library, or even the Vatican's archives.

John continued with the tour of the locked cabinets, pointing out notable artifacts and documents dating back to the founding of the Enclave in the seventeenth century. When they reached the end of the cases at the far wall, he turned to face Dan and grinned.

"Don't look so glum. This is just the tip of the iceberg; what everybody knows we have." With that, he turned to a narrow door, almost hidden, that was tucked between the last cabinet and the back wall.

He drew a badge from his wallet and held it in front of a card reader barely visible behind the last cabinet. He then reached his hand into a hidden keypad and entered eight digits. A subtle click was the only sign that the door had unlocked.

"You'll get your badge tomorrow, along with an absurdly long passcode. You'll note that the keypad, which you can't see without sticking your head behind this cabinet, doesn't have any numbers. There're not worn off. Our security director insists you learn the passphrase by muscle memory.

When he registers you tomorrow, he won't let you leave until you've done it right four times in a row."

With eyes wide with anticipation, Dan followed him through the door onto the landing of a metal staircase. The stairs hugged the wall to the right as they descended to the floor below. The landing was encased in thick Plexiglas, which Dan was pretty sure was bulletproof.

Confirming Dan's suspicion, John wrapped on the barrier with his knuckles. "They tell me it will stop anything short of a fifty-caliber round." He then turned and looked into a video camera mounted in an upper corner of this enclosed mantrap. "John Haviland." The side of the bulletproof mantrap facing the lower stairs slid silently into the wall.

After they had both passed through, the panel slid back in place with a barely audible click.

"He'll also record your voice over and over. He insists that a mixture of several authentication factors is better than just two."

"Authentication factors?" The top-notch security intrigued Dan, and he grew increasingly more eager to see what it was all designed to protect.

John descended the stairs while talking. "Yes, they are different ways to make sure you are who you say you are. Something you have—your key card, something you know—your passphrase, and something you are…"

Dan was more interested in checking out the room spread out below him than listening to a lecture on identity management. He was so engrossed in his examination of the room that it took him a couple of seconds to realize John had stopped talking, and that he still stood on the top step. For a moment, he kept examining the room from his perch on the stairs.

Eyeing Dan appreciatively, John asked, "OK, tell me what you see."

Dan looked at him quizzically. He thought he would get a tour instead of giving one, but he composed his thoughts as he descended the stairs, then began.

"Well, this is obviously an examination room. This table," it was about ten feet long and five wide, "is for examining documents. I'd say you could use those microscopes to make high resolution 3D images." John nodded and Dan continued.

"And, oh my. That," he pointed to a large machine in the corner, "looks like a SEM—a scanning electron microscope." He was getting more excited as he walked around the room. "Those," again he pointed, this time at some glass-fronted cabinets hung on the wall containing labeled bottles, "are probably reagents for testing the chemical composition of the documents' paper or vellum, the ink, and whatever."

He spun around, looking for something else. When he couldn't find it, he turned to John. "What, no Carbon-14 dating equipment?"

John was grinning broadly. Clearly, Dan knew his stuff. "Actually, we can do both beta counting and accelerator mass spec, but the sample prep lab and the measurement equipment is in another location."

Dan looked behind the staircase they had just come down and found another door with a card reader and keypad. "Down a level?"

"Down several, actually."

Dan examined the rest of the room. He saw several computer workstations and large monitors against another wall, and a closed door set in the wall opposite from where they were standing.

"Are the archives through there?" He pointed at the closed door.

"Some are. There are many more in lower levels. In general, the more valuable they are, the deeper they're kept."

Dan nodded and walked across the room to the computers. "You said our archives are computerized. This is where we access the records?"

John smiled at the pronoun shift. "Yes. We don't disturb the actual documents and artifacts unless there is a reason to gather more information about them. Our records contain fully indexed full-text transcriptions, 3D images in several wavelengths, X-ray images, as well as physical and chemical analyses, including the C-14 data."

"You said artifacts. We have more than documents here?"

"Oh, yes. We're more of a museum than a library. I'll give you a tour of the computer system tomorrow. If you've used online library catalogs—which I'm sure you have—you'll find it pretty intuitive. I'll also show you how to access similar records at other institutions."

"Tomorrow?" Dan's look of disappointment was exaggerated, but sincere. In fact, he was extremely excited and wanted to jump right into his exploration.

John chuckled. "Yes, tomorrow. It'll take quite a while to show you around in there." He nodded at the computers. "Besides, I told you there was something special I wanted to show you."

He walked towards the examination table.

"Something special? More special than all this?"

"These," John gestured at the equipment around the room, "are just tools. Very useful, and very expensive, but easily obtained. What really matters is what is not so easy to obtain. What no amount of money can purchase."

From a drawer in the table, he pulled two pairs of cotton document examination gloves and handed a pair to Dan. He then lifted a metal box from a shelf under the table and placed it on the table. Dan could see the pressure sensor mounted in the lid, and when John twisted the pressure latches, there was a hiss of gas.

Pulling on his own gloves, John said, "I have a bit of a project for you." He lifted a roughly bound book out of the box and placed it on the table in front of Dan. "This is a codex that we've dated to the middle of the fourteenth century."

He pulled out a thick folder from below the table as well. "This is the examination report. It has all the test results on the vellum, binding, cover, and ink. They all consistently show an origin of between 1320 and 1360. We ran the tests ourselves, then had samples verified by two independent labs."

Dan was a little perplexed as he pulled on the gloves. "What is the project?"

"Let me show you." John carefully opened the cover.

Dan leaned over to look at the book, then jerked back slightly. He bent over again for a much closer look, then turned his head to John, who was smiling broadly. "What is this?"

"That's what I want you to tell me."

The first page of the codex—the book—was covered from top to bottom with what appeared to be handwriting. As with any manuscript made on vellum, or lambskin, the sharpened point of the pen had scratched grooves in the page's surface where the ink had soaked in.

"Well, it's clearly a manuscript, and not done in a scriptorium, I think."

John nodded, but asked, "Why do you say that?"

"Well, first, it appears to be written using a combination of different languages. I see characters from Latin, Greek, Hebrew, and—oh, my—even Aramaic. Also, look at the irregularity of the angle and spacing of the lines."

Dan pointed at the page, but didn't touch it, even with his gloves. "A scribe, in a monastery for instance, would have used a rule to line the page before starting. Also, there is no art to the work—no illumination, obviously, but also the writer took little care to make the document as presentable as possible. Hmm, I bet the content was much more important to him than the presentation."

Dan looked up at John while still bent over. "Which itself is extraordinarily rare. Most books from this time were copies of the bible, or prayer books, or sometimes Roman or Greek classics. So much time and effort went into copying works that were already widely known that the beauty of the form and presentation was more important than the actual text."

He straightened up and continued. "In the fourteenth century, paper and quill pens were fairly common, although the ability to use them wasn't so much. Among the literate, paper was the everyday writing medium. On the other hand, books written on lambskin vellum," Dan rubbed the first page lightly between his thumb and forefinger, "were so rare they were more valuable than paintings. Lamb or calf skin vellum was used for documents that were meant to last through the ages. Using it for a, for ah, whatever this is…"

Dan looked closely at John, whose expression was blank. "But you know all of this already, don't you?"

"Actually, what you've said agrees with my conclusions as well. I know it's very important. What I want to know—what I want you to tell me—is what it says."

Dan bent over and carefully turned the page. As was typical of vellum manuscripts, nothing was written on the back of the first leaf. The second, however, was covered with more of the unevenly handwritten text.

"Who else has examined this?" Dan asked without looking up.

John hesitated a moment. "There are very few people still living who even know of its existence."

Dan took a magnifying glass from the end of the table and bent even closer. "Oh? How many?"

"Now—two."

Dan turned from the book to John. "Two? As in you and me?"

"Yes, just you and I." He let that sink in for a moment, then drove the point home. "This organization has thousands of members living on properties owned by the Enclave all around the world. The Enclave's wealth rivals that of many governments. But I believe all of that combined pales in comparison to the value of this one book."

Dan's hand trembled slightly as he carefully laid down the page he was examining. "How can you know that if you don't know what it says?"

John placed his hand on Dan's elbow. "This organization has been around for centuries. It officially dates back to the fourteenth century, but its roots go back much further. We have many secrets and many capabilities, some of which you may come to know, but many you will not. But our origin—where and how and why our Order was begun—is a secret known only to the founder. I believe this book tells that story. I believe this book can tell us why we do what we do. I believe it is our Genesis."

Chapter 37

The Enclave, March

Dan searched the Enclave for John. His office and apartment were empty, as was the library. This would be so much easier if cellphones worked here. The fact that his phone couldn't get a signal within The Enclave had annoyed Dan many times since he arrived the previous month. He finally gave up searching when the clock chimes indicated it was time for dinner.

When he asked about his cellphone in the dining hall that evening, the Head of Security, Karl Coolbaugh, who had actually made him enter his passphrase not four times, but six times in a row, gave him a cryptic answer.

"Why do you want someone else to be able to listen to your conversations, or read your text messages?"

Dan was a bit taken aback. "Who would want to listen to me talk to my mother?"

"Exactly." Karl forked a piece of barbeque chicken into his mouth. Chewing his mouthful, he saw that his response had just confused Dan even more. He swallowed and continued, "You don't know who might care if your mother tells you she's sick, like her insurance company; or that your brother's been arrested."

"But neither of those things has happened."

"Maybe not, but do you know what she is going to say next time? Or what you might say? Anyone can listen in on your cellphone calls and read your texts."

"There are laws…"

"Not for cellphones. Landlines are protected—sort of—but not cellphones."

"Aren't they encrypted somehow?"

"'Somehow' is the key. The encryption they use between your phone and the tower is so old I can break it with my laptop." Karl leaned back in his chair and crossed his arms. "And there's no encryption at all once your data is inside the telephone company's network."

The others at the table recognized his posture and knew a paranoid geek lecture was forthcoming. Lisa Stevens, with whom Dan often ate dinner, held up a hand to interrupt Karl.

To Dan she said, "Who are you trying to reach?"

Dan, who was feeling a little intimidated by Karl's attitude and his growing vehemence, was relieved by Lisa's reprieve.

"I've been looking all over for John."

Lisa nodded. "Ah, yeah, he's been out of town for the last couple of days. He should be back sometime tonight, though."

Lisa was dressed in hospital scrubs which, Dan noted, was unusual for dinner time. Just then, her pocket emitted an electronic warbling, and she reached in and pulled out a smart phone. When he saw what she had pulled out of her pocket, Dan's jaw dropped.

Lisa glanced at the screen, then stood and excused herself from the table.

Dan turned to Karl. "Tell me again why I can't use a cellphone?" His sarcastic tone reflected his indignation.

Karl responded, a little defensively, "Well, I said you can't use *your* cellphone. *Our* cellphones are totally secure."

"And how do I get one of our cellphones?" Dan's voice dripped with his annoyance.

"All you have to do is ask," Karl replied sheepishly. He stood to leave. "I'll have one for you tomorrow morning."

"Fine. I'll see you after Mass," Dan called to Karl's retreating back, knowing full well that he had never seen Karl at Mass.

The other two diners at the table, both young women whom Dan had seen around but didn't know well—one did regularly attend Mass—offered their apologies.

"Karl is paranoid, I guess, because that's his job. Still, somebody should have told you that we have our own phone system with a private cell site."

The other woman chimed in, "It's actually a private phone company. We plug into the outside world as an independent carrier. All the communications within our site are heavily encrypted. Anything that goes outside is…ah, let's just say it's not as private."

Dan looked from one to the other. "Less private?"

His companions exchanged a look. "If you use our phone system, you agree to relinquish a certain amount of privacy when communicating with outsiders."

"You're saying Karl can listen in on my conversations?" Dan's agitation was evident in his voice.

"He has software that listens for keywords." She leaned in conspiratorially. "If you want more privacy, there's an old pay phone in Kimberton, the village just down the road a couple of miles. It's outside Totally Organic, the grocery store."

Dan shuddered inside and felt much less comfortable with his new home than he had just a few minutes before and resolved to make regular trips to that grocery store.

After dinner, Dan headed over to visit his elderly parishioners in the Nursing Center, which was a wing of the Health Center. The Health Center also housed a small hospital and physician offices. The healthcare facilities were first rate, as everything else in the Enclave seemed to be.

He began to understand how members of the Enclave could be born here, live out their lives here, and happily never leave. The lifestyle was relaxed, but purposeful. Everyone seemed genuinely happy with their jobs, their homes, and their families.

Of course, there were conflicts and arguments. Dan was counseling a young couple struggling in their marriage, and an elderly couple dealing with the onset of Alzheimer's. Still, compared to his experience in Scranton, the level of contentment among the Enclave's residents was eye opening.

John had explained it during one of their chats.

"Everyone is bad at some things, good at others, and outstanding at something. Our philosophy is to sort out everyone's talents and help them excel. Usually, the things they love to do the most are the things they are best at. We believe that's the 'Secret to Happiness'. Most people spend as much or more time doing their jobs than you do with their families—you understand that more than most, I'm sure. So, we believe everyone should make a career out of what they would do, even if no one paid them to do it."

As he often did, Dan replayed that conversation in his head. It explained a lot of what he had himself perceived. This time, though, as John's words echoed in his thoughts, he was distracted when the Health Center came into view.

The roof of the hospital was ablaze with light, and he could see a group of doctors and nurses looking off to the east. An intuition struck him like a blow to his chest, and without a conscious thought, he turned and bolted for his apartment in the chapel.

The helicopter that the doctors had been waiting for had already landed when he came running onto the roof with his stole, prayer book, and vial of blessed oil. As the patient was unloaded from the flying ambulance, the amount of equipment that was unloaded with her astounded Dan.

Machines were breathing for her, monitors with squiggly lines marched across their screens, and her blood circulated through a machine at the foot of her gurney.

Placing his stole around his neck, Dan began the sacrament of Extreme Unction. Running alongside as they wheeled her to the waiting elevator, Dan anointed her forehead with chrism and recited the sacramental prayer.

Even with the intubation apparatus in her mouth, and the EEG patches on the side of her face and forehead, he could see that she was a stunningly beautiful woman. Her middle-aged features could have graced the cover of any fashion magazine and her jet-black hair, though tangled as it was, featured in any shampoo commercial.

Clasped at her neck was a gold chain from which hung a single charm bearing the numbers "355".

The doctors, Lisa among them, did not slow their rush as Dan ran with them into the elevator. Once inside, while the elevator descended, they stepped back to allow Father Dan the space he needed to complete the Last Rites. But when the doors slid open, and the gurney rolled through them, Lisa stopped Dan from following with a firm hand to his chest.

"Sorry, Father, this is as far as you can go."

With that, she hurried after the others into the hospital. Dan stood for a moment while the doors slid closed again. The elevator rose, and to his surprise, continued for several seconds before the 'G' floor indicator lit, even though the indicator above the door showed nothing below ground. "Yet more secrets," he thought as he folded his stole and tucked it and the other sacramental items into his pocket.

When the elevator didn't stop at the ground floor, Dan realized he hadn't pushed a floor button. Belatedly, he stabbed the button for the ground floor, but the elevator continued to rise.

"I guess I'm going for a ride," he muttered, as he watched the numbers climb all the way back to the roof. The door finally slid open to reveal John and the helicopter pilot.

John didn't seem surprised to see Dan. "Fancy meeting you here," he said as he and the pilot stepped inside.

Dan, of course, was quite surprised to see him. "How on earth…?"

"Steve here," he indicated the pilot, "was kind enough to give me a ride from the airport."

Dan knew, given the emergency treatment the woman patient was undergoing, that the chopper would not have waited for John. So, he must have been with her from the start.

"You and quite the entourage, it looked like. Who is the patient, and what happened to her?"

Steve, the pilot, looked apprehensively at John, but John responded without hesitation. "Her name was, er…is Kathleen Stridebach. She's one of our operatives. An outstanding one, actually. She met with a great misfortune while on assignment."

Dan silently offered a prayer. John continued, "The medical staff is not very hopeful."

The elevator doors opened on the ground floor and Dan again pulled his stole from his pocket, kissed it, and shrugged into it. John thanked Steve as they parted, but waited for Dan to finish his silent prayer. When Dan blessed himself and again removed his stole, he and John walked together into the early Spring chill.

Chapter 38

The Enclave, March

S o, tell me, what progress have you made on our little project?" John and Dan walked through the cool evening from the hospital toward John's office apartment.

"Well, that's why I was looking for you this evening." Dan got the vibe that John didn't want to discuss the injured woman or her condition. Figuring that he could tell him little more than Dan already knew, he decided to wait for the morning and to check with the hospital staff directly.

"Oh, you have news?" John's voice betrayed none of the anticipation he may have felt.

"Actually, no, I'm afraid not." Despite the disappointing news, John's face betrayed nothing. Dan continued, "I've tried everything I can think of so far. Statistical analysis on the frequency of symbols, substitution of symbols from one language to each of the others, even substitution ciphers using reference books that were available in the fourteenth century."

They walked on in silence for a few minutes. Dan was slightly embarrassed that this puzzle was beating him. John did not seem disturbed by either this news or the recent medical emergency.

As they came to John's front door, he said, "Why don't you come in, have a glass of sherry, and tell me what you know?"

Dan didn't need to voice his assent. He simply followed John inside. When they were comfortable in overstuffed club chairs in John's office, with petite crystal glasses in hand, Dan began his report.

"Let's see. What do I know about this document? Well, a single person wrote it. It was probably a man. The handwriting is consistent throughout. And it definitely has a masculine form."

John interrupted, "You can tell the gender of the person who wrote it?"

"Oh, definitely. Especially with a manuscript from this time period. Remember that very few men could read and write, and even fewer women. They were taught very different styles, the men being much more regimented in their education—often reinforced with a rod across the back. On the other hand, women were taught a much more artistic, flowing style."

John nodded and Dan continued, "Whoever wrote it, wrote it in haste, or under some kind of duress." John raised his eyebrows to ask for an explanation, and Dan obliged. "Typically, they scratched rule lines into the pages before starting the writing. And a stick or pillow to rest the wrist on would have been used to prevent smudging. But neither of these techniques were used. The script wanders a bit across the page, and there are many areas that are smudged with ink and dirt."

Dan paused when he saw John had a question. "So, this isn't an official document?"

Dan thought a moment. "It certainly isn't a Church document. If it was, it would have been written in High Latin.

It's most likely not a government document either, because unless the code was well known, no one could read it. No, I think it is either a very personal or family book—perhaps the code was passed down through the family?

"Or," Dan smiled a little, "perhaps it is an ambassador's or a secret agent's report."

"A secret agent? You mean like James Bond?" John was smiling, too.

Dan chuckled at the image. "Remember what was going on in the world in the fourteenth century. A succession of kings ruled Europe, who fought wars with each other pretty much non-stop. The political intrigue made James Bond's Cold War look like a tea party by comparison."

"It seems awfully long and involved for an ambassador's missive. And a secret report won't have been bound into a codex like this, would it?"

Dan thought a moment. "Those are good points. I hadn't thought of that. That supports the notion that the book is probably something more personal. A travelogue, perhaps." Dan's tone suggested he wasn't convinced of his own suggestion.

John wasn't convinced, either. "Why write it on vellum? The vellum for a codex this size must have cost a pretty penny."

"Well, he clearly wanted to preserve it." Dan stopped to sip his sherry. The mysterious book thoroughly stumped him.

John sipped from his glass as well, but kept prodding. "What else do we know? I mean, specifically about the code?"

"I told you, I have no idea how to break the code."

"OK, not how to decode it, but the code itself. Looking at it linguistically, for example."

Dan nodded. That was his area of expertise, after all. "That's the first thing I did. The text comprises a mixture of characters from four different languages: Latin, Greek, Hebrew, and Aramaic. There does not seem to be any pattern to the use of one language's character set over another."

John looked puzzled, so Dan continued, "In other words, sometimes there will be one, two, or three characters from the same language—Greek, say—then there might be single characters from Hebrew and Aramaic, followed by two Latin letters. There are never more than three symbols from any of the four languages in a row."

"Interesting. What does your statistical analysis say about the distribution of the four languages?"

"Not much. The four languages are pretty evenly represented, with a slight abundance of Hebrew. It's probably not really significant, though."

"Why?"

Dan was getting excited despite himself. He loved linguistics, and even though he wasn't any closer to finding an answer, talking through the problem with someone else might help. If he could get his mind out of the pattern of thinking— the rut—he was stuck in, that would definitely help.

"Well, I wouldn't expect them to be perfectly even. Assuming the codex has semantic value." John raised a questioning eyebrow. "I mean, I'm assuming the codex means something and isn't just random symbols."

"Probably a safe assumption," John said dryly.

"Yeah, right. Why go to all of this trouble if he wasn't saying something important?"

John nodded, stood, and walked across the room to an antique cabinet, from which he drew a crystal decanter. Returning to where Dan sat, he raised the decanter to Dan, who nodded, and John refilled both of their glasses.

"So, there are no patterns to the groupings of the symbols?"

Dan looked surprised. "Oh, there definitely are. I guess I didn't say that. There are two, three, and even four character patterns that recur with some frequency."

"Well, that's a start." John sounded encouraged.

"More like a dead end." Dan sipped his sherry.

The two sat in silence for a minute, each sipping from their glasses in silence.

At last, John spoke. "Let's go back to basics. Tell me more about the document itself. I mean its physical characteristics."

"OK. It definitely dates to the mid-fourteenth century. Three independent analyses at three different labs confirm the carbon dating of the vellum, the wooden cover, and even the linen threads used to bind the pages. The composition of the ink is also consistent with that time period. Do you know anything about its origins? Like, where it was written?"

"As I said, it's been locked in the Enclave's archives for centuries with no explanation. I've never found another document anything like it, and none that even reference it. It is unique, as far as I know."

Dan nodded thoughtfully. "I haven't found any reference to it in my searches, either. It's almost as though it was dropped here by aliens!"

They both chuckled and Dan continued after a pause, "There is one odd thing, though."

"One odd thing?" They both chuckled again.

"OK, one more odd thing." They laughed and sipped. "The form of the characters doesn't match the language forms that were in use during the fourteenth century."

John looked puzzled again. "I don't understand."

"Starting about the middle of the thirteenth century, the great secular colleges started appearing. Oxford's University College was founded around 1250, for example. They taught Latin and Greek, primarily, although advanced students could find professors to teach them Hebrew and Aramaic."

"That's consistent with our timeframe."

"It is, but the form of writing isn't." John still looked puzzled. "They taught a very formal, almost rigid style of writing. Our codex was written, or at least the characters were formed, in a much more colloquial style. The way a native speaker would write them, not at all how they were taught in schools of the day."

John nodded. "So you're saying our mystery writer wasn't formally educated?"

"Not only was he not formally educated, he learned to write these languages 'on the ground' among native speakers."

Dan got very thoughtful and seemed to drift off into a fresh path of investigation. John let Dan's mind go where it chose to without interruption. After almost a minute of silence, Dan refocused and continued in a much more thoughtful tone.

"Perhaps our 'mystery writer' as you call him, didn't just learn to write from native speakers, perhaps he learned to speak from them as well."

"What does that tell us about him that we didn't already know?" John failed to hide his excitement.

"It tells us he was a polyglot like—well, like both of us. If he could speak these four very different languages, along with probably French or English, it also tells us he was very well-traveled throughout much of Europe and The Levant."

A vein in John's neck revealed how hard his heart was pounding. "Perhaps he was a trader."

"That's possible. Or a pilgrim. Or even a Crusader."

Suppressing a gasp, John kept his voice level. The dim light prevented Dan from seeing his flushed cheeks and the gleam in his eye.

"Weren't the Crusades pretty much over with by the fourteenth century?"

"Mostly, yes, but that brings up another anomaly about the writing." John looked even more exasperated, which made Dan chuckle. "But wait, there's more!" They both chuckled again. "The characters are in the style that was common in the twelfth century, not the fourteenth."

This time, John gasped. "How could that be? How could twelfth century writing end up on fourteenth century vellum?"

"I'm assuming this is a copy, not the original. It was probably copied by someone who didn't know any of these languages, so he copied the letters verbatim."

John looked distinctly disappointed and, avoiding this line of thought, he changed the subject a little.

"If they wrote this in the twelfth century, it can't have anything to do with the Enclave. There's got to be another explanation. Besides, wouldn't a copy be more carefully done?"

Dan thought for a moment. They were good points. "Perhaps the writer had learned these languages, not from native speakers, but from a school that preserved the two-hundred-year-old style? No, that seems kind of far-fetched. The copy theory makes more sense, I think. Maybe the monastery or library where the original was kept was being threatened? Maybe the original was copied quickly to preserve whatever the message was?"

John nodded reluctantly, as if he did not want Dan to think of the codex as a copy. "It makes more sense, but please keep an open mind. I really believe this document is important to the Enclave."

Dan felt sympathy for John's hopes. "Maybe the origins of the Enclave go back even further than you know."

John shrugged, but looked a little more hopeful. "That would be an amazing result, too. Please keep an open mind in your analysis."

Dan nodded vigorously and downed the rest of his glass. "Oh, I will. This conversation has certainly opened up several new areas for me to look into." He paused a moment. "And I may have a new theory to work with."

With that, he thanked John for the sherry and headed for the library.

Chapter 39

The Enclave, June

F ather Dan wearily climbed the spiral stairs from the Vault to the Library. His eyes were sticky with lost sleep, and yet they burned with an excitement he hadn't felt in months. If he could have gotten a cell signal in the Vault, he would still be there. But the security shielding surrounding it blocked all radio frequencies. So, instead, he roused himself from his work and made his way up to the surface. Reaching the top of the stairs, he looked around the library and was mildly surprised to see no one else there, so he fumbled his phone from his pocket to check the time.

3:38 A.M. He groaned, knowing he would have to say Mass in three and a half hours.

Despite the hour, he opened the Locator app that came with his Enclave phone. John Haviland was at the top of his recently found list.

Out of town? Again? I have to let him know, though.

Tapping the phone icon under John's picture, the Enclave's high-security encrypting messaging app opened. He had turned off the annoying auto-correct feature previously, mainly because his spelling and grammar were normally meticulous. Tonight, however, with his dry, exhausted eyes, he could barely see the tiny letters on the screen as he tapped them.

Majr breakthru!!!! Native spekers was the
clue. Text needs to be spokn—in Arabic.
Arbic wis the missing key. Pronouncng the
chars phonetcly comes out in 12th c. Arabic!
I have most of the intro now…

That should bring him home.

Dan hit SEND and looked down at the sheets of notepaper he still clutched in his hand, still amazed at the ingenuity of the writer, not to mention the depth of his knowledge of the world. To speak and write at least five languages, when most people never strayed ten miles from their homes, marked him as a very well-traveled man.

Even though he had checked and double-checked his work, Dan couldn't help reading again this message from centuries past. A message that seemed to have been written just for him. He couldn't wait to uncover what lay waiting for him within the remaining, still undeciphered pages.

How do I begin a tale such as the one I wish to tell? There is the beginning, my youth before I came to know, though not necessarily understand, a few of the many mysteries this world holds. But I will get to that part of the tale soon enough. There is the middle, when I was pursued across the face of Europe, charged with protecting a most precious artifact with the power to change the course of human history. Then, there is the end which, until this last year, I thought might never arrive. We will get to the beginning and middle,

*but let us start here at the end, what may well
be the end of all things.*

Dan checked his phone again. With another three hours until Mass, he might get another page decoded. He spun on his heel and headed back down into the Vault.

PART V

The Fall of Jerusalem
Autumn 1187

"Then began the fiercest struggle imaginable; each side looked on the fight as absolute religious obligation. There was no need for a superior authority to drive them on: they restrained the enemy without restraint, and drove them off without being driven off...They challenged [us] to combat and barred the pass,...they slaughtered and drew blood, they blazed with fury and defended the city, they fumed and burned with wrath...They fought grimly and struggled with all their energy, descending to the fray with absolute resolution...they made themselves a target for arrows and called on death to stand by them."

— Ibn al-Athir, Ayyubid chronicler

Chapter 40

Jerusalem, July—September, 1187 A.D.

Stewart relegated grand Master de Ridefort and Seneschal Hurson to servants' duties. They accepted their punishment in silence and spent every free moment prostrated in the chapel. In the meantime, Stewart rallied every able-bodied Christian—men, women, and children—to the defense of the city. The resident Muslims he offered a reasonable wage to work under close supervision, mostly shoring up the walls and sealing all but one of the many of the city's gates and posterns.

David's Gate, adjacent to the Citadel and King Guy's palace, was the only remaining access into and out of the city. Stewart placed a heavy guard there, tasked with inspecting all shipments into the city and all people, camels, and wagons leaving. Guards manned all three of the watchtowers in shifts throughout the day and night, the city's location on a plateau giving them good sightlines to the surrounding mountains a few miles distant. Upon the peaks of the surrounding mountains, signal bonfires were prepared and staffed, stretching several miles to the north and east—the expected direction from which Saladin's forces would arrive.

Thus, from mid-July until the end of September, did we live and prepare under a self-imposed siege. I did, however, mange to ensure that the merchants from whom I bought whispers had free passage in and out of the city. It was from them that we learned that Saladin's concubine Moira pressed him daily to being the march to Jerusalem, as she claimed that we Templars had found a relic of great value that was hidden there. She implored The Sultan to take the city before we spirited the artifact away.

I, of course, thought about the bundle that Hurson had strapped to his side in the desert. I never mentioned this to Stewart, because the merchant from whom I bought that whisper also told me that the Ayyubid forces were already on the march. Sure enough, I could see the smoke from bonfires to the north that afternoon, and their glow lit the sky that night. With frenzied final preparations underway, the she-devil's motivation seemed unimportant.

Chapter 41

Jerusalem, October 1, 1187 A.D.

S aladin's strategy was much more subtle than we had expected. Instead of heading straight for the high walls of Jerusalem, Saladin had led his armies of fresh troops across the Levant, capturing towns and cities at every turn. Nablus, Jaffa, Beirut, Toron, Sidon, and Ascalon all fell or surrendered outright to the Sultan of Egypt.

In the span of less than three months, Jerusalem and Acre stood alone as the only remaining Christian-held cities of import. Stewart, his lieutenants, and the few remaining knights drilled every able-bodied man left in the city. In the last days of September, de Ridefort and Hurson began attending Stewart's War Councils in the Templar headquarters on the Temple Mount, though by his order they remained silent. I observed these meetings from my hidey hole and saw them exchange knowing glances every time the concubine Moira was mentioned, thus confirming my belief that Hurson's bundle was the relic she sought.

Saladin arrived, finally, on the twenty-third of September. It was almost a relief to have the anticipation broken. At least we would engage the enemy and meet our fate.

As we had expected, Saladin positioned his army opposite the Damascus gate, where we had concentrated our defenses. For six days, his troops rolled siege machines and belfries up to the city's mighty walls. And for six days, Stewart led sorties through the gate and drove the attackers back. When dawn broke on the seventh day, we peered through the ramparts to see no soldiers or machines outside the gate.

Our moment of exhilaration was short-lived, however. Sentries overlooking the Mount of Olives, where Our Lord suffered his final temptation and ultimate betrayal, raised cries of alarm. During the night, Saladin had moved his forces there and had mined the city wall. With no gate to sally forth through, the Golden Gate having been sealed, we watched, nearly helpless, as his machines battered the formidable wall while his miners dug at its roots.

Stewart rallied all abled-bodied Christian men, whether soldiers, smiths, or merchants, to where the inevitable collapse would occur. On the second day of the unrelenting barrage, the wall, which had stood for a thousand years, crashed to the ground.

Now it was our turn to surprise our enemy. As they tried to pour through the breach, a rain of arrows, stones, boiling oil, and flaming pitch rained down on them. The bodies piled so high in the crack that the remaining attackers had to withdraw.

Further bombardment that night brought more of the wall down, widening the hole beyond our ability to stopper it with the bodies of our enemies. When the attack came again at dawn, the first waves fell as they had before, but eventually, by climbing over the corpses of their fellows, the Ayyubids entered the city.

We expertly executed the plan Stewart had devised. When our pikemen pulled back, allowing some attackers entry, Stewart's knights and sergeants sliced into the enemy from both flanks, cutting them off from the breach, and breaking the momentum of the attack.

Knights, soldiers, and any man who could wield a sword or axe fell upon those trapped in our encirclement and hacked them to pieces.

With their thrust thwarted, again, the attackers withdrew. We let loose a great cheer, and our spirits were raised for the moment, but when the siege machines started up again, and the walls again shook and crumbled, so did our joy.

Within a few hours, the third attack came. The breach in the wall was now wide enough to allow twenty men through shoulder to shoulder. When, for the first time, we could gaze through the wall to see the extent of the army massed against us, those who were not professional soldiers, and many who were, turned and bolted for their homes.

We who stood our ground grumbled about their cowardice, and some threw a few stones and threats at the fleeing men. But Stewart would not stand for such treatment of those who simply wished to protect their families.

Instead, he relieved them of their duty, shouting to all the defenders, "Thank you for your service. If you have families to protect, go now and hide them and yourselves."

When those who chose to had left, most with their heads bowed, Stewart addressed those of us that remained. "The rest of us have no families but the brothers we stand beside." Heads nodded all around. "Make those brothers proud to die at your side!"

A great cheer arose and echoed from the remnants of the city walls until the beating of the war drums overcame it as the Ayyubid horde descended from their perch.

Stewart placed the few remaining Templars in the vanguard, but as they were engaged by the first attackers who swarmed through the wall, a second wave followed immediately. These attackers seemed to target Stewart himself.

Their pikemen thrust relentlessly at his steed, and their archers pelted his armor. With me at his side, we felled dozens of the enemy and, for a moment, stopped their advance. Our success was as short-lived as we knew it would be, however.

For the uncountable time, Stewart raised his sword to cleave off an attacker's head. That time, however, an arrow slipped under his armored sleeve and through the ring mail he wore underneath. He completed his downward swing, separating the man's head from his shoulders, and for a moment I thought his steel shirt had stopped the missile. But, to my horror, I saw Stewart's sword fall from his grasp as his body slipped sideways in his saddle.

My reaction was quick and without thought. I rode up next to his charger, and as he slumped down, I dragged him across my saddle. Without further thought for the battle, or for the city, or for any of my brothers still fighting and dying there, I turned Almae and galloped to our headquarters.

Behind me, I heard a cheer rise from our attackers. They had seen Stewart falter, and a matching groan of despair arose from the defenders as they dodged out of our way.

The guards at the door to our headquarters helped me carry Stewart into the Council room, where de Ridefort and Hurson cowered. We lifted him bodily and lay him on the long table in the center of the room.

I stripped off his breastplate and upper body armor to see how severe his injury was. Only a third or so of the arrow's shaft protruded from his armpit. Stewart, brave until the end, made not even a whimper, even when the blood bubbled from his mouth. Seeing that, I fell over his chest and sobbed.

"Steady, Brother," I heard him whisper. "Our family has done its duty here."

I lifted my head and wiped my eyes clear. Stewart's eyes, however, were staring at something far off that I could not see. After a moment, though, his eyes cleared and focused on mine.

"We have done our duty," he repeated. "Escape here and go home." I nodded, though without real understanding. "Tell our mother the good work we have done here, but nothing about this day."

"I will have the minstrels singing songs about your prowess and wisdom."

Stewart smiled, though I was not joking. "I don't care what the minstrels sing." He coughed violently, and dark red blood spurted from his lips.

When the coughing fit subsided, he gathered his strength once more and grasped my arm with an iron grip.

"Promise me," his voice barely above a whisper, "promise me Mother will see at least one of her sons again." I nodded, but my voice could make no sound. Stewart's glazed eyes could not see my assent, however, so he shook my arm. "Swear it."

"I swear," I croaked.

I thought he had breathed his last, but this last word he said to me, "Brother."

"Brother!" I answered as the life left his eyes.

From behind me, I heard Hurson, the seneschal, say, "Only Stewart can hold off the invaders. If he dies, we will have no time to escape."

I turned my head. He placed his hand on his side where I am sure he still wore their precious bundle, whatever it was.

"He is already dead, you fool!" I yelled. Was this man an idiot? Could he not see what lay before him? But Hurson was not looking at me or at Stewart. He and the Grand Master stared at each other. Finally, de Ridefort nodded and began a mumbled prayer.

Hurson turned to the guards standing at the door. "Remove Brother Liam."

The two guards each grabbed one of my arms and dragged me to the door despite my struggle.

"Why am I being dismissed? Let me grieve for my brother," I pleaded.

But the guards were relentless and carried me into the hall, then slammed the door barring my entry.

I knew many things about our house that these guards, and probably neither the Grand Master nor his seneschal knew, however. Feigning despair, I ran down the darkened hall and slipped into a storage room on my left. At the back of the room, I slid aside a loose board and reentered the Council room behind a hanging tapestry. I had spied on many a Council meeting through a slit I had made in the hanging rug in just this fashion.

From my vantage, I had a clear view of Stewart lying on the table. What I saw frightened and disgusted me. de Ridefort yanked the arrow from Stewart's body and dropped it to the stone floor while Hurson placed his linen bundle on the table and gently unwrapped it.

At least I will see what could be more precious than the lives of thousands of good men, I thought.

Hurson handed a long, thin object to de Ridefort, who then lifted it high above his head as the priests lift the host at Mass. What I saw appeared to be simply the broken shaft of a weapon, either a spear or a lance.

"Oh, Lance of Longinus! Oh, Blood of Christ! Save this man so he may save Your Holy Blood!" de Ridefort cried.

I watched in awe, a gasp nearly escaping my lips. Was that truly the Lance of Longinus? The lance that pierced the side of Jesus Christ while he hung on the cross. My awe turned to horror, however, when de Ridefort lowered the lance and thrust it into Stewart's side.

Without thinking, I burst from my hiding place.

"What are you doing?" I screamed. I reached for my sword. "Why do you maim him further? He is beyond your petty revenge."

In my haste and fury, though, I had forgotten Hurson. Before I could fully draw my weapon, he fell on me from behind, pinning my arms in a bear's embrace. I struggled, but being nearly twice my weight and a full head taller, he held me easily.

The Grand Master pulled the lance from my brother and turned to me, Stewart's dead blood falling from it in black drops.

"I maim him not." His eyes burned red with a fervor I had never witnessed before. "I have infused him with the blood of our Savior, which clings still to this relic."

"But, why?"

"Brother Liam," de Ridefort's tone was gentle towards me for the first time. "Do not despair. You are about to witness a true miracle. One that lies at the heart of our Order. One that is, in fact, the very foundation of our Order."

He placed his hand on my shoulder. "Every Templar knows the story of the birth of our Brotherhood. How Hugues de Payens brought eight of his kinsmen here to the Holy City to protect Christians on their pilgrimages."

"Yes, yes, and they luckily found a remnant of the True Cross, which *you lost* at the Horns of Hattin!"

Hurson snickered, and de Ridefort scoffed at my outburst. "That old piece of wood came from a horse stall in the stables beneath us. What the First Nine Templars found, after years of searching, was this most holy relic, instead." He held before me the supposed relic. "Look at the miracle it has wrought so far."

Again, his eyes shown with wonder. I imagine mine did also after I saw the change that had taken place. Where once it was coated with Stewart's dead, black humors, it now gleamed a bright crimson, painted with fresh, living lifeblood. My heart filled with awe, and I had an inkling of what was transpiring.

From behind de Ridefort came a stirring and a sharp intake of breath. I was right! The miracle they promised was coming to pass. Stewart lived again.

Hurson must have been awed, as well, because his embrace that held me captive loosened and, breaking free, I ran to my brother's side.

His eyes fluttered, and a smile came to his lips, but when they came fully open and he saw where he lay, the smile disappeared, and a look of horror overtook his face.

"What have you done?" he roared as he rolled off the table and rose unsteadily to his feet. He looked at me from across the council table with terror in his eyes.

"Brother, what have you done?" he repeated. "I was gazing upon Our Lord, and he beckoned me into Paradise."

Tears sprang from his eyes, eyes that had witnessed the worst horrors one man can inflict on another without shedding a single drop. The tears made tracks in the dirt and sweat on his face.

"As I crawled over the threshold and reached out to touch the hem of His robe, I awoke back here in this hellhole!"

My joy at Stewart's rebirth instantly forgotten, I shared instead the anguish he felt. That he could blame me for his renewed torment was unbearable to me. Perhaps he saw the pain his words caused me, or more likely his sharp mind had registered the entire scene before him, including whom it was who held the Lance.

"Ah, of course," he turned his fury from me to de Ridefort and Hurson. "It was not my sweet brother who worked this necromancy. It was *you!*"

He pointed a hand that trembled with rage at the Grand Master. "Our Lord himself has freed me. You no longer command me!"

With that, he drew the short sword, which still hung from his waist, and burst from the room.

After the moment it took me to recover my senses, I ran after him, but I heard Hurson yell, "Stop the boy!" to the guards who were shocked by Stewart's rebirth and sudden departure.

As I ran down the hallway to the main entrance, I heard the clatter of their armor as they lumbered after me. I had easily beaten Stewart in footraces since we were boys, and I expected to catch him in a few more steps.

Instead, as I reached the double doors that opened onto the stairs leading down to the courtyard in front of our quarters, my right foot slipped in Stewart's blood—the blood that had spewed from him when we carried him inside. As if he had commanded it to prevent me from catching him, the blood proved too slick for my running foot.

I fell, face forward, onto the landing at the top of the stairs. Before I could arise again, the guards were upon me and pinned me to the ground.

Unable to rise, I looked down at the scene below. The remaining defenders had fallen back to this very courtyard. The rest of the city must have fallen, because only a small force of Ayyubid fighters pressed the attack against our headquarters. I could see, however, that Saladin himself sat on horseback amongst these men.

It took but a moment for me to find Stewart within the melee. He ran forward through the bedraggled Christian defenders to the very front line where, to my horror, I saw him launch an attack with just a short sword and no armor above the waist.

Upon seeing him return to the battle, our men raised a cheer and they, too, went on the attack. His presence shook the Ayyubid soldiers, as well, and they fell back, thinking they were in the presence of a ghost. I suppose they were.

The shift in the tide of battle was only momentary, however. As the guards pulled me to my feet and again dragged me, this time backwards toward the Council chamber, I saw the first blow strike Stewart.

A pike pierced him high on the shoulder, rendering his left arm useless. His right arm, his sword arm, kept swinging though, until it too was struck. An axe removed it above the elbow. The last thing I saw as the doors slammed shut and were barred, was Stewart's headless body crumbling to the ground.

Inside the Council chamber, I stood in shock as the Grand Master placed the hastily rewrapped bundle into my arms. "Brother Liam, you have seen the power of this Lance today. Perhaps we were wrong to use it as we did, but God alone will judge whether that is so. You are a smart boy—no, clearly you are now a man. You must understand how dangerous this holy relic is." He licked his lips, and a look of frenzy contorted his face.

"The temptation to use it, whether for good or for evil, is too great for any but the most pious. Imagine the horrors that could be wrought if it fell into the wrong hands. Saladin, the Christian kings, even the Pope would not be immune to its promise of resurrection."

I again found my voice. "You should burn it. Now. In that fire." I pointed to the room's hearth where a fire was kept burning day and night.

When their heads turned to follow my finger, I grabbed for the bundle. Before I could wrestle it from de Ridefort, though, Hurson again pinned me in a bear hug.

"You'll not burn it, Brother. This you must swear. Although dangerous, it is the most powerful and miraculous relic in the world. Not because it can restore the injured to health, or the dead to life, but because it is proof that what we believe is Truth. The Lance itself is but the branch of an ancient tree. Our Lord's blood is the miraculous instrument. Without it, this Lance would surely have rotted to nothing centuries ago."

The events of the day had left my mind reeling, but de Ridefort was correct on one account. I was smart, and I knew the only way I would leave this room alive was with the bundle strapped to my side beneath my cloak. The secret they revealed was too great to let me live without the burden of the embodiment of that secret.

"I agree, Grand Master. This relic is too sacred to be burned." But not because it proved what must be believed on faith.

"Then you must swear to take it safely to Templar headquarters in Paris."

"I swear to you, and to God, that I will take this holy relic to safety."

De Ridefort eyed me warily, for I had not promised exactly what he wanted. In that moment of silence, the clatter of steel on steel echoed from just outside the doors to the chamber. Deciding, he nodded to Hurson to release me, and together they lashed the bundle to my left side. Being much shorter than Hurson, it hung awkwardly from my armpit to mid-calf.

While securing it, de Ridefort instructed me, "I am sure you know many escape routes out of this deathtrap. Use the most secret way, and your most stealthy skills, and go now!"

Without a word of parting, for I was already planning my escape, I bolted for another hidden passageway out of the chamber.

Before I could slip out through it, however, de Ridefort called out, "Brother Liam, I free you from your vows. Do what you must to hide your burden in secret until it may be called upon to fulfill its purpose. Whatever that may be."

The import of his words fell upon me like a great weight. Although freed from my obligation and the oaths of the Order, I bore a new one—the oath I had sworn to my brother. As I ran through the hidden corridors of the ancient palace, I knew that oath and the bundle strapped to my side would be burdens that would hold me prisoner for the rest of my days.

Chapter 42

Jerusalem, October 1, 1187 A.D.

The escape route I had chosen took me deep into the keep and down several staircases to the dungeons. The dungeons were unguarded since all guards had been called to the defense. The men held there yelled for food, water, and release.

I had no regard for any of the deserters, thieves, or cutthroats chained to those rough stone walls. I cared not whether they died of thirst, or at the hands of the invaders. There was one captive held here, however, that I did care about. Indeed, I liked and respect him as a teacher—Yusef.

Yusef's lodgings, though Spartan, were much more comfortable than those of the common criminals around him. I had tried to secure him a room above ground, but no one trusted him as I did. Failing that, I furnished his cell as comfortably as possible.

When I unlocked the door to his cell, I found him in a fighting stance, a double-edged long knife in his hand. I pointed at the knife.

"Which guard *misplaced* that?"

He smiled and seemed to relax, although I knew his muscles were still ready to pounce, if necessary.

"Not a guard's, *Yutqin*. They would notice and search. That would be bad."

"Of course not. Some unsuspecting fool, you passed in the hallway, no doubt."

Yusef just smiled and changed the subject. "My ears tell me the battle is not going well."

"Your ears do not deceive you, my friend." He raised his eyebrows at my choice of address. "The city has fallen, and this last stronghold is even now being taken."

The sound of the fighting came clearly from inside. "You have served me well, taught me many things that might yet keep me alive. As repayment, I give you your freedom." I stepped back out of the cell and Yusef really relaxed. "You may choose to stay and join your Muslim brothers in victory, or accompany me," Yusef looked surprised, "not as my prisoner, but as my guide."

"An interesting choice...ah, Liam," he replied, addressing me as an equal. "I share a God with these Sunni pigs, as I do with you, but little else. To them, I am as infidel as you. Since we both need to escape their grasp, we might as well do it together."

The shouts and clangs of weapons grew louder. His eyes flashed. "But we must do it now."

"Agreed. This way."

The next several hours saw us crawling through hidden tunnels and wading through rank sewers before emerging after dark outside the city wall. The sewer drain we crawled out into the cool of early evening was east of the south-facing, and still fortified Mt. Zion Gate.

Thankfully, we were out of sight of Saladin's encampment on the Mount of Olives. The city, having outgrown its protective walls, had spilled houses and merchants through this gate and down the hillside.

As we rested against the stones of the city wall, Yusef looked at me appraisingly. "Your armor is more dangerous than helpful to you now."

"Yes, and we both stink to heaven. We need new clothes."

"And water, and food. It is a long journey to where we are going."

I nodded, and Yusef turned to look out over the houses on the hillside.

Without looking at me, Yusef said, "Liam, you are moving without your usual grace. Were you injured in the battle?"

I shook my head. "No more than the usual bruises. I am hindered by a burden I carry."

"I am sure your brother fought valiantly, but he rests with your God now."

"How did you know—"

"If he still lived, you would be at his side." His voice was heavy with sadness.

I was surprised by Yusef's sincerity, but puzzled by it, also, until I realized he had misinterpreted the nature of my burden.

"It is a physical burden that I carry," I patted my side, "as well as a heavy heart."

"This burden must be valuable for you to let it encumber you so."

I did not like the look in Yusef's eyes. "Valuable only to me and my family," I lied. I drew back my cloak. "It is the shaft of my brother's lance. I carry it back to my home to bury with our ancestors." I gulped back tears. "It is all that is left of him."

Yusef looked at me dubiously, then his face softened. "Well, even if that is true, the linen that wraps it in is worth a knife between the ribs to a thief. You are lucky I am not a thief." His eyes and smirk told me he joked. "We need clothes, food, water, and a poor man's sheepskin, so you can carry your burden on your back."

"And how will we get these items?"

"Night is coming, Liam. That is my time—and yours. Any of these houses contain what we need."

I untied my purse and withdrew two copper and two silver coins. "I cannot sneak about in this armor." I handed the copper coins to Yusef. "And I will not become a thief this night."

Yusef frowned but took the coppers. "And the silver pieces?"

"They made many horses riderless today. I suspect at least some have been gathered up by those who have no use for them." Yusef nodded, and I placed the silver coins in his hand as I continued softly, "I trust you will return to me."

Without taking offense, Yusef replied, "An infidel boy hobbled and took me prisoner." He paused. "Yes, you were but a boy then, although a man now. And though my limp is slight and no longer hinders me much, there are those in my village who will mark me as one who has dishonored his family. Some night, to reclaim the family honor, a cousin will slit my throat while I sleep." He slashed his right hand across his throat.

"However, I can regain my honor if I return to my village with the boy-man who maimed me as my captive and slave."

Alarmed, I pushed back from Yusef and drew my knife. He simply raised his hand, though. "This is the bargain I propose. I will 'buy' us clothes and horses this night. Then we will travel as companions to my village in the mountains north of here. You will then become my captive and servant until my honor is restored."

I interrupted him, "Your slave, you mean."

"Servant or slave makes little difference in my village. The point is, you will do as I command until I am accepted again as a member of the tribe. Then you can 'escape' into the night."

Now I was skeptical. "And how long will this restoration of your honor take?"

"Who knows? My cousins are not a trusting lot. Weeks? Months? Even so, it will be but a small part of your long journey home."

Seeing the truth of that, I sheathed my knife and held out my empty hand. It took Yusef a moment to understand, but then he grasped my wrist, as I did his. "We have a bargain, then. Let us sleep until our 'sellers' are themselves asleep."

Exhausted from the momentous day, I drifted to sleep straightaway despite the stench enveloping us.

PART VI

Codex Cognito
Present Day

But first, let me set expectations. If you, whomever future you may be, are reading this, I congratulate you. I have written this chronicle in the most devious cypher I could devise, hoping that one day someone with your skills would see through my subterfuge and decode this most unusual manuscript. So, I say, "Well done."

Now that we have finished congratulating ourselves for being so clever, let me teach you lessons that are so strange as to be at first unbelievable, but which will seep into your mind and erode whatever faith in the Almighty you may hold dear. Let me assure you that no harbor is safe from the momentous revelations contained in this missive.

— Codex Incognito

Chapter 43

The Enclave, June

Two days! What could possibly be so much more important than The Chronicle?

Dan's thoughts even sounded petulant to himself. He knew nothing of the Order's work outside the Enclave, so he couldn't judge whether John was ignoring him, or simply too busy to come home. John's response to Dan's repeated messages had been curt.

> Say nothing to anyone until I return in a few
> days.

Dan had obeyed, although his heart and mind were bursting. Bursting with pride for having cracked the code and bursting with wonder at what his translation had revealed so far. Although it was untitled, Dan thought of the book as The Chronicle. Despite the introduction's adamant insistence on the authenticity and first-hand nature of the story, it was probably a compendium of tales the author had accumulated through the years. Regardless, the book was a historical document of immense value. If even a tenth of it was true, it represented a new, original insight into medieval times, places, and events.

He had come to the dining hall very early in the morning to avoid the company and camaraderie he normally sought. The last two days had been torture for him. Everyone he encountered seemed about ready to ask him about the book. He knew the feeling was silly, because, according to John, no one else even knew of its existence. Still, the feeling was so strong that more than once he had to stop himself from blurting out the latest details of his translation. So, upon waking after a scant four hours' sleep, he resolved to avoid everyone else until John returned home.

Keeping to that promise, when someone sat across the dining hall table from Dan, he kept his head down to avoid eye contact. But the subtle scent of expensive perfume caught his attention, and before he realized what he was doing, he looked up from his bowl of cereal. His gaze fell upon the face of a stunningly beautiful young woman. She smiled a dazzling smile and extended her hand.

"Father Dan, I presume."

He could have sworn her eyes actually twinkled. He felt his cheeks flush and he could simply nod as he took her offered hand. She continued her introduction while Dan recovered.

"It's so nice to meet you. I'm Elizabeth Webb."

"It's nice to meet you, Elizabeth." As he looked more closely at her lovely face, she seemed strangely familiar to him. "Have we met before?"

"No, Father, I'm here at the Enclave on, ah, family business."

Her smile melted into a more melancholy, though no less pleasant, look, and her eyes fell away from his. Dan, in response, dropped his eyes from her face, but only as far as the hollow of her neck. There, dangling from a simple gold chain, was a pendant he had seen before.

"355?" he said and nodded at the pendant.

Elizabeth's right hand clutched at the necklace. "Oh, yes, it's a…a family heirloom, I guess you'd call it."

Dan remembered back to the night the ambulance helicopter had brought in the critical patient, herself a beautiful woman, even in death. He had said her Funeral Mass two days later. The resemblance between Elizabeth and the older woman on the gurney was now clear to see.

"Margaret was your relative? I'm sorry for your loss. I didn't know her, but at her memorial, John spoke very highly of her."

A smile, a sad one this time, returned to Elizabeth's lips. She reached across the table and took his right hand in both of hers.

"Thank you for your kindness, Father. I hadn't seen Aunt Peggie for several years and didn't know I was the only relative she had left. Apparently, it took them a couple of weeks to locate me—I was camping up north—and by then she was gone and buried, so there was no reason to hurry back."

Dan squeezed her hands but didn't break contact with them. "Again, I'm sorry for your loss. I prayed for her smooth journey to Our Lord." Elizabeth smiled. "Margaret—Peggy?—was your aunt?"

"My mother's sister, yes."

"And your mother has passed, also?" Dan squeezed her hands again.

Elizabeth returned the squeeze and released his hand. "Yes, she and my father passed away many years ago. I stayed with Aunt Peg on school breaks, when she was home, that is."

Dan leaned back from the table and tried to lighten the mood. "The number 355 seems like an odd family heirloom. Do you know what it means?"

Elizabeth touched the necklace at her throat again and chuckled. "Apparently, my great-something grandfather was a baseball player. 355 was his lifetime batting average. It sounds silly, and it's really more sentimental than valuable, I guess."

"Sentimental things are often the most valuable of all…" Dan paused when something over Dan's shoulder drew Elizabeth's attention.

"Well, well! Glad to see you two have met."

The woman was so mesmerizing that Dan had not heard John approach, even though he stood directly behind him.

Elizabeth rose as Dan turned. "Yes, Father Dan was offering his condolences." She extended her hand to Dan again, and he rose to his feet as he clasped it in both of his. She continued, "I'm glad we met, Father, and thank you for your kind words."

Again, Dan's eyes seemed to be drawn into hers, and he had a bit of a premonition that they would meet again.

"I'm glad we met, too. I hope we meet again soon."

Elizabeth's brilliant smile returned. "I suspect we will," she shifted her gaze to John, "although I doubt it will be 'soon'. I've packed Aunt Peg's things and I'll be leaving this afternoon."

Elizabeth's smile had faded completely.

John offered her a smile, however. "Safe travels, my dear. You know you are welcome to return anytime you wish, of course."

"Of course." The sarcasm in her voice was incongruous with the previous conversation.

With a curt nod to Dan, Elizabeth turned and strode from the room.

John drew a deep breath and sighed. "Well, that went as well as could be expected." Dan raised a questioning eyebrow. "It's a long story, Father, which I—or she—may tell you someday. In the meantime, I believe you have a story to tell me. One that warrants a more private setting, I think."

John looked at Dan with a rue smile, and Dan responded in kind. "Indeed, I do."

Chapter 44

The Enclave, June

J ohn wouldn't let Dan speak until they were locked in the Vault deep below the library.

"You haven't taken any of your translation out of the Vault, have you?"

John's voice was flat, without emotion, but Dan knew him well enough by then to know that meant the opposite of what it seemed.

"Only briefly, when I first translated the introduction."

"And you left nothing up there?"

"No, I never would have taken even the intro upstairs if I hadn't been so excited, and so tired."

John relaxed a little. "You look like hell, you know."

"I've been working non-stop these last couple of days. I've barely been able to remember the Mass the last two mornings."

John chuckled. "Well, tonight you must get a full night's sleep. This thing," he gestured to the sealed case containing the codex, "has waited a long time to be read. It can wait a little longer." Dan nodded and John continued, "Besides, haste and exhaustion cause mistakes. It's got to be hard to decode."

"It is, indeed. If it was modern Arabic, it would be much easier. But it's written in colloquial twelfth century Arabic."

"How do you even know how to pronounce twelfth century Arabic?"

Dan chuckled a little. "The Society of Dead Languages." John looked very skeptical. Dan smiled. "Seriously, it's a real thing. A bunch of us nerd linguists try to keep dead languages from disappearing altogether."

Smiling, John shook his head as Dan continued, "We research pronunciations back through time and extrapolate backwards century by century."

John's smile faded a little. "You didn't consult any of these 'nerd linguists', did you?"

Dan shook his head. "Of course not. Besides, I just taught a seminar on thirteenth century Arabic at our last meeting. Going back another hundred years was simple." Dan thought for a moment. "Come to think of it, that might be why I finally figured it out. It was fairly fresh in my mind."

"So, it really is originally from the twelfth century?" John's voice reflected his excitement.

"Oh, I would have said definitely so, ah, until I read the text." Dan's brow was furrowed.

John's voice hinted at his confusion. "I don't understand. The text contradicts your analysis?"

"It does, yes. As I told you before, they wrote the characters of the four languages in a late twelfth century style. And, when you pronounce them as in the vernacular of that time period, you get twelfth century Arabic. Rather informal Arabic, actually. Not a form that was used by the nobility, or taught in any school."

"So, it all sounds consistent with a fourteenth century copy of a twelfth century document, given the age of the vellum and ink. I don't understand what the problem is."

Although John said he was confused, Dan didn't hear it in his voice, piquing his suspicion that the young man knew much more than he was telling. Of course, nobody told him everything around there. Filing these thoughts away for later, Dan pulled the papers containing his translation of the introduction from a folder and handed them to John.

"Read the intro. Then you'll see why I'm not so sure."

With raised eyebrows, John took the papers from Dan, then he began to read.

How do I begin a tale such as the one I wish to tell?

Dan watched John intently as he read the translation. He could tell almost word-for-word where John was reading by his face. When he finished, John set the papers on the table and gazed off into space, deep in thought.

After a minute or so of silence, Dan interrupted John's reverie. "I can show you the Arabic, too, if you want to check my work."

John shook his head, both to answer Dan and to clear it. "No, I trust your translation. The author claims he's writing in 1350, based on your editorial note, right?" Dan nodded. "And that's consistent with the vellum and ink – mid-fourteenth century."

Again, Dan nodded. He was letting John work out the conundrum. Maybe he would have a better answer.

After a pause, John continued, "Could the copier have written the introduction? But then he would have had to know the code, right?"

Dan nodded and frowned. He had wondered the same thing. "The intro is consistent both phonetically and stylistically with everything I have translated so far. The same man certainly wrote them. Someone who could speak and write colloquial twelfth century Latin, Greek, Hebrew, Aramaic, and Arabic."

"Could it have been passed down orally, in an older form of Arabic?" John looked sideways at Dan. "Like your dead language nerds?"

This was a new way to look at it, and Dan considered it. "Then why use the old forms of the characters?"

John shrugged. "To be consistent?" John didn't sound like he believed that himself.

"Maybe, but both the form and the text show the author was in a hurry and was probably afraid he wouldn't finish before either he died or the world ended." John nodded his agreement. "So, why would he care about being consistent? If this was some kind of hoax, which we know was written in 1350—both the text and the radiocarbon dating attest to that—who was the author trying to fool? It's well documented what the Black Death did to Europe, and particularly England. It would have been a pretty macabre joke."

"Agreed. And one with no punchline, or even an audience, for that matter. But you've made a hell of a breakthrough. You've accomplished something that many have tried and failed at over the centuries." Dan beamed with pride. "So, what else have you translated?"

"Quite a bit, actually. I've got it down to a process of reading a line or phrase of the text aloud, writing it down in Arabic. When I've finished a section, I go back and translate the Arabic to English, although I could translate it verbatim now. Writing down the Arabic lets me, or you, double-check the translation. It also lets me translate it into colloquial English more easily."

"Are you recording what you are reading?"

"No. I didn't think you would want any extra copies around, especially easily reproduced ones." This was something Dan had not been sure about. "I've just got the Arabic and the English."

But John nodded in agreement. "Good thinking. Until we know the complete story this book contains, the more tightly we control it, the better." Seeing Dan nod, he continued, "Why don't you read me what you've translated so far, after this introduction? I'd like to hear your interpretation."

"OK." Dan pulled the handwritten sheets from the folder and began.

Our story, or at least this part of it, begins in the twenty-eighth year of the reign of King Henry II of England. The year was 1178 Anno Domini...

Chapter 45

The Enclave, Late Summer

Have you double-checked the facts?"

John sat reclining in the overstuffed club chair he had brought down from his office to the Vault. Dan sat in a matching one opposite him, with his sheaf of hand-written translations in one hand and a glass of sherry in the other. John had insisted that if they had to spend hour after hour in the hole, they might as well be comfortable.

Ruefully, Dan wished he had thought of that when he was working down there by himself. The days of tedious translation had fallen into a routine. Taking John's advice, Dan was less fanatical about the pace of his translating, as he had been about cracking the code in the first place.

For a couple of hours each day, he translated the codex in the Vault, which fit comfortably into his schedule. Every few days, he and John gathered so he could read aloud his latest bit of translated text.

"Yes. The dates fit once you adjust for the start of King Henry's reign. The names all seem to match with the historical record, too." Dan sipped his sherry. "And a lot of that history wasn't written until decades, or even centuries, after our anonymous author put pen to vellum."

John looked up, his glass halfway to his lips. "So, it's possible the author witnessed these events first-hand?"

"Either that, or this is the first recorded history of the time leading up to the fall of Jerusalem. He could have written down stories he heard from his elders."

John swallowed his sip before objecting. "But, given the typical lifespan in those days, he would still be seven or eight generations removed from the actual events. Even if his great-great-grandfather told him stories, which wouldn't be likely, given their short lifespans. That's still a huge gap."

"I know. This...thing...keeps getting stranger and stranger."

"How much more do you have tonight?" John checked his watch, which Dan noted with some annoyance. "I'd like to hear all you've got so far. I have to leave in the morning for, ah, some Enclave business. I'm afraid I'll be away for an extended period of time."

"Oh? How long do you think?"

"I can't tell for sure." John shifted in his seat before continuing. "It could be several months. It'll be a few weeks at least."

John frowned and raised his glass again, and Dan frowned in response. He would miss these nocturnal meetings. But then John smiled. "Don't worry, I'll leave the sherry down here."

Dan chuckled. "And the chairs?" John laughed and nodded. "Well, in that case, have a nice trip!"

They both laughed while Dan scanned his papers to find his place again. "Let's see. Last time Saladin had crushed King Guy and the Templars at the Horns of Hattin. OK, here we are..."

*Darkness had fallen by the time I made my way
into Saladin's camp. Using the ruse I had
employed previously, I took up a waterskin and*

> *followed a wandering path through the Ayyubid
> camp. My goal was the officers' tents, of
> course, but I picked up snippets of gossip at my
> stops along the way.*
>
> ...

When Dan finished the account of the *rescue* of the Grand Master and his Seneschal, he looked up at John expectantly. Rather than the praise he usually heaped on Dan, John sat lost in thought for several moments. When he spoke, the subject surprised Dan.

"This Moira woman. What does the historical record say about her?"

Dan nodded appreciatively at the direction of John's interest.

"Absolutely nothing."

That got John's full attention. "Nothing? Anywhere?"

"I've run searches against every database I have access to—which you know are quite a few. There isn't even a hint that a woman was behind, or even present at any of Saladin's victories, let alone the most critical one." After a pause, Dan continued, "I have to say, though, that it is not unusual for powerful women to be erased from history. It's a shame, and a sin, frankly. The sin of pride."

"Indeed. She sounds like a formidable woman. What do you make of the assassination story?"

"The *failed* assassination, you mean? Clearly, Saladin's nephew bragged about it a little too prematurely."

John eyed Dan intently. "I find it odd that a man of your faith, a Jesuit whose Order was founded, frankly, in the spirit of the Templars, would discount a resurrection tale, so out of hand."

Dan was taken aback. "Christians were at war with the Muslims. Why would God give such power to one of them?"

John laughed. "First of all, I doubt Moira was a Muslim woman. If she was, she would have been shrouded and locked away in a harem. But more to the point, didn't—don't—Christians and Muslims worship the same God. Through different intermediaries, perhaps, but ultimately the same omniscient, omnipotent, wondrous being. If your God took sides in that war, it's clear which side he backed. Isn't it?"

Dan sat stunned. He had no counter-argument for John, and he felt the rock of his faith, which had always rested on sand, not stone, shifting underneath him as if a wave of doubt had turned that weak foundation to mud.

After a moment of stunned silence, John smiled and cocked an eyebrow. "You're right, it must have been a braggart trying to impress his fellows."

The hollowness of John's words rang in Dan's ears, and his rock tilted yet a little more.

PART VII

Flight
1187 – 1188 A.D.

What defines a man? Is it his physical nature—the color of his hair, the strength of his muscles? Or is it his intellect—the knowledge he carries, the languages he speaks? No. It is the responsibilities he bears—those thrust upon him and those he takes willingly upon his shoulders.

— Ruminations on Being

Chapter 46

Syria, Autumn 1187— Spring 1188 A.D.

Yusef and I traveled through the desert and mountains for two weeks. I admit, to my shame, that not all the food we ate, nor the water we drank, was paid for. Yusef refused to give the 'stupid herders' any of my copper or silver, insisting instead that we would need it once we reached his village. He was correct.

When Yusef left his village to murder King Guy—for that was his intended target the night we met—his wife, Sirrah, moved in with her sister Nieva and Nieva's husband, Ibrihim. When Yusef failed to return after a few weeks, then months, Ibrihim was enlisted to join a raiding party. Normally, Yusef was the one chosen from his family, since his skills far exceeded those of Ibrihim. But in his absence, Ibrihim and five other men set out to stalk a passing Christian army as they marched to Acre. Only two men returned, and Ibrihim was not among them.

The survivors told of how they split up to sneak into the army's encampment late at night. Ibrihim's party were set upon by soldiers who had been keeping watch from hiding. Yusef, with his greater experience, may have anticipated the trap, or at least sensed the guards' presence in time to escape. Ibrihim had not been that smart or quick.

Ibrihim's death left the sisters destitute. The dishonor brought on by their missing and dead husbands meant no one would take them in, even as servants. The village of a hundred or so inhabitants, most of whom were related through blood or marriage, turned their backs on the poor widows.

One relative, an aunt only a year or two older than Sirrah, agreed to give them an occasional meal for working in her family's garden. With the onset of fall, and the subsequent harvest, however, even that source of sustenance disappeared. The sisters could do little more than beg in the dusty street.

So, Yusef's homecoming was less joyous than he had hoped. The contents of my purse helped Yusef wash away some of the stain on his honor, since he could pay for the food grudgingly given to Sirrah and Nieva. I, as his captured "slave", also raised his standing among the men of his tribe.

Yusef had upheld his side of our bargain, getting us safely to his village. I, in turn, upheld my side by becoming his servant. He never treated me cruelly—he knew I would not stand for that. But when within earshot of the other men, he always spoke to me harshly and ordered me about.

We moved Nieva and Ibrihim's tent and joined it to Yusef's. With this arrangement, I slept under cover, which was a blessing when winter fell on those bleak mountains.

The first night, I watched from my bedroll in the tent where we took our meals as Yusef made a show of tying the door flap to a copper pot balanced on a high stake.

Trying to hide my amusement, I whispered, "What in our God's name are you doing?"

He threw me a sharp look, then scanned the area for anyone within earshot. Satisfied that we were alone, he chuckled and could barely keep a straight face when he said, "I'm setting a trap to keep you from escaping into the night."

I covered my mouth to keep from laughing out loud. "I could just lift the edge of the tent there," I pointed to the back of the tent facing away from the rest of the village, "and wriggle out that way. Don't you trust me to keep to our bargain?"

"Oh, I trust you, my clever friend, but no one else here does. A wise man pens up his goats. Not to keep them in, but to keep the desert foxes out."

That sent a chill down my spine, but it made perfect sense that the other villagers saw me as a threat.

"Then you should set the same trap on your tent, to keep me out here."

He winked and raised his hand, holding another pot and stick. Nodding, I settled into my bedding, feeling at least a bit more relaxed than I had in months.

We passed the winter this way, mending broken tools, patching roofs, hunting, and telling stories over the cook fire. As spring approached and the days lengthened though, my thoughts turned to the long journey to reach Sowich, my home in fair England. The vow I had made to Stewart weighed heavily on my heart.

Yusef must have seen the faraway look in my eyes too many times because he pulled me aside one day.

"Liam, I know you long to continue on your way, and I will not break our bargain. I ask only that you stay long enough to help with planting our meager garden. A few more weeks is all."

I looked at Yusef in dismay. I came to think of him as a brother, though he publicly treated me as his slave.

"I will have to think on it, but you agree I am free to 'escape'?"

Yusef nodded reluctantly. "Yes, our bargain is fulfilled." He held out his hand, and I grasped his wrist as he had grasped mine when we struck the bargain back in Jerusalem. "But, please, a few weeks more."

That night, while I lay next to the banked coals of the fire, I was awakened from my sleep by the faintest of sounds. Opening my eyes to slits, I saw a hand reach through the flap to the inner tent and gingerly lift the pot from its stake. A small, slim figure slipped through the opening and huddled over the remains of the cook fire. It was Nieva.

I will admit that this young widow had been a daily distraction to me since I arrived. There were many nights when I was glad of the day's hard labors that took me quickly into a deep sleep without time to think of her sleeping only yards away. When I realized she was shivering in the chilly night air, I raised my head.

"Why are you out here in the cold instead of sleeping in your warm bed?"

The dialect of Arabic these Assassins used came easily to me.

She grunted disgustedly. "I cannot sleep when those two are rutting like goats."

I chuckled, knowing exactly what she was complaining about. "But they finished their romp hours ago," I replied. I could not keep the smile from my voice.

Nieva smiled and chuckled, as well. "But the stink they leave behind would keep a horse awake."

I could barely keep from laughing out loud, which would have wakened the rest of the household. When I met Nieva's eyes, though, the laughter caught in my throat.

Although she was already a widow, Nieva was younger than my seventeen years. The other men in the village loved to gossip, so I knew her face, though normally veiled in my presence, to be very handsome. I could see by the faint glow of the fire's embers that she was indeed a beauty. Her eyes, which, by then, I knew very well, were blacker than the blackest night sky and seemed deeper than the deepest cave. But it was her biting wit, usually aimed at Yusef or myself, that I found most attractive.

Shivering only an arm's reach away in her thin nightdress, I was overcome with desire. Her eyes bore into mine, and I believed I could read in those eyes a desire that echoed mine.

Knowing my life would be forfeit if I was mistaken about her intentions, I lifted my blanket and barely croaked, "It is warm in here."

My heart leaped when her face broke into a leering grin as she stepped around the fire pit and lay down next to me. We spoke no more words that night, though our eyes, mouths, and bodies made each other solemn promises.

When I awoke in the morning, Nieva had snuck back to the other tent, and all was quiet. Arising and rebuilding the fire, I heard Yusef rising, as well. With head bowed but eyes raised, I watched for any sign of disapproval as he entered the outer tent. His body was tense, as mine was, both of us ready for a reaction from the other. When I raised an eyebrow questioningly, he just shrugged and fed a few pieces of wood into the fire.

A knowing smile crossed his lips when he said, "At least she slept quietly last night…once she fell asleep."

Every night for a week I lay awake, hoping Nieva would join me again. That hope had dampened my desire to escape, and I committed to staying with Yusef and his family until the planting was done. After several days, though, I had to admit that either she regretted her forwardness, or our liaison had simply been a ploy, probably orchestrated by Yusef, to keep me around longer.

So it was that after a hard day working the rocky soil of our garden and a hearty meal, I fell into a deep sleep straightaway. I awoke in shock when Nieva slid beneath my blanket and pressed her naked body against my back. My shock turned to joy when she whispered my name against my neck, and joy flamed into desire when I rolled over and took her in my arms.

Nieva did not return to her own bed that night, or any night after that.

I should not have been surprised when Nieva announced she was with child. Sirrah certainly was not. Her attitude toward me had shifted from tolerance to brusqueness when Nieva began sharing my bed. Now it flared into open hostility.

Although I wanted, with all of my heart, to marry Nieva, Yusef patiently explained that the villagers would never accept me. In their eyes, I was a slave, and now a rapist.

"Liam," he said simply and coldly, "they will stone Nieva to death, then they will castrate you and make you wear your balls for earrings while they flay you alive."

After the many atrocities I had witnessed since coming to that godforsaken land, I knew that he was being completely honest.

"Then we must leave. Together, if Nieva will go with me. Tonight."

Yusef studied my face and read the depth of my sincerity there. Slowly, he nodded. "Yes, you will leave and take Nieva with you, whether or not she wants to go." He grinned a little now that we had made the decision. "And judging by her moans in the night, I have no doubt she will want to."

I blushed until my ears burned. Yusef, serious again, continued, "But not tonight. She will not show for a while yet. The moon will be new in two weeks, and the garden will be planted. You can make your escape then."

I considered this, then nodded. "Will you grant me the horse I 'bought' and rode here?"

Yusef shook his head. "No, my brother. If you steal away with a disgraced widow, my cousins will scoff and make jokes at my expense. But if you steal a horse, you will offend their honor, and they will hunt you down."

I could see the wisdom of Yusef's words, though I was not convinced our departure would be ignored. The sense of honor being very strong among the *Hashashim*. Then another idea came to me.

"Perhaps a raiding party will take you and your cousins away for a few days? If we must go on foot, that would give us a head start, at least."

It was Yusef's turn to nod. "Yes, it is time for me to regain my standing here. I will suggest that we ride out in five days when the moon is dark."

That night I told Nieva our plan, and Yusef told Sirrah. The sisters embraced and cried, but both understood that it was the only solution.

We used the days until our departure to good effect, stowing gear and hording some necessary supplies. Before leaving with the raiding party, Yusef returned to me both my long dagger and my short knife. He also gave me a crossbow and set of bolts that his cousin had brought back from a previous raid. The other raiders had laughed so hard at his 'trophy' that he threw it away. Yusef had seen the effectiveness of such a weapon many times, though, so when no one was watching, he had retrieved and hidden it.

When he placed it in my hands, our eyes met, and I could see that Yusef had something to say. He had seemed hesitant in our banter for several days, so untied his tongue.

"Yusef, say what it is you wish to say, but cannot."

He sighed, but looked relieved. "I have come to know you like a brother, Liam. You are an honorable man. Taking Nieva with you is ample evidence of that fact. I wish you success on your quest to fulfill the vow you made to your brother."

He made a sign with his fingers next to his ear that I echoed by making the sign of the cross.

"I leave today with two others to scout for a suitable target for our raiding party, so this is goodbye, my brother."

We embraced, and my heart felt heavy with sadness, but also light with the joy of starting a new life and family.

That was not the last time I spoke with Yusef, however.

Chapter 47

Syria, Spring 1188 A.D.

Anticipation kept me awake, despite the comforting presence of Nieva, most of the next two nights. So it was that I lay restless when a rustling of the tent brought me fully awake. In a flash, I grabbed my dagger and knife and crouched protectively between Nieva and our attacker.

"Peach, Brother Liam," I heard Yusef's voice whisper. I did not relax my fighting stance, however. Yusef crawled under the tent's edge but stayed out of striking distance. "I bring you a dire warning."

His voice, even when whispering, carried a note of dread.

"My cousins and I met a small force of Saladin's men on the road to Damascus. They were dispatched by the order of The Sultan's she-devil whore to find the Templar who carries with him a linen-wrapped bundle. She is offering a tremendous reward for that bundle."

My heart froze. How could she know about the lance and its power over death? If Saladin could restore fallen Ayyubid warriors to life, no army, Christian or otherwise, could stand against him. I held my silence and my stance, waiting for Yusef to continue.

"I know it is you she seeks, Liam. My cousins will suspect it soon, too, I expect. When they do, they will come for you and *your brother's lance*." His tone told me he no longer believed that to be my burden, if he ever did.

I found my voice. "What will you do?"

In the dim light of the dying fire's coals, I saw Yusef shrug. "I bring you this warning at great risk." I knew this to be true. "But when I return to our camp, I will join my cousins in their hunt for you. Tomorrow."

"Thank you, brother Yusef. Go now and awake your cousins. By the time you return, we will be gone."

"And the burden you carry?"

I knew what he was asking. If I left the lance behind, he could present it to Moira and collect the reward, greatly enriching his village and raising his status immensely. There would also be no reason for him and his cousins to pursue an escaped slave and what they would believe to be his pregnant whore. I admit that, for a moment, I considered lightening the load of my life that way, but those thoughts were fleeting.

"I think you know my response," I said, and Yusef nodded. "I will bear my burden to the end."

He nodded again. "As I expected. You wear your honor well, Liam."

"As do you, Yusef. Return to your cousins and do what you must."

Without another word or gesture, Yusef slipped out of the tent. I turned to Nieva, who rose immediately and began dressing for our journey. Without the need to exchange words, we gathered our cache of supplies. I slung the bundle of the lance in its wrapping, tied with a leather strap, onto my back, and within minutes we slipped out of the village.

If I had known then what I later came to learn, I could have avoided many years of doubt, tragedy, and hardship.

Chapter 48

Syria, Summer 1188 A.D.

The night in late spring when Nieva and I started our marriage, that was not a marriage, we were like two thieves slinking out of the village under a moonless sky. Yusef's village was to the north and west of Jerusalem. From there, we headed north toward Antioch, staying mostly in the mountains. I hunted with the crossbow Yusef had given me, taking desert hares and the occasional mountain goat. Nieva knew the edible plants that grew wild, so between us we kept our strength up.

We traveled overland for several weeks, avoiding the roads as much as possible until the rough terrain became too difficult for Nieva. Our baby grew inside her, which brought us great joy, but it also made her tire more quickly. Although it would be more dangerous to travel on the road to Antioch in the open, we had no other choice.

One morning, shortly after having broken our fast, we quietly bundled our meager belongings for the day's hike. Our cook fire burned low as I stood looking out across a ravine next to our campsite. Behind me, Nieva gathered up our blankets. The summer was almost past, and I was hoping we would find a village soon where Nieva could rest until our child was born, and where I might find some work during the harvest.

Perhaps I was lost in these domestic thoughts, or perhaps our attackers were quite stealthy. Regardless, I was completely unprepared when pain worse than any I had suffered on the battlefield gripped me in its talons. An arrow pierced my lower back. My left leg gave out, and I pitched forward onto my knees.

Seeing me fall, and the reason, Nieva screamed and rushed to my side. As she did, I heard hoofbeats approaching at a gallop. Struggling to get up and draw my long knife, I pushed Nieva away rather roughly, just in time for the horseman's club to miss her head. It did not miss mine, however. I glimpsed it out of the corner of my eye as it met the right side of my face. The force of the blow knocked me senseless to the ground. I never saw the ground coming up to meet me, nor did I feel my head crash into it.

It was Nieva's cries of pain and anguish that brought me back to my senses. As my eyes cleared, the scene I saw before me chilled my heart. One bandit had Nieva's arms pinned to the ground and was brutally raping her, the other stood and watched, grinning while waiting his turn.

The bundle I normally carried on my back lay open on the ground at his feet. He bent and picked up the bundle, separating the wrapping from the Holy Lance. He clutched the wrapping covetously to his chest. He then looked at the lance, shrugged, and broke it over his knee. He then fed one half into the remains of our cook fire. Seeing him destroy the lance brought me fully alert, and hearing Nieva's screams drove me to action.

They must have counted me dead already, as I still had my head, and they ignored me as I gathered my strength and prepared for the pain I knew I would suffer when I moved.

In one motion, I rolled to my side—the pain in my head and back was excruciating—drew my short knife and threw it at the beast raping Nieva. My aim was true, and it struck home, slipping between his ribs on his left side.

His howl of pain was satisfying, but even more so was Nieva's reaction. When the beast freed her arm by reaching for the knife, she grabbed it before he could, yanked it from the wound, and screamed, "You son of a whore!" as she drove it into the side of his neck.

I saw this out of the corner of my eye as I struggled to rise on my one working leg. To my horror, I also saw the rapist smash Nieva's head against the hard ground with his last breath. Knowing I had but one chance, I lunged for the other bandit with my long knife. Glimpsing my motion, he spun and thrust with the only weapon in his hand, the remains of the Lance of Longinus, just as I thrust with my knife.

My aim again was true, and my knife slid in below his jaw up to the hilt. His aim was equally good, though. His thrust drove the broken and jagged wood of the lance straight into my chest. We both stumbled backwards from the impact, and I tripped and fell backwards. The last image I saw before tumbling backwards into the ravine will be forever burned in my mind.

Nieva lay with eyes wide open, but clearly dead, beneath the equally dead rapist, covered in his blood. The other bandit spewed his lifeblood into the dirt, and the fire flared as it consumed half of the most holy relic in all of Christendom.

Chapter 49

Syria, Autumn 1188 A.D.

I know not how long I lay there. Months, I suspect. You, my clever reader, know I did not die that day. You might think the bandit did not deliver a deathblow, only grazing me with the lance handle. I admit, I thought the same when, to my surprise, I awoke lying among the rocks on the ravine's slope. I was very confused when I first came to my sense, but slowly my mind cleared and the horrible memory of how I came to be there came flooding back.

When the lance pierced my chest and I fell backwards over the ravine's edge into space, I had no doubt that I was dying. And I knew I wanted to. My love and our child that she carried lay dead beneath a foul beast of a man. The ancient and holy artifact I had been entrusted with, the lance that had pierced Our Beloved Lord while hanging on the cross, was all but destroyed. I knew I would die, and I welcomed it. I had no wish to survive, for all reasons to go on living were gone.

Regaining my memory brought with it a new confusion and many questions. Beyond being alive, other aspects of my circumstances were very strange. The first sign that something very odd had happened, aside from the fact that I awoke at all, was the state of my body. Why was the fragment of the lance, which had slipped from my attacker's hands, not still piercing my chest? Why were my arms, legs, and even my skull not broken to pieces after my fall? And why was I not in excruciating pain?

Although dried blood caked my tunic and cloak, my wounds no longer bled. Stranger still was the fact that the arrow that had pierced my back and the lance that had penetrated my chest were no longer inside me. And, strangest of all, both my back and chest wounds were completely closed.

My hands found the scars from what should have been mortal wounds. They itched as scars do, but the pain I felt throughout my body was akin to the soreness one feels when awakening on the stony ground after a night's sleep.

I took stock of the condition of my body, noting that there were none of the broken bones I should have suffered from my fall. Instead of broken bones, I found knots beneath the skin. I had seen many similar bumps and ridges on the limbs of soldiers whose broken bones were not expertly set.

I also found what appeared to be animal bites, probably from scavengers, that were also fully healed. I felt no pain from any of these many healed wounds. Amazingly, I felt only stiffness from lying on the cold ground. And it was cold. The air had the distinct feeling of the oncoming winter. Given that it was high summer when the attack occurred, how could the weather have turned so cold? I did not understand why until I climbed the slope back up to our campsite.

As I rose, first to my knees, then onto unsteady legs, I found the remaining part of the lance, basically just the handle, lying by my side. The arrow, broken into pieces, lay beneath where I had lain.

The strangeness of the day made me wonder what else I would find at the top of the slope. I expected to find three dead bodies. The state of their putrefaction might give me a hint of how long I had been unconscious on the slope. But instead of decaying bodies, I found only the desiccated and dispersed remains of my beloved and our attackers. Scavengers had picked them apart, and all that remained were scattered bones and mummified skin. Seeing the condition of my beloved Nieva, I understood many weeks had passed between my demise and my reawakening. Weeks of lying insensate while deadly wounds miraculously healed.

It was miraculous but, to me, not incredible. In fact, I had witnessed the same my last day in Jerusalem. But, while Stewart had revived in only a few minutes, my resurrection—for I had been truly dead—had taken weeks.

Perhaps the fact that the arrow and the lance handle remained embedded in my body had greatly lengthened my recovery. Or perhaps being the handle of the lance and furthest removed from the tip, only a stray drop of holy blood had enchanted this wood.

My opinion on this has changed drastically over the years, but at the time, I could only drop to my knees and pray. I was truly born again, and for this I thanked God, but I could not help also asking Him, "Why?"

I could tell as many tales about my journey home as I have told you so far. But I fear the Great Mortality that is consuming my homeland and the extent of Europe will cut my time on this Earth too short to relate even a tenth part of the trials I overcame during my long journey home. Instead, I will relate only what I learned and came to suspect during those long eleven years that culminated with meeting the she-devil who pursued me during my wanderings.

My failure to protect my young family cast me into a state of deep melancholy. I knew my shattered dreams of domestic bliss were in complete contrast to the realities of the brutal world around me. I also realized that my age and small stature would mark me as a target for the lawless and Godless.

Before leaving the scene of death our campsite had become, I buried what remained of my beautiful Nieva, and scattered the bones of the dead bandits. Of my unborn child, there was no evidence. Even so, I said prayers for both. The campfire that had flared so brightly when fed by Our Lord's lance was long dead, of course, and the ashes that had once carried the blood of Christ which had revived Stewart had long since been blown away on the wind.

Looking about for any other remnants of my prior life, my eye fell upon a spot of white caught in the sparse branches of a desert bush half-way down the ravine. Memories of how the bandit had clutched the linen cloth that had wrapped the lance, while ignoring the real prize—the lance—made me scrambled down the slope to recover it. Why did he value the simple cloth more than the relic that I held, broken, in my hand?

For the first time since I had taken it into my hands, I looked closely at the cloth itself. I had never unwrapped it the entire time it was in my care. I was surprised to find that the wrapping was only a hand span across, yet it was four or more paces long. Rather than a sheet, it was actually a ribbon of cloth.

The ribbon's linen threads were finely woven in a herringbone pattern. Three sides were expertly hemmed, while the other was more roughly closed, as if it had been rent from a larger piece, then repaired. Along its length were several rows of markings coloring the linen a light brown. The markings were not of an alphabet or language with which I was familiar, and still am not to this day. In my travels across the wide world, I have never encountered other symbols like those on the cloth—except once, and that was but a single mark cast in gold.

I folded the cloth over the remains of the lance and wrapped the remaining length around it from one end to the other, making a bundle for my back. Gathering up the knives and the bandits' bow and arrows which still lay about, and with a last, longing gaze at the mound of stones over Nieva's grave, I set off once again, heading north.

PART VIII

Doubt
Present Day

Or perhaps being the handle of the lance and furthest removed from the tip, only a stray drop of holy blood had enchanted this wood.

My opinion of this has changed drastically over the years, but at the time, I could only drop to my knees and pray. I was truly born again, and for this I thanked God, but I could not help also asking Him, "Why?"

— Codex Incognito

Doubt
Present Day

295

Chapter 50

The Enclave, Late Summer

Dan and John sat in silence for several minutes after Dan finished reading his latest translation.

Finally, John spoke, a rasp in his voice. "That's quite the story, if it's true."

"If it's true? How can you doubt it?" Dan felt offended by John's suggestion. When he had translated the last passage, and each time he had read it since, he felt an overwhelming sense of wonder.

John, though clearly affected by the telling, sounded skeptical of the tale itself. "Well, it is pretty fantastic."

Dan did not appreciate John's condescending tone, and his voice clearly showed his annoyance. "It's not fantastic, it's miraculous! Clearly, this document is itself proof of the power of Holy Blood, and the divinity of Christ. It validates all of the Church's teachings!"

Alarmed by Dan's zealous reaction, John tried to inject some humor. "Whoa there, Father. Let's not get ahead of ourselves. Even if this story is true, it just speaks to the power of the lance, doesn't it?"

Dan was a little embarrassed by his outburst, but still adamant. His voice rose almost to a whine. "The Grand Master explained the source of the lance's power. It was infused with Christ's own holy blood while he hung on the cross."

"That's the explanation the author attributes to some supposed Templar Grand Master…"

"Gerard de Ridefort was the Grand Master when Jerusalem was lost to Saladin," Dan interrupted.

John was undeterred. "OK, so he got that part right, but it still doesn't prove that de Ridefort's explanation was accurate." Dan huffed derisively, but John continued before he could interrupt him again. "Set your blind faith aside for a moment, please."

Dan crossed his arms in defiance, but remained silent as John continued. "What evidence is there that any part of this tale is true?"

Something in John's attitude told Dan he was being goaded, which broke through his enthralled enthusiasm. He took a deep breath and gathered his arguments.

When he spoke, his voice was even, and his words measured. "We know the writer's style is consistent with the twelfth century timeframe." John nodded for Dan to continue. "But the manuscript itself is at least a hundred years younger."

"A hundred and fifty, at least."

Dan nodded. "OK, even better."

John shook his head and interrupted. "The writer's style doesn't prove his age. We have no idea how or where he learned those languages."

Dan was undeterred despite John's continued objections. "The simplest answer is that he learned them—all of them—from native speakers in the late twelfth century, just as he relates in his story. That makes more sense than some unknown teacher in some unknown school of ancient writing styles."

"You learned these ancient styles from someone, right? And they were only a century and a half out of date when written."

Dan wasn't convinced, but he had to consider John's objections, and so he became a little more thoughtful as John continued, "Lots of 'schools' teach old techniques. The Church itself maintains traditions that are much older than just a hundred and fifty years."

Dan had to admit the truth of what John said, though reluctantly. But John surprised him when he seemed to take Dan's side.

"Still, your theory is a good working hypothesis. The next question is, how do we prove it? Until we can, and even more so *if* we can, what we have learned must remain a secret."

Being a priest, Dan was used to keeping secrets, so John's admonition didn't strike him as odd. But, if they could prove beyond a doubt that Christ's blood could raise the dead, it could change the world. There would always be doubters, of course, but many whose faith had faltered, and many who had never known Christ could be brought into the fold.

"There is another equally valid hypothesis," John said. "The lance itself, or the wood it was carved from, could be the mechanism of this 'miracle.'" Dan started to protest, but John spoke over him, "If we believe the lance resurrected the two brothers in your story, it is quite possible that it resurrected another person eleven centuries before."

With the fire of faith burning in his eyes, Dan asked John, "So, what would you consider irrefutable proof?"

The change in Dan's countenance was obvious. John had lit a fire that, if controlled, could illuminate this and the Enclave's other deep mysteries. If left to rage uncontrolled, though, it would surely consume them both, along with the entire centuries-old Enclave. The implications were dangerous, but the die was cast. John's new job was tempering and focusing Dan's enthusiasm.

"First, finish the translation and see what other 'wonders' it claims." Dan nodded his agreement as John continued, "I have to travel again for a while. When I get back, we can discuss this further. But again, I ask you to keep your findings between us, at least for now. Agreed?"

Dan nodded, but with a distant look in his eye. He was already planning his next round of research.

Chapter 51

The Enclave, Autumn

*A*fter that fateful day when my world changed, I examined every curve of grain, every fiber, every pore of the shaft that both killed and restored me. I knew for certain that there was not even a single drop or splash of blood not my own on it. It was but the handle, after all. I could draw but one conclusion, namely that Our Lord's blood had played no part in my resurrection.

That left only the lance. Could it simply be that? Was it simply the wood itself that imparted this strange power to me? Was this branch, straight and true with a grain unrecognizable to me, the source of such fearsome power? These thoughts led me to a terrible conclusion. If this mysterious shaft could raise me, and Stewart before me, up from death, could it not have also raised from the dead man who hung on the cross on Golgotha? Could The Resurrection be not the cause of the lance's power, but rather its effect? Did it, in fact, expose as a lie the singular article of faith

*that has caused so much strife and suffering for
so many centuries? Did it, in fact, belie the
divinity of Jesus of Nazareth?*

Father Dan put down his pen and bowed his head in prayer. He had gone over his translation three times, hoping to find an error or another way to interpret what was written. But it always came out the same.

"Father, are you testing me? How could someone blessed by Our Lord Jesus himself come to doubt Your Son? Father, I'm so confused. I want so much to follow this thread, to understand this mystery fully. But I'm afraid of what I may find. I fear it will test my faith beyond its breaking point."

Without an answer forthcoming, Dan sat back in his chair, ran his hands through his hair, and stretched. John had posed this same conclusion as possible. Was the healing and resurrective powers of Christ's blood responsible for the miracles this chronicle reported, or did the power live in the lance itself? Could he even be believe this tale? All the forensic evidence pointed to it being authentic, but was it one of miracles, or magic, or something else? Could Liam and John be correct? Dan felt the rock of his faith crumbling even as waves of doubt eroded its foundation further. He sighed heavily and rose to seek the clarity of the cool night air.

As he walked the calming streets and fields of the Enclave, he recognized that something about John had been bothering him, plucking at the back of his mind. He thought back through their meetings, especially the ones when Dan had read to him what he had translated. On several occasions, something about the way John reacted to Dan's translation just didn't seem right.

Nothing about this tale caught him off guard. It affected him. Dan could see the flush in his cheeks and the tears in his eyes, but nothing ever seemed to shock or even surprise him. It was as if he already knew the story. It was as if…

Dan stopped dead in his tracks and stood frozen in place like a man struck blind. It wasn't possible, was it? Dan didn't know, but he knew how to find out.

Recovering from his shocked paralysis and with a renewed, but different purpose, Dan practically ran back to the library and down into the Vault. Instead of resuming his examination of the codex, he strode straight to the desktop PC in the corner. He thought for a moment, planning his search strategy, then hunched over the keyboard and let his fingers fly.

PART IX

Mariel
1189 – 1199 A.D.

After he had expelled the man, the LORD God placed winged angels at the eastern end of the garden of Eden, along with a fiery, turning sword, to prevent access to the tree of life.

— Genesis 3:24

Chapter 52

Europe, 1189-1199 A.D.

My trek home took over ten long years, several of those years learning more lessons in stealth and killing than I can recount. Though the route was circuitous with many interruptions and adventures along the way, always, I trudged toward England, intending to fulfill my vow to Stewart.

During my journey home, I worked in fields and towns, shared many meals, and many beds. The years and the miles were hard. Hard on my body, and harder on my soul. But I learned many useful skills as an assistant to many masters. Architecture and engineering, apothecary and alchemy, even anatomy and astrology. When not working, I sought out poets and artists, for after a first life of dealing out death, I was drawn to those who instead celebrated life.

I occasionally heard of or felt the presence of pursuers, searchers who sought the Templar Ghost, or simply the traveler with the mysterious bundle. Often, simply listening to loosened tongues in taverns, or through the whispered warnings of the many friends I made along the way, I learned of plots to find and capture me so I that torture might reveal wherever I had hidden my burden at that stop. When I arrived back in Christian lands, and was able, again, to dress, act, and speak as my true self, I thought I would be safe, but still the she-devil's minions pursued me. They usually came in twos or threes, and always I let one live long enough to answer my questions.

Where and when did they learn of me? What did they know of my burden? How long had they been searching? How many others were seeking me?

The answers, often blurted out simply to end the suffering I was imparting and given knowing that they would be their last words on Earth, followed a pattern that was worrisome. In each case, their pursuit began closer behind me than the last, recruited by a beauty with raven-black hair. Moira was closing in.

During my journey, I learned of the many changes that had happened while I was in the Levant. The fall of Jerusalem shocked both the Church and the kingdoms of men. The pope called for a great crusade, and the three greatest noble houses of Europe responded.

A few years after Yusef and I slipped out of Jerusalem, Philip II, *Phillipe Augustus*, of France, Richard I, *Coeur de Lion*, of England, and the German, Frederick Barbarossa, all took the cross, attempting to recapture the city. Though they reclaimed Acre, which had fallen shortly after Jerusalem, they lost their will to continue and turned back. Barbarossa's army, devastated by disease and desertion, even turned back before reaching the Holy Land. Philippe, having bankrupted his country, returned to France after only a few months, where he tried to recoup his losses by seizing the Pope himself and holding him hostage in Avignon.

Richard remained in The Levant long enough to recapture some of the towns, forts, and cities that the Ayyubids had taken, but he did not have the men or the stomach for the long siege that would have been required to drive Saladin's forces out of Jerusalem. So, despite the exhortations of the Pope, the combined strength and wealth of the three greatest kingdoms in Christendom, and the suffering and death of tens of thousands of men, women, and children stretching back over a century, our struggles were all for naught. How Saladin must have laughed in his palace.

Many times, in addition to those on a mission to capture me, I encountered bandits as I wandered across Europe. Other times, soldiers waylaid me, usually Christians returning from Crusade. Although I dispatched all those who set upon me, I was often wounded. Many of those wounds should have been fatal. They all healed extremely fast, however, and the scars they left faded, though none left me completely.

I slowly came to realize another strangeness about my condition, besides my amazing, perhaps even miraculous, healing ability. Although I was nearly thirty years of age before I again saw the green fields of England, I arrived there without a single gray hair on head or beard. My joints did not ache in the morning, or even after a full day working in fields. None of the changes that would normally overtake a body during those eleven years of labor and travel afflicted mine.

I came to realize that I was, in fact, not aging at all. My hair, face, and body remained that of a ripe seventeen-year-old.

The only explanation, of course, was that the Lance had done more than just restore my life, heal my wounds, and repair my broken bones. It had imparted to me some form of agelessness, the power to survive almost any injury, even those imposed by Father Time himself. I imagine if someone severs my head from my body, or I am immolated and reduced to ash, that I will finally find out what lies beyond this hard life. Until such happens, however, it appears I am immortal.

Rather than bringing me joy or deepening my faith, this power has had the opposite effect. I know I do not deserve such a gift. It came to me purely by chance, since if my legs had been stronger, or the bandit slower, I would have killed him straightaway, then I would have died a slow, festering death from the arrow that pierced my back.

Instead of these powers filling me with awe, they instilled in me a feeling of deepening guilt for undeservedly surviving torment after torment. The guilt drove me into the depths of depravity. I sought out the whores in every town I visited. I stole from the drunken and the weak. And, although I swear I never did murder, I did not hesitate to dispatch an opponent when angry words turned to blades. I did this gladly, even when I deserved the curses that were thrown at me.

My self-hatred brought clarity to my mind, however. If it made me unbreakable and perhaps even immortal through pure chance, how could the lance be truly holy? I even questioned the mechanism of my transformation.

After that fateful day when my world changed, I examined every curve of grain, every fiber, every pore of the shaft that both killed and restored me. I knew for certain that there was not even a single drop or splash of blood, not my own, on it. It was but the handle, after all. I could draw but one conclusion, namely that Our Lord's blood had played no part in my resurrection.

That left only the lance. Could it simply be that? Was it simply the wood itself that imparted this strange power to me? Was this branch, straight and true with a grain unrecognizable to me, the source of such fearsome power? These thoughts led me to a terrible conclusion. If this mysterious shaft could raise me, and Stewart before me, up from death, could it not have also raised from the dead man who hung on the cross on Golgotha? Could The Resurrection be not the cause of the lance's power, but rather its effect? Did it, in fact, expose as a lie the singular article of faith that has caused so much strife and suffering for so many centuries? Did it, in fact, belie the divinity of Jesus of Nazareth?

Chapter 53

France, Autumn 1199 A.D.

As I made my way across Christian lands, I often visited Templar commanderies and castles, not as a Brother, since Grand Master de Ridefort had freed from my vows, but as a traveling merchant or pilgrim. I admit that when short of funds, I would write out a *cheque* in the Templars' code that they used to hold and transfer wealth. When a pilgrim set out on their pilgrimage, they could deposit a portion of their wealth with the Templars close to their home, then recover its equivalent upon arrival. This way, they traveled humbly and were less of a target for the many marauders on their route. Since, through my stealthy activities, I had learned the nature of this code, I forged many a document that kept me fed and sleeping in warm beds—usually not alone.

I felt justified in these thefts as my fee for keeping their most precious treasure hidden. It was not long, however, before I thought of my Burden, not as theirs but as my own. By comparison, the coin I stole from the Templars' vast treasuries was but a drop in the ocean against the theft of the *Holy* Lance itself. My soul had become debauched and hollow.

I repaid my debt in kind, however. Whenever I took lodging with the Templars, I made a show of practicing the forms of solo combat I had learned and developed myself where the brothers could observe. Invariably, this led to questions and often challenges to my prowess. After I had bested all challengers with blunted weapons, the local weapons master usually sought my instruction. In this way, I spread my methods of stealth, secrecy, and the *attack sinister* throughout the Templar holdings—methods that stood them well in the betrayal and downfall that was to come.

My belief in the lance's holiness was shattered, so I sought explanations for its powers among the purveyors of potions and those who claimed they had secret knowledge of the mechanism of death and resurrection. All but one of these were surely charlatans who knew less about immortality than I. There was one who did impress me, however. He was an old Jew living a hermit's life on the coast of France.

My intention, when I arrived in Havre, was to, at last, cross the narrow sea to England. While buying provisions for the crossing, trade goods for my journey home, and gifts for Mother and Cecelia, I had the most interesting encounter.

An old man, Jewish by his look and speech, tried to buy peaches from a stall in the market next to where I was haggling over a basket of apples.

"Get your Jewish ass out of my place," the merchant said. "Your copper is tainted."

The merchant tried to strike the old man's hand to knock his meager coins flying, but he snatched his hand back and muttered, "Steffan, *yimakh shemo*," from under the hood of his cloak. He turned and shuffled away.

Casually adding a sack of peaches to my apples, I paid and strode nonchalantly down the aisle between stalls, keeping an eye on the old man. I gradually quickened my pace until I drew abreast of him.

"His name will surely be erased from the memories of his progeny," I said in Hebrew as I held out the sack of peaches.

Without breaking stride, he turned his head and his sad eyes looked me up and down.

"You are not of the tribe of Israel," he continued in Hebrew.

I shook my head. "No, but I counted many among your kin as my friends once."

This brought him up short, and he turned to face me fully. I still held the sack of peaches out to him. He looked me up and down again, then said, "Your accent places you from Jerusalem, but your kind have not held the Holy City since before you were old enough to fight for it, boy."

I chuckled. "I'm older than I appear. I spent many years battling our mutual nemesis, and just as many trying to get home." He raised an eyebrow at that and I continued, "Take the peaches. They are probably sweeter than those you were refused by…what was his name again? I seem to have forgotten."

A wry smile curled his lips, and he snatched the sack from my hand with a speed that impressed me. My own raised eyebrow told him so.

"I cursed the bastard you bought these from," he shook the sack, "yesterday." We both laughed, but then he said, "Why extend me this kindness? Or do you seek my last coppers?"

I shook my head. "I have no need for your French coins."

"Ah, English then," he said in my native tongue.

"Aye." I nodded. "I sail with the tide tomorrow."

He turned and continued walking, but looked back over his shoulder. "Come, I'll share my newfound bounty with you." He shrugged. "It is the least way to repay you."

I served as his proxy as we made our way through the market, buying a wineskin here and a clutch of eggs there, always with him looking at another merchant's wares while I paid. By the time we passed out of the market, we both carried heavy packs.

His stride became longer and brisker as we walked the streets and passed through the city gate. When we were clear of the crowds and any unintended listeners, he spoke.

"I am curious how you have maintained your youth, despite your obvious military experience."

"My obvious military experience? Is my past written so clearly on my bearing?"

"Everyone's past is written on their bearing," he said. "Yours reminds me of the proud, yet humble, knights I encountered during my own stay in Jerusalem."

I nodded at this admission, which confirmed my own suspicions. "I thought so. You matched your accent to my own," I said. But aware that the conversation was approaching a very dangerous topic, I shrugged and said, "I have lived a hard but lucky life."

As he had before, he stopped and turned to face me. "Let us not lie to each other," he said, switching back to Hebrew. "Your life has been hard, true—as has been mine. But lucky? I think not."

I frowned, thinking of all that I had lost—Cece, Stewart, the Brotherhood, my Nieva, and our child. I nodded.

"I have lost much, and I hope to regain some," I responded in Hebrew. Then switching to Arabic, "I have found many things, as well." Then in French, "Some are useful." I switched to Italian. "Some are less so." Finally, I finished in English, "And some are very dangerous."

The old man actually smiled, then turned and continued along the path leading up into the hills overlooking the coast.

He responded in Greek. "Knowledge is always useful, and very often dangerous." We both fell silent for a few heartbeats, then he continued. "I had a very curious visitor yesterday."

He glanced sidelong at me, but I just raised a questioning eyebrow.

"*She* came with two guards, but she walked alone into my hovel."

At that point, we crested the trail, and he pointed to a lean-to shack built against the hillside. It appeared to be made entirely of pieces of driftwood, hardened by saltwater, bleached by the sun, and scoured by sand. Its gray blended in with the rocky hillside as if it had grown there. But to my experienced eye, it was only a façade.

"I thought we were not telling lies," I said, a touch of chiding in my voice.

"Not everyone is as…understanding as you seem to be."

"How far back does the cave go?"

He shrugged nonchalantly. "A few feet? Or all the way to Provence? Who can say?"

At that moment, the sun broke through the overcast sky and he drew back his hood so his face was fully illuminated. What I had taken for gray in his beard and hair was simply dirt and dried mud, and what looked to be deep wrinkles in his face were, in fact, streaks where sweat and perhaps tears had carved tracks through the dirt of his face. This *old man* was actually young enough to be my brother.

He turned his back to the sun, and his wild, backlit hair formed a halo around his head. Awed by the sight, I had the almost overwhelming urge to drop to my knees at his feet. He broke the spell, however, when he laughed.

"Close your mouth, young man, or the flies will bite your tongue."

He turned and walked to his door. I followed on shaking legs. Once inside, he poured wine into a wooden cup and bade me sit at his small table. Then he drew a peach from his sack, whispered over it, and tossed it to me. It was ripe and sweet, and I wiped the juice that ran into my beard with the back of my sleeve.

Finding my voice at last, I said, "Tell me about this visitor, this woman."

He produced a small knife from a hidden pocket of his robe and sliced off sections of the fruit.

"She was quite beautiful," he said around a mouthful. He let the juice trickle into his filthy beard without seeming to notice. "Stunning, actually."

My heart sank. "Black hair?" He nodded. "A medallion of a strange symbol worn around her neck?"

Again, he nodded, but this time said, "Strange to you, perhaps." I looked at him questioningly, but he shook his head slightly and remained silent.

Resigned to another fight, but this time with the *jinn* or *anaha shaytan* herself, I muttered, "Moira."

Strangely, the Jew smiled. "Is that what she calls herself now?"

I spread my hands as if to say, "Are you going to tell me?" but he shoved another piece of peach into his mouth.

Chewing slowly, he said, "She sought information from me. About *you*, I suspect." I nodded. "She wants the burden you have carried since our holy city fell to the Ayyubid horde." He stopped chewing and grabbed my arm just below the elbow. His grip was powerful. "You must not allow her to obtain it." I remained stoic as his grip tightened even more. "I tell you, the fate of Man rests on your shoulders. Your Burden is far more powerful than you think."

My mind whirled. How could this hermit, living in a shack and cave on the coast of France, know anything about the Lance? A relic that had lain under the Temple of Solomon for over a thousand years. Tentatively, I spoke.

"I know she could raise an invincible army of the undead—"

He shook his head violently and squeezed my arm even harder.

"No! Its power goes far beyond raising the dead."

There. He said it. He possessed knowledge that I thought no one but myself knew. And more, apparently.

His eyes bored into mine. "Your Burden could enslave the whole of humanity to a race of beings that were driven from the Earth millennia ago."

He released my arm, sat back, and popped another peach slice into his mouth. I sat silently, trying to absorb his words. What, exactly, had he revealed? Not much, in truth. It could all be a lie, like the *faux* wrinkles and driftwood shack. Or his warning could be dire. The next few moments would be telling.

"What did you tell her?" I asked, trying to keep any emotion out of my voice.

He shrugged, as he seemed to do when giving me an answer that wasn't an answer.

"I had not met you yet. What could I tell her?"

"And if she comes back?"

He shook his head. "She won't. That I'm sure of." He picked up another peach slice but paused with it halfway to his mouth. "Which means this place," he spread his arms, "would make a perfect hiding place for your Burden."

I stood swiftly with my dagger in my hand. The Jew looked disappointed, but then nodded.

"It was worth a try," he said with a wry smile. "Good luck on your journey, Young Man, but beware. Whether or not you believe my warning, Mariel is probably lying in wait for you at this moment."

'Mariel?' I wondered, but I held my tongue and slowly backed out of the hovel. I took his immediate warning to heart, however, and eschewed the beaten path back to the town. Instead, I headed overland toward the cave where I had hidden the Lance.

Chapter 54

France, Autumn 1199 A.D.

I didn't need to go back to my lodgings in Havre. There was nothing there that I couldn't do without. I knew the inn was probably being watched, if not by Moira herself, at least by her minions. It was those guards that I sought. Perhaps I simply wanted an end to the eternal chase. Perhaps I thought this *jinn* could end the purgatory I found myself in. I know not. All I know is I felt compelled to meet my pursuer face-to-face, and eliminating those who stood between us was the first place to start.

The two who watched the inn were easily spotted and dealt with. One simply stood in a shadowed doorway across the street. The other waited in an alley further up the street. I took him first. A hand across his mouth and a knife across his throat sent him silently to Hell.

The other was not so simple. I had to lure him from the doorway into the open. This I did by simply walking, whistling, down the street. Like a bull, he came charging from his hiding place with sword raised, ready to lop off my head. Instead, using a trick Yusef taught me, I flipped the loose cloak I wore spinning into the air. It flattened into a wall of coarse cloth that blocked my assailant's vision, then wrapped around his face and head.

I moved with the cloak, ducking under my enemy's wild, blind swing and slashed deeply into the back of his left thigh, cutting his hamstring. As his leg collapsed and he fell sideways, I followed him down with my knee on his back. He dropped his sword from his right hand and reached for a knife at his belt, but as he drew it forth, I pinned his wrist to the ground with my ever-faithful Luisa. To his credit, my attacker never howled in pain, but instead let out only a whimper.

With my left hand, I placed the point of a stiletto against his neck and whispered in his ear, "Where can I find your Mistress?"

The only response I received was a grunt. I switched to Arabic. "Tell me where the *anaha shaytan* is, and I'll let you bind your wounds." This was a hollow promise, as blood spurted from the severed vessel in his leg, and he knew it.

"My life was forfeit the moment I was sold to her," he replied. "You cannot kill her, you know. She is indeed a devil sent by *Alshaytan* himself."

"Where?" I asked again.

He shrugged and his voice grew faint as his lifeblood poured out into the street. "She will find *you*."

"I'm sure she will," I muttered as I drove my blade upwards through the sinews in his neck into the joint where his spine met his skull. I felt him stiffen, then go limp.

I made quite the scene as I burst through the inn's door into its tavern, covered in blood, with both daggers drawn. But it was a time for speed, not stealth. I flew up the stairs to my room in the back of the second floor, a tiny rectangle with a door at one end, a window at the other, and a narrow cot against the side wall. I intended only to grab my travel bag and leave through the room's window, but before I could do even that much of my plan, the door burst open behind me. I fell into a fighting stance automatically as a figure stepped lightly into the room, her back against the wall.

Moira faced me with a slight smile on her features. Even in the dim light cast by the night's half-moon, her beauty was manifest, and I admit a small gasp escaped my lips. This broadened her smile, though her black eyes were unreadable in the shadow of her long, loose hair.

"You know what I want," she murmured, barely above a whisper. Her voice was a siren's call. "And I have what you want."

She spoke in a husky tone as she ran a hand across her breasts and undid the clasp of her cloak. It fell from her shoulders to reveal a courtesan's dress tightly encasing the body of a Greek goddess.

"A simple trade is all I propose. No need for—"

She moved like the wind, impossibly nimble yet deadly. A feinting step to her left to give momentum to her spinning kick that would certainly have rendered me senseless had it struck my temple. After my initial gasp, however, I had closed my ears to her taunt and focused entirely on her body. Not lustily, as she intended, but instead watching the minutest shifts in the muscles visible beneath her sheer garment. She moved with such speed that I could not avoid her attack altogether. But the blow she struck with the side of her foot was but a glancing one.

Diving sideways, I rolled along the length of the bed, then back to my feet. Moira continued her spin, so we ended up in exchanged positions, her back now to the window, and mine to the door. I probably could have made a momentary escape, but that would have simply prolonged the chase which I wanted so desperately to end. So, I chose instead to stay and end, one way or another, our *danse de la mort* that had taken us across the whole of Europe.

Moira's eyes flared red, like a wolf's at the edge of a campfire's glow, and I read in the tightening of her tendons that another attack was coming within the next beat of my pounding heart.

"Mariel," I said, remembering the old Jew's name for her.

Her surprise gave me the momentary pause that I needed to flick Luisa from my right hand straight to her beautiful face.

Faster than my eye could follow, she snatched Luisa from the air, a mere finger's breadth from her open mouth. I did not wait for Luisa to do her job, however, as I was moving even as the blade flipped over on her mission to deliver death.

Anticipating Moira's impossibly fast grab and the instinctive blink of her eyes gave me the opening I needed to plunge the stiletto in my left hand into the side of her neck.

My satisfaction at the fountain of blood that drenched me and the room's low ceiling as Moira stumbled and fell onto the bed was only momentary, however. A searing pain exploded in the right side of my chest, and I looked down to see Luisa buried up to her hilt between my ribs.

"We join each other in death," Moira croaked. She made no attempt to stanch the blood that by now was merely pulsing with the last of her life. "But I will rise again in the morning to find you clutching in death the prize that I seek."

The pain was excruciating as I drew Luisa, scraping my rib bones, out of my chest. Blood dribbled from my mouth as I said, "You should study your target more carefully." But the light had already faded from her black-as-night eyes.

The pain was severe, but I had lived, and died, through worse. Already, I felt the rush of heat that accompanied the miraculous power of healing the Lance bestowed upon me. I knew I would not die that night, or at least not until I was ensconced in the hold of the Templar ship I had hired for the crossing to England.

Lifting the loose floorboard where I had secreted the Lance in its wrapping and slinging it across my back, I hung from the windowsill and dropped to the ground.

PART X

Reckonings
1307 A.D.

I have documented the events of my life thus far as recent events have shaken my comfortable faith in the continuation of my long life. Indeed, I fear the world, or at least a large portion of it, is dying and the End of Days may be upon us. In the past year, the population of my fair England has diminished by nearly two in three. A pestilence lays over the land that strikes men, women, and children, regardless of the height nor depth of their station nor of their piety. Entire villages stand empty. Fields of wheat, barley, and beans all lay fallow and untended. Cattle wander feral through the land, and the lords of those lands, those few who remain alive, have no bound serfs to collect and husband them.

Even I, who has survived most of two centuries, was taken to Death's door, once again, by this plague, this Great Mortality. Either my blessing, which is also my curse, kept me from knocking or, more likely, Death himself was busy elsewhere. In either case, I awoke in my sickbed, which I had fouled, a stinking, sweating near-corpse. The buboes that are the hallmark of this disease subsided, leaving behind black scars that mark me as a survivor. Reports that have come through my network of spies tell me these scars, which fade slowly, are believed to be either the blessed fingerprints of God Almighty or as the mark of Cain, depending on local superstition. I can tell you, rather, that they are simply the flesh proudly proclaiming victory over this most vile pestilence.

Thus, you know the circumstances in which this codex has been so hastily written. You know the When, Where, and How of it, but you have yet to learn the Why, the reason I have put quill and ink to the finest vellum and written this history in the most obscure way I can imagine.

Bending over the vellum, trying to decide in what language I should commit these words, The Fever again overtook me and I fell, senseless, into another delirious dream.

In this fever dream, I met again companions of mine with whom I have not conversed for many years. Each spoke in his own tongue, but the words that came from their mouths were gibberish spoken in a halting stutter. As I strained to make out what each was saying, their faces blurred and merged into a single countenance. Their mouths, still speaking nonsense in their own tongues, now complemented each other, filling the gaps and combining into a single voice, as their faces had. It was the face and voice of a man I had once thought of as my brother, though we were born worlds apart and had, at different times, each called the other Master.

His voice spoke to me clearly in his native Arabic, "Your story is too precious for any but the most enlightened, and too dangerous to far too many. Use my voice to tell it, and I will keep its secrets until the one with the proper talents is ready to hear it."

My purpose is simple, yet contradictory. I write to preserve and protect, yet also to reveal to the worthy, a secret. A secret that could, and perhaps should someday, if revealed, change forever the course of humanity on this Earth. Whether that change is for good or ill will depend entirely on the enlightened one who decodes and reads this missive. Will they use the secret to gain power over the rest of humanity, as this secret could certainly facilitate? Or will they use it to benefit all the people across this wide world? This knowledge and the physical manifestation of it can accomplish either of those goals. Or, as I so fervently hope, will the reader pledge to keep the secret hidden and safe, as I have these many decades?

This illness has shaken my complacent belief in my immortality. I no longer believe in that false and unearned blessed-curse. I return to the understanding, as all others of humanity come to realize, that my time on the Earth is finite, and that someday I may well have to answer for my earthbound failings.

Until then, I present my story, written, not as a memoir, but as a history, a travelogue of sorts. It is, fundamentally, a test. A test of erudition, a test of intuition, a test of forgotten knowledge. But most of all, a test of faith. You will be forever changed when you read it. That I promise.

— Codex Incognito

Chapter 55

England, Summer 1199 A.D.

I t was high summer when I, at last, stood again on the shore of my beloved England. Fully twelve years had passed since I set sail as a Templar recruit at seventeen years of age, and much had changed in England. King Henry was dead five years by then, succeeded his son Richard, known throughout Europe as *Coeur de Lion*, the Lionheart.

He was called thus because of his love of battle and his skill at leading men. But, in England, he was known simply as "Richard the Absent". After his coronation following the death of his father, Richard never again set foot on English soil. In his stead there was a parade of regents who ruled in his name. When Richard died while laying siege to yet another castle, the last Regent of England, and his successor as king, was his younger brother John.

John, known as "John Lackland" because his father, Henry, had left him no lands to rule himself, was the opposite of Richard in every respect. John ruled England with an iron fist, taxing rich and poor alike. His practice of elevating minor nobles and even commoners to positions of power as his sheriffs angered the barons and earls of the kingdom. They saw this as an infringement of their God-given right to rule their fiefdoms.

He also angered the poor common folk by confiscating and enclosing lands for his personal use that had traditionally been public hunting grounds. To be caught poaching, gathering berries, or even gathering brush or sticks for the hearth in one of these King's Forests meant the loss of a hand. As a result, the prices for meat, berries, herbs, and other fruits of the forest were soon beyond the reach of many common folk. The exorbitant prices lined the purses of John and his cronies, while the poor starved. Once could see many one-handed beggars on the streets.

Tales of John's brutal reign were whispered in every tavern in every town I visited as I crossed England. Only by eavesdropping on my tavern mates, though, could I hear these tales, for to speak openly about such grievances could mean prison, or worse. Sitting with my head bowed over my cup of ale or feigning sleep in a corner, I caught snatches of whispered conversations.

"The Lacklander took my cousin Johnny's hand."

"Hisself?"

"O'course not. The sheriff's men, drunkards all, accused 'im o' takin' a rabbit."

"A stinkin' rabbit?"

"Aye, it wouldn'a even fed his wife and six little ones. Then they botched the job, anyways. Didn't heat the axe properly, so the infection set in. Barber says he's like to lose the whole arm."

The two men fell silent, so I feigned sleep by letting out a snore, but they remained silent.

Even when the words were too quiet to be understood, the undercurrent of resentment was unmistakable. But no one spoke openly against the king for fear of being overheard by the local sheriff's spies.

Being a stranger in my homeland, without having yet recovered my English lilt, most folk viewed me with suspicion and treated coldly, though not unkindly. Afraid that I might be one of the King's men, no tavern owner or patron would chance offending me, but neither did they want to be seen as being friendly towards me, for fear of losing the trust of their neighbors.

Needless to say, I was disappointed that my return to England was not the joyous occasion I dreamt of for so many years. Thus, it was that I was on watch for trouble while making my way through one of the newly enclosed King's Forests in Nottinghamshire. If I had been more relaxed and simply enjoying a walk in the woods, I would not have carved a walking staff of my own height from a straight and strong beech sapling, and had a smith fit it with an iron foot.

Being on guard and thus armed, when bandits ambushed me on a game trail deep in the forest, I brought one of them down with a quick strike of my staff to the side of his head. I disarmed another before being surrounded by at least a dozen men armed with all manner of weapons. Swords, knives, long bows and quarterstaffs were held at the ready on all sides.

Curiously, rather than attacking at once, or even being angered by my surprising success with the staff, they laughed uproariously at their disabled companions. While they laughed and hurled jibes at the two who moaned over their injuries, I assessed my opponents.

They stood in postures that showed they were very practiced with their weapons of choice. A few wore chain mail under their jerkins, and the swords held at the ready were of a military type issued to sergeants and valued for their strong yet light manufacture. I knew from these few observations that I faced a band of well-trained and experienced warriors.

My mind and tongue were the only weapons that afforded any chance of escape.

"Heigh ho," I called when their laughter subsided. "I hope I knocked some sense into your friend for startling a humble traveler."

This repost resulted in more chuckling and even a few guffaws, but no one relaxed their readiness.

"It would take more than a goose egg on the head to enlighten that one. Perhaps next time he will give the humble traveler a wider berth."

The speaker, who was clearly the band's leader, stood directly in front of me on the path, feet spread with his body turned to present his left shoulder and arm while in his right hand he held a sword tipped upwards. His posture showed me he had learned to fight with a long shield on his left arm. Without that protection, though, his stance left him open to a feinting attack. I knew I could take him in the space of a heartbeat, but the remaining eleven would surely bring me down.

"I have to wonder why hardened warriors returned from their Crusade would live as outlaws in the King's Forest," I said, keeping my voice low and steady.

This brought cautious glances among those arrayed against me, and a shift in the weight of a bandit armed with a short sword to my left. A slight flick of my staff told him I was aware of his intention, though, and he stilled.

"What does a youth of your tender years know about warriors and crusades?" The leader said slowly, reassessing me as he spoke.

"Oh, I am not as young as I may appear." While I spoke, the anxious bandit to my left drew back his sword to strike and lunged toward me. Before his foot landed, however, my staff broke his arm with a resounding crack and my staff's tip snapped upwards under his chin. His mouth clamped shut with a second crack. The attacker dropped like a stone as blood and broken teeth leaked from his mouth.

Before anyone else could even catch their breath, I was back in my ready stance. I expected that the remainder of the band would fall on me in earnest, and I would find out if my powers of healing would resurrect me yet again. Instead, the leader lowered his sword and relaxed his stance, placing his left fist on his hip.

"Regardless of your age, you are clearly well-trained. We both know that my fellows and I have the advantage in numbers, but I fear several of us will fall before you do. I would rather not lose any more men unless it is well warranted."

Several bandits, now clearly less enthusiastic about our encounter, nodded their heads. "So, I would ask you, Humble Traveler, who you are and why you are here in the King's Forest."

As a show of good will, I also relaxed, though only from a position of attack to one of defense. My muscles remained ready, however, should another attack come.

"I am Liam of Rollingford, second son of Edwin of Rollingford, nephew of the Baron Geoffrey of Sowich."

Many of the bandits exchanged shocked looks, and their leader tensed again. It felt good, however, to use my own name after so many years and aliases, so I continued, "I am returning home after many years of battles and many long journeys."

The leader stood silently for a moment, weighing my words. "That is hard to believe, Traveler. Liam and Stewart of Rollingford left Sowich Castle a lifetime ago, as Templars."

"Aye, we left as Templars, and Stewart died as a Templar when Jerusalem fell. As the filthy Muslims beat on the door of our headquarters, I received a mission from Grand Master de Ridefort who released me from my vows."

I knew the whole truth could not be told, and would not be believed, so I continued with a lie. "I completed that mission and have walked across Europe to return home."

"You invoke the names of persons long dead. Baron Geoffrey of Sowich succumbed to the wasting disease before King Richard took the cross, and the Templars have had two Grand Masters since the fool de Ridefort lost all of the Holy Land to Saladin. Besides, I have never heard of a Templar knight being released from his vows."

"Well, you see, I was but a sergeant, serving at my brother Stewart's side. I may look young, but I assure you I carry the knowledge and scars of nearly thirty years."

Since I knew I would either walk from that wood with this leader's blessing, or die there, I fully relaxed my stance and drove my staff into the soft loam to the side of the trail.

"It is a three-day journey for a caravan to travel from Acre to Jerusalem. Two full days, from dawn to dark, for an army on forced march, and a full day by horseback." I saw heads nodding around me. "Pita is the Arabic word for bread, a scimitar is the Ayyubid cavalry's curved blade that beheads with a single stroke." More nods. "In Arabic, a stallion is called *hisan*, and a whore is *sharmuta*." Several grins appeared around the circle. "Ayyubid horsemen attack in groups of seven, which is a holy number to them."

I looked around the ring at each man in turn, before staring into the leader's eyes. "These things I could have learned from drunken soldiers' tales. But these," I shrugged off my cloak and slipped my shirt over my head, "I earned in battle."

Several gasps rose from the men as the dappled sun fell across the scars that crisscrossed my torso.

After a moment, the leader sheathed his sword, stepped forward, and extended his now empty right hand. "I am Robert of Locksley, known now simply as Robin of the Forest. I, too, was a sergeant and bowman, but in the army of King Richard, may God rest his soul."

I could hear murmurs of agreement around the ring. He extended his left arm to indicate his men. "We fought with Richard against Saladin in The Levant, so we know you have spoken true evidence of that godforsaken place."

I gripped his extended wrist as he gripped mine. "And now you hide in the forest as outlaws?" I asked.

Robert's expression darkened. "Like you, we returned home after many years only to find England ruled by a madman interested only in power and wealth. He steals from both rich and poor, so all but those he has heaped favors on suffer and hate him for it. Most of us were freemen when we left, and those who were not followed their liege lord. But when we returned, the Regent John had confiscated our lands, turned our families out of our homes, and enclosed for his own personal use the forests we hunted and the streams we fished."

Around the ring, men grumbled and muttered curses and epithets at the king. Robin nodded to his fellows and continued, "In order to live as free men, we must live as outlaws."

These men had real grievances against the king, but they were not mine to share, at least not yet. I was solely interested in safely leaving their midst and completing my journey home. When I told them this, Robert bid me to stay and join his band.

"We have need of one with your skills." When I shook my head, he continued. "And I warn you, there is nothing for you at Sowich or Rollingford."

"Why do you say that? I am the sole heir to the Rollingford estates. I am certain that my cousin Sir, ah that is, Baron Gerald, will restore my estates to me."

Robert sadly shook his head. "Of course, you would not know of that either."

"Know of what?"

"Sir Gerald of Sowich took the cross and also marched with Richard on crusade. Alas, he died in battle during the siege of Acre. When the news of his sons' death reached Geoffrey, he was already on his deathbed. With no apparent heir, since both you and Stewart took the Templars oath, the entire Barony reverted to the crown. John granted the estates to his sheriff Robert Enderhite. To win back your title and lands, you must prove your identity—and fight Sheriff Robert for it."

This last bit of news was shocking to me. I had assumed that my cousin Gerald, once he recognized me, would restore me to my ancestral estate. Perhaps that was simply a fantasy that had lodged itself in my soul, but something else weighed on my mind.

"If this is true, what has become of my mother and my cousin Cecelia?"

The bandits exchanged glances around the circle. Robin shuffled his feet before finally speaking.

"Your mother and Cecelia ran off to the Savior of the Fields convent. To protect themselves from Robert Enderhite's designs, they took their vows many years ago."

"The Sheriff's 'designs'?" I did not like Robin of the Forest implied by that phrase, and my voice betrayed my growing anger.

At this, none of the bandits would meet my eye until finally Robin, to his credit, met my gaze.

"The first night your uncle lay in the cold ground, Sir Robert had Cecelia dragged to his bedchamber." I knew how men, especially those with newfound power, treated the weak, but I forced Robin to continue with my stare.

Drawing breath, Robin continued, "It is said her screams were heard throughout the castle, only drowned out by his laughter. The next morning, while Robert slept, your mother spirited Cecelia away to the convent."

I did not want to show weakness to these warriors, so my face remained stoic. But inside I felt my heart break into pieces, leaving only a stone pit. My rational mind had told my hopeful heart over and over again through the long years that Cece was certainly married off to some noble landowner. But there remained a faint glimmer of hope that kept my feet moving toward home. That silly, childish wish that she would wait for me to return snuffed out, only to be replaced by the flame of vengeance.

"This convent has the protection of the King, then?" I asked, and Robin nodded. "So, no one dares to violate its sanctuary?"

"Aye. If they live still, they live unmolested."

That, at least, was some comfort. My plans changed in an instance. I would journey to visit Cece and my mother at this Savior of the Fields convent while I laid plans to confront Sheriff Robert and reclaim my title. My heart still hoped that perhaps Cecelia could be released from her vows, as I had been. But I needed information to make my plans.

"Tell me, if you will, all that you know of this Robert Enderhite. I would know my opponent before facing him."

Robin looked deeply into my stony face before answering, then he looked to the reddening sky. "A wise decision. Join our camp for the night, and we will tell you all that we know."

I nodded and followed as Robin and his men melted into the deep forest.

That night I heard tale after tale of the abuses heaped upon the people—rich and poor alike—who did not lick the boots of the Sheriff and his men. While hearing their grievances, a plan formed in my mind. I only sipped the wine offered me, so I rose before dawn and slip out of the camp undetected.

Chapter 56

England, Summer 1199 A.D.

I went straight away from the forest to the convent of the Savior of the Fields, a journey of two days. I arrived at the convent gate when the eastern sky was barely lightening. But, despite the early hour, I could hear that the industrious sisters on the other side of the high stone wall were already leaving the chapel following their matins prayers.

The young novice who answered my rapping on their tall gate stared wide-eyed at me through the viewing window set into the gate for a moment after I explained the purpose of my visit. She then slammed the window's wooden door, and I heard the heavy latch bar drop into place. I admit that I was taken aback by this reception, but within the span of a hundred breaths, I could hear the bar of the main gate being raised. This time, the door swung open, and I faced a phalanx of cowled nuns.

A sister who was almost as wide as she was tall stood before me, blocking the doorway.

"This stupid wisp of a girl," her hand flicked toward the novice, now standing with her head bowed off to the side, "says you claim to be our late Mother Superior's son, Liam."

My breath caught in my throat to hear my mother referred to as the *late* Mother Superior. It saddened, but did not surprise me to hear of her passing. After all, it had been nearly twenty years since I had seen her. Life for a widow or a nun in a convent was extremely hard.

I bowed my head and blessed myself. When I raised my head again, I spoke as the disbelieving Sister paused to catch her breath.

"Your novice speaks the truth, Sister, although I did not know we shared a mother."

"We do not entertain liars here, Sir." The Wide Sister reached to swing shut the door once again, but my extended arm stopped its advance. She tried to force it closed, but my strength surprised her, as I easily held it open.

"I'll not enter your premises if you do not invite me, Sister, but at least let her third-born child pay my respects to your Reverend Mother."

The nun's eyes opened wide, her nostrils flared, and her mouth opened in a triumphant smile.

"You are caught, Liar. The Mother Superior bore only two sons before fleeing to this sanctuary."

My trap thus laid, the Wide Sister had stepped right into it. But, before I could correct her with knowledge only her son would know, a voice called sharply from the back of the group of nuns.

"Silence, Sister Ruth." Wide Sister's mouth snapped shut, and the nuns parted as a tall nun, herself wearing the vestments of a Mother Superior, strode forward.

"Mother Superior Sadie's second child, a daughter, died of the croup while still a babe in her arms."

"Aye, my sister Katherine, may God bless her and keep...her." My voice caught in my throat on the last word, not in grief for a sister I never knew, but rather because I recognized the face, still beautiful, beneath her cowl.

Without a thought, I dropped to one knee and bowed my head, afraid to show the tears that had sprung unbidden from my eyes.

Barely above a whisper, I breathed the words, "My beloved Cecelia! How I have dreamed of this day."

The gathered nuns let out a collective gasp as Cece bent, placing her hands on my arms, and bid me rise. When I lifted my eyes to meet hers, I saw my tears were matched by those streaming down her cheeks.

Although I would have gathered her into my arms if we were alone, her face showed me a mixture of joy and sadness, and her arms, which had gently pulled me to my feet, now held me stiffly away as if to prevent both of use from falling into a mutual embrace.

Without another word to me, Cece turned to Wide Sister, whose vein bulged in her forehead.

"Sister Ruth, prepare a room for our guest Liam, son of Edwin of Rollingford, and the true Baron of Sowich."

Again the sisters gasped, except for Wide Ruth, who spun on her heel and pushed through the press of habits.

Now the Mother Superior turned to me and spoke. "We break our fast in an hour. Will you join me in my study until your room is ready?"

"It would be my honor, Mother Superior."

I followed her to the convent calefactory as she shooed the sisters and sent them back to their chores.

Over her shoulder she spoke, barely above a whisper, "I am known as Sister Mariam now, but please call me Mother Superior when the other sisters are around."

When we sat before the unlit fireplace and Cecelia—I cannot think of her as anything else, even now—had poured us each a draught of sweet wine, she took my hands in hers.

"Liam, you cannot imagine the joy and the sadness I felt when I saw you standing at our gate. I gave up all hope of seeing you again long ago. That is when I petitioned to join the Sisterhood."

"My journey has been long and hard, but it was the thought of seeing you again," I looked at her hands clasping mine, "and the touch of your hands, that kept me going."

Cecelia looked at me askance and dropped my hands from hers.

"Many other men, men who left years after you, returned long ago."

Her tone chided, and I could see why the sisters had elected her to lead them. Her gentle and sweet nature sheathed a steel will.

"Aye, but they did not carry the burdens I have born."

Unimpressed, she merely raised an eyebrow skeptically.

"The Templar Grand Master himself released me from my vows and sent me out of Jerusalem on a mission. A mission that has taken me across the breadth of Europe, and which continues to this day."

Before Cece could speak, I raised a hand to silence her. My sleeve slid down my forearm, revealing a circle of scars around my wrist.

Seeing her eyes widen at the sight of them, I nodded to them and continued. "I have worn shackles as often as boots and gloves. Not for crimes I committed, but simply because I looked different or spoke differently or did not know the local customs. But always, always, I saw your face before me."

Her lips turned up at the corners in just the hint of a smile. "And now you find an old woman running a poor convent filled with a gaggle of nuns who cluck and gossip worse than the hens in the yard."

We both chuckled, but I could tell from her voice that she loved those hens as if they were truly her sisters.

"I would offer to spirit you away from those hens, and from these walls," I looked around at the roughhewn stone of her room, "but something tells me you would not accept."

Just for a moment, I saw a wistful look cross her face, but then it was gone, although the faint smile remained.

"Though I am sorely tempted, you are correct. I have not been released from my vows as you have been."

I nodded in understanding. "Indeed, and I have not yet completed my mission."

"Then rest here in our guest house until you are ready to pick up your burden again." With that, the convent bell rang, signaling the morning meal, and we both rose to join the other sisters.

I stayed only two days at the convent. The proximity to Cecelia was too painful, and I felt I had a long overdue debt to pay. So, on the morning of the third day, while the sisters were again at matins, I took my leave, silently, leaving only a brief note of goodbye. When the sun brightened the forest enough, I spent an hour searching for certain roots and the leaves of the plants I needed to execute the plan that had formed in my mind.

Two days later, I entered the town of Sowich. When I left years before, the townsfolk had walked about with their heads proudly held high. When I returned, though, they scurried about with heads bowed and shoulders hunched. Adopting what was to me this most unnatural attitude to blend in, I found lodgings in a rundown tavern at the edge of town.

I spent the next few days assessing the defenses of the castle occupied by Sheriff Robert. The Sheriff and his men had clearly never been in hostile territory, for their guard was extremely lax. I found at least three unguarded portals that would allow me easy access into the keep. On the fourth night, I set my plan in motion.

Over the next fortnight, Sheriff Robert took to his bed with a weakness in his arms and legs, accompanied by a general malaise. The barber surgeon bled the malignant humors from him, which of course only made his condition worse.

Finally, when he could no longer rise from his bed even to piss, I slipped into the castle, past the sleeping guards, and into his chamber. The room reeked of sweat, shit, and imminent death.

Walking silently to his side, I leaned in and whispered into his ear, "You will meet Our Lord this night, and I have no doubt you will not like his judgment."

Robert's eyes flew open as I placed my gloved hand over his mouth and pinched his nose closed. The poison with which I had been dosing his nightly draft of wine had done its work well. Unable to raise his arms against me, his feeble struggles did not deter me in the least. When the light had left his eyes, I left as I had come, a murderer in the night.

At dawn the next morning, I appeared at the castle gate dressed and in the attitude of a man of nearly thirty years. My youthful face I subtly smudged with soot to give the impression of wrinkles and, affecting a limp, I demanded to see the Sheriff.

As expected, the guard, whom I had roused from slumber, made the mistake of drawing his sword to chase me off. A moment later, as I stood over his limp, senseless body,

I called out my name and title, and claimed Castle Sowich and all the lands it commanded as my own.

This caused quite a stir and, when the half-dressed captain of the guard ran to rouse Robert, they found out that they no longer had a Sheriff.

The next two weeks brought challenges from Robert's son, nephew, and finally his decrepit brother, who was nearly twice as old as I made myself appear. Of course, none of these soft men who were knights in name only were a match for the fighting skills I had honed over two decades.

A few of my father's retainers still survived, including Francois, the old stable master. Being nearly blind and unable to see my face, he quizzed me in French about my youthful lessons in his stables. When I answered his queries and added anecdotes of my own, he joyously declared my claim to be true.

King John soon heard word of my return, and when the king's man arrived to investigate my claim, it seemed everyone in the town over the age of thirty years came forward to swear they recognized me the moment they laid eyes on me.

So it was that I gained a Barony, and my people avoided the rule of another of the Crown's Sheriffs.

I have neither the time nor the space here to relate the happenings of the next sixteen years. Suffice it to say that I tried to ease the suffering of my charges, serfs and freemen alike, as much as I could. This very often brought me into conflict with John, and more than once, I had to balance on the edge of the headsman's axe. I suppose what saved me were the knights and sergeants whom I trained in the ways of both the Templars and the Hashashim.

My army, though small by comparison with my peers, was the strongest, most disciplined fighting force in all of England. So it was that when my fellow Barons, who thought as I did about the King's tyranny, needed a fearless rebel to bring the King to heel, they approached me.

I parleyed with the wisest of King John's advisors—indeed the wisest and most renowned knight who had served John's father, mother, and brother—William Marshal, the very same knight who had unseated Stewart at his knighthood joust. We were of a common mind, for William understood that John's abuses of his subjects would surely lead to rebellion. So, instead of pledging my fighting men as both sides wished, we offered to bind the King with laws rather than chains.

Force of arms were employed, of course, but only to bring John to the treaty table to recognize the rights of noblemen. On the fields of Runnymede, we did just that, and King John affixed his royal seal to a charter of rights and laws that William and I had authored.

But John, being the scoundrel he was, soon broke his vows and reverted to his pettiness and tyranny. Disappointed but not surprised and knowing that a civil war that would kill thousands of innocents was soon to follow, I dispatched my best student of the Assassin's Way with a specially prepared vial of fouled water.

Dysentery took King John within a week. The guilt I expected to feel after arranging the murder of an anointed king never overtook me. This lack of feeling frightened me more than the sword or knife ever had, and I realized that if I could kill a king without remorse, the temptations of power that my title, and my mysterious affliction afforded me, would lead me down a very dark path.

Also, my continuing youth had become increasingly difficult to disguise. Whispers of sorcery were spreading among the ladies and whores whom I took to my bed.

In all those years I spent wandering and the more as Baron of Sowich, I never married, and none of my amorous partners ever brought a bastard of mine into this world. It seems the price I paid for my longevity, or immortality as I came to think of my condition, was the inability to father any progeny.

Once I thought through the future paths my life could take, it was easy to make a life-changing decision. There would be no more Barons of Sowich. King John's death and the succession of his nine-year-old son Henry III, far from stabilizing the kingdom as I had hoped it would, instead caused another rebellion among my fellow power-hungry nobles.

I was truly tired of war and the choices a leader of warriors must make. Also, my Burden, the broken fragment of that mystical lance, which had lain hidden in Sowich castle, now seemed to kindle a wanderlust in my heart. So, late one night without a word to anyone, I packed a simple bundle, including the lance of course, and I made my way to the coast. There, without my aged disguise and looking like a young man again, I found work on a ship bound for France and once again left my homeland, not to return for nearly fifty years.

Chapter 57

England, Late Summer 1307 A.D.

D uring the fifty years I was absent from England, I am certain I wandered farther afield than any other Englishman before or since. The places I visited, the people I met, and the adventures I had—for good and ill—could fill an entire library. So, I will give no details of them here. I wish, however, to offer this summary.

I did not wander aimlessly throughout the world for those fifty or so years. Everywhere I visited, I watched and listened for like-minded people. In particular, I sought those who felt, as I had come to believe, that the accident of their birth should not separate and classify men.

No child was ever born into the family of their choosing. They did not decide they would be rich or poor, highborn or low. They did not choose to grow to be a man or a woman, nor did they choose the color of their hair, nor the tone of their skin. Why, then, should they be judged from birth to be deserving of respect or to be reviled, simply because of the station of their parents?

Indeed, everywhere I traveled, I met blacksmiths and farmers, millers and grooms who were brilliant of mind. Likewise, I met noblemen and their ladies who could not compose a poem or keep the simplest accounts. To me, it was clear that everyone should have the chance to create their own destiny, rather than have it thrust upon them, or endowed to them on the day of their birth.

Discussing such views in the open was quite dangerous, of course. The highborn, dim though they may be in matters of letters or numbers, generally were, and still are, quite adept at keeping the lowborn in their place. But, on the rare occasions when I met people whom I suspected might share my views, I discreetly broached the subject, and often we agreed. After much clandestine discussion, some among the enlightened decided we should try to reshape the world to match our ideals, each from our own position of leverage.

To those who were so inclined and positioned appropriately in society, I taught the wiles of political intrigue and some of the secrets I learned while traveling, but never the secret of my own continued existence. To others, I taught some of the more subtle ways of the Assassins. Two of these I called upon to avenge the torture and burning of my former brothers, the Knights Templar.

I was warned of the coming calamity a month before that fateful night in October of the year 1310 when Philip the Fair, the king of France, in collusion with Pope Clement V, tried to steal the treasures of the Templar order. Throughout France, all Templars: knights, sergeants, and even simple serving brothers, were rounded up and imprisoned on that most unlucky of days, Friday the thirteenth of October.

After building a network of intellectual colleagues throughout Christendom, I returned to England and took up residence at a hospice for those poor souls afflicted with leprosy. Shunned by the general populace, they lived out their days in small enclaves where they cared for each other as best they could. Dependent on the produce of their labors and the charity of relatives and the Church, their lives were hard and short.

Confident in my immunity, I took work as a laborer in one such village. Over the years, the afflicted villagers passed on and new ones took their place. Few noticed the young man who, despite living in their midst, never got sick. Those who noticed did not seem to care, as they passed on to me more and more of the responsibilities associated with the hospice. Whether they believed me to be angel or demon, I knew not and cared less. It became my mission to make the few years left to my charges as comfortable as possible.

Within a decade or two, I became quite comfortable living in the shadows behind the veil of contagion that kept the outside world at bay. So, when two knights of my former order knocked on the village gate in the summer of the year 1310 and asked to see the master of the hospice, I was quite shocked and dismayed.

The two stood before me in my study and introduced themselves as Sir Charles and Sir Andre, making secret signs of recognition and greeting known only to members of the Order. The insignia hidden in the knots of the ropes about their waists marked them as seneschals to the Grand Master himself, Jacques de Molay. Unsure of their intent, I feigned ignorance of their subtle gestures and made none of the expected signs in return.

Looking discomfited by my lack of response, the one named Charles spoke. "Master William," for I had adopted that name of late, "we understand that a predecessor of yours was, at one time, our brother, before being released from his vows."

I answered this statement with a blank look and said, "I'm afraid you have been misinformed, Good Knights. While

I admire the good works your Order does, I have no affiliation with you and yours."

The two exchanged glances, then Charles nodded and continued, "The one we refer to has long since passed to his reward, of course. The person we seek is one to whom a secret burden that he carried was passed. That burden fell to him for safekeeping in a moment of extreme crisis."

Charles raised a questioning eyebrow, expecting, I think, to impress me with his knowledge. Clearly, in the century and more since the fall of Jerusalem, my mission had become a legend within the senior ranks of the Templars, though if they knew what my mission was protecting, I am certain they would have sought me out long before. I maintained my blank expression and instead offered them wine, which they happily accepted.

Undeterred, after refreshing themselves, Sir Charles continued. "It is our Grand Master's wish to know that the secret—of which you have no knowledge, apparently," he smiled and almost winked, "remains so—a secret, that is."

They had piqued my curiosity, which drew a small smile to my own lips. "I find it strange that your Grand Master would inquire about a supposedly long-held secret after so long. What has prompted your quest?"

Again, the knights exchanged a look. Then Sir Andre nodded, telling me he was the one actually in charge. It was Sir Andre who spoke next.

"Both the Pope in Rome and the King of France have been corrupted," he said, dropping all pretense of innuendo. "A demon has taken control of their minds and poisoned those minds against our Order."

This tale sounded hauntingly familiar, so I interjected, "Tell me about this demon."

Charles spat on the ground, and Andre shook his head and made the sign of the cross. "She appears as a woman, as beautiful as any I have ever laid eyes on, with hair and eyes as black as night, and a soul to match. She has convinced Clement and Philip that we, the Templars, hold a secret, a weapon that can bring down the Church and all Christian princes. Our spies tell us they are preparing the most drastic actions against our Order with the purpose of finding and stealing this secret weapon."

I fear the astonishment I felt reflected on my features. This demon, this she-devil of which he spoke, could be none other than Moira, Saladin's *djinn*.

Recovering my countenance, I said, "This is quite the tale, but what does it have to do with a poor hospice keeper like myself?"

The set of the knights' shoulders and the way they lifted the wine goblets with their left hands, keeping their right ones in their lap, told me they had come there prepared for a violent end to our conversation if they found it unsatisfactory. I closed my hand, hidden under my work table, on the handle of the dagger whose sheath was nailed to the underside of the table.

Andre's eyes bore into mine for several heartbeats, then he seemed to come to a conclusion and nodded. "Grand Master de Molay simply wishes to ensure that it—whatever this secret is—remains so, despite the coming storm."

I returned Andre's steely stare. "As I am sure you and your brothers know, a secret is not a secret unless it remains unsaid."

Both knights visibly relaxed, and switching their goblets to their right hands, they drained them in unison and stood. Keeping the table between us, I stood as well. They bowed and Sir Charles spoke in the friendliest of tones.

"I see we were misled, Master William. Thank you for your time and the excellent wine." They both offered a salute one would make to a superior, then strode from the room.

Within a month's time, word came that all Templars in France were arrested, and the Pope issued a Bull commanding the other Christian kings and princes to do likewise. King Philip clearly sought the Order's vast hoards, but when the king's troops searched the Order's commanderies and castles, they could find none of the wealth and spiritual treasures. Forewarned, the Templars spirited it all away. Frustrated, Philip resorted to torturing hundreds of Templars, most of whom were stable hands or masons and who knew nothing about finances or secrets.

Those who refused to betray their oaths suffered hideous deaths. When two of my compatriots, whom I had contacted through my network in Paris, witnessed Jacques de Molay, the last Templar Grand Master, being burned at the stake, they took to heart the curse the Grand Master pronounced upon King Philip and the Pope.

De Molay proclaimed that within a year, both would answer to God for their crimes. And so it came to pass that Clement died within a month, and Philip followed him five months later while hunting.

True to the secrecy I had taught them, the two young fellows never admitted to me that either had been the instrument of de Molay's curse. All they would say was that they had lived their lives true to my teachings. So, it is possible, indirectly at least, that I am responsible for the deaths of two anointed sovereigns and God's own voice here on Earth, the Vicar of Christ. If so, and these are truly the Final

Days, then I fear my judgment is at hand. Perhaps the good works I have done for those who were cast out, and now for the widows and orphans of this great pestilence who come to my hospice still, will help balance the scales.

PART XI

Closings
Present Day

And so, I close this Chronicle with a few notes about the long intervening years between the great and treacherous fall of the Knights Templar and what appears to me now to be the end of the world.

Knowing that Moira, or Mariel as the old hermit called her, that anaha shaytan, *that she-devil that haunted me for years, still lived over a century after our last meeting, gave me great pause and worry. That she had achieved similar influence over both Pope Clement V and King Philip the Fair that she had over Saladin was not surprising. But the realization of how powerful that influence was—that she could bring down the strongest religious order of knights that had endured for almost three hundred years—shook me to my core. I felt the noose tightening. But having sensed the trap, I was also determined to avoid it.*

I had faced the dilemma of whether to use the lance to heal the poor souls in my charge when I traveled throughout Europe establishing hospices for the infirmed of all sorts. Their suffering weighed heavily on my heart, but the consequences of healing even one of them weighed equally on my mind. I imagined the attention from Church authorities and the attendant flood of pilgrims should rumor spread of miraculous cures. Instead, I steeled my heart and offered

353

comfort, not cures, to the afflicted. That decision still weighs on both my heart and my mind.

As I prepared to slip away, again carrying my Burden, I hit upon an idea to help soothe my conscience. I whittled from the shaft of the lance the tiniest sliver of wood, then dropped it into the well that provided the hospice's water. I hoped that whatever the mechanism of the lance's miraculous powers, once dissolved into the water source, though diluted, would still provide some measure of health to the unsuspecting residents.

A sea voyage of several years took my Burden to a far corner of the world, unknown to all but the most adventurous and those possessing the secret of its location. Of this sea voyage I will say nothing else, as its purpose and execution was, and remains, of the utmost secrecy.

When I returned from carrying my Burden to the far side of the world, I found a much heathier and more hopeful populace. It seems the lance shard may have had a positive effect. It certainly had the desired effect on my conscience.

Alas, the pestilence that has befallen the whole of Christendom and beyond has erased those modest gains against the tide of disease and suffering that seems to be mankind's lot. Is it the punishment bestowed upon us by a mean and vengeful God? Or a natural result of man's avarice and thirst for what others possess? Who knows the truth? Certainly not this humble chronicler.

Now I must bind this codex before this Great Mortality, which lays upon the land and which has taken most of this country and the world, takes me, as well.

Humbly,

Liam, son of Robert, Templar Sergeant, Baron of Sowich, Wanderer, Keeper of the Sick, Cursed.

1350, A.D.

— Codex Incognito

Chapter 58

The Enclave, Late Autumn

Dan split his time between finishing the translation and continuing his research. He delved deeply into the Enclave's copious records. With his evidence mounting, the final piece of the puzzle fell into place on the day John returned from his latest travels.

When John asked Dan to brief him on his progress, as had become customary upon his return, Dan was ready. He had completed the translation, but he was also armed with the evidence that unraveled the complete mystery of the Lance, the Enclave, and its founder.

John was already in the Vault when Dan descended the steps. The lights were turned down low, and the Enclave's master sat, legs crossed at the knee, in one of the club chairs. A glass of the ever-present sherry was in his hand. He gestured over the table that separated the two chairs, where another full glass rested.

Ignoring the invitation for the moment, Dan said, "Welcome home. I trust your trip was fruitful."

The tension in his tone and attitude were plain for John to hear and see.

He answered warily, "Indeed it was. You seem a little pensive, my friend. I trust you've made progress with the translation."

Again, he gestured to the empty chair.

Still tense, but oddly relieved that John could tell something was bothering him, Dan gathered his thoughts as he slowly sank into the offered chair, looked at the crystal glass of sherry, but resisted its temptation. He knew this conversation would change their relationship, for good or ill, forever.

"I've finished the translation, actually." John smiled, but remained silent, allowing Dan to continue. "And I've done some side research that sheds a great deal of light on the story, the Enclave—and you."

Unable to remain silent as he realized this could be the moment he had been waiting and hoping for, John asked, "Oh? What sort of research? I didn't know *I* would be the object of your impressive talents."

His tone was light, but his eyes were piercing. Dan returned his stare with an equally intense gaze. Their eyes locked for a few heartbeats.

"I've been delving into the Enclave's archives." John's look of surprise was quite genuine. "You know about my previous work that traces the authorship of otherwise anonymous manuscripts?" John nodded warily, but remained silent, so Dan continued, "And I've made some interesting correlations."

A vein pulsed in John's neck. Dan knew that tell and saw the minefield of emotions he was walking—hope and fear—flicker across John's face. Uncharacteristically, John stalled for time.

"Well, why don't you read me the rest of your translation, then we can discuss what else you've uncovered."

Now it was Dan's turn to smile, though it was a rueful one. "I think we both know I don't have to read it to you. I'm now positive you already know what it says, considering you're the one who wrote it."

The blood drained from John's face, and Dan worried that the young-yet-ancient man's heart had stopped. But after a moment, John bowed his head and closed his eyes. What he murmured could have been a prayer.

"At last! This is what I've wanted, what I've needed for so long. So, why am I so scared?"

His heart, which of course had not actually stopped—which could not stop of its own volition—continued pumping and the color returned to his face. Wiping the tears—whether tears of joy or relief Dan wasn't sure—from his cheeks, he cleared his throat and met Dan's eye with a mixture of gratitude, relief, and fear.

"Yes, I did, but it has been so long since I wrote those words."

Chapter 59

The Enclave, Late Autumn

S o, do you think me a liar? Do you think this is all a joke or a hoax?" John asked quietly.

"Oh, I don't believe it's a hoax. In fact, I believe every word written. Both written in this story," Daniel pointed to his translation which lay on the table between them, "and written by the same hand in a continuous series of journals, reports, and letters saved in the archives over the last six and a half centuries. My authoring analysis software confirms that the same person who wrote this Chronicle," Dan again laid his hand on the printed translation, "has also Master of this Order and this Enclave since its inception."

John, who sat hunched forward, hanging on Dan's every word, relaxed and leaned back in his chair. A broad smile crossed his face.

"Congratulations, Father. You have accomplished a task that many, many others have tried and failed to complete."

Dan just shook his head. "What, you mean solving a mystery that you already knew the answer to?"

John shook his in response. The eminently self-confident persona of John Haviland was again fully present.

"No, I mean passing a test. A test I created to find a scholar who can solve a riddle that is not of my making."

Dan sat back, aghast. "My labors over these many months, an entire year, have just been a test? Why would you have me waste my time?"

"Has it really been a waste of time for you? Think of the things you've learned and the secrets that you have revealed, the living history that you now know."

John's eyes twinkled at his pun. It took Dan a moment, but he got the joke, too. That seemed to ease the tension and gave him a moment to reflect on John's words as they both chuckled.

"You're right, of course. This is life-changing for me. To witness the work of God first-hand, and to call one of his agents a friend."

Their eyes met, but the near reverence in Dan's, made John start and tilt his head warily.

"Hang on. I'm not an agent of God. Far from it, since I don't even believe in Him anymore."

Dan wasn't swayed by John's denial. "When Paul set out on the road to Damascus, he had no inkling of the path his life would take. You may just be starting down your own road."

John shifted uncomfortably in his chair. "I'm way down my road, Son. It is you who are just starting his journey." He stared hard at Dan, trying, it seemed, to burn the adoration out of him. When he saw that he couldn't, he sighed deeply. "I am nothing to gaze at so adoringly, Father. But let me show you the thing that got me started on this road."

He rose and went to a row of filing cabinets against one wall of the vault. Wrestling the end cabinet off to the side, he revealed a safe set into the wall. The front of the safe held a blank panel, a camera, and a keypad. Placing his left palm against the panel, he looked into the camera lens. Without taking his eyes from the camera lens, with his right hand he entered a long sequence of digits on the keypad.

Dan heard a mechanical whirring, accompanied by a hissing sound, as ambient air replaced the inert argon gas in the safe. Then a series of clicks and whirs sounded as the locking mechanisms slid back. The safe swung open with a slight pop.

Reaching in, John withdrew a cloth-wrapped bundle about three feet long. Carefully, he laid it on the examination table in the middle of the room and gently unwrapped its contents.

When Dan saw the remnants of the Lance lying there, he gasped, blessed himself, and mumbled a prayer. Glancing sidelong at Dan, John smirked and unceremoniously picked up the lance and handed it to him.

"Here, hold this a second." Completely surprised by John's casual attitude toward this most holy relic, Dan almost dropped the precious artifact.

John just laughed, though. "Trust me, you can't hurt it."

Dan smiled sheepishly, but his hands shook visibly as he held the ancient piece of wood. Through those trembling hands, he imagined he could feel it pulse with a living warmth. He looked at it with awe to see that this instrument of death, which had been fashioned from the branch of an unknown tree thousands of years ago, looked as fresh as a newly cut sapling.

Though smooth and hard, as you would expect such a weapon to be, it was not dry or brittle as its age would suggest. Still in awe, but feeling a little more comfortable, Dan ran his fingers over the nicks and cuts that it had suffered through the centuries.

"I can't believe I'm holding proof of all that we believe."

"Ha! Proof? I hardly think so."

Dan's face revealed the hurt he felt at his friend's attitude. "You, yourself, have witnessed and felt firsthand the power of Christ's blood. How can you deny its power?"

"Oh, I don't deny the power of this branch. As you say, I have felt it myself, and seen it work its magic on others. But I don't believe its power comes from any man's blood. In fact, I believe the opposite is true. The branch itself is the source of this 'magic', and it by no means proves anybody's divinity."

The heat rose in Dan's cheeks. "It is a source of miracles, not magic. Clearly, the lance was transformed by Christ's blood into a miraculous relic. What other explanation could there possibly be?"

John smiled. Dan had asked the right question. "Am I divine then? Was my brother Stewart?" Receiving no answer, he continued. "Of course not. I am a man. My brother was a man. We were resurrected from the dead by being pierced by *this*."

He grasped what remained of the original lance—the handle—and shook it.

"Does that sound familiar to you?" This time, Dan tried to respond, but John cut him off. "There is no reason to believe that the blood of another dead man transformed the wrong end of a Roman lance into an instrument of miracles. In fact, the only evidence that I can believe points to the lance itself, or actually the wood of the lance itself, as the magical element."

It wasn't John's argument that gave Dan pause, but rather a single word. That word "lance" was a key that unlocked a sequence of memories that washed over Dan one after another.

He pictured the *pilum*, a long throwing spear or javelin. The *lancea* was a shorter version that could be thrown or thrust into an opponent during close-in fighting. It was not, however, a weapon that legionnaires in garrison would have carried. Dan pictured the scene on Golgotha in his mind's eye as represented in grisly detail by the statuary in his chapel.

Christ, having given his soul up to God, hung limply on the cross while the two Marys, kneeling at the base of the cross, begged for his body to be taken down before sunset—the beginning of the Passover Sabbath. And the centurion, Longinus, thrusting a—. This made no sense.

A centurion, in command of one hundred legionnaires, would not be carrying a foot soldier's weapon, certainly not one used during pitched battles on the open field. The only weapon he would carry during the mundane assignment of overseeing the execution of a common criminal would be the one worn by every Roman soldier, namely his *gladius*, his familiar short sword. No, the traditional depiction of the ultimate moment of the crucifixion had to be wrong. Longinus would have reflexively reached for the *gladius* on his hip to ensure Jesus's death.

John was the only gospel that mentioned this event that was seminal to Liam's story. Thinking back to the oldest existing version, Dan retranslated the ancient Greek λόγχη—*lonchi*—definitely "lance," but John, being the most evangelistic of the canonical gospels, contained descriptions of many events not reported in the other, Synoptic gospels, Mathew, Mark, and Luke.

As his theology professors had always said, the *prose* of the gospels might be suspect, being copies of copies of traditional stories one or more generations removed from the actual events, but the *literature* of the gospels, their meaning and message, was holy writ.

But if the story of Longinus was an invention or a misrepresentation of the act, what was this piece of wood now in John's hand? From where did its powers originate?

Dan shook his head violently, too overcome with this looming tidal wave of doubt to speak. These, again, were the doubts seeded in his mind by the words he had translated. Words, of course, that came from the same person who stood before him now, and amplified by his own disturbing musings.

"Our statue is wrong, as is the root of the Order."

John, who had waited patiently for Dan's response, was taken aback by the priest's statement.

"Oh? How so?"

When Dan explained the incongruity of the use of a Roman lance, whether a *pilum* or a *lancea*, John nodded but frowned.

"I wish I could say you've proven my point. But your logic has a flaw, as well."

Dan raised an eyebrow, and John continued. "Longinus could not reach Jesus hanging high on a cross with just his *gladius*."

"Then…"

"I hate to say it, but he needed something longer. Maybe this was close at hand."

Dan took the artifact from John. He ran his hand along the tight, smooth grain of the wood. His fingers felt the smoothness interrupted by ripples in the wood near the end. He turned it in his hands until he held it as if thrusting it forward, but shook his head. Instead, he spun it around until the broken end pointed to the ground. His fingers fit the worn grooves perfectly.

He looked at John, surety in his face and voice, "A staff. It was a walking staff."

John nodded appreciatively. "Makes sense. The soldier probably grabbed it from an onlooker."

A sense of wonder overcame Dan in that instant. Could this be Christ's own staff? Could he have held it just as Dan was in that moment?

"Which means it was nothing special before that moment. Just somebody's everyday walking stick."

John's mouth fell open in shock, but he quickly recovered. "We're just guessing. We still don't know where it came from."

The revelation came to Dan in a flash. In that moment, that insight turned the whole meaning of his life upside down. He grasped the reason God had led him to this point.

The Lord has a plan for John, but he refused to acknowledge it. He had refused this calling for over eight hundred years! Now Dan knew, as surely as he had ever known anything in his life, that his mission was to bring this stray sheep back into the fold. He offered a silent prayer of thanks for finally being shown the way.

To John he said, "I have Faith. You may have lost yours, but I have Faith enough for us both."

"Faith? Just Faith? Where's the proof?"

Dan's voice was the calm one now. "John, sometimes having Faith means choosing what *not* to believe."

As an argument stopper, there could be no better statement. Agreeing to disagree just didn't compare. The two stood in silence for a full minute before Dan broke the standoff.

"I believe God has made my mission clear to me."

John chuckled ruefully. "What, to convert me back to being a good Catholic?"

About to agree, Dan realized that their relationship stood at a crossroads. The wrong word now could send them each down opposite paths.

"No. I believe the source of the miracles you have experienced is the blood of Our Savior. You believe otherwise. I think my mission—our mission—is to find the truth of this lance. Whatever that truth may be."

As John smiled and nodded, Dan felt a profound sense of relief mixed with terror. His simple declaration was a leap off a precipice into the unknown. It was terrifying, but he also felt liberated by his words.

He whispered a prayer, "Give me strength, Lord. Give me strength to find my path in the Truth."

John's smile widened, and he took a deep breath and extended his hand, glad that the confrontation had passed. "On that, we can agree."

Dan took the offered hand in both of his, and their handshake forged a bond between them and a partnership with a common goal.

Taking the lance from Dan, John set it aside on the table.

"It truly is something to behold, whatever its source of power. But this," he indicated the linen wrapping that lay in a heap, "is what your test was really about, what the codex was about. I think it is the first step on our quest."

With that, he handed Dan an end of the strip of cloth, and they stretched it to its full length. It was about four inches wide, but nearly seventeen feet long. Once unfurled, they could see a pattern of light brown symbols staining the fabric. Though clearly meaningful, the collection of straight, interconnected lines did not resemble any language that Dan had ever come across.

"This cloth is still as it was when thrust into my hands that day in Jerusalem. I swear that I have never added or subtracted from these strange markings. I believe them to be some form of language, but in all of my travels throughout the world and down through the centuries, I have never seen another like it."

Immediately fascinated by this new puzzle, Dan casually pushed the lance aside and they set the cloth on the central examination table. They had to fold it in half to fit. He bent to examine the markings more closely, and after a minute or so, he straightened up and looked at John.

"I have to admit I've never seen anything like it, either. This, I suppose, is the real riddle you want me to solve?"

John just smiled.

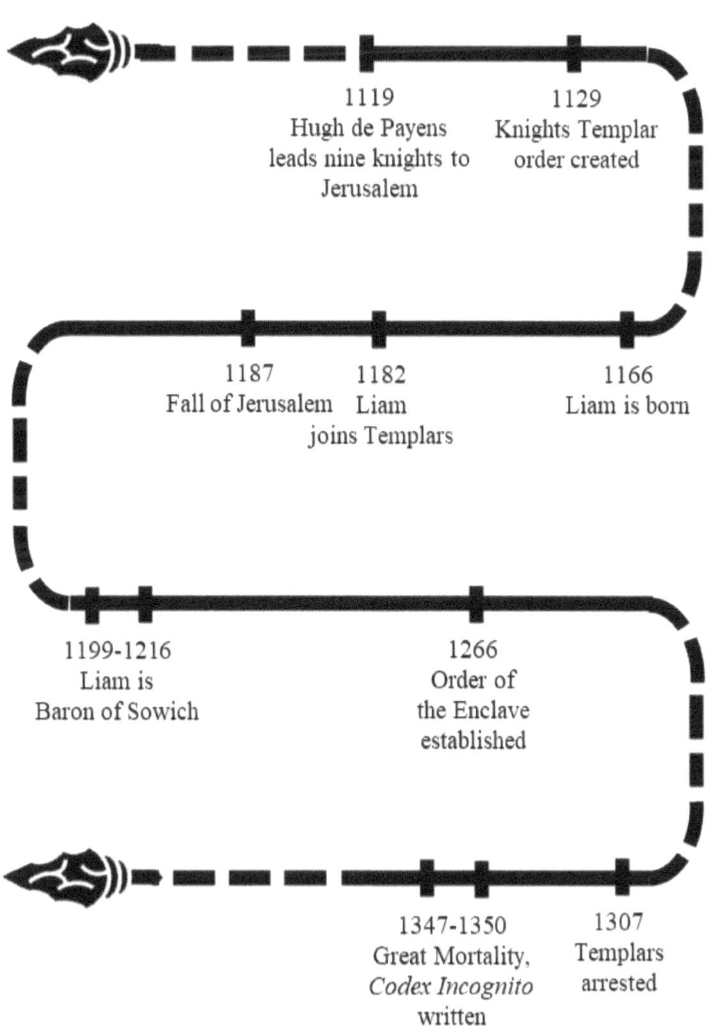

1119
Hugh de Payens
leads nine knights to
Jerusalem
1129
Knights Templar
order created
1187
Fall of Jerusalem
1182
Liam
joins Templars
1166
Liam is born
1199-1216
Liam is
Baron of Sowich
1266
Order of
the Enclave
established
1347-1350
Great Mortality,
Codex Incognito
written
1307
Templars
arrested

I have always found the Knights Templar to be the most enigmatic group in the history of the West. Most discussions around the many mysteries they left behind deal with either their "missing treasures" or whether any of the trumped-up charges leveled against them—various blasphemous activities, homosexuality, holding heretical beliefs, etc.— were true.

But those mysteries, although interesting, I believe are secondary to the mystery of their founding. How did an obscure group of nine knights convince a pope to grant them unprecedented powers, essentially making them an independent, sovereign state? What did they discover during those nine years they spent in the stables below the Temple Mount? Was the papal bull that established their Order a reward, or a pay-off for keeping their discovery secret?

The Templar Lance is my fanciful solution to that mystery. I hope you enjoyed it—if you've read this far, I assume you did—and that you will tell your friends.

As always, you can find me, my flash fiction blog, newsletter sign-up, and anything else I post at
https://robjohnsonwriting.net

Thanks, again, Faithful Reader, for taking some
time out of your day to spend with me and this ancient form
of mental telepathy called storytelling.

Faithfully,

R.A. (Rob) Johnson
Pennsylvania, U.S.A.
September 2023

ACKNOWLEDGEMENTS

So many people have helped me over the years it took to perfect (as much as possible) this tome. Dave Dodgson gave me great feedback and copy editing help. Sarah Inforzato was an early reader of the first edition and provided suggestions that greatly improved the story. Emily Shoup was so very encouraging during the whole process. Emily, we all miss you very much.

Also, my daughter, Carly proved to be a wonderful sounding board for ideas throughout the process of creating this final revision. She continues to provide firm, but necessary feedback on story structure, characters, and every other aspect of storytelling.

Finally, a heartfelt thank you to Joanna Penn (TheCreativePenn.com) who, despite having written dozens of books, decided to heavily revise the first two novels in one of her series. It was her very public discussion about that decision that prompted me to do the same with The Enclave series. Thank you, Joanna.

A note about the tools I used to put the various formats of this novel together. I write in Microsoft Word and rely on he ProWritingAid plug-in to point out many of my common typographical and grammatic issues.

I also used Word for all of the interior layout and formatting, including the internal illustrations at the beginning of each Part. For the cover, I prompted the AI tool MidJourney to generate four separate images—the faces, background Templar flag, and a manuscript containing Latin, Hebrew, and Aramaic script. I then blended those images, modified their color, contrast, and other attributes, and added the back cover blurb, all within Microsoft PowerPoint. Many thanks to my professor and Western Colorado University, Allyson Longueira, a wonderful cover designer.

To connect with me, check out my website www.RobJohnsonWriting.net. There you will find my blog, which contains dozens of flash fiction pieces, and you can join his email list to get monthly newsletters, bonus stories, and special offers.

I am also active in the Fiction Writers Group on Facebook, the APEX Writers Group, Superstars Writing Seminars (yay, Tribe!), the Western Colorado University's Creative Writing/Publishing MA program, the Pottstown Writers Group, The Writers of the Future Contests, and various other challenges and competitions.

You can contact me directly at:

rob@robjohnsonwriting.net.

Other Titles by R.A. Johnson

FICTION
The Enclave Series
#1 *The Templar Lance*
#2 *Lady 355: Mother of Freedom*
#3 *Shroud of Doubt (coming soon)*

Ghost Stories
The Ghost of Mackey House

Fantasy
Tales from the Wood: A Modern Fairytale

NON-FICTION
Mental Crudites – Appetizers for the Creative Mind Series
#1 *Helping Science Fiction Writers Get Their Stories Off the Ground*